Ian Holding was born in 1978 and lives in his home town of Harare, Zimbabwe. His critically acclaimed first novel, *Unfeeling*, was shortlisted for the 2006 Dylan Thomas Prize. In 2009 he was awarded a Hawthornden Fellowship. *Of Beasts & Beings* is his second novel.

www.ianholding.com

# of Beasts
and Beings

IAN HOLDING

SIMON &
SCHUSTER

London · New York · Sydney · Toronto

First published in Great Britain by Simon & Schuster UK Ltd, 2010
This paperback edition first published by Simon & Schuster UK Ltd, 2011
A CBS COMPANY

1 3 5 7 9 10 8 6 4 2

Simon & Schuster UK Ltd
1st Floor
222 Gray's Inn Road
London WC1X 8HB

www.simonandschuster.co.uk

Simon & Schuster Australia
Sydney

A CIP catalogue record for this book
is available from the British Library

ISBN: 978-1-84983-014-0

Typeset by M Rules
Printed in the UK by CPI Mackays, Chatham ME5 8TD

Man is the most formidable of all the beasts and the only one that preys systematically on its own species.

William James,
Remarks at the Peace Banquet, 1904

1

He is taken captive on the outskirts of the city. He's picking among the ruins for food when they take him unawares on this hot gauzy morning. The sun tracks his seizure from above; he is a speck in the sweep of desolation about him. He had just come across the miracle of an unscathed vegetable patch studded with cabbages and beets and pumpkin and the bulbs of some sweet potatoes buried down hard in the ground. His mind is lost in an uncoiling rush of relief, his tongue and mouth unclotting. It is only a small vegetable patch. It's someone's sacred prize, their last oasis. Hemmed in with tall walls of bush and the skeletal stubs of hacked trees. He is busy gnawing at the stalks of the beets when a rope lassoes him taut around the throat. His breath is lost to an instant panic; he staggers on his feet but does not fall. A moment of blind senselessness overtakes him and then he glimpses the posed attitudes of three men brandishing machetes. They gather in, surround him. Their feet dig firm to the sod, their hands grip the rope as if taking part in a tug of war. He doesn't try to fight or flee.

One of them shouts something but he cannot understand what. Something crude and direct. He does not comprehend anything they say. His tongue is locked somewhere down his throat, his breath constricted by the snare staving into his vertebrae. A firm pair of hands clamp him by the neck and a foul stinking rag is stuffed into his mouth like a muzzle. Ragged and ropy, it smells of filth baked crisp in the sun. Or something fetid, something scum-like. Then the deeper odour of fear spikes his nostrils and a rapid swell slops up from his stomach. He stumbles about, moaning, shaking his head, but the harness they have him by is unyielding. He panics, sensing he is going to heave and choke, be over-whelmed from the inside out. The ground and the sky and the haggling bodies rove jaggedly, fusing in an odd cabal against which his actions are futile. He tries a feeble kick, to draw from inside himself and surge against them. Too little too late. They have him tight now, tighter.

They lead him off without a further word. His stomach is crouching in his throat; his wide eyes are burning. They lead him through the charred fields and the smoking debris of a shanty town recently levelled to the ground. He has to pick his way over a mangled pile of corrugated tin and shattered asbestos roofing as if dodging jetsam on a river-bank. The shards are sharp underfoot and stabs of spiky pain jerk up his shins. The shells of a few brick hovels stand here and there but the mud huts have been returned to the earth in an incendiary slew and the thatching lies thick in the black-yellow ash.

It hasn't rained for some time. Frayed canvas tarps are draped amongst the ruins and the air is thick with the smell of burnt plastic sheeting, the reeking tar of blistered tyres. They pass a creosote-stained wood shack with rows of pit latrines that have been bombed. The ruptured sewers snake in dark, wet runnels and lie drying in caked crusts of shit-soaked earth. The sick and emaciated were here not long ago. The pot-bellied, balding children, the grown-ups squatting on the ground gripping their cramped stomachs.

Now the smell is stiff and sits in his nose beyond the gag like an elastic fume. Between everything, a sporadic spread of tin pots and utensils has been unearthed and scattered. Upturned stools and old bits of bedding with coils of springs jutting out like disused antennae. This is all that escaped the torching and the advancing rampages of the horde, barbarians at some ancient bloodletting coasting on the shanties.

*

They march him on. As they veer round a cluster of shelled shacks they see the bodies of a family lying roasted on the ground, composed in a kind of petrified flux. The flares have pulled the skin tight across the faces and the whiteness of the teeth glints like slits of plastic or polyester grinning up at the smashed world. They pass on. The men don't comment or exclaim or bemoan. These fallen dead may have been members of the opposition or a household loyal to some rival faction. This is just a sight thrown up from a newly adjusted reality, a commonplace thing.

Their mismatched combat fatigues singles them out. Stalking effigies of violence, intimidation, fear. They may be from various factions of the militia. They may be offshoots of the army, the police, the opposition – on the rampage for anything they can loot or plunder or hijack. They wear camouflaged trousers in an array of mottled shades as if they have attempted to band together but the rest of their attire is indistinct: a frayed cotton shirt embossed with florid insignia; a grubby white vest torn at the side; a bare black chest muscled and sleeked with sweat. Their footgear is random too: a pair of dark leather boots, a pair of worn track shoes, a pair of old slops fixed over with wire gnarled around the toes. They have tied bandanas to their heads but with no legend or flag or colours of this side or that. In some ways they look like a comic trio out of a travelling circus, these teenagers rampaging as men.

On they lead him. Out of the spill of the shanty town and across a dead vlei burnt black and still sighing a wisp of smoke akin to the morning mist across the lowveld lands he may have come from. Or may not have. He has little clear memory of anything. He walks uneasily, fearing his feet will scorch. But they don't: the ash lies thick, a carpet of silken blackness into which the field now seeps. Nothing moves in this vacant rink but themselves and the rising smoke. On the turf there are bodies lying across the spiked scrub, rutted slits on their backs from the machete strikes and gobs of flesh scalloped from their buttocks.

They continue onwards and all the while he thinks of precious little beyond the discomfort of the gag and a faint pulsing alarm at his predicament. He thinks of the vegetables left bedded in their neat, prim rows. He had come so close to their sweet pleasures. He had sensed them and sniffed them out and been brought to them perhaps by some act of providence. They were his for the taking. He had found them and for those moments he owned them. There in that theatre of chaos he had stood relishing such gifts before his luck ran out.

They may have stumbled upon him by chance, out scouting for opportunities. What luck for them. Their brutal strength, the rope their weapon. Or they may have knelt in the scrub waiting for his hunger to send him creeping from the barren bushes. Like a fisher in his skiff, lobbing baited hooks to the dark reedy pool, hooking him in their creel. This small victory would always be theirs. A small battle they had won in a war that was too big for them.

It's bizarre to think they didn't plunder the vegetables before him. That they weren't sat there on the ruffed sod with that blanking ecstasy drawn across their tear-stained faces, the relief, the joy, clawing at the bulbs and tubers and leaves as he was. There must be some ill-gotten source that keeps them fed in these desperate days of famine. The dry ashen lands, the unyielding skies. The fertilizer rotten. The pumps rusted, stripped to the core and the water pipes ripped whole from the ground a long time ago. There must be something that keeps their stomachs full and their minds

ticking and allows them to plot their treachery. Some strange
devil's bedfellows they must be.

Until they approach the main highway leading directly
into the city he plods along in their grasp diffidently enough,
as if time itself has muffled his mind against the blows of the
heat and the carnage. Now, though, he begins to tense. He
senses the danger of walking a path travelled by every bandit
and his brother. He knows to avoid the sight of roads. When
stumbling on a stretch of asphalt he has always stopped and
turned round and slunk off. Here, they are poised to
encounter one faction of militia or the other, intent on guarding the entry and exit of the city for their own travails, as if
they were savage trolls at a sentry posting. He begins to strain
against the rope. He feels it tighten at his throat and his eyes
widen. The man leading him shouts *Ewe!* and yanks on the
rope and shoots him a threatening glance. On they pull him.

The road is deserted of all traffic save the occasional sweep
of jeeps that thunder by, laden with men shouting victory
songs and waving their AK-47s in some futile celebration.
The jeeps are military, though other factions drive similar
ones. After several convoys pass without incident, his mood
eases and he walks on again. No one will stop them and ask
questions of the militia who have taken him hostage and are
leading him off with a rope bundled round him and a gag in

his mouth. There will be no spate of fighting in the midst of which he may be able to wrestle and break free. The jeeps drive on past their ambling band and it is possible they may not even see him. If they do then they obviously don't care a passing moment for his plight, such is the new order here flexing its iniquitous brawn. So much for that.

The battery of convoys come and go and the road is lined with the carcasses of burnt-out cars heaped here and there. No one else strolls about. They approach the forlorn grey city. Even from a distance it exudes a clouding eeriness. When they reach the outer suburbs there is a sense of desertion which becomes tangible and oppressive like a vast sweaty palm stretched low across the sky. A weight bears down on them. The air dense and insufferable now the bustle of movement and the throes of active commerce have been blown from the city's vortex, succeeded by this stale and stupefied redundancy. This is not a sight anyone would care an instant for.

He has not been into the city itself since fleeing a week back. How the atmosphere has changed since then. He had left in a deluge of panic and chaos with cars and lorries and buses thronging the streets and backing up along the highways to make their escapes, hooting and jamming each other in. Then the streaming hordes were loping out along the highways on foot or on bicycles, all straddled with the wares of their lives. Children being dragged at heel and babies bundled tight to their mothers' burly backs. Some lugged a clutch of chickens aflutter in makeshift coops; others yanked skittish goats along behind them. Others just left with nothing. The old, the infirm, the sick and dying, too. All souls with half a whim left for life scuttled out like crabs along an oil-slicked beach. He didn't leave with the masses along that shambling noon highway. Too encumbering, too startling. He chose the back road warrens. It turned out much easier that way.

He had woven through the suburbs and then out on the quieter roads. At this point the fighting hadn't broken out fully in the city and the shanties orbiting it, but everyone knew it was coming. He walked and walked and covered a fair distance in a short period of time. He took refuge in a horticultural plantation on the city's outskirts where he kept himself hidden low in the cool green growth, among the lush stalks and rows of budding icebergs, the fragrance ripe and full at his nose. For a while this was heaven. He would have been content to live out his last days in such a place, surrounded by some vague notion of beauty that he hardly understood; untouched, unhampered by man and his war machines.

Then the sounds broke in the still hot air. One moment, late on a cloudless day. The low concussions of mortars and grenades rocking through the ground and the tight chill to the skin in their aftermath each and every time. In the evenings he crept atop a small kopje that was well treed and from there he could look over towards the city. As the sun sank in the sky and the pining evening blueness came to being, he stood there and stared out at the plumes of smoke, the flashes of gunfire, listening to the booms and roars and spatter.

After a few days the noises stopped although great wafts of black smoke still rose over the city, so thick at first they looked like thunder clouds smudging the calm paleness. When it seemed certain the volleying blasts were over, he dislodged himself from the kopje and scrounged around the plantation for food and water, finding little. There was a reservoir he could drink from; what a travesty he couldn't eat roses or sunflowers. He was feeling weak and nuzzled with delirium.

On the fourth day his confidence rekindled and he moved into a well-kempt garden to scrump some plump peaches from a tree. He picked them and was savouring the sharp sweetness on his tongue when an elderly white man came charging at him from the confines of a grand old Cape Dutch house. He was startled because such a stillness had been awash over everything and the plantation seemed long deserted. The man shouted and picked up a handful of stones from the gravel driveway and started pelting him with them, waving his arms and yelling so much his bald head flushed a sweaty crimson. All for a peach or two. In that moment he knew of no way to implore the man to some sympathy and so he ran off into the undergrowth. He roamed around panic-stricken for a while looking for food before coming across that oasis of a vegetable patch on the edge of the shanty town.

They lead him into the city centre. The danger here is inestimable and for a while his trepidation builds again until he can feel his feet grow heavy, wanting to dig into the tar. His whole body recoils into itself. The rope tautens. One of his captors looks back and grimaces at him. He sees a hand tighten round the handle of the machete, its gore-stained blade briefly shimmering as it draws on the sun. There is a grunt and a hard yank down on the rope. It digs into him as the lasso bites. One fear outstrips the other; his legs soften and passively he walks on.

In the city some of the buildings stand shelled, their windows blown out and their roofs caved in from the intense pressure of the fires that have ravaged them. Paint has been singed off large tracts of walls and in some places the structures have begun to collapse, leaving great snaking shafts of bent metal struts bare through the crumbled concrete. Occasionally, a gaping hole through which he can see the remnants of an office appears, as if some keen child has swung open a doll's house. There are charts still pinned to the walls, desks and swivel chairs and pot plants and water purifiers and filing cabinets, all standing there as if in states of shock. Other buildings are untouched, their neat outer facades prim and pristine and their silver windows emblazoned where the bright sunlight of the afternoon smashes into them, dazzling the eyes of onlookers below. But over everything there is a great aura of stagnant alarm as if a vast omnipotent hand has reached out and pressed a pause button in the middle of some urgent action.

The aura of desertion saturates the city entirely. Beyond it there is the sense of something festering in the air, the remnants of some frenzied chaos which broke full into the streets and spilt across the roads and sidewalks and alleyways. On both sides of the street the shop fronts stand battered, their iron girders mangled and their chains hacked. TV sets, hi-fis, DVD players – such easy pickings when the shopkeeper has long fled and the police are busying themselves for the army's assault on the city. Those few days must have felt like paradise. Lugging out their booty and sloping off bleary-eyed or else standing along the pavements guarding it and bartering it off and fighting amongst one another in ways learnt only in the gangland shanties and ghettos. There has been no food on the shelves for many months;

DVD players, not food. It is possible to believe that the tatty children were there nonetheless, crawling about the old bakery floors or chain stores and rummaging in storerooms in the back to scoop up the spillage from a long-popped chip packet or a ripped bag of millet, maize, soya.

Then this great vacant space is broken by rapid gunfire blurts from the depths of the rubble. Electric disarray. The fracturing pavement, the blistering tarmac. The trio shout, darting and yanking him. In the flourish of confusion they sidle into an alleyway and duck down behind dustbins spilling with shredded paper. The absurdity and the fragility of it. Agitated exclamations and brief grimaces from one to the other of some unknown fear. No dustbin for him. He tries to press himself against the wall but realizes the stark prominence of himself there. A step into the alleyway and the shadowy marksman will have him sighted. But the gunfire spurt is brief; silence now but for the spreading ring of panic in his ears. The report is a distant hammering quake in his chest. He huddles into the dank slimy stockade and together they all crouch there for some time, looking and listening out at the empty, voided street.

Most likely they're unseen rival factions who have laid siege to this particular quarter of the city. Anything to defend their territory. Or snipers lying hidden behind overturned cars taking pot shots at the legs of pedestrians. For some time anyway he had been walking gingerly, somehow sensing to fear having his kneecaps blown out or his shins blasted. The sound of the gun has been lodged in his ears these last few days: its pop and rip an instant fright to him. How foolish of these men to have ventured into the very sinews of a battle-field.

He had begun to sense what it was like to be shot at, to be shot; there in the blooming plantation when he heard those first faraway booms volley deep towards the shielding sky, then the crackling peal of the automatics in ever responding raps, the monotonous drone purling towards him in faint pulses as if the ground beneath him were giving up murmurs of its deepest self. The back of his throat had a dryness not entirely down to thirst. Some parchment of dull anxiety, the thickening settlement of fear. He would sleep in snatches, curled in the undergrowth, his flesh all the while tingling to the half-expectant stab of wayward bullets. Something falling out of the air. He would feel his eyes flicker in their sockets, knowing the unease of his mind. The nerve endings in his flesh stabbed at him.

When he was chased from the plantation his trepidation grew more marked and at times, when the blasts burst out again and the rifle fire responded, he found he could hardly put one foot in front of the other, so overcome was he with an instant paralysis. He had faltered on, tramping along in his own marcescent way. It was surprising that he made it to the vegetable patch at all. Surprising, too, that at the point of capture he didn't feel so afraid. Perhaps by then he had sated all his dread and the dull quaking in his throat was just plain hunger and resignation.

After some time they disengage from the bins and regroup in the alley. There is anger and frustration between them. He stands looking on but it doesn't occur to him to take the chance to flee. He isn't thinking like that. Scampering out of the alley and into the sights of the snipers is no option. He doesn't move. Something keeps him nailed to the spot and for the smallest shred of time there in this dark corridor he may have stopped breathing altogether.

One of the militia crawls to the end of the alley, then crawls all the way to the other end and looks out. Crouched like a lizard, he scans the area thoroughly. Not a glimmer to be seen. After a while he returns to give his report. There is much discussion in whispered, agitated tones. Then what sounds like an argument between two of the men, leering at one another with fists clenched. They find themselves trapped and have little way of knowing what to do next. One of them leads the way towards the back end of the alley.

The still, starched air draws them closer to the vacuum of no man's land, a dimension of space where perhaps not a single living entity dares draw a breath. Inch by inch they sidle out, the men scanning the holed-out windows of the adjacent buildings, looking up to the canted rooftops. There isn't a sound that man would know; just the horror of emptiness and silence. He takes a deep breath as the rope yanks him forwards into the open light. The men hurry now, scurrying rats in the undergrowth. He is not as agile. He lumbers behind, dragged by the last of the three men, the rope cutting into his neck, his feet making a noise on the concrete. He thinks he feels a certain heat open up on his back, a radiating space big as a target board so conspicuous that any bored enfeebled sniper would be mad to pass up a pot shot at. But he keeps on moving. There is nothing else to do.

They round the side of the building and emerge onto an adjacent street. They make a dash for another alley and run its dark tunnel, then work their way around the back of a building and then another alley until they have networked well away from the city centre. They do not encounter another human being. The air at last softens and finally they stop and rest against a tall redbricked wall. They are panting and clearly relieved. But they don't hang around long. On they go, dragging him in their stern by the rope. Out down a deserted street heading west and then down a jacaranda-lined road where the soft scatter of purple flowers is a pleasant distraction, a luscious carpet under his feet. The air is infused with a citrus scent which burrows deep into his nose – even beyond the stench of the gag – and makes him think insatiably of food and those vegetables he was cruelly deprived of.

Eventually they leave the city centre behind and move into the rolling suburbs where high walls, green pavements and lines of tall firs hem their path. A strange sense of calm pervades here. The white people had quietly packed a suitcase, loaded up their cars and driven off to avoid the bother and tedium of the revolt. They are now sitting up in the lush wooded highlands, in stone chalets or log cabins, sipping gin and tonics, snacking on cheese biscuits while looking out over the grey receding tranquillity of a lake. In a while, when the evening chill rises, they will move indoors in front of lilting fires, spitting and crackling through wet logs of pine. They aren't thinking of the civil war, but they are. They are telling one another it's all going to be fine, but they don't believe it.

It was different for him. He wasn't able to pack up and drive off. Caught up in the sudden wave of confusion, things suddenly escalating about him, he walked around for some time not really sure of anything. It was all a fraction removed from him; his mind clouded with an irrepressible despondency, lost in some catalepsy of thought. For a while it was as if things were happening around him in quick, sporadic glitches of unravelling importance which he failed to grasp. Only some days later did he come to the understanding that he ought to sidestep the hubbub and pace his way out of the city before it was too late altogether. Before someone saw him and hewed him down. Before someone in their inhuman desperation (God forbid) ate him. Before a bunch of thugs threw a lasso and captured him.

As they lead him past the houses he looks in at the high electric gates and occasionally he can see the large houses hidden away in the shadowy splurge of the gardens. But there is no sign of life. No sign, therefore, of possible rescue. Every now and then a pair of large, jaw-snapping dogs comes charging the gate as they pass, salivating and foaming at the mouth from lack of food and water. They have been left behind in the panic, or maybe on purpose as a deterrent to the looters. There is something redundant about their fierce loyalty. They will be dead in a day or two, hacked down mid-bark or leap, their bones licked clean for meat, their hides scraped, salted, baked dry in the sun, stitched into clothes that the limping survivors of the genocide will strap around them.

Past the expansive suburbs and beyond the manicured golf course where the flags on the greens still wave when the wind blows; they walk the roadside and encounter few people. Those they do come across veer to the other side of the road and slink past them cowering. Or they are seen in the distance and are gone in an instant, slipping down the side roads, creeping down into the ditches where they disappear behind a mesh of bush. No cars. No rickety bicycles that are easy targets for three thugs to chase and snatch. They walk for some time. The sun licks the asphalt, spooling back at them in refractory waves. It is midday or just past it. Other bandits may have quartered themselves away from the nakedness of the noontime blink, holing up in shacks and makeshift shanties, but they carry on walking as if on a journey out of the world itself. He is tired but doesn't falter. His captors are tired, too, but they don't show it. The man who leads him tugs on the rope. It makes a tight line between them along which runs a constant menacing pulse. He can feel the vibration at his neck.

They turn off the main road, make a few turns down side roads and continue walking. From behind them a lone figure appears, hobbling along the track and gesturing to them, calling out for them to stop. The men halt and draw their blades and call back. The figure comes limping up, his bare hands raised in the air. He is an old man with bad hips or a bad leg and a silvering mat of hair. He wears the khaki uniform of a domestic servant. His cheeks are fat; he has large pale eyes which are genial and carry no threat. The men relax. They stand and talk for a while. Gestures are exchanged. The old man points up the road and beckons them to follow. After a while they turn around and walk with this old man who keeps chatting amiably while looking him up and down out the corner of his eyes. All through the short journey this man casts a constant possessive glare over him and he doesn't like it.

They arrive at the gate of a large property, slab-walled with a concreted seal of broken glass. The gate is high and barred. The old man wheels it back and ushers them in. The yard is vast and vacant. No dogs yap at their arrival but he has a feeling still that this is marked territory. The brick drive winds elegantly to a double-door garage and, beside it, a house that looks cool and newly whitewashed. It has a black roof and wide French doors and windows with rose-bushes sprawling beneath them. The lawn has begun to overgrow. The dead flowers in the beds lining the driveway droop from their stalks or have fallen and lie crushed on the tarmac. The pool has begun to turn green; its rim heaves with a mulch of leaves. Otherwise it's an ordinary suburban home. They make their way up to the house and stop by a long glitter-stone porch with white-enamelled railings.

They tie him by the rope to a pole and he stands there looking on. He has no comprehension of what they have come here to do. He tries to inch back on the rope but the knot only tightens. He can only stand and watch what unfolds, bear witness to acts from which he is excluded. His dimming mind is growing ever more passive as the day wears on. It rests somewhere on the edge of indolence, nestled blissfully in a vegetable patch or a peach tree. Only skittering motions of violence or danger will dislodge it. The old man fishes a key from his pocket and shows it off to the men. They crowd round as he unlocks the door and burst into the lounge. The old cookboy is knocked to the ground.

They comb the house, the old man piteously wobbling after them in turns, calling after the beasts he has unleashed on his master's home, pleading with them to restrain themselves. He can see them from the porch, streaming up and down the passage, in and out of the lounge. They push the old man out of the way and dismiss his pleas. There are tall framed photographs of smiling white faces sitting on the TV cabinet until they're brushed off with an urgent swipe and shatter crisply on the ceramic floor. Books are pulled from shelves, ornaments go flying, furniture is shunted about.

The old man backs away to the porch door and stands there looking on.

The house is trashed from the inside out. In the orgy of looting a spate of fighting breaks out: two of them have laid claim to a DVD player and tug it back and forth between their clenched fists, their voices snarling at one another. One strains forward and slams the other into a wall. There is a thud; an oil landscape tilts on its hook and slides to one side. It takes the third man to calm them down and stop an all-out brawl. In the relative sanity that follows, they gather their booty and bring it out onto the porch. A small flatscreen TV, a laptop, a digital camera, the DVD player. The old man stands, his face and eyes glazed over. The hard lead weight of his betrayal. He looks at his trade, tied there frail and meek to the pole. He looks over the stack of merchandise. There is a grim silence as the men make one last sweep of the house. Then they lug their pickings off down the drive, an easy swagger in their step. The old man watches them disappear up the road and then locks up the house, slips the key into his pocket and unties him from the pole.

He cares little for what has just happened. He has no great opinion about it beyond the raw facts, its bland happening. The old man limps away with him round the back of the house, past the garage and down a little narrow path towards the kias which are nestled behind a spilling compost heap and a tin garden shack with tendrils of moss growing up the base. The old man hardly looks at him now but ties him to the branch of a lemon tree and then sits down on a shoddy wooden stool outside the door to the kia room. Now that there are only two of them he begins to moan and struggle in the grip of the rope and the foul gag, but the old man doesn't seem in the mood for granting a little sympathetic respite. Just a little hunched man sitting there brooding and staring ahead as if the world and its sins has suddenly blinded him, as if he stares on nothing but darkness now, tanned with the dimmest infusion of the sun.

After a while, the old man gets up and limps to the side of his kia and bends to scoop up a sadza-caked pot. He carries it over to a tap spurting like a flower from a patch of green button weeds and begins to scour it with a wire brush. The suds of sadza clot and loosen, pooling into scum which he tips down a drain, speckling it white with dripping slime. He leans the pot against the wall and peels some shoots of rape which he heaps into a bundle. He lumbers off his stool again and shuffles inside the dark cube of his room.

He is quiet for a time. The gloom furls out, an insidious gas, vaporized instantly by the chinks of sun piercing the lemon tree and the hedge against the wall. Suddenly there is a great sharp whack of a blade against a chopping board. It slices through him. He shudders from the inside out. A grey dove takes flight from the tree, scatters up against the blueness of the day and vanishes. Another pelt of the blade and this time he hears the steel rend. He strains in the harness and pulls hard against the tree. The rope jams and grips his neck and his shoulder blades. A sharp pain cuts into him. The thin bow of the trunk lilts but will not give. He starts shaking his head but the ropes are unforgiving. Now the old man is at his side shouting at him and grappling at the ropes to steady him. From the corner of his eye he catches sight of the meat cleaver raised and ready to strike and he cowers down against the tree.

The threat is enough to still him. He stands uneasily, breathing heavily and panting through the gag. His breath is steamy and hot, wheeling about his mouth. His feet feel impermanent. The old man moves back inside his room. Soon there is the dull clanking sound of metal bashing against brick. When the man walks out again he's carrying a stainless steel dish which he places on the ground. Inside lies the rump and hindquarter of some small beast glistening darkly in a stow of blood. It looks muscled and lean with a pointed foot that's been half hacked away. Blood pools from the flesh in an accumulated silence. The old man squats by the tap and fills the pot to half. He presses in the rape and sets it aside. Then he moves over to a small paraffin cooker stacked atop some charred bricks and fiddles with the valves before taking a box of matches from his pocket and lighting the plate. It flares in a low blue flame. The rape boils away and when it's reduced some he adds more water before laying in the hindquarter. It bubbles and spatters. The stench of the dark meat gluts the air.

The old man tears the withered rape leaves and picks at the grey hindquarter. He rolls them into balls and chews them strenuously. He sits consuming his meal while his new acquisition stands tied to a tree looking on it all. When he is finished lapping up the juices with the last of the leaves he rinses out the pot and stands it to drain. Then he takes the bone over to a garbage pile heaped up beside a vegetable bed where limp green stacks of rape sprout. He tosses the bone and a pocket of flies bursts out and scatters momentarily before diving back to a small pelt of beige and white fur that hangs over the branch of an avocado tree. The old man limps back again and looks him up and down and then goes off to his room. There descends a long and rigid quiet.

*

He looks at the tap and the circle of damp beneath it and can feel the thirst harden in his mouth. He has been standing for some time. His legs are tired. His mouth is numb. There is a dull ache nudging the corners of his eyes. He manages to shift his stance and turn himself around. He eyes up the garden, the back of the house, the driveway running crisply to the gate and can sense the open road. He knows he should try and make good an escape before the old man wakes up and comes out of his room and starts looking him up and down with vague insinuations. He looks closely at the knots that bind him, he bends forward and tries to gnaw at one with his teeth, but the gag is too tight: he can barely open his mouth. Shifting, he strains again, trying to bend the branch to a point where it will snap. But it won't. He eases up and stands there. Then, ahead of him he sees two youths standing and watching. They have jumped over the wall from the neighbouring house.

They are in their early teens but look hardened, carrying sacks on their backs with machetes belted to them. They whisper to one another and he can't hear them. These boys look surprised to see him tied there; disbelieving, in a contented sort of way, as if they'd stumbled on a store of wealth. As they come towards him his body tenses up. He tries to cringe into himself but he is unable to. Then there is a sound

to the right of them and the old man is standing at his doorway. He starts to shout and gesticulate, lumbering forward,
but one of the boys has already lunged out and struck him
across the throat. The blood thickens quickly. The old man
gargles and splutters, staggering back against the wall where
he slides to the ground leaving a swathe of blood smeared
bright against the brickwork.

In the racking stillness of those next moments, neither boy seems to know what to do. They look at the old man's body slumped against the wall, the blood still spilling in jets from the gash at his throat. It seems that only when the jets slow to a trickle do they register their act and are quick to extricate themselves from it. They untie him from the tree and pull him along with them. In shock, his legs stumble on mechanically and he doesn't put up any protest.

They had come to ransack houses but they are leaving with a bigger prize – a living being. They move down the driveway and pull the gate back on its coaster, relieved to find it's not locked. It's as if they want to get out quick so the next marauders who scale the wall won't find what they've found. It is bewildering to him why they would want to take him hostage. He has no concept of his value in this order of things. Still, the three of them move briskly down the deserted road and quickly make a turn left and then they turn left again onto what seems like a wider, more public road. But it is deserted. The hot eeriness of a fairground park after hours, thronging with the buzz of its daytime crowds.

They hurry along, almost at a trot, pulling him behind them. It's as if something may swerve round the corner at any second and store them in their sights: some murderous, militant gang. They quickly veer off towards a small shopping centre. It too is deserted save for the odd car caught unawares in the lot, windscreens webbed and sagging from a pelting. The ransacked bottle store; the butchery; the fruit and veggie mart; the pharmacy. Red plastic shopping baskets lie cracked, scattered at the entrances. Giant dominoes of white enamelled shelves lie toppled into each other. The mannequins in the small boutique lie naked and grotesquely abused on beds of glass. He is pulled round the back of the complex where a stinking stretch of potholed tar covers the ground between the delivery zones of the shops and a whitewashed wall now grey with grime and graffiti. The puckered tar has blades of beige grass sticking up through it like sails on paper boats and litter spills from large drums and lies decaying in the stagnant sun.

An agitation of flies and then the slimy belly of a rat slides through the scatter and he hardly notices the odd pair standing there in the lot. They seem somehow the limp and tatty product of its squalor. A stocky man of middling height with a stern expressionless face comes striding forward, opens a toothless mouth and a raw sound spews out, some alien lingo. He is strangely drawn to the workings of the man's mouth, opening and closing on a darkness, certain night hours never yet witnessed. For a moment he is scared to his skin. And when the man ceases talking a sudden stillness sweeps down. Motions and actions he wasn't aware of stop and fall silent and he feels a malign and concentrated attention push towards him. For an awkward time no one says anything. Not the boys, his captors. Not the strange cast staggered about in this weird and random tableau.

He looks about and surveys the people around him. There are four altogether now: this man, the two boys, and a woman. She is pregnant. The last time he saw a woman was one stone dead in the bushes. She is crouched on the ground, weary eyed. She ignores him. He stares at them all for a heavy moment which may be quite a passing of time or almost none at all.

He senses the man is very pleased with the boys' find, their catch. The boys are smiling, basking in their triumph. He stands there in that dusty quarter with the rope dangling from his neck to the tar. He is a specimen they talk about, scrutinize. They are studying his bones, his physique, his condition. Together they are making an appraisal of him, saying what an asset he will be when the time comes for them to need an asset. Yet despite the humiliation, the conveyed indignity of it, the drive to turn and run from the shopping centre and back down the roads through the suburbs somehow seems devoid in him. It's curled tightly into some wrought place. Perhaps he simply lacks the energy to do so. He stands asunder from the group and watches them with his tired eyes. The rope dappling on the ground. His unshackled being. The gag still packed in his mouth and sitting acridly on his tongue and in the mayhem it seems he has almost relinquished its existence.

The man mutters to one of the youths who walks towards him and picks up the end of the rope and walks him ten paces before fixing it to an iron pole cemented into the concrete ground. The pole forms the corner of a large storage bin and the rotting smells instantly stain the air. Even the boy recoils in disgust and walks away quickly. If only the gag was removed he could at least breathe through his mouth. He should feel sick but he doesn't. He stands there for some time tied to the pole and the discomfort of it and the tiredness in his legs starts to make him moan a little. The muffled sound he invokes is pathetic. No one is roused an instant.

He watches the woman crawl about gathering waste in the lot. She scoops it up in the bow of her baggy dress and hobbles over to a heap of ash and scalded bricks where she stacks it into a tripod, ready to be lit. The man brings out a box of matches from an inner pocket of his trousers. He extracts a single match and strikes down. The match flares and wanes and flares. Some relief is evident. The fuel is lit. The woman squats next to it and begins to roast four maize cobs she has skewered with the spokes of a plundered shopping trolley. He looks on in amazement. Such wealth: a store of cobs casually spiked and stacked atop the flames; the pale yellow gleam of their kernels gently browning, blistering. The smell of charred sweetness.

Still, the smoky whiff of maize may drift too far in the cauterized air and alert some prowling famished gang to their whereabouts. Here any conception is possible. All is stoked by desperation of the lowest order. Some ravaging troop may come bursting over the wall or pounce on them from the tops of the shop buildings. The gangs of rival militias may come across them and their four little cobs and blast them all away. Or the approaching wave of the military – surely at last regrouped and mobilized – may storm the area, round them up and have them declared guilty of treason. They'd be shot in the head at dawn or struck in the gut with a panga if their bullets had by then run out. It would be no small wonderment.

*

For a while he studies this group with a cautious eye. The man has a sprouting of grey in his beard and his hair. He is fairly well built but thin with a firm gaunt face and eyes that hint to some steeliness in his character, some depth of soul not for the turning. He wears faded tweed trousers, a grubby white shirt, threadbare at the collar, and a pair of dusty leather shoes. He sizes this man up, scrutinizes him: it is his turn now. It's possible the two adolescents will prove to be the most combative. They seem to be of similar age, twins possibly, and they sit about bare-chested, their charcoal skin drawn tight across their firm bodies, their thighs bulging, their biceps prominent, their calves sculpted and sanded and pumiced from some great hulk of ebony.

The man chats to the boys as if telling stories round a bonfire while the woman continues to turn the browning cobs over the smoky flame. They seem at ease. They seem to believe in their own sense of infallibility, here in the back alleyway of the shops, nestled cosily. The woman presents them with their blackened cobs and then withdraws into the shade of some awning strung up from the back of one of the shops and sits looking out over the cracking asphalt. He sees them biting into the cobs and a first touch of despondency breaks within him. He remains standing for a while longer and when it seems acceptable to do so he sinks to the ground, the rope just loose enough to allow him the flexibility to lower his head and catch a moment's rest.

They sit round all afternoon stoking and feeding the waning fire. Sometimes talking, mostly not. Sometimes listening as a rare truck roars close by, sounding as if it has driven into the parking lot. They wait for the military choppers that blade overhead. They are listening, too, for the blare that comes from the trucks that had of late rolled across the streets and suburbs, loudspeakers wired to their cab tops, a continuous disembodied drone wavering out at the few people who remained, like the grave voice of an embittered god. The trucks had inched street by street, the strange electric voice echoing all about them. Some of the citizens may have thought Armageddon itself was at hand. Some had drifted about dazed and aimless and catatonic, defying the decree to leave the city and return to their tribal lands. They wanted the city flushed. Then some who had dallied were shot on sight and kicked into ditches. Everyone else went into hiding.

The day has been hot and the long walk from the shanties has taken its toll. His shoulders are tight and his limbs ache. His body hankers for a patch of rest but as the sun finally dips down and a dim amber glow spools over the cooling asphalt, they all rouse themselves at the command of the man. The youths have been snoozing on flattened cardboard boxes, the woman at rest under the spread of the tatty awning. One of the youths comes over and unties him from the pole. Not a word is uttered; the boy hardly even looks at him. The men gather themselves. The woman remains sitting. From a stack of sacks and plastic bags one of the boys extracts a broomstick broken in half with a bob of hessian bundled round the top. The boy lowers this handmade torch to the fire and in an instant it flares in a quick wave of blue, then settles down to a weak pulsing flame. The smell of methylated spirits briefly sours the air.

They set off at sunset from the back of the shopping

centre. The man, the two boys and he. One boy carries the torch, the other swings an empty twenty-litre plastic water container. The man carries a bundle under his arm, wrapped in a white shopping bag with a red logo on it, but he soon slips it under the inner sleeve of a thin navy tracksuit top which he puts on and zips up. The three of them move out, pulling him in their wake, plodding along the quiet roads of the suburbs once again. The branches of trees intertwine overhead tunnelling them in and dousing them in a syrupy light which seems all too confining. It's growing dark quickly and apart from the darting whine of a mosquito, nobody else is about. Even the abandoned dogs have given up their gate patrol.

Over everything there's soon a great spill of darkness and no glimmer of a moon. Not one of the houses seems occupied and when night falls and the crickets finally sing from the lawns, there are no dotted gate lights. No slow flickering street lamps overhead casting waves of dimness up through the netted branches and down on the grimy road. Not even the lowing of a generator breaking the dead stillness of the air. It is just them: four dimly illuminated figures plunging into the darkness. The torchlight is a comfort. He feels a sense of relief that because of the glow he can see what surrounds him. At least things have vague form and the group are not these bodiless beings haranguing him in the dark and pulling him along in the depths of some stuffy dream.

They turn down a road. The trees on the pavements have thinned out and an immediate sense of exposure floods over him. The sky opens up on a covering of dull, distant stars. The lack of light across the city renders the night naked and raw. The sky used to look different – cool and calm and chaste – not this random screen of chaos which now seems to exude some force of misalignment, some pretension. Of course the truth is that the sky is the sky and really it's the blotted fuzziness of his mind that drops it so sharply from focus.

At a T-junction they make a left and then soon afterwards a right into what ends in a close, the road circling a small island of spiky indistinct grass. Three large properties arch around it. They make their way to the one in the middle and stop outside a tall wall stitched along the top with a coiled electric fence and a squat nest of cacti shrubs planted along the bottom. Even in the dark he can see the tips of the thorns glimmering like nails and trace the erectness of the rubbery shoots towards a blurred mass of black. The others stand awhile conferring with one another. The man approaches the tin-boarded electric gate and taps three times. Then he stands back and waits. Whistles quietly. Nothing happens. He knocks. Finally a soft coarse voice calls out from the night and a faint, fluid conversation starts up. He can't understand a word and tension nudges its way into his stomach.

Eventually the gate rolls back a short way on its coaster. The man enters and then the gate rolls closed again and they are left waiting outside those teethed walls. A space of time passes. That dark disjunction of being. Something cold across his soul. At last the gate slides ajar and a whisper brings them in. The property at once gives off the rich scent of wet soil – he is alarmed at the comfort of this. The humid smell fills his lungs and draws him along the driveway, no one need prod him or yank him now.

The moisture is such a pleasant change to the dry dustiness he has been accustomed to that gets up his nose and sits there along with the nebulizing muzzle across his face. The whole garden seems to drip coolness from every branch, from every shrub, fern, plant. Immediately he senses a flow of water nearby. His mouth prickles with anticipation and he is drawn to the sight of a man in tatty overalls and gumboots standing by a flowerbed, holding a hosepipe, drenching the plants and the soil. There is no muffled roar of a generator; there is only an inexplicable silence that incites his bafflement.

Oblivious to constraints, he trudges his way over and stands beside the hose, silent and breathless. No one says anything. The man withdraws the plastic bag from under his tracksuit. He opens it and brings out a bag of crushed dried fish. Someone comes up behind them along the driveway. A short man in a grey overcoat. He takes the bag of fish and holds it, running his fingers over the clear plastic, stroking the flaky fillets. Finally he nods to the man holding the hose, slipping the fish underneath his coat and disappearing up the driveway. The man and the boys come forward and drink their fill and then they dip the nozzle of the pipe into the container and they all stand about listening to it drum against the plastic. It curls full to the brim. They screw the cap onto it tightly and one of the boys walks off with it, lopsided now, down the driveway and into the bleary darkness.

All the while he stands there looking on patiently and desperately. It is impossible they will forget him. He is aware of an exchange of bemused glances and then the other boy is beside him, fiddling with the gag. Its release is such relief his vision fuzzes slightly and he feels light on his feet. When he regains focus the man with the hosepipe is looking at him. A moment later he steps forward and brings the nozzle to his mouth like some apostolic baptizer of the night. The spray juts out firm and steady and gushes round his mouth strong as an avalanche.

He drinks and drinks until the hose is pulled away from him. He watches it continue to drench the dark colourless plants. He stands there and gapes bewildered about him and allows the damp night air to be drawn towards his sated tongue and wet face, to sink its soft balminess into his tired brow. Indulged in this luxuriance, his guard lowered, he feels adrift from the actions of his captors. They have disappeared down the driveway and left him. He hears muted voices punctuating the steady spray throbbing from the hosepipe but nonetheless he feels alone and distantly, blissfully frightened. He stands regarding the man watering the flowerbed.

They walk back down the driveway. They pick up the rope and reattach the gag. The gate rolls open and lets them slip out and rolls closed again. There a couple are waiting outside with an array of empty juice bottles, whistling softly for some attention. Briefly their eyes all meet in the bluish halo of the hessian lamp, invisible lasers scanning one another with the deepest scrutiny. Not a sound is uttered between them. They move away from the property and tread along the road. The boy lugging the water container falls some way behind and the man lingers with him. The risk of being seen in the glow is too terrifying to contemplate, so the other boy leads him on and carries the torch as a decoy. He looks like a medieval monk on a lone crusade, stooping across the outlays of some heathen land.

They take a few turns and walk for some while before stopping outside a property with a high brick wall and a line of shadowy palm trees along its pavement. It has an ornate entrance with concrete statues of miniature sphinxes guarding the gates. The boy with the water cowers behind the palms. The man whistles and taps on the high wooden gate. Someone pulls back one half of the unwieldy gate and they step inside. The man moves off at once, sidling along the darkness of hedge. One boy follows after him and then the other boy comes sidewinding into the entrance, rolling the drum of water. The gate closes. All is quiet.

He moves along the driveway to seek his captors out, following the distant hum of voices. There is no inclination to flee: the streets beyond the gate are serpentine, inked with malice. So he moves forward. There is a garage draped in creepers and behind it a shed made from planks, with a strong stench of creosote. He spots them deep in negotiations. His captor and another man. They gibber animatedly.

At times voices are raised and exclamations uttered before they remember themselves and the volume of their speech lowers to an expressive whisper. Then the two men move off behind the house and follow a small brick-lined path towards the rear domestic quarters. He stands looking about. The house is an imposing double-storey; the darkened sheen of the windows gives it an eerie presence. It is possible people may actually be behind those windows even now looking down into the garden at his shape in the dark and wondering strange things.

There is squeaking along the path. The men return pushing a weird and cumbersome contraption. It lollops ungraciously along the uneven brickwork and then comes into full view. Two small wheels with fat tyres are attached to a chassis and the chassis is welded to a frame of sorts on which is fixed a wrought-iron cab or compartment. It looks exactly the same as the ice boxes the ice-cream men used to push or the portable bread bins the bread vendors used to station at street corners. Just bigger. They draw it to a halt near him. He looks down at the compartment which is decked out with warped wooden plywood planks. Leading from the chassis are two poles in an A-frame and where the two poles meet, a toe hitch. Its creator stands over it protectively, still prodding bits into place, holding a complex network of ropes and harnesses. He has some inclination what is about to happen next.

The two youths come behind him, grip him by the shoulders and turn him around. He tries to struggle but they shout, *Hey hey hey,* and he feels the flat of a hand slap him across the back of his neck. The pain inches into him so he stands still. The gag is reattached and tied tight behind his head. A weight comes down on his back, straddling his neck. Within a few seconds the whole thing is fixed, the ropes bound round his chest and shoulders. An unknowing feeling of despair comes over him. There is a thud behind him and he sees they've dumped the water container into the compartment. Someone pushes him in the back; he feels a sharp punch to his ribs. *Shoo, shoo,* the boy says, gesturing him to walk. Wide eyed and startled he moves forward and feels the weight of the contraption strain against him. He tries again. The boy slaps him in the ribs once more and he lunges forward grimacing as the whole ungainly mechanism moves along the driveway after him bobbing like some gangly old chimp in a circus show.

Even the short trip back to the shopping centre is taxing. The wheels are fat but slight in circumference and the sheer inconstancy of them fails to grip the tar. They have not been mounted properly; they wobble and shake.

The chassis has no suspension to speak of so the weight of the compartment and the axle pounds into him whenever the tyres slip into the smallest divot, sending a battery of shocks through his spine. Hitting a pothole will be calamitous. He walks with his eyes trained to the tarmac, scanning in the dim glow.

Back across those goffered tracks they tramp in the dark, through the cavernous tunnels of trees, beneath the icy distant spew of stars, the absent moon. Nothing moves out there except their motley troop. Those three stooges and he and the cart behind him whining and slurping over the black pool of roads. Some way before they reach the shopping centre the hessian torch hisses, flickers and burns out and that weak blue flame is extinguished forever. So they inch onwards unsighted in the shudder of those night-time sounds.

At the hideout the woman squats again over a small flame roasting cobs behind a screen of cardboard boxes. The boys extract the water container, undo the cart and wheel it parallel to a wire cage which towers with crates of empty bottles. They tie him again to the pole and soon he sinks to the ground, exhausted. His breathing is laboured. The men chew on their cobs and if they speak at all he cannot hear them. Blood is drumming in his ears, everything now a fraction removed from him, a fraction distorted, dulled, deadened. The woman retreats into the dark. He cannot see her now; only the men chewing away.

He lies there at his uncomfortable station, edging his weary spine against the grooves of the cage for some support. He looks about with listless eyes, the stencilled shapes of the figures blurring now and then, the fire's pull weakening. On occasion he hears odd sounds close by: the scurry of vermin, probing mosquitoes. Once an empty bottle topples on concrete somewhere, shattering the taut stillness. One of the boys is sent to investigate and comes stumbling by, swooned in lethargy, his eyes half succumbed to sleep, a line of drool crusted down his chin. He tries to extend his hearing beyond the lot and out into the wide furling night but there he can only determine a warm thrumming stagnancy. He tries to spool his senses into the asphalt to discern the distant shudder of tanks rolling quietly into town or the collected thud of soldiers' marching boots stamping crisp across the roads but he can detect nothing.

Some indistinguishable time later a low hiss bores its way into his ears and he looks across the lot at a figure hunched in the dark. His eyes accustom themselves to the sight of the man cradling a small radio, thumbing at the knob. The boys sit round like elders at a tribal council. A slew of words here and there between the hissing and bleeping. All gibberish to him. They thumb on. Then finally a string of speech. The set is raised to the man's ears. He lowers his head and closes his eyes and they all sit listening. They exclaim intermittently. The occasional shake of the head. Some stuttered disbelief. Then the words dissolve into strains of traditional music, tinny and jerky, and they click the radio off and fold up its aerial, slipping it back into a sack.

The group sit mumbling. The odd tune hummed in that hooded cloister. Phrases of bush lore. Perhaps some calling on the ancestors. One by one they drop off, lying curled against one another on the cardboard tarps and raggedy bags. He puts his head down and allows the world to dislodge around him. He dozes. He wakes. He dozes.

At some point he hears whispered discussion and raises his consciousness from the dank concrete terrain to see the man standing and instructing the boys, gesturing and pointing. The boys clutch something pliable and the man bends towards the clutter round the fire and brings out the length of a machete. He sees its cold blade glint in the dimness and something in him stiffens. One of the boys takes the machete and together with his cohort slips off into the dark while the man looks on after them. He

stands there for a long time watching, even after their dis-
seminated bodies have waned in the shroud of night and
there is nothing except the presence of their actions reeling against the fears of his mind. It is some time before the
man breaks his stare and steals back to his cardboard
mattress.

He may sleep only lightly after this. He may not sleep at
all. Probing shivers of anxiety and fear spill across his flesh.
Hours later he hears a distinct whistle and thinks it must be
birdsong heralding the dawn. Nothing so innocent. The man
leaps up from his curled state and rushes from view. A pause
in which every imagined horror riles him. He huddles
against the cage. As he cowers down, the rope tautens. Then
they all return – the man, the two boys – tramping in a line
like silhouettes shorn of the soul.

They lug bloated sacks across their shoulders like gross
deformities. They swing them from their backs and the
staccato clank of tin against the iron casement of a rubbish
dumpster placates his thoughts, wanes his fear. He loses
interest in their operation and from then on he is only
conscious of odd movements about him and at times a
strange flitting presence which seems to be standing over
him and observing him. Perhaps it's one of the group checking to see he has not fled in the night. That he has not bitten

through the gag and wrestled free from the ropes and slunk his furtive shadow into the abyss. Or maybe all this is some machination of the mind, some conjured fear made tangible on the sterile night air.

Dawn comes in the end. Then the blaze of the full morning sun, cruel and bright on the grey turf. No birdsong in the suburbs that he can hear. No jostling sounds from the streets: the sweep of morning traffic or the brisk rush to work. He fixes his eyes on the ropes that dangle round him and drape on the asphalt where he lies – the stolid assurance of his reality. Already the men are up, sitting on the boxes with the loose sacks swathed across their shoulders, staring out over the vacant lot as if this moment dawned over each of them with the full weight of some unsolvable quandary. There is no sign of the woman.

They dig about in the guts of a large waste dumpster and unearth a heap of tatty bags and plastic packets. The bags are stuffed with rags and clothing, spilling with food the boys have plundered in some vicious raid he doesn't care to think on. Tins of relish, baked beans. Bags of dried fish, rice and grain. One or two luxuries: a bottle of cooking oil, a tin of paraffin, a black cooking pot. He stands there as the boys wheel out the cart and station it behind him. They hardly glance at him. The harness is attached; the ropes bundled tighter round his chest.

The woman appears from round the back of the dumpster and hobbles across the asphalt, gripping the ball of her swollen stomach as she idles towards him. Her breathing is laboured. Screeds of discomfort flush across her face. She stands by the cart, her hands pressed into her back. The man packs the cab with cardboard and rags and then slowly helps her ease her way in. The cart sags under the immediate strain of it; the wheels buckle some. She sits with her legs raised over the edges of the compartment, the weight of her pregnant stomach rising from her like a bulb.

The rest of the group gather themselves, the provisions slung over their shoulders or somehow tied to their backs. The heavier sacks are stashed beside the woman in the cart and the water container is wedged between her legs. The wheels strain and fret, the chassis bulging beneath it all. One of the boys slaps him on the back with the flat of a machete. Pain darts towards his spine and splinters outwards across his body. He lurches forwards, digging into the ground with his legs. The strain of it. The cart rocks gently back and forth. He lunges again, feeling the ropes cut across his chest, neck, shoulders.

All he knows is fear for the flight of the machete through the quickening air at his straining neck. There is nothing comprehensible about what lies ahead. The distance is unknown to him, the scale of the torment yet to be borne. The woman grits her teeth and grips the cart, legs flung immodestly outwards. How long, in her condition, can she tolerate the thumps of the ride before her womb yields and her waters soak the planks beneath her? He has no assurance that within a mile, maybe half that, she won't be screaming in pain or that the birth, messy and fatal at the side of the road, will be the only way they realize their stupidity and draw a halt to the journey before it has begun.

Off they go, shuffling from the stinking shopping centre and onto the side roads. No matter how shaky the ride becomes and how many divots the cart falters through, the woman hangs on with a steely resolve, holding her stomach and pulling wearisome faces, leaking the odd anguished groan. Her muscles must be as tough as rubber, her tendons as strong as wire.

Once momentum is established, the cart is not unbearably heavy to pull. The problem arises whenever they slow and the cart's centre of balance is disturbed. Then, the whole con-traption comes careening into his legs, or the front tilts abruptly, digging into the ground and causing the woman to shout out in anguished discomfort. It is not his fault. The men don't always see it this way and on occasion they grow petulant with him. He is hit hard across the side of his head and for a moment the grey road floats and froths as if a hot spring pooled beneath his feet. His eyes water over and he has no words to protest his alarm. He staggers on.

The city is flat for the most part, straddled atop an expansive plateau. It only undulates occasionally, rising and dipping over moderate inclines or hillocks. When they face such a rise it's a labour and a half. He feels the cart begin to strain and its weight moil and then the harness bites into his shoulders and a ten-tonne granite boulder may well be what he drags in his wake. The world is at his shoulders. But such slogging is nothing compared to the perils of any descent. He is lucky not to suffer serious injury to his legs. The boys walk alongside and when they see the cart wheel out of control they step in and pull backwards on it to ease the descent. Sometimes it's a close call. Sometimes they put stones under the wheels to act as a brake. Sometimes after such ordeals they bring the whole trap to a halt and allow him a moment to compose himself.

They go on like this for some time and the woman hunkers down and holds steady. She doesn't cry except for the occasional burst of whimpering. The rest of the group plod on grimly. On the flat stretches the boys run some way ahead of their path and, gripping the machetes in their fists, they survey the terrain for bandits lying in wait to ambush them. The man keeps a steely eye about him. If the boys lower the machete parallel to their legs then passage is safe. If it is raised to shoulder height it's a signal to halt whilst the boys make further investigations, often hunched down and crawling to the nearest cul-de-sac or gate post or hedge and then inching forward like spies or snakes in the undergrowth. When they come to a T-junction, they halt automatically some thirty or so yards before whilst the boys make a full reconnaissance of the coming bend or turn. The whole while the man glances behind them to make sure no one is sneaking up on them from the rear.

Sometimes the man drops the rope and walks alongside the cart and mutters words to the tender-bellied woman. For the most part they take inconspicuous back roads, sometimes winding round in a near circle to avoid the obvious dangers present on the main highways. Sometimes they encounter slim streams of pedestrians but long before their paths cross, the boys have confronted them and made them account for their intentions. Sometimes they are wary of approaching groups and quickly make a turn or a detour. Mostly the roads are deserted and so they inch onwards.

Then they are set on by a trio of militia. Tall, striding men dressed in long grey khaki coats leer towards them on their left flank. They appear from nowhere and the fright of it is instant, a shock through his whole self. He stops dead in his tracks. The woman's panting screams blunt the air and he sees the boys running back to them, brandishing their blades and yelling, but the attackers already have theirs poised and gripped double-fisted, trained within a few feet of them.

There is a stern holler and the boys freeze mid-motion, standing posed in attitudes half-ready to lunge or flee. They look to the man and the attackers alternately confused and frightened. The man steps forward with his bare hands held out and tries to talk, but the machete tenses in the bandit's fist and he stills himself. The trio circle in on them, glancing over their strange set-up with the blankest interest. His breath punctures into quickening gasps but outwardly he remains passive and immobile as a snake in the grasses. The negotiations are tense and frayed and it is only when the man points to the woman and she presses the outline of her belly do the bandits utter the briefest of exclamations. One of them strokes his chin and nods indifferently. Waves of relief spread over them all. The boys lower their machetes; the bandits do, too. There is some savouring calm. They poke around the knapsacks and prod at their pockets, helping themselves to two bags of dried fish and a jar of peanut butter before waving them on again. The group totters forward and no one looks back for an instant.

Their progress is even slower after this. The man mutters to the boys and scolds them. They look ashamed at the encounter and walk on sulkily. After a few hours they come to the edge of the city. The sun is blazing down now. They don't come across any other trouble. Only two cars tear by the whole morning, neither one military or police.

When they get to the outer suburbs the houses start looking more battered. Gates have been bashed down and the slabs of concrete walling smashed in with what looks to have been the rams of armoured vehicles, exposing the houses which show their injuries like victims lying destitute after some natural scourge. There's a barrage of damage: broken windows, tiles torn from the roofs, grids bent in, burglar bars contorted. No animals here. No scampering dogs. No fowl aflutter in the gardens.

Once or twice one of the boys is sent into the more affluent-looking properties to scavenge for provisions, but he comes back empty-handed. There is nothing left that could be carried by the hands of man; these places were scoured clean days ago. But a few houses later a pillow and some bedding are unearthed. The boy comes running out with glinting eyes, a widening grin. The man glances over the prize. The pillow is smeared with a crust of red which flakes off crisply when the man scratches at it with his fingernails. The dark mottled blanket hides its defilements. He folds the pillow onto its stain and tenderly packs it behind the woman's back. The blanket he folds and eases under her buttocks. On they tramp.

On the edge of the city some houses are mere shells, black and buckled, scarred wide across their red seared brick, roofing collapsed into great sooty cavities where the tiles lie shattered like scorified sprees of larva. Over everything this mordant splurge. When at last these properties thin out they cross a narrow plain – a dumping ground interspersed with clumps of dry grass – and beyond that the levelled expanse of a shanty town comes once again into view. These towns are different to the ones he traipsed through yesterday. Still there is little difference to the sight here. The smoke billows from the scorched metal and thatch and riddled plastic sheeting. The smells sour the air. They halt for a good minute and look over the carnage, sullen and bewildered. They mutter and exclaim. The extent of it all, the scale.

They seem glum-struck by it. The woman begins to sob, gently at first, and then breaking into loud, breathless wailing. Slowly, amidst this anguished requiem, they move on.

They do not stop again to dwell on the destruction but keep a stoical poise throughout their trail across the wasteland. Occasionally here and there they come across the grim sight of a limb sticking up through the debris, an arm or a leg, sometimes a stretch of skin that may be a belly or a back, always burnt crisp, the blood dried black. Always the man stiffens first and tries to veer them off onto another route or path but sights of the genocide are inevitable. The image of flesh gorged by flames, hardly inseparable from the rags and sheeting and scorched tin, yet always an instant pull on the eyes as if the brain is being drawn there to register the bloody and evil ways of man. The stench is unbearable; the air stained with tarry flesh smells blazed in the open, the heady congealment of blood and fluids, the harried soul spilling into the stagnancy, newly fled from a slashing or a beheading or a burning. Hanging there intermingled with the smoke, dumb and befuddled.

There in that great vacancy is the bareness of being. Plodding through those once-peopled killing fields, they inch along the tendrils of some encompassing dread.

Nothing they have ever known matches the senselessness of that sight. The sheer scar of vitriol. There seems no other way to go now they are in the middle of it. They have not chosen a route around the cooling inferno to avert bearing witness to this display of misery and desolation: they are amidst it, fording it. The boys keep having to clear a way for the cart, moving tin and brick and a clattering of junk spewed into the dirt tracts. In some areas the trail is smoothed by natural attrition. In others its tedium is over-bearingly torturous. For some stretches then he may close his eyes to the carnage and place one foot in front of the next and think of walking hapless along some soft-trodden way, furry reeds underfoot, or a lush flooring of marula leaves, the smooth wind across his brow, caressing his soul in muffled whispers.

This escapism cannot last long. The group grow easily impatient with him now. If he veers off-track they yank the rope and whoever is leading him turns and yells or else comes close to him and thumps him on the top of his head or punches his shoulder. It's a rude awakening. Then the reason for crossing the wasteland becomes apparent. On the far end of the shanty, quite some distance from the remains of the shacks, there is a narrow path that opens out from a dense swagger of bush and leads them round to a small series of huts. They have not been destroyed entirely, though the thatching of one has caught ablaze and collapsed into ash. They make their way to the end hut and stop. It's partially shaded by a tall wilting msasa, its dry mottled leaves have scattered a carpet across the pale dirt. The man circles the hut and looks about with some concentration. There is not another being for miles and the man is sure of this, but isn't taking any chances.

He signals for the boys to come towards him and together they start jumping up and down. It is not the end of the journey. They are not jubilant, nor have they cracked and gone mad. Their jumping is mechanical, stiff, pragmatic. After each jump they stop and move a step to one side and then jump again. After five or so jumps there is a metallic thud that booms out from beneath them. Something hollow, something cavernous beneath them sounds that strident note. They stop and drop to their knees and claw at the dust. A great russet swell plumes the air from their furrowing. They scoop off the top layer of gravel and squat next to a rectangular strip of metal sheeting nailed to what seems to be the frame of a door. They heave and push it aside and a dark, dusty cavity opens on them like the restive darkness of some tomb. The boys drop themselves down and burrow in this pit. All he can see is the swells of red dust rising and dissolving.

Soon there is the sound of metal against metal. A shaft of iron points out to the sky. The man grabs it and brings it out fully into the hot shiny day, smoothing off the dust with his shirt. He stands there looking down on the weapon cradled in his arms.

The sight of the gun draws all eyes to its stiff metallic bearing, the caveat of the barrel. An automatic rifle. An AK47. Across them all echoes the splintering silence of such an unearthing. There is a stilled shudder hardening against the hotness of the day, as if none of them seems certain how to bear up in the presence of a gun. The boys feed out the beads of ammunition. Two belts in total. Hardly an arsenal to gloat about.

They pick themselves up from the pit, dust themselves off and pull the metal grid across the cavity. With their feet they rake waves of gravel over the entire enclosure. Just the bare blanketed ground now. Just a man and a gun, belts of bullets.

They gather themselves together and without a word between them they trundle on, back the way they came. The threadbare path, the ash-soaked shanties, the carious fields. This time their track is easier to traverse but the sights are no less scaring. When they veer towards the puckered roads of the outer suburbs they digress across a forking channel of paths and here the cart occasionally gets wedged between the flange of narrow bush and it's a struggle to pull it through. He strains and stamps ahead and the cab surfs through a sea of falling vlei and the woman clutches on. When he peers back he sees her scrunched grimacing face, though he doesn't hear her wail.

They diverge sharply from their path and progress northwards through the tussled bush toward another line of huts, their kerbs puddled with clay, thatched and arched in a semicircular clearing of pale, cracked earth. The huts stand unscathed but seem deserted. The same stillness levitates over them, the same quivered fright. They stop at a hut in the middle. Its entrance is bordered with bones hanging from plaited shoots of grass attached to the jamb. There is a wooden stool placed at the entrance of the door, the wavy grain of its seat top polished to a smooth glow, its sides puckered with deep vermiculate borings. There are pots and skins and cleavers scattered about.

Inside the hut a mustiness settles over everything and beyond it the smell of crushed herbs, ground bone and blood. The bare feet of an old man are just visible, the crisp skin of his calves veined and creased and almost white in the wash of sun which licks over them. Then the figure of a small boy comes through the door gripping a spear which he flails and pegs to the hard ground before them. The boy disappears into the darkness as if he'd never been present. Just the spear dow-elled to the turf. The old pair of feet haven't moved an inch.

From their group the man calls out and drops to his knees and the boys behind him drop to their knees too. His calling trails into a tune he hums or incants. He moves towards the cart and fumbles in the sacks, pulling out a packet of soya chunks and a 750ml bottle of vegetable oil. He crawls over to place these offerings before the spear. They wait a long time before the small boy appears and in a single movement he withdraws the spear, scoops up the offerings and backs into the hut again. After a while there is the sound of a rattle stir-ring from the cavity. The boy emerges, the spear held out, and behind him, with a hand on the youth's shoulder, the stooping figure of an old man, his eyes sunken in his shriv-elled face, pale blue, milked over, unseeing. He has a gourd in his hand, which he shakes in a perpetual dirge and across his chest is a velvety leopard pelt. He wears faded blue denims ragged at the knees.

When the old man speaks he spits as he has no teeth, just tiny pins where teeth once were. His whole face curls into the cavity of his mouth. He stands unsteadily on his feet, his hand gripping the boy's shoulder, his guide, his support. The sage talks and as he does the boy draws lines on the ground with the tip of the spear. Lines indistinguishable to anyone but those well versed in bush lore. The man looks down with deep scrutiny, listening, training his eyes on every angle, every line the boy carves. The wise man does not point but the boy points for him: a direction southwards and he animates with his hand certain things his mentor says. Then the rattle starts up again. The boy turns, the wise man turning after him and the pair trail off slowly back inside their hut, the map he has drawn on the ground erased with a single swash of his foot across the dust.

They pick their way deep into that broad sink of land and eventually the smell of the burning and the stench of the dead is lost to the sweet waft of the fields. The city sprawl is soon screened behind by the tall ridges of bush. The lone broadcasting towers and the tall buildings fade gradually from sight as if their candescence was only temporal, faded now into some hazy oblivion of existence. No one else may ever look on them. Some clearings are low and open and only random clomps of scrub clutch at the hard, cracking turf. Here the cart and he sail along with little in the way of obstacles to deter them. The luxury of a wide berth either side, the way ahead open to them.

At other times the path narrows. The bush sprouts and thickens and staggers over them, hemming them in and then it's almost impossible to know what predators, man or beast, stalk them from the webby camouflage of the veld. But they encounter no one. Not a sound breaks from the outback. Just their thumping along. Just the rickety yammering of the cart wheels.

He has no notion where they are headed and no understanding of the scale of the journey ahead. It has taken them almost an entire day of the earth's good sun and they are barely a few miles out of the forsaken city. He hauls the woman along and she gets shunted back and forth, her tender, ripe body bashed and blasted. Still they press onwards into the unknown.

It's getting hotter and hotter. The sun's scorching rays spool over him in unfailing flashes, each one more prying, more sapping. His shoulders are knotted in balls of clay where the harness straddles him. His flesh is chaffed and goitred by now, he is sure. The rope they drag him by is ever taut and repressive. He feels as if he can't breathe at times; his mouth is numb, the gag is utterly deplorable but there is no taste now that would summon any vile reaction. It is past that. Instead the whole thing sits there across his teeth, a nebulous sheath, its filth and fetor having drained onto his tongue and dripped down his throat, dissolved there into him. His eyes are sore and sting with the sun's glare, the ever wavering gusts of dust. His back is stiff, strained, smarting. Such a catalogue of woes and they would be never ceasing if it wasn't for the fact that each foot onwards atop the crusty malm is at least a step towards some end point in this intolerable saga.

He kneads his discomforts into some general malaise and the sun overhead belts down regardless. They inch ahead, stopping occasionally for a blotch of shade under a scraggy tree where they drop to their haunches or squat against the trunk or stand doubled over to catch their breath. The woman is helped off the cart and she wobbles over to some sacks they bundle for her on the ground. No room for him under the steamy shade. He stands looking on. They carefully angle the container, trickle out some water into a Coke bottle and pass it round, sipping modestly. He begins to get agitated. The very sight of the water drives him insane. He shakes his head and moans and eventually one of the boys comes over to him and undoes the gag and raises the bottle to dribble some drops onto his expectant tongue. Each globule explodes over his flesh and kindles a thousand shudders of relief in his parched mouth.

The path ahead is blocked by a body strewn on its back, its rigid arms composed around its head, the pose of a statue knocked over on the ground. There is some noble antiquity

about its demeanour that doesn't plunge their guts this time.
The guise of a warrior god dumped here in its loamy tomb.
Flies have flown in and are busy sucking at its opaque marbled eyes with their proboscises and as the boys are ordered
in to shift its bulk their rustling wings pester the solemness
of the air. The boys are quick about their business and dump
the body further afield, withdrawing expressionless from the
bush. A sad indictment sits over them now. So soon these
horrors are absorbed, the brute indifference of a death. They
strain ahead.

The ball of sun finally begins to fall out of the distant sky. The spattering ledges of clouds that had until then been bleached spumes faint across that epidemic screen. Soon, they glister purple and red and stand out like scars against the oozing cosmos. As the light dips and darkens, their raggedy shadows begin to reel against the veld bush and the scabby marl, diluting painlessly into this vast sweep of dusk light across the land. At any moment now he will raise his weary eyes to the formless horizon, and maybe somewhere he will see the first glimpse of a night-time star that will guide them onwards.

Still no stopping. Not yet is he spared the toil of it. They buckle down through the enveloping darkness and grope along their singular path. A sudden implosion of mosquitoes darts in feverishly, driving him to quick distraction with their constant droning. They are all victims; the others slap and curse, faltering in the darkening light, but he just walks on, too tired and too tied up to fend off the invasion.

Small flying beetles dart into him, bouncing off and falling to the soil defeated. Some drill in his ears or claw against his body. He shakes his head to dislodge those phantom voices, but is unsuccessful.

The coolness of nightfall is a tonic, a languid spill across his weary muscles and bones: the vast exhalation of his entire being. In the next clearing they come to a halt. They look around and at one another and then the man signals the boys to dump their loads and to help the woman off the cart. They support her under the arms as she limps off clutching her bulbous stomach and whimpering, brushing tears from her cheeks. The trauma of the day has finally broken on her. The man ignores her, muttering instructions to the boys who mope about. In time the cart is unhooked and an inestimable weight falls from him. He stands there panting hard and feeling sick from the pain and exhaustion.

They rummage about for kindling and just before the full fall of night they knock together a pyre, screw strips of old newspaper into balls and strike a single match which flares the fire into crisp jagged flames. Soon the woman is crouched over, dangling skewered maize cobs above the smoky heat. They gnaw sullenly, one cob each. They pass the Coke bottle round and sip at the water. He looks on and finally one of the boys comes over, undoes the gag and shunts him to the side of the clearing to allow him to feed. He drops his head and scoffs his lot. It has been a long day.

They tie him to a tree for the night but make one concession and remove the gag. Gradually the numbness in his mouth retreats and he keeps it open, lapping at the ambrosial night air to allow the coolness to salivate his raw rubbery tongue. The group is quickly asleep, curled up on sacks, rags, card, newspaper. The fire pit has been sanded over so the mosquitoes relish them all. He is too tired to fend them off, too tired to contemplate that perhaps tonight he might worm his way out of the ropes that bind him and slip off unseen into the wilderness. There is a strong smell of peat nearby – stiff, rich, reeking – and perhaps there is a shanty or a village close by. He lies there tied to the tree and nurses the pain in his back as best he can. Soon a fuzziness takes hold of his vision and a light ache inches its way up though his skull and lodges behind his eyes. He lowers his head to the chalky turf and somehow, unfathomably, he drifts off.

A gravelly hissing burrows its way into his resting thoughts and levitates there, waning and then levelling out to a high continuous bleep. His droopy sun-sore eyes quiver in response and he raises his head to see the man's hunched back towards him. He is crouched over the radio, thumbing the knob, angling the aerial at the iron blueness of the sky-line. The boys are curled on the sacks. He cannot see the woman. The man sways backwards and forwards on the balls of his feet, his head moving with him as if he is medi-tating or working himself into a trance. There is nothing but a line of hissing, bleeping, squawking. He slaps the receiver impatiently, its frequency drops and blares but he cannot pluck the sound of the spoken word from those static, imper-vious airwaves. It is as if the whole world has gone silent; as if everyone has just crept away from them and curled up in a ball somewhere. He turns the knob until it clicks and is quiet suddenly. Laying the receiver on the ground, he con-tinues to rock on his heels and look around him at the still void of night.

After this no sound sullies his sleep. The distant quake of dreams dims in some distant palpability. He sleeps for the most part, undeterred by the openness about him; the feeling of vulnerability; the nerve chill of the militias swooping up on them from their camps in the bush and slitting their throats. Such fears only nudge the outer periphery of his mind now and then, ebbing and flowing. Once or twice he may hear footsteps across the grasses but when he opens his muggy eyes, all about him is still. The calmness of the night-time terrain. Every resting thing. At times there is just the whine of mosquitoes and at other times the sound of indefatigable beetles darting.

He dozes off and later glimpses the sight of the woman limping into the sparse scrub; squatting down, clawing her baggy dress about her waist and spewing jets of urine at the foaming earth. The sound gushes at his hazy mind. Then a leaky silence. She drops her dress and lumbers up and moves gingerly back to her repose. When he wakes again the air has greyed and warmed, the mosquitoes have vanished and there is a sweet smell of wetness leavened on the ground. The blades of grass are licked with dew. Their spiky definitions sharpen in the coming light.

The others are up and rustling about the sacks and bags. The boys pick in the bush for kindling. Soon the fire is ablaze and the woman is kneeled over it with more maize cobs. They sit huddled round the gritty hearth, each with a look of bleak resignation. Though their eyes are resolved to the slog ahead, their minds have not forgotten the pains of yesterday. They consume the meal in silence, then sand over the fire and restack the bags and sacks. The boys wheel over the cart and attach the harness to his tight stiff shoulders. They reattach the gag, which inches down across his teeth and eases against his tongue. They set off with the cool morning air coalescing about their bodies. In the distance the

77

renascent sun stokes the sky and it turns and furls in its immensity, flushing a brief spree of puce before the pure blueness of day itself.

Then they are moiling hard, the early heat fanning down on them in this never-ceasing plain, out over the monotonous silence of the bush. The cart seems heavier this morning. The woman is still her grim self. She barely makes a sound now and her face is a waxen effigy of some stricken abhorrence. The man is strapped with the rifle, the belts of bullets like fat fingers wedged in a knuckleduster. The gun stirs a fear in his belly that does not subside. The lanky spurning boys walk on beside them. The sacks strung to their backs seem no small burden today. There is a strange dynamic to the convoy, some permanent absurdity that will never be quelled. All this and they keep walking, walking. They walk all morning and they do not see another living thing, no birds or mammals or snakes sprawled in the fanning heat.

They walk for long hours. The sun trails them from above, a sterile eye behind a microscope. The muffling bush gathers up the heat of the day and discharges it at them in some cruel osmosis. There is no breeze. The sky is still and evasive. There is not even cloud stacked across the far spheres; just a gauzy scrim and the seeming nothingness between it and the unfaltering ground they trek. It seems to them there has never been such a vastness between two points on a map. There is delirium in the air, some risen doubt. This path must lead to somewhere that is a place, to somewhere that is an end result to their labours, to something that is a release of the pain. It must lead some-where.

The mind plays tricks. It speaks in riddles and suggests they may not have even travelled a tenth of what their aching limbs tell them. Pulling the cart is slow and tedious and draining. When its wheels jar on the unlevelled land and it can't be shunted by him alone they have to crawl to a stop yet again. The men all heave and lift and he goes charging forward to break them free from the rut. It takes some time away from the whole unending schlep of it. Then they have to stop for a snatch of shade and a rest. The woman has to dislodge and weave off into the bush to relieve herself frequently, such is the brutal bashing her bladder suffers with the weight bearing down on it. The squat chassis is blunt underneath her. The babe kicks away in a tirade of unease. At these intervals they tip the container and slosh a bit of tepid water into the Coke bottle and pass it round; all this under the steamy heat. It is quite likely after all that they have only covered some twenty or so miles.

Sometime in the early afternoon they come to a village, which resembles a wasteland burnt flat to the ground by some apocalyptic scourge no one has told the world of: a place sanitized by burning. They are weary. The boys are sent ahead to survey the area, their machetes raised. Bit by bit they creep forward towards its charred circumference, akin to a space scorched deep on the ground by a rocket launch. So intense has the inferno been here that there is nothing distinguishable beneath the black clumps of debris, the sagged mulch of melted things that have fallen to this slurry pit. All is soot and ash and a splay of blackness which shifts in sheets off the periodic breeze. Even the bones that lie here half buried within it are sure to be charred, glazed and incendiarized.

There is nothing of value that they can scrape up from this pit – the fields are already plundered of their scabby crops, the livestock wired up and yoked and hauled away – so they make a cursory inspection of its perimeter and then move on. Such an episode scores itself tangibly into the still whiteness of the coming afternoon hours and for a while afterwards they all feel drenched in a fine crust of slag, those last finite remnants clinging to them. They walk for a long time and do not come across another such village that day.

It is just the veld they plunge into and it is so thick it could well be virgin bush that parts its arched walls and opens up its tunnel to them as they press ever forward. Its stooping hood is staggered over them; growth that no eye can penetrate. There may be swags of trees festooned out in the vastness of this beige sea, their tasselled tips frothed like surf, but their struggle is in vain; they are swamped and sunk. Only the path cuts through it, trodden threadbare and compacted smooth beneath them like a slip of balding skin.

Along the path there are other paths: the turf has splintered and webbed into a network of crevices that open up in miniature cavities. Here ants and termites may nest but they are seldom to be seen. They may be down there in those cool recesses. They may be hidden away from the foot of man. Or perhaps they are already attuned to the perils of the path.

When in the late afternoon the sun's eye finally breaks its concentrated stare and begins to droop into the far corners of the horizon, the light blurs and smirches the tufted tops of the rooi grass and their red inflorescence is lost in a blink. He has lost track of time and its beady accentuation of his plight. Each step of the day pulling the cart is a mark of some penance served. Some penance or sacrament he has no knowledge of. He has just been walking and the cart has lumbered on behind him in his shadow and mounted in her cab the woman has, like him, dropped off mindlessly and lost the hours. He hasn't heard a sound for some time that isn't the grating whine of the wheels slurping against the axle. Even this has become at one with the forbidding silence of their progression, the stilled land that stands mute as their creaking presence rolls over it like an unwelcome heathen skulking across the town square to the vaulted doors of a church.

At the man's command, they come to an unexpected halt. There is little space on the path to rest and recline. The man mutters to the boys and they drop their sacks and move to the back of the cart and stand over the woman, who reclines in her barge as a queen attended by her eunuchs. If they had palm fronds they may have fanned her flushed and sleeted face. The man has gone. He has crept away ahead of them all along the path and they must wait for his return.

He is gone for a while. The tired boys drop to the ground and sit, resting against the cart. They may fall asleep. Occasionally they swipe at flies that zoom in on them in their prime stillness and feast and suckle the sweat on them. He cannot lie or rest and so must stand there laboured with the weight of the cart on his back. His legs ache in spasms. The pain is centred at the very pith of his bones and it quivers outwards criss-crossing the fibres of his flesh. His back is stiff, his shoulders throb. Where the ropes bind him he is chaffed and tender; it may not be long till the skin breaks and the ropes dig into his thinning blades, scouring flush against the bone.

When the man comes back the boys try to get to their feet but they are too slow. He has caught them at their sloth. He dives on them from above in a spurt of rage. He pegs one of them to the turf and stands over him kicking the point of his shoe into the boy's ribs as he squeals in a half-broken voice and tries in vain to fend off the blows. The gun swivels from his shoulder and the belts of bullets flap a rhythm against his hips. The man breaks off and turns on the other boy in a flash, slapping him about his head and yelling and pushing him till he keels into the bushes. The woman's screams increase until he yells in her face, raising his hand above her. She cowers and stiffens, swallowing her cries in a gulp of fear.

There is relative silence now. The stifled breaths, the muted whimpering. The man stands back, breathing hard and looking down on their failings as a father does who knows the stack of his unsung sacrifices. The kneeling boys

84

look up at him like dogs scorned by their master. Then all is broken. The man sulks away and scoops up the rope and pulls him on and he staggers forward, the cart wobbling onwards; the boys pick themselves up and limp after.

They move along the path for a good half hour before they stop again. The man raises his hand to silence and still them. He stands looking ahead, knowing well that the eye can't see through the pall of bush. He drops the rope, lowers himself to his haunches and not for an instant does he break his stare. He signals to the boys and in unison they drop to the ground too, squatting over the low spiky tufts of the glimmering scrub grass. Here they wait, hushed, inhaled, hidden.

There is the threat that even a single breath stolen from this inimical air will warn some stooping unseen foe of their presence. The air has thickened, furling overhead in an elastic splay of tension. Twisted and muscled and knotted. Off to the side of him he alone can observe the last struggling arcs of the raddled sun slipping under the fuzzed surface of the horizon, sinking like a vessel ablaze after some drawn, unconscionable wrecking. Then a grim iron gloaming shudders across the sky in its dying moments, hanging nebulous and bleary before the fullness of night.

The man has been sitting cross-legged at their helm,

staring into the impervious screen that is shunted ahead of them. The boys, too, are sat on the dust of the path, their sacks beside them each balanced on the scrub. They wait patiently and don't dare render up a moment of their tiredness or boredom. They nurse their wounds in silence. Saddled in the middle is the woman reclined in her tub. She has not made a sound in ages nor moved a muscle. Perhaps she has even slipped away into a world of the unconscious where the full extent of her indifference can be borne. He can only stand there harnessed to the cart; as much as he would like to he can't hunker down and lay his body across the coolness of the threadbare path, spreading his aching tendons and dipping his throbbing bones into the soothing emollient of the earth. He must stand there and wait.

When at last the man is convinced that the night is at its deepest, he crawls from his post to the cart and fiddles silently with one of the sacks. His face is inscribed with some deep concentration, a fixed, determined stare. He draws out a reel of steel wire and unravels a length in his hands, feeding it into a thin groove on the iron frame of the cart, working it as a blacksmith may until the piece wears through and weakens, coming away clean from the coil. He must have a good metre stretched in his hands. He deposits the reel back in the sack and creeps along the path without a word. The boys strain and look on, but within seconds his body has slipped into the dark tunnel of the path and has been enveloped by the seeming nothingness beyond it.

They wait there for what seems a painful passing of time. He can no longer bear the strain and finally begins to shuffle on his feet, pulling against the harness, feeling the fullness of the weight of the cart like a lead sarcophagus behind him. At once the boys are at his side and one of the machetes is raised and angled at his neck, though it means nothing to him now. The other boy is behind him and punches his hip to stop him from scuffling on his feet. He feels his midriff splice through with a pain that quakes his very innards. He can barely stay upright, but the boys have him at the harness, holding him up. He tries to struggle free and snap his head at them but the gag is tight and wedged firm into his mouth, paralysing him. In their grip he cannot lash out and overpower them so they stand there rather absurdly, the three of them, jostling silently amongst themselves as if they were all small children squabbling over a toffee apple.

Then through the slim darkness the man runs towards them. The boys drop their grip and stagger back. The man repeats something in a breathless, urgent rant and the boys jump into action, scurrying for their sacks. The man picks up the dangling rope and pulls on it with a violent jerk. It shunts his neck and he almost trips in his precarious balance. He groans through the gag, straining against the rope out of some primitive protest. He tries to dig his heels into the turf and recoil his whole body from the force that pulls on him, the prepotent tension. The man tugs, yanking at him but as tired as his legs are he manages to grip his heels against the earth and hold his course. His stubbornness comes from some sudden welled loathing. His captor is beginning to panic. He can sense his advantage over this man who keeps looking ahead at the path he has just returned from, pulling at him with a desperate urgency. He calls to the boys and they come swooping in and push him from behind. His weight topples forward and he is forced to give up his stand. The cart edges along. All the while the woman lies there, her expressionless face screened from the mayhem.

The man leads them with haste along the path. The wheels of the cart slip along the cooling earth, the chassis wobbling in waves from side to side – it has perhaps never managed speeds like this before. They are almost at a canter. Their quickening breaths are fuming the air, curling back on their flushed faces. The man mumbles something incessantly – he may well be talking to himself or he may be urging them on. The others don't seem to react either way but just press along with their sacks strewn over their shoulders and their raspy breathing grunting all the while. Soon they come to a sudden clearing. The man halts and raises his hand and they all come to a sharp stop behind him. Like cartoon characters they could well have rammed into the back of him. The man paces and looks right and left. He beckons and the boys come forward, pulling him. They cross a short levelling of stony ground and weedy shrubs and then the path dips through an incline that's as deep as a ditch. He struggles to ascend it. The belly of the cart wedges itself briefly in the cupped hollow but the boys are behind it at once, heaving it up and onwards, pushing while he staggers ahead.

On the other side, they find themselves on the edge of a wide tarred road. It looks like the miracle of some unearthing, some lost and ancient place. The stretch of asphalt grey and granular, long like a lick of tongue. On either side of the road there are two petrol drums painted in white and grey stripes. A wooden log runs atop them in a beam. The man hurries them on and they step onto the road, then edge onto the stony clearing and trail down into the ditch, re-entering the hooded tunnel of the path.

Lying there in the trench as they pass they do not see the two slender strips of mottled camouflage, warm and still, posited there in their ready-made graves. They have been hauled limp and lifeless across the tarmac, each one taken from the tedious silences of their dreary watch, and the corners of the heels of their boots may be glassed over with the powdery whiteness of attrition. Otherwise they look asleep; hardly touched or throttled. The swelling at their throats is insignificant. One of them still has the coil of wire wrapped tight round his windpipe.

They carry on a good distance in the dark. After a while they ease into their step again. The boys slouch along with the weight of the sacks bearing down on them. The woman is awake now – he can hear her wistful sighs behind him, the occasional deep-bellied groan that cracks on the back of the stiff night air. The cart wheels climb over the skewered tracks and then thump down into the recesses. The wheels slam against the frame and send a hammering through her numb and prickly rump. It has been a long day. She has had enough.

At the front the man leads on, the freakish fifth limb of his rifle flat against his back and protruding above his head. He seems determined to get them as far away from the road as possible. Perhaps cast jaggedly across his quiet demeanour is the quaking heart that beats in his chest like a drum. Its off-beat racing rhythm is pivoted at the moment he flexed the wire in his hands and took a deep breath and slipped from the roadside bushes, a bodiless force towards the first of his lazing victims. How he managed to pull it off only he can ever know.

They walk so far into the night each step becomes nothing but a mechanical placement on some ever revolving treadmill. The scene never changes. Tall staggered shards of bush encumber them. It may well be a painted backdrop awash with long blotchy strokes which they troop in front of in a pantomime scene. Or it could now be the far somnambulism of the mind. Some ether where they tread on vapours and the cool air sings some hymn of emancipation.

Finally a glade opens up to the left of them. The man staggers into it and stops and looks about. He signals to the boys. They drop to their knees and an audible sigh from them all breaks into the soft openness of this place. They sit, heaving and sucking in air as if they have at last crossed the tape at the end of a marathon. Attached to the cart, he must stand and endure the torture a while longer.

Later they are curled on the sacks and cardboard, dead to the world. They finally got round to unbinding the ropes and loosening the gag and wheeling away the cart. He staggered on his feet; the relief was pulverizing. He scoffed his food and drank the water they spared him and was content to be led into the low grasses and tied to the thin pole of a tree. His legs collapsed from under him and he lay there against the trunk, his mind already blanking as he drew his head to rest.

When he wakes the full sun is up and wood smoke drifts towards him, settling in his nostrils and stoking his brain to consciousness. The woman is hunched over the pyre turning skewered maize cobs in the rounds of her stubby swollen fingers. She looks sullen, her lips downcast and drawn, her eyes marbled with some distant dappling of despair. The boys perch by her close as puppies, waiting for the bony maize stalks to brown, char and soften.

The man sits hunched on his feet drawing lines in the soil with a stick. Some personal cartography. He is preoccupied, lost in his own imaginings, his own calculations. He whispers to himself. He closes his eyes, mutters, draws deep into the well of his memory. He opens his eyes again and counts on his digits and scrawls in the dust. Then he turns to a jagged cutting of card and scribbles something with the blackened tip of a twig cooling now like the greying filament of a poker rod. After breakfast and water they reset the gag, wrap the ropes about his shoulders and wheel round the cart. And so another day becomes them all.

They mope along. Well past noon the woman finally breaks the static silence and curls into a heaving mass of hysteria. Low rising cries at first and then she bawls a wrenching tirade. She clubs her fists against the sides of the cab and screams, crying as if she were giving witness to some revelation scored in the sky. The man tries to snatch her wrists but she lashes out at him. She scratches at the air like the victim of a swarm. The boys rush to her and they all grip her arms and steady her swipes and try to mute her screaming. She struggles under their arrest. Finally they lift her from the cart and drag her into the bush. He hears a sharp slap and then her steady whimpering behind the khaki veil of the grass. Her gibbered plangencies surrender to a steady hiss of sobs and pleading.

There is nothing and no one about. The snaking path lies open ahead. He stands listening. They come staggering out of the bush and plop her back into the cart. Stern words are uttered at her. The man scolds the boys and mutters angrily to himself as if everything is a conspiracy against him, against his vast deplorable scheme. He is still murmuring when he walks in front of the cart and hits him across the back of the scalp and his mind dims to the blow, his vision swimming but he finds he is walking on regardless.

She hunches down in the cab, silent and sulking. Her

master stoops on, a thrawn stoic begrudging his obligations. They trundle through an unravelling sameness of place. Nothing has ever changed in this world of soil and grass and sky. It is like something elemental stabbed on a frieze, on a slip of canvas, its infinite permanence hewed at the beginning of time and forgotten. The taut afternoon air suckles on their bodies and shadows the distemper of the group. Five forlorn beings it has made of them. Deep in that landscape there is a path that leads onwards to some distant purpose; forged and weathered by the feet of time.

Still they nudge on. Their weary limbs; their downcast moods; the pester of the errant flies that come sometimes and at other times are wholly conspicuous by their absence. They walk and stop and rest to measure out a dram of water into the Coke bottle and reward themselves the relief of it, an elixir measured on the tongue as if in pitiless spoonfuls. Then they put away the bottle, screw the lid tight on the water container, and walk on again.

They are perhaps only fifty miles away from the city. How can they tell? How can the tiredness of the feet and the aches in the limbs measure distance? Maybe they had travelled seventy miles, their collective minds dulled into weary submissiveness. All that toil and only this meagre smattering of distance to show for it.

Deeper and deeper into the heart of the country they go and with each passing step their minds get lost to the unfathomable terrain they travel, the delusions it conjures. They stay clear of main roads. They bypass all the little dorps that are dotted along them, if the dorps are not all levelled to rubble, brick, ash, burnt beyond all recognition. They skirt road signs, if there are road signs left to tell them anything, if their iron poles are not yet yanked from the ground and carted off and smelted down. They sidestep all the compass points they may have known; the familiar assurances of the road, the chartered course. Instead they plunge the forbidding trails of bushmen and peasant farmers and rural dwellers, the man always stopping them to consult his scrap of card and screening back in his mind to the fast-fading words of the wise man. But it leads to nothing at all that is certain in the mind. No placement of the foot along the path that is anything but a thumb suck in the vacant wind.

The day passes in a haze of heat and bleached bush and the silences of this hermitic land. Noon comes awash on the consciousness and in the hours afterwards, memory swims beneath the skull and only surfaces to acknowledge the occasional dim sting of a lashing they issue him when he stumbles from his path. Only later in the afternoon, when the sun at last curves away, does he re-emerge to the tedium of the day now racked up against him, the tension so great it feels as if his brain may pop. Then he would be just a dazed stream of simplicity; his body and the cart plodding along until finally the twitching nerves realized their fate and the whole contraption fell to a great heap in the bush.

At last the dusk air thickens before his nose, grey against the metallic horizon. They walk and walk. All day this crawl across hard soils. An aimless journey. Rocks against which his feet succumb to numbness and stones to which his skin is hopelessly reconciled. There is little to hurt him by now. Thorns of the scrub are no longer vehement. Spiky branches part before his chest so easily it's as if he is wading through water, plunging the mystic depths. His body is a vessel. Of what he does not know. His mind is sun-battered and his brain is shrivelled to nothingness beneath his crisp scalp. His head is just a shell during this unending trudging and the heat of these daylight hours. A space within a space where if one stopped him and pressed their ear to his ear they would possibly hear the ocean there. The wavy lapping hollowness breaking in primal rhythms on a blonde shore.

They may walk like this for many hours and many days and still not stumble across another village or kraal or being. They may walk one whole day of this unending solitude and then be tricked at the end of it to assume they have travelled more. So easily the heat dapples with the mind and its convictions. Such is the drag of the foot upon the rutted turf, the clomping assimilation of distance, the sense of disorientation now scoured into them. Some force in the air is sucking the sanity from them little by little, minute by minute as each lone second passes.

The woman lies in the clutch of the trap he drags her in. Her legs are splayed immodestly over the sides and she is hunkered down there on sparse rags and bedding, the sacks and container between her thighs. She is inert, sometimes like a mannequin, something to be plopped down between the clutter or folded away. Her gaunt face, her tightened mouth grinning inanely at the vapid air. Her bulging stomach rises from her bony torso, a pocket of fluid in which her child flicks about like a fish in its confinement, its lungs filled with waters from the deepest of seas and plumbed from the most endless, the most unfathomable darkness. Pooling and pooling into the essence of existence. Here it flashes about, it flinches. But it may never surface into this realm of the living.

She grows ever more despondent. Sometimes she is completely unresponsive and her body lies there in a static heap whilst she has slipped down into the depths of some catatonic moroseness. She is no virago. When they stop now it sometimes takes all three of them to ease her out of the cab and carry her off into the bush where she slumps on her haunches and does her business and is carried back stinking of shit and crying feverishly. Sometimes she hoists herself up on her arms and vomits over the side of the cart and its aftermath dribbles down her chin and settles in the hollow of her neck, drying there, crisp, in the sun.

The man loses his patience and doesn't heed to her heaving or hurling. The boys try to rig up a canopy of some sticks wired to the cart and an awning of sack stretched across a rickety frame to shelter her. She slumps down completely in its mottled shade and is lost even further to the world. They don't hear a sound from her for hours until the wheels get rammed on a ledge or a protruding root and the canopy comes swooping down on her and she wakes with a shudder, whining and wailing, clutching her gut.

As for him, his back hurts more and more from lugging the load behind him. His captive's dues. His spine aches with stiffness. The thing is so unwieldy, so infirm, so unbalanced, that he has not been able to grow accustomed to it. He should become used to walking how he has to walk nowadays, carting this burden behind him. There ought to be a sense of balance in his posture or a levelling out of weight distribution. The load should by now be absorbed into his own weight and his own body; becoming one with him. But he can never get used to it. Things no longer make sense. Out here, in this world.

So the pain is always there, sunk like a coldness into his bones and there is no respite for it, not even in sleep. Sometimes he thinks he dozes off while walking. His legs just keep trundling, spokes in a machine, and his mind becomes dulled to the whipping they issue if he slows down or veers off-course. At least his captors have no option but to realize he serves them little purpose if his legs buckle and he drops in the vlei dead or stumbles off the edge of a kopje. If he goes down what will become of the woman and the child in her belly? Here perhaps there is a certain degree of leverage between himself and them, so at last they do stop for a while. They give him a gulp of water, momentarily relaxing the rope bound round him, knowing he won't run because he would rather have the water brought to his lips instead.

But every day there eventually comes a point when the sun plummets red into the dust-filled distance and in the strip between the black haze of seething earth and the furling blueness of sky something kindles there which may just be the first inkling of nightfall. How much longer? How much more plodding along this unnerving path before some gift of respite? The grey air thickens. The strip of night widens.

When the heatwave dips entirely he surfaces from his shrunken malaise of isolation and begins to detect slow shifts in the rhythm of travel, sloth in the motions of the group. He knows soon they will think about resting and start to look for a place to stop. His eyes are sunshot but he will still be able to see the grey stalking figures of the group ahead in the duskfall. He will be able to see them halt and scan the orange flush for promising campsite locations. They will mutter to one another, standing there contemplating the bush, the tense electric air.

When they do settle down for the night it's at some makeshift campsite. A clearing or a cave if they are lucky to find one. They come to a halt and he stands and watches as they unravel their backpacks and rummage in the sacks and spread their wares. They do not command his assistance in this. The woman of the daytime and the evening are two separate people. She suddenly comes alive in the absence of the sun. Or she is simply energized by a sense of duty or guilt. She clambers off her perch in the cart and stretches her aching spine and peels back the sacks. She deals out a cup of mealie-meal or skins four small figs. The boys mope about collecting kindling for the fire. The wood is dry and the grass

burns easily; it is no great effort. The mealie-meal she steams
in a cutting of sack because they cannot afford to squander
the water on boiling it. It comes out like wedged slabs of clay
they mould in their fingers and bury the figs in. Or else she
cooks it a while longer till it looks close to chinks of slate,
hard colourless cakes that snap in the hand, sometimes dis-
integrate.

They make no attempt to wash or attend well to their
toilet. In the end the reek of stale odours grows into a musty
fogginess and is forgotten and forgiven by the wild. It matters little out here. The men stop and turn aside and piss the
little water their bodies hold out at the glinting stalks of
grass. He is the same. Or else they reel into the bush or round
a tree and squat and defecate, the waste dropping from their
emaciated torsos with grim reluctance. If the wind should
pick up at night it carries the stiffness of their stools wafting
back towards them but otherwise it is lost in the expanses
forever.

They bed down on blankets and rags and are able to drift
off as if it were the most natural thing in the world. They
make a bonfire which can only be to ward off the notion
that a pack of hyenas may sniff them out or a leopard may
be crouched in the trees above them as they hardly ever sit
about it and commune. They're too tired and so they drop

off soon after. Predators of the wild never come. There probably isn't an animal left native to these parts that isn't already a stiff shell bedded in the ground, its flesh scraped clean by poachers.

Sometimes they mutter for a while and then drop off. What they talk about, what complaints they level, what fears they share is unknown to him. Sometimes it happens that even in the midst of all this the night stirs unlikely passions. In the deep ends of a cave one night, where the firelight dashed dimly off the reddened walls, she pleasured the man orally, pitying him because he can't get any while she's in her state. Or the night he knelt before her and slipped a finger into her slack cunt and stimulated her gently, and the look of teetering pleasure she exuded completed her bewildering metamorphosis from the figure who writhes in pain all day in the cart to the figure who lies together with her man propped up against a rock or a tree. All this before she remembered her condition or it became uncomfortable for her to maintain such an intrusion into her burgeoning body and she stopped him.

The boys are active too. In the late darkness they sometimes wake and restively fumble at their trousers or shorts and out jut their stiff erections. They lie there jerking off until the inevitable spasm grips them. They pan the effluent whiteness into the palm of their hands or it specks the sweaty blackness of their stomachs – they are of an age where the seed is eager and flows free and fast – and then they fall at once to rest and the quickening pull of sleep.

Such voyeurism invokes no guilt. No feeling that's uncomfortable to him, no sick desire, no illicit longing. He looks on brazenly, not even registering fully what he sees, his insular mind adrift in some desperate lodging. The long lonesome nights with nothing to do. The sheer exhaustion of the day pressed over him, a hand that muffles the consciousness. Stiff and unable to get comfortable he stays awake for an inestimable time. He peers at them from across the raggedy bonfire and sees the flickers dart on their sleeping faces, the sweat-glow of contentment. If the wind picks up it grows bitterly cold and the pain eases into something akin to an icepack on his back followed by eventual numbness that is not numbness itself but another type of pain altogether. He can't win. He tries to creep as close to the fire as the rope will allow him until one of the group rouses from sleep and shouts at him or throws a stone at him to move away into the cold and the dark. At such times he could shed a tear. If he knew how to weep after all this or if it were possible, he would cry for the pity of it. He would cry for a good night's sleep, a barn of dry hay.

But he can't weep and so he nestles down there to another restless night chained to a tree or fixed to a biting outcrop. He cannot despise their primitiveness either: that they can lie down anywhere and fall asleep in a second. The night wears on steadily enough. Occasionally the man is up and about stooping round them, the rifle clutched at the ready. But mostly all is still and quiet and just his mind is spooling.

2

12 October

Veronica came & put up a sign outside the gate today. My initial instincts: crude, tasteless, tacky. An insipid orange with that rather unimaginative logo of her agency stencilled onto it, 'For Sale' scrawled diagonally across it in a thick blue screed. So much for discretion. As soon as I saw it something in me numbed: I suppose the tangible realization that things are going ahead. Concrete steps & all that. Sixpence pegged it into the flowerbed, just beside the gate sign with the family name on it. Somehow it seemed to eradicate it, possess it. Felt as if I'd already packed up & gone.

'That'll get things ticking,' Veronica said, her customary pre-conditioned smile flashing away.

'We'll see,' I murmured.

13 October

A weary Saturday. I woke up in a downcast mood & remained in one for much of the day. A constant, irritable drizzle falling outside & the grey skies bleak & glum. The rains are v. early this year, though I still suspect the food crisis will be blamed on drought. Drought & illegal sanctions imposed by Western neo-colonizers!

Spent much of the morning reading in bed, too indolent to get up. Heard Tobias clattering about in the kitchen, then the old familiar smell of chicken casserole wafting down the passage. It rekindled in me some heady nostalgia, taking me at once to memories of my youth & the smells in the house of Mom's cooking. I didn't get up & go into the kitchen, but from bed I imagined the scene all too vividly: Tobias frying the onions & the peppers & the ginger, mixing the special sauce which comes from no cookbook, but is ingrained from years of Mom's tutoring.

I wonder if in Australia she still makes the same casserole? I wonder if the ingredients blend in the same way, whether the spices fuse as they do here in Africa? I don't suppose you can get Viljoen's All-Wors Spices in Perth. Unless Viljoen himself also left in the great migration & continues plying his trade to every homesick African? What a clever little enterprise that would be. Come to think of it I haven't seen Viljoen's Spices in the shops since the meltdown, but that isn't so surprising.

I wonder if Mom too, smelling the whole thing baking

away in the oven, is ever kindled with thoughts of Zimbabwe & this house (that was after all her mother's house) & how she taught the then green Tobias how to cook from scratch? Before any of us were born & when she & Dad were just married & taking on a household of their own.

'That old munt didn't know a thing I didn't teach him,' she used to boast. 'He came to me straight from the bush.'

Yes, I wonder if she too is moved to the same pangs of longing & melancholy? If she knew how to send an e-mail I'd ask her. If the phones here were a bit more reliable I'd probably be able to tell from the tone of her voice, albeit crackled over with static noise & a five-second delay.

Later I found I wasn't hungry. Tobias took the dish from the warming drawer & proudly set it on the counter alongside a steaming bowl of rice. I looked at it & then waved him off, telling him to put it into a Tupperware dish for later. He stood there looking stunned & bemused as if this slight signalled my displeasure with him. He said, 'What is wrong, baas?'

Of course he wouldn't know. 'Nothing,' I snapped, 'I'm just not hungry.'

Went into the lounge & watched TV & felt low for the rest of the night.

14 October

It must be the sign outside the gate that is putting me in this mood. As if, somehow, that fat stake has been hammered into me, into my skin, slicing the roots that bind me. Feel unsettled & unsure. Have given to doubting my decision to sell up & leave. If the truth be told I struggle to find an actual reason, to pinpoint the moment or act that triggered off the impulse to chuck it all in. It wasn't something very definitive that did it & this I suppose plays on my mind.

It wasn't, for instance, another vitriolic presidential speech blared out on the TV or hateful headlines in the state paper that did it. I like to tell myself I'm too immune to all that after thirty-odd years even though I know deep down it still riles my guts each & every time. What they say to us, the way they paint us all with the same brush because our skin is white & halfway across the world there's an island they blame for everything where people happen to have white skin. Just once I'd like to stand up & tell some fat party boy that we both have common links – more, comrade, than you'd like to think. I'd say: you who fought the British in the bush thirty-five years ago & never let anyone forget it, well a century ago my mother's father's father fought the British around the kopjes of Magersfontein, had his family rounded up into a concentration camp in Mafeking, his fields burnt, his homestead looted. Where does that leave us now, comrade, in this strange disposition? What does that say, face to face, eye to eye? Somehow I can't see my claim being v. penetrating!

Maybe I am just contaminated by the same unplaced, nebulous infectious spirit that seems prevalent amongst many of my kinsmen? The mindset that says we deserve better than this, that for some reason greener pastures are justly deserved, a birthright of the pale-skinned & that we needn't tolerate this mindless ineffectual chaos a day longer. So we sell up & pack up & dissipate ourselves far & wide where we just expect to carry on, one day to next, one country to another. That's what Mom & Dad, Alex & James did. Dad just threw up his arms when the company went under & had Mom sign the house over to me & they just took off as soon as they could get visas, severing all ties. But I am fearful of this weakness most of all. Of being the willing victim of a trendset, one of the flock, the rambling pack. But still I find myself inching along with my intentions, pulled in this wake & with no real appetite to stop myself.

When the rain stopped in the evening I decided to go for a walk around the neighbourhood. Maybe I could walk off my sullenness, so I thought. Everything was dripping in green & the trees on the pavements were heavy with water.

The aroma of coolness, of damp African dust v. prominent. Down Argyle Rd, there were no less than seven houses with 'For Sale' signs up, all glinting in the late breaking sun, vying for attention. Somehow I doubt if Veronica's orange & blue effort will be able to compete.

15 October

The power went off last night. That sudden plunge into blackness is always startling. I was up late preparing notes for the lower six when they went & for some moments I just sat there, the spools of dark gyrating around me & an instant feeling in my stomach of something I can only describe as dread. But dread at what, of what? When one is plunged into the dark the dread is instinctive, it's of the unknown, the formlessness about you, sightlessness of a known reality. Everything has gone but in a way that is only relative to you, your lack of sight. It is difficult to describe in the clear light of day now, but for a few moments then, something dreadful did come over me, something I sensed is linked to my precarious situation. I wonder if this darkness & dread embodies 1) the dire situation of this country, the abyss it's in: in a nutshell everything I'm trying to escape or 2) my own unshaped, undecided future. Perhaps everything is around me, just as it's always been, the structures & parameters of my

114

life, just that I am presently stumbling along it in the dark unable to see the light at the end of the corridor? Well in the end I groped my way down the passage & clawed into bed, moody & embittered, though I ought to be used to this by now. The power has yet to come back. When I got home today & walked into the kitchen I could already hear the silences of the fridge & freezer. Ominous looming quiet. The water in the geyser is still tepid enough for a bath of sorts but if this carries on it'll be back to the cold water bucket & sponge. Thank God it isn't winter.

16 October

Still off. I'm not going to worry about it today. Earlier I was invited to Hedgehogs by a group of the staff, the outgoing bunch. I'm surprised they even still ask me as I usually decline at once, fumbling for some excuse, even though I often regret it later. But today I accepted without hesitation. I thought: why not? Anything is better than the dark tedium of the house. When I got home in the evening I told Tobias to go off. He looked a little shattered. He had assembled the gas & scottle braai & was preparing to fry me a pork chop & heat some sweetcorn. I said, 'Don't worry about that, I'm going out,' & left him standing in the kitchen, no doubt looking down glumly at the braai disc.

So this is how it is to be, he probably thought, *now that the boss is selling up & heading for the horizon. Am I to be thus discarded? My efforts disdained, my loyalty brushed aside?* Already I've told him to chuck the chicken casserole from Saturday, completely untouched, as the fridge isn't holding up in this power cut.

Hedgehogs was dreary. As I was pulling up in the car park a moment of apprehension clouded over me & I had the sudden nervous thought that I'd made a mistake accepting & thinking I'd enjoy myself. Something pitted in my stomach, hard like a stone. I don't know why this happens. I can't recall when it started, so long back I don't care to remember. But something in me recoils when the prospect of contrived human contact looms. Mingling with people I hardly know & hardly care an iota for. I sat there, the car parked, the engine off & a brisk vision of the night before me rolled across my mind. All the familiar resentments & loathing. I wasn't enthused.

Didn't stay long. Had two beers & an argument with that irrepressible flirt Stacey Brisk over something intellectually trite. Seemed as good a barrier as anything I could concoct. Then as I was leaving I thought I glimpsed a familiar face at a table in the far corner. The light was dim there & I can't be sure, but I could have sworn it was Alicia Wall.

Now at home in the candlelight I'm writing this entry & wondering if it really was her. But what confounds me more is this: why am I wondering? Why didn't I just go over to the table & if it was her, greet her? Show my pleasant surprise at her return from abroad, catch up on old times? What is it that makes me retreat so from those around me, the society that inhabits the same space as me? Why is it that I'm rather drawn to the insulation of these pages, the walls of this house where I am incubated from the outside by fragments of the past?

17 October

The power has been off for three days now. When it went I hoped it was just the usual load-shedding cut, but now I know to reconcile myself to the inevitable. Have tried to phone to report it but of course can't get through or they don't answer. The previous fault lasted a month, the one before even longer. Can't bear to think how long this one's going to drag on for. The usual story I presume: no money for spare parts, no technicians to carry out repairs. Suppose you can't blame them for doing a runner if they've hardly been paid a cent for six months, can you?

I don't mind the quietness so much. I've realized this. I rather like the silence in the house, that vibe not sifting through the walls of things humming, rattling, bubbling away. A certain peaceable remoteness one gets. I can live without appliances too. That's the joy of the book, this journal, the piano. From another age where quietness reigned, where calmness presided. It's just the whole hassle of the fridges & freezers, the meat going off, the milk souring, etc. And I'd just gone & stocked it up. I can ill-afford to but rumours abound of the prices going up again next week. (Funny how in Africa, in such times, even the US dollar attracts such a rate of inflation!) Someone told me that if you wrap a blanket over the freezers they keep iced for longer. May have to try it.

18 October

No change. Tired today. Before the sun slipped away (the rains seem to have abandoned us) I was reading out on the veranda & felt my eyes growing heavy. The garden is so lush this time of year. Traces of Mother's touches everywhere still, though they've been gone almost ten years already. A lot of the plants flowering now she planted herself. Cut them back in the winter & they just spring up again in summer, like some force that can't be vanquished. Something I'll certainly miss. Am trying to put all other thoughts to the back of my mind re. the move, leaving, etc. I suppose the danger is of getting lost in the escapism of a world whose landscape lies across the pages of a book. Or the deep engrossment of the mind: I have been thinking pleasurably in the dark of Alicia these last two nights, her face ingrained in my mind as I drift off, that specific scent of her effusing in my memory with astonishing ease.

19 October

I've heard nothing further from St James' College about my job application, not a word from Veronica about the house. Tonight I fired up the old genny for a few hours. Thought I'd resist longer this time but the freezers are my main concern & justification. Plus it's just so miserable once the sun sets sitting here by myself in the candlelight or the dim glow of the hurricane lamp. Tried to read by it the last few nights but got too tired too quickly. The orange glow falling over the page does it I think: too soporific. So I got Sixpence to fuel it up & ran it for a while. The house lit up like a Christmas tree. An island in this suburb of dark. I caught up with the cricket highlights on TV, watched a bit of BBC news. All the while I could hear the chug of the diesel motor outside. Suddenly I felt an alarming guilt. Quite unquantifiable. As if the glower of lights, the blare of the TV, were tantamount to a type of gluttony. This when everything has been so frugal of late! I suppose I was thinking about the fuel & how I really can't afford to squander it. So I stomped outside & turned it off. Rather embittered that I was made to feel so shameful by such an insignificant luxury as a few hours' electricity.

20 October

In the upper-six lesson I got into a spat with Edwards, something that seems to have deepened this stupor of late, not lifted it. Factors attributing to the rise of fascism, etc. All v. racy stuff, as far as the history syllabus 3108/8 goes. Mostly the boys lapped up my preamble with no real reaction, but I could detect Edwards sitting there weighing up everything with that blank, dispassionate look of his I've come to know not as arrogance but as some sort of osmosis, some kind of intellectual digestive process. Sometimes I wonder whether I'm looking at myself when younger & I marvel fondly at the similarities. I remember discussions when my teachers often thought I wasn't even present in the room & passed biting remarks about my conceited aloofness. The better ones knew of course that I was normally biding my time, processing the information before seizing the eventual moment to argue back. Sometimes I said nothing & then spilt it all in essays or papers. Sometimes Edwards does that too.

I was hoping today he'd just shut up. Truth is I haven't really felt up for a fight of late. Something about pulling a carpet of security away from under your own feet is unsettling intellectually. It's been said of me that I've wasted my time teaching a mixed bag of schoolboys the scant shallowness of A-level history when I could have carved out a promising career as a university academic, a professor, lecturing the crème de la crème at the best institutions abroad, penning scholarly texts on my field of expertise – Africa & its litany of problems. That I'm over-qualified for this job is an understatement. I just started studying one day, drawing deeper & deeper into that murky well of the past & no one told me when to stop, no one drew my head up for breath. I was left there to drown in my own notions of a bygone reality. The degrees stacked up from the correspondence university with alarming ease & time & the normal progression of life seemed to saunter by with only a passing nod.

I suppose I have no one to blame but myself. All the while this house got flooded with books, extensions of my cerebral haemorrhaging I couldn't stop & even when Mom & Dad were still here they'd complain about being overridden with bulky volumes I'd plunder cheaply from car boot sales, dusty second-hand shops, flea markets. Books on anything & everything. A house of books: a house within a house.

How am I going to dismantle it? I could never afford to truck them all down to South Africa. My lodgings at St James' will probably be woefully inadequate anyway. And some yuppie upstart graduate will point out to me the virtues of the Internet in such a smarmy way my books & I will be stigmatized forever after.

I shrink at the prospect. I have carved out a comfort zone here. Even if Mom & Dad could have afforded to send me to Rhodes or Cape Town I think I'd have rather stayed here & gotten on with it myself. Now I am established, I'm something of a stock figure, no one questions my methods, my results speak for themselves, the Head keeps his weary distance from my turf. I am not particularly personable with the boys but I know they respect me. I like to think over the years they have even appreciated the rigours I put them through, beating into them the rectitude of academic integrity. They'd never say so of course & I don't really mind that. My harshness & hostility become me with something of a legacy I'd hate to tarnish, even now as the last days draw near.

So Edwards was biding his time & I wasn't really up for it. When he finally reacted I was almost half fearful of the challenge. We exchanged blows for a good five minutes with me barely holding my own before I was saved by the bell. I haven't felt as loose-footed in the classroom for many a year.

I think Edwards sensed I was off colour as well. As he left he gave me one of those wilful smiles of his, brimming with adolescent triumph, yet hesitant too, almost a glimmer of concern if I read him correctly.

'Don't worry – I'll have a comeback for you next lesson,' I said, joking to reassure him.

'I'll look forward to it, sir,' he said & was gone.

What is to become of me? Above everything I fear death at the chalkboard, pinned up & left hanging there in a final moment of humiliation when one day I just won't have the answer, the next step in the argument. I'll stutter & stammer & thumb nervously at the pages of a text book I never use. All will be so utterly undone.

21 October

Every day when I drive in from school I tell myself the electricity's come back & every day I'm disappointed. Accompanied by a sudden rage that only lasts a moment. My general mood plummets thereafter. Can't seem to stop it though I feel it coming on.

I got home today & found myself quite supine only moments later, sprawled on the bed, fighting back the waves of sleep that flowed in a wash of tedium, moroseness, lethargy. I lapsed into a deep sleep & woke much later with the dark around me. Tobias had locked everything up & gone off for the night. I fumbled for the candle he always leaves by my bed when this happens – I suppose he stoops in while I'm dead to the world, snoring my lazy, indolent head off. Truth is I'm lost in some distantly breaking desperation that I am somehow managing to keep just at bay. It's as if I know it's there somewhere, just beyond the fringes, a bend in a path, or a wall of some description, beyond which is an allusive entanglement, something in the grey mists. Only I know at this stage not to ford it, to hold back. The school term still has four weeks left so I know not to go there. I've got to tell myself to maintain my rigid demeanour in front of the boys. Don't go cracking at the edges.

Maybe just a bad day. Maybe I exaggerate.

23 October
V. tired. Still no news from Veronica re. the house. No update from any of the neighbours re. the power outage. Really must sort out the meat situation tomorrow! No news of the ongoing political agreement saga. Haven't picked up a paper in days. School weary. The return 'match' with Edwards never materialized in the upper six today. I set them an essay question from a past paper & then watched them moodily get on with it. Felt like a cop-out. Felt like a fucking coward.

24 October

School taxing – these long, tedious Thursdays. The double lower six, followed by the double upper six. Got v. hot by lunch so everyone was in a steamy, foul mood. By 8th period the boys were playing up, hot & bothered themselves. Wanting to talk about sport & girls & parties, etc. instead of work. They ought to know better with me, but sometimes too I tend to forget they're only youngsters. Really, the term can't end soon enough. For those of us who are leaving, this is especially true. Lots to tie up before then – year-ends to mark & grade, reports to write. How does one say encouraging things about the next term when one is deserting the sinking ship? The crew is jumping, the passengers are left on board. 'This was a pleasing examination result for Johnny. I wish him all the best for next year's finals.' Somehow seems patronizing. Seems as if a trust is being broken, a bond forfeited. Feeling low about it.

I overheard snatches of a conversation in the staffroom: someone thought they saw Alicia Wall in the distance at the shops. So is it true? Could it be so? I admit I sit here & am aquiver with thoughts of the tantalizing possibilities. Images of her throng my head, desire runs strong in my blood to have her one more time, to sate myself with lust. But I remember our chequered past. The awkwardness of our prior break-up. Then it hits me, as if it were a completely new realization: I'm to be gone from this place in a mere two & a half months. What room is there for courting in an agenda of upheaval & chaos?

25 October

New domestic woe on the horizon I fear. I got home & Tobias put a pot on the gas cooker & brought me tea. I noticed that he hovered for a moment before withdrawing back to the kitchen. I knew right away something was up. I can understand their edginess: I must have it out with them about the future, what happens when I'm gone, etc.

Only it wasn't that. He was mincing garlic – the God-awful smell permeated the whole house & determined not to fall into my usual afternoon stupor, I went outdoors & walked about the garden for a bit. It's been raining more often than not lately but the sun was out, piercing the thick swabs of clouds. The late-afternoon light drenching the lawns, glistening at angles off the shrubs, etc. Once I'd rounded the house I saw Tobias standing outside the kitchen door & noticed the poise of his stance.

'Excuse me, baas,' he began.

I sensed this was coming. He rolled up his left trouser leg & showed me a small sore on his shin, just above his ankle.

Didn't look terribly serious. My initial reaction was to fob him off. It looked to me like a mosquito bite, albeit a bit inflamed, with a distinct puckered dot at its centre. Slight swelling. But he told me he's had it now for over a week & in the last few days his whole leg has begun to ache.

'Ah, very sore,' he exclaimed, 'very very sore, baas.'

I didn't take this remark at all seriously. I know he's a good old munt in that sort of way, but I do know he's given to exaggeration. (I remember the whole 'Big, big nyoka, baas, big, big!' fuss when I was a boy which turned out to be a tiny brown house snake coiled in the garage.) Endearing in a way & harmless, but slightly devious in others. (The day he came running to report that Sixpence had been on an all-night binge again after pay day, though he hadn't really.)

So I gave him two Disprin from the bottle in the pantry. It never ceases to surprise me how it always does the trick with any of their ailments. They're none the wiser. Could be the placebo effect. Let's see.

26 October
Nothing to report. Dug out my old portable radio & thumbed about trying to pick up the BBC World Service. No luck really, not helped by batteries which soon ran down.

Rumours abounded in the staffroom at lunch about a whole truckload of opposition activists being rounded up in the night & marched off to the cells. Unnerving development. The wavering, tottering unity government can hardly stay together under normal circumstances, let alone when pushed to the brink by such a blatant provocation. It's all such a scam. Who do they think they're kidding? It's more clear now than ever that they never intended to enter into the spirit of power sharing, of reconciliation. The opposition were mad to do a deal, sign up for this abuse, water down their principles by hopping into bed with the enemy. Everyone seems to forget – I think they forget too – that they won the fucking election. One is tempted to grab them by the scruff of the neck & yell, 'Get off your timid bloody arses & fight for your rights. The people spoke loud & clear!' But I guess they had little choice when virtually every neighbouring head of state chooses to turn a blind eye. Anyway, all I write is irrelevant as the preserve of politics in this place takes no account of the will of the people, esp. a young white male. I ought to be furious that beyond the pages of this journal I don't have a voice, but I'm not really. There's an indifference that sits over me like a cloud all of a sudden. I used to care, I used to be passionate about the outcome of events which I – as a citizen of this country by birth –

thought I could help determine. But there is no easier killer of an optimist than the cold cruel workings of an African 'democracy'.

27 October

Yesterday – increasingly desperate over the state of the freezers – I siphoned ten litres of petrol from one of the jerrycans into a small container. Just before cricket practice I stopped off at the area depot for the electricity authority. Went through all the formalities. Waited in line, made my official report, got the standard lowdown: fault in the area, no fuel for their vehicles, shortage of technicians, etc. I anticipated all of this. So when I offered my ten litres to fuel their truck (I know, I know), I expected they would accept the offer, thinking I'd gain some leverage to try to pin the operations manager down to a specific pledge to fix the fault at the earliest opportunity, etc. All went according to plan & I went away under the impression that by lunchtime, the power would be restored.

And when I get home today . . . ?

I flew into an unimaginable rage. Slammed the car door shut, strode to the house, chucked the clutch of house keys at the bread bin & swore at the top of my voice: 'Fucking arse-holes!' Added to this, as if on cue, I could smell that all too familiar fetid odour starting to drift from the freezer. I'd been meaning to pack the meat into cooler boxes & take it round to Ron & Linda, but thought I'd get away with it one day longer. I stormed down the passage & sat on the bed. I could feel my heart thudding in my chest, my breathing was sharp, laboured. I thought to myself: it's days like these when I know exactly why I'm getting out of this dump.

Everything is quiet & still & mournful without the power. No thrum of energy about the house, about me. Everything lifeless. Ironically exactly the opposite of what I felt a few days ago. It's no longer romantic. Just then Tobias hobbled into the bedroom carrying tea on a tray. My initial reaction was to think he was overplaying his limp, I'm sure to goad my attention & sympathy. I must've looked at him coldly because he stopped dead in his tracks, unsure what to do next.

'Just put it there and get out,' I hissed.

I fell into my mattress, cussing & cursing the world. I lay there on my side staring at the walls. Soon I felt numbness come over me & swiftly my eyes were pulled towards deep nothingness.

Now I'm wide awake & it's late & I'm feeling rather ashamed. It's raining: in the stillness I can hear the water drum on the roof.

29 October

Tobias has been wary of me for a few days. My attitude: so be it. I haven't paid too much attention to him, whether he's limping or not. The power's still out & to rub salt into the wound, that ten litres I wasted could've run the generator for close on eight hours. Have chucked all the meat from the upright – ominous watery pools of blood started to appear, leaking from the trays. When we opened it up the smell was putrid. 'Just throw everything away,' I instructed Tobias. I've decided the loss in monetary terms is not worth the loss of sleep I'll have if I actually worked it out. No word from Veronica – must remember to give her a call. Nothing new breaking on the political front. Apparently the activists are still imprisoned. Rumours rife of torture in the cells. Totally outrageous! Am reminded of Plutarch: 'Draco's laws were written not with ink but blood.'

Lots of rain today. Tinkled the ivories a bit: tried to pick out snatches of Chopin, Liszt, Debussy on the piano in the dark but didn't get v. far.

30 October

Finally got round to Ron & Linda's to store what's left of the meat in their big freezer. The first thing Linda said to me was, 'Ian, you've lost weight.'

'Have I?' I replied. 'I hadn't noticed.'

Should I be flattered or concerned?

As warm as ever they invited me to stay for supper, insisting when I tried to back out. I'm glad I did. Linda produced the most amazing spread – roast fillet, Yorkshire pudding & veggies. How the other half live. I sat there, tucking in & realized just how much I've been missing out on over the past few days. It doesn't occur to me to feel deprived when I'm on my own at home, but in comparison to the splendour of the Wilsons', with their grand mansion in the hills & all the electricity you can shake a stick at (for now), I did begin to feel a little resentful. A hot meal in a man's stomach, a few lights to brighten the night-time, a good soak in a hot tub – not much to ask for, is it? Life's little luxuries. Suppose it's a grand deal more than the poor so-called liberated sod gets living in the shanties & squatter camps.

'Touch wood, the power's not so bad here,' Ron said. 'I think there must be a fat cat living up the road, so we're more or less taken care of by default.'

Lucky you, I felt like saying, living in an area where every other NGO executive & gvt minister has a luxury pad.

'So is it true,' Linda said, 'you are definitely off then?'

'I'm afraid so.'

'No turning back this time?'

'No. The house is on the market. I've resigned. I've applied for a new job. It looks as if it's a done deal. Hanging on any longer just doesn't seem an option anymore.'

'Such a pity. I'm sure the school is kicking themselves.'

I shrugged. 'Don't know really. They'll replace me I'm sure.'

Ron said, 'Can't be easy, after sticking it out all these years. But don't think South Africa's the golden ticket. Their problems are only just beginning.'

'Surely you've thought of Australia?' Linda asked.

'I have. But the passport issue & the immigration process is just killing.'

'Come on – someone as educated as yourself?'

'Well, they're not really in need of academics I don't think. Hairdressers & refrigeration technicians yes. And I'd never want to teach there – I've heard the kids have no respect for authority. Besides, I don't really feel I can leave Africa entirely. I don't know, it's sort of my domain.'

'Your poor mother, I'm sure she'd have loved to have one of her sons close by.'

This carried on for some time in a similar vein. All v. nice & tidy. Then Ron said, 'News is they're trying to get rid of all us NGOs. So the honeymoon is finally over. Apparently we're seen as spies of the West now, sympathizers of the opposition.'

'Christ, it's like the bloody Cold War,' I said.

'I don't know, truth be told, if we'll manage to hold out much longer here ourselves the way they're carrying on. Everyone & everything is an enemy threat to them. Their own paranoia is what's driving them now. We're the single largest aid donor in sub-Saharan Africa & what thanks do we get? I'm convinced I've got the CIO tailing me day & night, our trucks get stopped, searched, regularly looted & diverted exclusively to the loyalists they're desperate to keep happy. It's all about food control now. Who has it & who can give to who. And all they rant about is how Britain has imposed illegal sanctions against their nation! How can you call sixty million pounds a year in aid "illegal sanctions"?'

'It's tunnel vision, Ron,' I said. 'The only reason they call it sanctions is because they perceive targeted travel bans & asset freezes that only apply to a handful of them as being the end of the world. They assume by extension they apply to every citizen because they care about no one but themselves. Plus, it's all just an excuse to try & get the European banks to unlock their accounts.'

'It's the height of selfishness,' Linda added. 'They have no idea what charities & aid organizations do for this country, how they prop it up, keep it going.'

'Indirectly,' I said. 'I mean no offence, Ron, but it's such organizations that prolong the misery in the long run, that keep giving the dying beast a further breath.'

'True, but it's catch-22, Ian. What are we supposed to do? Sit back while three-quarters of the population starve to death because a bunch of thugs has decided to prolong its glorified plunder of the country's resources?'

'Yes, yes, quite right,' I said. The conversation was getting a little heated. In the end I couldn't help but sympathize with poor Ron. Despite the protected executive lifestyle, despite having a passport at his disposal that gets him back to Britain in a flash, it's still tough when you're being pushed out of something by forces beyond your control.

In all the years I've known Ron & Linda, going back to the days when Ron was Dad's regular fly-fishing pal up in the Highlands & we all used to have family trips together to the National Parks cottages by Mare Dam, I don't think I've ever seen them as despondent as tonight. What is wrong with everybody?

1 November
Went to school, taught badly, came home. Exam revision – boring as hell & I think the boys can sense my indifference.

Tobias cooked up something for me on the gas plate for dinner. Spaghetti with tomato & bacon sauce. Hope the bacon hasn't gone off. Stopped off on the way home & bought four big ice blocks. Crazily had to go to three different garages at three different shopping centres: the first two had power cuts! For a bag of water shoved in a freezer overnight they certainly charge a premium – been muttering all evening about it. Still, it keeps the big freezer going for a bit.

Tried to reread bits of *Antigone*. Why, I don't know. Lessons in tyranny, etc. Ancient & modern: man has never been more the same! Anyway, candlelight too weak. Can barely see what I'm scrawling here. Will go off & wash in the water Tobias leaves in the bucket that's so cold it shocks the flesh like a zap & soaks down to the bones.

2 November

Phoned Veronica during a free at school. 'Oh, my darling,' she said, 'I was just about to call you.' Good appeasement strategy. 'Great news – I have an interested viewer. Would tomorrow afternoon suit?'

'I suppose,' I said.

'Two thirty?'

'Fine. But I must warn you – the power's been off for days. Things aren't as pristine as they could be.'

'But, darling,' she retorted, 'what's new?'

Have been living in dread ever since.

3 November

As expected, the day was a trying one. Arrived back home at 1.30 already in a state of some anxiousness. Can't exactly say now what I felt, or explain why I felt it. Almost the knowledge that I'm wedged in a paradox of sorts: the defensive instinct of being wary of strangers in one's home & yet the simultaneous need to make them feel they can possess it. I walked around certain rooms thinking I'd rather they didn't see this photo, or this painting, or snoop around my bedroom or peer at the toilet seat. Tobias & I went to some lengths to spruce the place up, clearing away the clutter. (As it turns out such considerations appear redundant: they only seem interested in the physical construction of the house these days, not its ambiance, its homeliness, so Veronica tells me. 'They'll probably just rip it all out anyway, darling, and start over.')

I guess what really upsets me – apart from my space being invaded – is that I still don't have a really clear, absolute reason for deciding to sell. Just as in the same way, I couldn't confess to this journal – or perhaps 'express' is a better word – in *real* terms a reason for the day I walked into Muller's office & handed in my notice. I cited practical reasons only: economics, remuneration, the prospect of all-out anarchy. He sat there looking shell-shocked. Poor sod.

I was the fourth member of staff so far this term. Maybe he thought we were calling his bluff: he knew that we didn't really know the real reasons. He knows that we've survived so far on the salaries we get, & have put up with the decline for so many years that we could probably carry on doing so indefinitely. The lot of the stoic. We'll always make a plan to overcome the odds: that's what's defined us Zimbabweans for so long. It's what makes us a breed on our own.

Along came Veronica, all kisses & hugs, the usual fawning fatuousness. Stuffed into a short, tight, denim skirt. After her a Mercedes came in. A bald Greek businessman. Pale grey suit & dark shades. Looked very severe, critical, stony. Sweaty face. Veronica fell all over him but he wasn't moved. He made a cursory inspection, grumbling & groaning in heavy Greek. At the end of it he stood in the driveway shrugging his shoulders, his palms upturned, weighing his opinions from hand to hand.

'Sure, it's an okay place,' he announced. 'But I have to ask this – does Tasso want to buy property at this time in such a country? Such a basket case? Possibly Tasso does want to take a risk. Does Tasso want to pay top dollar for such a place in such a country? Hmm . . . Tasso is unsure.'

So he was off, Veronica shrugging, saying, 'You can't

please all of them, darling, but don't worry, something will come up soon.'

It still seems somehow unreal. Kept thinking I was standing in a scene from a Greek version of *The Godfather*. So I haven't been too dispirited about the whole encounter as yet. I haven't felt as if my world is being ripped from under my feet.

4 November

V. hot all day. Cricket practice almost unbearable so took boys for swim instead. This evening Edwards came round. He'd asked me some while back if he could go over a few of the common questions on Paper 2. Not that he needs it. He came racing up the drive in his little blue Starlet, all done up with flashy rims etc, & the most God-awful music blaring from what must be the most massive speakers. We sat out on the veranda. It was only 5.15 & plenty of sunlight left. I put out some crisps in a bowl & opened two warmish beers & then tried to remember the last time I'd actually entertained anyone. Must be the better part of the year. V. shameful.

We went over a question on the Napoleonic wars, one on Nuremberg & one on the decolonization of Africa. We talked a great deal, much of it getting v. philosophical & beyond the brief of the syllabus or the reasons he had come. I recall saying something like, 'History, Nicholas, is simply a matter of strength. Its only function is to detail the collective power of muscle. The strong dominate the weak. The powerful conquer the powerless & then exploit them for their own gains. Colonization is the history of the world in one form or another. What the propaganda machine that runs this place now conveniently forgets is that dozens of African tribes were doing exactly the same thing for centuries before the dreaded Cecil J. Rhodes showed up.'

One day I really ought to finally put pen to paper, fulfil that early promise. Flesh out some polemic on this blighted land & stir a thousand hateful voices in my ears. Anyway, I found it v. stimulating. A fine evening of conversation. Feel much better for it. Before we knew it the light had fallen & we had another warm beer & by candlelight he was regaling me with the current woes of his love life. Juggling two girls at once, it seems. I'm hardly surprised. I'd imagine he's quite a charmer, young Nick Edwards, he has that smoothness of talk & manner. Then he realized it was getting on & went home.

Now all quiet, still, dark.

5 November

Have been missing music on the stereo in the house. When I got home today I had Vaughn Williams' 'The Lark Ascending' on the player in the car & I just killed the engine

& pressed back my seat & slumped there, listening to it. I dozed off under a weary, ethereal fog. The solo violin climbing, soaring to the top of my mind, the emptiness. I woke to Sixpence tapping on the window. The sun was setting. I stumbled groggily into the house.

6 November
Morning

I woke in the dark this morning when I heard the rain drumming on the roof. Fumbled for the candle & struck a match. The room wavered greyly in dim snatches of light. Hadn't slept well. I was still half sunk in a restless stupor when I sloped off to the bathroom. As a madman lost in his own catalepsy of thought, I stripped bare & soaked the sponge with soap & lathered the bitter coldness in the bucket to my body. Wrapped the towel round my waist & lay in the dark again, thinking through those still hours till dawn. I was recalling tracts from *Paradise Lost*. I don't know why. 'And in the lowest deep a lower deep still threatening to devour me opens wide.' The mugginess seemed to linger long after the dark had dispersed.

Evening

Drama of a sort. At six o'clock this morning Tobias was nowhere to be seen with my breakfast tea. His lateness annoyed me but I shaved with the cold water left in the basin & got dressed & left for school. In the fourth I felt a hollow grumbling in my stomach. I was drumming into the dreary lower six the need to reference their essays properly when I felt light-headed but it quickly passed. By break I was starving.

Later, at home, I noticed at once that the house hadn't been cleaned. In the bedroom, the bedding was all rumpled & creased from last night. I walked down to the bottom of the garden to the servants' quarters in something of a temper. The ground was all squelchy & muddy & the rain had pooled into small rivulets beneath my feet. Sixpence was sitting under a yellow plastic tarp knitted together with old fertilizer bags, tied like a sail between the branches of the lemon tree.

'Where's Tobias?' I asked. He pointed to his room. I banged on the door & called out but there was no response. The rain was falling harder, perhaps I didn't hear him. I was getting drenched. I pushed the door open & it grated over the slate stone floor & stuck. I kicked it impatiently. The red brick and mortar gloom. The sense of perpetual dankness, made considerably worse by the tall piles of clutter & junk. I've never been in Tobias's room before. In one corner stands an old iron wood stove & I saw instantly how caked it was in a thick muck of coalesced black soot. I was drawn to the line of black singed up the brick wall. The ceiling was speckled with a black & grey mould. Disgust filled me. On a small cot pushed against one side of the room, Tobias lay.

'Why haven't you been at work today?' I demanded. He was shirtless, his wrinkled flabby skin hanging loosely from his bony chest as I suppose it does on an old man.

'Sorry, baas, very very sorry.' He pointed to his leg. 'Very very sore it is.'

I took a step forward & squinted down at his ankle. The bite was still there, but it didn't look any bigger. The muscle around his shin was drawn tight & shining a light coppery brown. I don't know if this is usual or not. As far as I could tell it wasn't swollen. By now the rain was thumping on the loose tin roof & in the corner above his cot I could see it was leaking in & dripping down the wall in a neat silvery stream.

'For God's sake,' I began, 'why don't you look after your room properly, hey? Look at this mess in here! It's filthy. No wonder things bite you and you get infected. It's because of the dirt. Now clean this place up.'

I made my way back to the house, trudging through the streaks of mud, getting utterly drenched. I traipsed through to the bathroom & dried myself & lay down on the bed, tired & irascible. I may have begun to snooze, but a while later I felt a presence next to me & a voice said, 'Baas, your tea.'

Later I felt bad. I watched him from behind & his limp is quite pronounced now. I gave him four Disprin. I scoured the medicine chest & found some antiseptic lotion. I gave him the tablets & squeezed a dollop of the lotion onto his finger & told him to rub it in. He looked at it curiously but was grateful nonetheless. I hope this will be the end of it.

7 November

Started marking exam papers. What a bore. What a way to spend the weekend. News on the grapevine that the opposition has demanded the release of all political detainees or else it will withdraw from the unity gvt. As if on cue, the army has apparently intensified intimidation & fear tactics in the southern strongholds. Rounding up villagers, beating them up, pillaging their food. Seems now that whenever a demand is made on them they step up the brutality. And from a party apparently 'committed to a peaceful, political solution to resolving the political stalemate in the nation'. Added to this, someone was talking of a fresh cholera outbreak this morning. All this while here in relative sanity I plough through largely unpromising history essays.

8 November

Marked all afternoon. Neck stiff, eyes strained. The stress intensified by the arrival of night which puts a sudden stop to progress. Then groping around in those waiting hours, knowing there's so much to do. Later this evening, just before it was totally dark, Tobias brought me my supper of tuna in a white sauce with pasta. When I took the tray back to the kitchen, he was sitting on the back step, clutching his foot in clear anguish.

I called to him but he didn't respond. The pain must have been very pronounced. He just sat, quietly humming a woeful tune. I could see his teeth were gritted.

'Just stay here,' I said. 'I'll go call Sixpence.'

I walked halfway down the garden & yelled. Sixpence came running.

'Come,' I said, 'we need to get Tobias to his room.'

Tobias muttered something to Sixpence, shaking his head.

'What's the problem?' I asked.

Sixpence said, 'Baas, he says he needs to go to clinic.'

I must've shaken my head unconsciously or shown some impatience because Tobias looked up & started pleading with me.

'Please, baas,' he said several times, 'it very sore now. Very sore.'

I sighed & thought about it, but I was not at my most

145

sympathetic. I was tired from marking. The thought of getting into the car & going on a trek round town for the sake of an aching leg wasn't one I welcomed.

'No,' I said, 'we can't go now. It's too late. All the clinics will be shut. I'll give you some more tablets. Sixpence can help you get back to your room. We'll go to the clinic tomorrow if it's still sore.'

He half nodded, though I could tell that he was disappointed. Rather than feel any more sorry for him, I became annoyed. I walked inside & shut the kitchen door behind me, leaving the pair of them in the dark.

9 November
Lunchtime

Have received an invitation to a 'drinks reception' at the O'Connors' on Friday evening. A few of the staff have them, hand-delivered to our pigeonholes. On very elegant white card, it says, 'Tony & Michelle O'Connor cordially invite you to a drinks reception at 7.00 p.m. at our residence, no. 15 Beaton Close, Greystone Park, on Friday the 11th November, to show our appreciation for your efforts in teaching Michael in his final year.'

Funny how it's always the dimmest prospects who end up being the most gracious. I may well attend.

Otherwise I have finished all scripts. Entered marks on the database & began reports. I can see light at the end of the tunnel. Today I got an e-mail from St James' College confirming my appointment as head of their history department for the start of next year. Details of my package were outlined. A flat in the school grounds, adjacent to the boys' hostel. Basic furnishings included. Meals at communal dining room at a nominal cost, if desired. Medical benefits. 35 per cent pension contributions. The salary nothing exceptional, but certainly a marked improvement. Seems things are falling into place. On the back of this I posted an advert on the web server: 'Household goods for sale. Good quality, tasteful. Cash offers welcome.'

Later

On my way home I stopped off at the electricity depot & tried to pin down the operations manager. Apparently, or so they told me, he'd been called away to fix a fault in a minister's neighbourhood.

'I wish I bloody lived next door to a minister!' I quipped but the remark raised no response. So I asked about the fault they'd promised to fix when I donated ten litres of fuel. The man – some clerk or another – grinned & shook his head. 'Ah, sir, we have big problems here. We are short of spare parts. For that fault we need cable joiners & kits & we don't have any in stock. Also, our vehicle is off the road & needs a new ignition system.'

He took me round the back of a small prefabricated workshop. There were four trucks stationed in a line. Two had their bonnets up, awaiting attention. Another was supported by bricks & had no wheels. There were some seven or eight men in blue overalls – supposedly technicians – all lazing about. Two were playing checkers with bottle tops. A few were dozing in the sun.

'You see the problem, sir?'

'Look, is this fault ever going to get fixed?' I asked.

He looked at me for a while. 'Well if every resident contributes ten US dollars towards spare parts then we can fix it, no problem.'

'And how many residents are in the affected area – how big is the fault?'

'That one – about 100 residents sir.'

'So basically you want 1000 dollars?'

'Yes, sir. You bring direct to me & we'll arrange it to be fixed within the hour.'

'To you directly & you guarantee you can get the part & fix the fault in an hour?'

'Yes, sir, one hour.'

10 November

Where to begin? I was dead tired last night & fell asleep in half an hour, though it was only seven o'clock. I slept well & when I woke it was brighter than usual. The clouds had cleared, the sun was up. Knew at once I'd overslept. No Tobias. I got up & hastily dressed & left the house. By the garage Sixpence came running up to me. Already late for my first lesson, I wasn't in the mood to dally. He wanted to know whether he should go & bring Tobias out so that I could take him to the clinic. I had to breathe in deeply to stop myself from yelling.

'Can't you see he's already made me late? I don't have time now.' He stood there stone-faced. 'Okay, look, here's what you can do – you go with him this morning to the small general clinic on Second Street. It's only three kilometres away & it's free. Take him there & get him sorted out proper, see?'

I handed him ten dollars. 'If it isn't free this should be enough. If it is, bring the money back.'

When I reversed out he was still standing there clutching the note. When I got home from school at lunch he was weeding the grass by the back door. 'Well? All sorted?' I asked him. He stood up shaking his head.

'No, baas. There is no one there. Whole place empty & shut.'

This came as little surprise. I didn't react. But I knew I couldn't put it off any longer. I told him to help bring Tobias to the car.

'We'll try a different clinic,' I said.

It took an age for him to hobble – propped up by Sixpence – from his quarters to the garage. I could see now that he was in some pain. He could barely manage to put an inkling of pressure on that foot & whenever he did, his face convulsed into a tight ball of anguish. Eventually we got him to the car & he shuffled in.

Drove to the semi-pvt clinic in Glen Lorne. I'd thought they'd gone bust but when I was relating the whole saga to Janet over break, she mentioned she'd recently taken her maid there & that she'd found them 'good enough'. About a ten-minute drive away, over the hills & past the school & into the affluence of Glen Lorne. Lots of expansive, ostentatious mansions of the nouveau riche have popped up since I was last in the area. Towering colossal above lines of fir trees, acres of rolling, manicured grass, etc. V. distasteful.

Found the clinic easily enough. Only a few cars in the car park but a long line of people snaked towards the entrance. An ominous sign. Already I could feel my temper flinching (a psychosomatic reaction to the mere sight of a queue?). I parked & told Tobias to wait & walked to the entrance.

V. shabby inside. Weak-green, plastic-coated tiled floor, peeling in large chunks. Grubby plastic chairs which were all taken. A few people squatting on the floor. A nice little pastiche of chaos. A muddle of the sick & ailing. The screams of a snotty-nosed baby. The wail of a delirious woman lying half unconscious on the floor. It stank of stale perspiration & sickness. A nurse was giving orders from behind a counter in a raised voice, trying to keep control. I waited, already ruing the decision to come at all.

She proved difficult. Party loyalist I suspect. She found the circumstances – of an employer bringing his worker for treatment – to be most irregular.

'No, no, no, he must come & register himself,' she said. 'If he is not a juvenile he can come on his own.'

I explained to her why he was waiting in the car but she was even less impressed.

'No, no, he must come. I need to see all patients in person.'

I gave her a bemused stare & started walking back to the car. The queue had lengthened. I turned & went back in.

'Look,' I said, 'how long will it take to see the doctor?'

'The queue is there,' she said, 'you can see yourself.'

'Right, so if I bring him in & he registers & then I pay a little extra, would he be able to see the doctor a little quicker?'

She looked at me sternly. 'What are you saying? Do you think you are special? There is a queue. Can you not see the queue? That is where every patient must wait their turn. Is it because the colour of your skin is different to mine that—'

There was nothing for it. You just can't corrupt some people. I went outside to the car & fetched Tobias. He was limping but he could walk. We went back to the desk & he registered. Took an age. Not an easy task for a man who has never had a formal education. The nurse seemed belligerent every time I tried to help him. I paid the nominal ten-dollar fee & we went outside.

'Just join this line here okay, & wait to see the doctor,' I said. 'You'll be okay to wait here?'

He nodded & didn't protest & went limping off to join the queue which was some thirty people long. I sat in the car & tracked down my CD of Chopin's *Nocturnes* & let it pipe about me. Nothing like a little genius to sate the wounded soul.

I was listless for a while, despite the music, & I became tired quickly, saturated with boredom. I slipped my seat back & soon found myself slumped against the window, my head tossed back for a while, then rolling about my shoulder. I was drifting off, curiously sedated by the warmth of the car's interior, the light fragrant smell of the lavender spray Sixpence uses to polish the dashboard, the vanilla cream he uses to shine the leather seats. I wasn't unhappy there, my mind free to drift, my body absent from school & the quiet restiveness of the unpowered house where the tensions of life lie exposed, those open wounds. With the CD playing I was hardly aware of the figure standing beside my window, tapping at me.

The light had dulled. I opened the back door & Tobias prized his way in. He was panting hard. His jaw clenched, his cheeks drawn in, his eyes burning hard. One hand clutched his ankle. In the other he held something.

'What did they say?' I asked. He opened his palm to reveal a small plastic packet of tablets. I looked at the label: Paracetamol. 'Is this all they gave you?' He nodded. He turned his head from me, hiding some inner fury or maybe a gleam of emotional strain. Strange to suddenly have that intimacy exposed between us after all these years of being committed to the distant aloofness of our master/servant trope. I leant over & patted his knee.

'They didn't say anything else?'

He shook his head.

'Don't worry,' I said. I tried to sound reassuring. 'These tablets are good. Better than the ones at home, hey. Much stronger.'

153

He said nothing, nor did he turn to look at me. I was tired now & started the car & reversed out, past the patients reeling off from the queue. I didn't make any conscious observations of them at the time, although now, when I think over it, when I sit here in the dark & confess to my own insensitivities, I can swear they were all looking down at the packets of painkillers in their hands. Each & every one of them treated the same. Cattle in the kraal, getting vaccinated, getting shunted through the run.

Past midnight

Can't sleep a wink. Keep tossing & turning. Some close dread in the outer dark. Got up & fumbled for the candle & stalked down the passage to my desk. Everything in these lone hours seems invested with some pretence, some rejection of my presence. It's as if the air objects to my woken conscience stealing from it that which I'm only entitled to by day. Strange observation. Shakespeare's *Twelfth Night* – 'There is no darkness but ignorance.' Maybe that's it. Maybe I'm just ignorant. Maybe the absence of light in my life – not just the physical light of bulbs & lamps – but a light, *the* light, light itself, is the manifestation of my tantamount ignorance to all that surrounds me. The degree certificates framed & hung on the wall beside this desk where I write exonerate me from nothing, nothing at all. How stupid to assume they lift me above anything. I really ought to haul myself back to bed.

11 November

Have finished reports, tied up all loose ends re. admin. Now it's just a waiting game. Tap, tap, my fingers on the desk. I floated the idea of trying to text Alicia's old number, test the waters, try my luck. Something was holding me back – perhaps fear of rejection, or even worse, silence.

Since the trip to the clinic I haven't heard much about Tobias's ailment. To be honest I'm reluctant to ask. Trying to avoid engaging him in too much conversation. We seem to stay out of one another's way as if by some unspoken agreement. He's still hobbling about badly but seems more resigned to it than before. I go about my routine & he goes about his chores & I'm beginning to think that I've heard the last on the matter. I hope this is the case: strangely, the whole affair's been playing on my conscience.

12 November
Saturday mid-morning.

Slept well after a rather heady evening. The notion of a sedate 'drinks reception' at the O'Connors' turned out to be a lavish bash, with no expense spared on catering (the most scrumptious spread imaginable), a full bar, a disco & a whole cross-section of guests ranging from other parents, O'Connor's mates (almost the entire upper six), a whole bevy of young girls clutching onto them & several fellow staff. The house is a huge sprawling affair perched on the side of a hill with substantial rolling gardens. All lit up with angled spots. Long, classical-style pool & a wide terrace too where everyone was congregated. The accompanying girlfriends all Lolita-like in vulgar miniskirts & tops that barely covered their midriffs. God knows what was going on behind the bushes.

Felt decidedly cringing at first, but soon mingled in with the staff & parents, all of whom I have come to know pretty well over the six years their sons have been at the school. More than one set came up to me & said how sorry they were that I was leaving after so many years & 'such a reputation', as that horsey Joan Henson said. Vicky Edwards said, 'Nicholas has just loved all the discussions you've had together.' Felt v. flattered, then a bit flat. Suddenly that first twinge of realizing I'm actually going started to flare up. Nonetheless I braced myself & continued to mingle. Muller & his Mrs were there, grim-faced as ever. Then that coquette Stacey Brisk latched onto me, glass of wine in hand & seemed determined not to let go. It seems she thinks our friends with benefits arrangement still stands, though it's been over a year since I ventured down that dark alley. (A whole year?)

A bit later we all started to mingle more. We all had far too much to drink. The boys were all v. hospitable & cheered us staff on, etc. This was after the Mullers had gone & even before we all played immature drinking games with shooters of neat lemon-scented vodka. Vile. Then a group of them disappeared into the house & up the stairs to a room, insisting I go with them. We went out through open French doors to a balcony. The lights of the city spattered rather thinly below us. Somewhere in that dark splurge was this neighbourhood, this house which hasn't seen a touch of electricity for three weeks. O'Connor, Ncube & Henson were fiddling on a wrought-iron table with a packet of something. I stood looking out, talking to a quite inebriated Edwards.

'Fuck am I glad school's over sir,' he said.

'What are your plans, Nick?' I asked.

He steadied up & said, 'Don't know, just get out.'

'Out where?'

He shrugged & gestured with his arms at the air. 'This fucking shithole, what else?' I knew at once he meant not only the city, the country, but the placeless redundancy, the toxic sterility, the contagious sensibilities of being a white boy in Africa. At once I saw in him the courage I'd never had when I was eighteen, bookish & antisocial, withdrawing into a shell & mistakenly thinking I had a place here, a future, instead of getting out into the real world where the history attached to the colour of my skin wasn't going to end up being a liability, a target, a weight of debt.

'Good,' I said. 'That's what someone like you needs, Edwards.'

'And you too, sir,' he added. He was looking at me quite intently across that limp sodium light & our eyes met in a moment of stern intensity as if things had been reversed now & he was instructing me & I needed to take heed of his advice. I don't think he was referring to just South Africa either. I nodded.

Just then the others came round all clutching spliffs they'd been busy rolling. They handed me one. I was hesitant to take it at first, but they all said, 'Come on, Mr H, live a little.'

Then Ncube said, 'We just want to say, sir, thanks for everything.'

I was completely taken aback.

'You weren't the easiest dude to have as a teacher but we'll never forget your lessons, sir. We sure learned a thing or two about life. Thanks from all of us & good luck in your new job.'

With that we all took a deep drag on the spliff. I didn't know what to say. I just smiled at them & nodded appreciatively. I'm sure they could see I was fighting back the gleam welling in my eyes. I knew it was time to leave.

I'm sitting here now plunging my mind for parallels with the classics, something ageless & vindicating that I can quote from the sages on the innocence of hedonism or the justification of excess. What I really ought to be doing is acknowledging the unbridled comradeship of man.

13 November

Two trying developments re. the house. Veronica phoned early to say she had another viewer. We set up an appointment at three o'clock. A Chinese man this time, short & stocky & dressed in a severe blue suit. My heart sank. My contempt rooted purely in the belief that they're only piling in here by the plane load to mop up everything we leave behind. (And the gvt rants & raves about the threat of recolonization!)

'I look to make Chinese lestalant,' he announced.

'Of course you do, darling,' Veronica replied, patting him on the shoulder. 'Now come this way, Mr Lin.'

He stood looking at the driveway. 'Must have big livelay for car park. Fifty car they must fit.'

Then in the kitchen: 'No, no, this kitchen too small.' He shook his head vigorously. 'We go now please.'

Later I phoned Veronica & told her bluntly: no more Greeks or Chinese.

'The market's dead as a doornail,' she tells me. 'No one wants to invest.'

'Just keep trying,' I said.

Then at about 4.30 I got a call from a woman looking to buy household goods. When she arrived at 5 p.m. she handed me a business card – 'Express Auctions'. Not what I wanted to see. She nosed about, prodding & poking at all & sundry. Looked as if she had a bad smell under her nose the whole time but I persevered with her. Made a few notes & said she'd give me a call.

Now I'm feeling very disconcerted about the whole encounter. I keep getting this flash-forward to some dingy, dusty, overcrowded warehouse where all the world & his dog gather to scrutinize & bid on the contents of your life. 'Lot no. 28, one queen-size bed, pine, with ornamental woodwork & side drawers, lockable. Posturepedic mattress. Slept in by thirty-one-year-old male, tall, educated, white. Only rare occasions of coitus. Not particularly adventurous sexually. No pets to compensate for lack of company.'

14 November

Tobias has been busy. When I got home I immediately sniffed mukwa oil & saw a light drying film of it across the parquet tiles. The smell always kindles an unplaced satisfaction: fuel & linseed & something organic altogether. Everything's been dusted & polished. A glint to every surface.

Then his motives were revealed. He was hovering again, just out the corner of my eye the whole time. I decided to broach the issue directly.

'How's your leg?' I asked him.

He turned from the sink & said, 'Ah, baas, it is still very bad.'

'And those tablets they gave you at the clinic – they haven't worked?'

He shook his head. 'They not work that well, baas. It still very sore all the time.'

We stood looking at each other for some moments. I didn't really have anything more I could say or offer on the matter.

Then he said, 'Baas, I think I go back to my homelands to get better.'

'Homelands – are you mad?'

'No, baas, I go to see traditional healer man.'

'Traditional healers aren't the answer,' I tried to tell him.

'He'll only rub some or another ointment on & rattle some bones & that'll be that.'

'No, baas—'

'Plus, have you not heard that the rural areas are not good places now? There's lots of problems there. The army, the cholera, beatings & looting.'

He looked at me blankly.

'Don't you listen to that radio of yours?'

'The radio say everything going to be good here again. It say all problems are fault of England & America.'

I sighed. I felt truly despairing for him. But nothing I say is going to get through to him. He's not going to be bullied by me.

'When will you come back?' I asked.

He lowered his eyes & didn't answer. I took this to mean: I'm not coming back. What's there to come back to?

'Well go,' I said sharply, 'but when your supply of tablets runs out, you'll be on your own, hey.'

The more I think of it, the more I fret. This strange limbo we're living through. No one knows who's coming or going. There's a troubled dispensation in this country & ever since that disputed election & the shaky power-sharing deal, we've all been paralysed, a void which resonates uneasily about everyone. Nothing's happening, but everything is. We're always on the verge of outright anarchy, but somehow not quite. Behind the scenes, in the depths of the country, villages that hardly have a name on a map are being levelled to the ground. I'm nervous thinking of Tobias caught up in it all. He's innocent & weak, just an old man wanting to get to a destination. He's been a loyal old soul. To my parents, to me. All these years.

16 November

No sign of power. Have almost given up worrying. In the meantime I've streamlined my life. Something tinned for supper, usually. Tuna, sardines, ham, lots of pasta. I'm ambivalent. In the end I've finally decided to text Alicia. Surprisingly I got a message straight back. Confirms she's back in the country after being abroad, working in London. Suggested we meet. Intriguing, but somehow, despite initiating it, I feel reticent. Still I replied: 'Of course, definitely, can't wait 2 C U,' etc. Probably sounded like some desperately horny teenager. We'll see.

17 November

Well that's that. He's gone. Went off this morning. I hadn't been expecting it to be this sudden. I thought of telling him to stay till the month's end, but what difference does it make? I squared up with him & gave him a fairly handsome gratuity & money for the bus fare, plus a whole lot of old clothes I was throwing out anyway in a tatty brown suitcase. He'd packed all his possessions into his little knapsack. The rest of his belongings, he says, he's organized for his nephew to pick up in a truck. He wore his Sunday church suit & looked dapper in his faded fawn trousers & tan checked jacket & a navy-blue tie. I noticed he was wearing the maroon shirt I gave him in his Christmas box last year & found this v. touching. He also donned a wide-brimmed hat, the kind a cricket umpire might wear, only brown, & held a wooden cane in his free hand which he used as a support for his bad leg. He docked his hat at me & smiled politely & we shared a few memories, a few anecdotes of his recollections of me as an infant, with my mother & father & my brothers. Then he hobbled off down the driveway & out the gate. Slowly down the road he went, walking away from thirty-eight years of service, from a place I'd imagine he called his home. For some reason I want to record this image v. precisely.

'Be careful, old man,' I called after him as he went away down the road. 'Get to your home in one piece, hey!'

He lifted his hat one more time in acknowledgement. I turned from the gate & went indoors.

18 November

Have been depressed all day. It isn't exactly the knowledge that he's not coming back, or that things are going to stack up beyond control, or that the power's been out for well over a month. It's the process that has started to unravel around me, the process of elimination. It's the atmosphere in the house, the atmosphere of rejection. By osmosis, it knows I'm abandoning it & it's gone cold, frigid, indifferent on me. It's the loneliness.

Yes, it's the loneliness & somehow, with Tobias now gone, it seems the last link to my childhood, my youth, my family has vanished for good. I sit here & can honestly say I have no idea when I'll next see Mom & Dad, Alex or James. For they are flung in all directions & I can't see how I'd ever afford to get to them all. I can't see myself arriving in Toronto to see Alex & the Canadian wife I've never met, the woman from a foreign icy place he's coupled with & produced two off-spring, a girl with cherry locks & a chubby boy, who'll both grow up in a welfare state & speak with a twang & not have an inkling that pumping through their veins is the sun & heat & dust of Africa. And James, in the crowded misery of London, working in the bland IT field. Screwing loose girls he picks up easily, drunk in overcrowded pubs. He moves amongst people who have no feel for space, for the wide expanses of the plains of the lowveld, the bush where man treads a tenuous step, ever subservient to the calls & beasts of the wild. He tramps the concrete streets & rushes for buses & is pushed along with the masses onto an underground train & in certain solitary moments he has unbidden memories – this I know to be true – of playing French cricket with his brothers on the big back lawn of this, his boyhood home, of roasting mealie cobs with Tobias over bricks at the back of the garage, of Mother's chicken casseroles.

3

All the while the provisions are whittling down. When they stop and tip the water container, the meniscus lowers ever more, and the angle at which they have to tilt it becomes more acute. It's almost painful to watch. The lip of the Coke bottle is too narrow and the prospect of losing even a drop of water is so grave that they make a funnel with an empty bean can that they squash and hammer into the shape of a cone. Their path has not taken them to any active river or stream. Coming down off a low knoll one afternoon they drew parallel to a riverbed, a bare grassless basin, the pale loam hard and dry. There where the bones of some beast had fallen into the sand as if its airy shell were still kneeling and burrowing its neck into the trough. The man stood and glassed over the dryness and a visible dejection took hold of him. A boy promised a toy he will never have. He had been expecting to come across water. He had been measuring out their stores bit by bit. They had little left in reserve.

The food must be running low too. Every time they dip a

hand into the sacks they bring out less and less. But each time they do something is produced that is more than nothing, more than the empty held-out palm. Their stores seem bottomless, blessed by some proverb or watched over by some atavistic numen. Or else they are simply thrifty in the extreme, pilgrim-like in their consumption and they know well the parable of division: a little broken into many, many parts. Sometimes when they aren't so tired the man will remember a word of thanksgiving before the mealie cakes or the mashed dried fish or the thin cobs are eaten. Sometimes he will hold out his upturned palms and raise them to the level of his face and, closing his eyes, mutter something which may be a prayer or an offering to the ancestors. At other times he forgets and they all sit hunched and drawn and melancholic, rolling the food in their fingers, pressing it into small balls in their hands and bringing it forlornly to their mouths. They take nothing for granted.

The boys' free time is set aside for the chore of scouring beyond the threadbare glades for trees they may pick and plunder. Once they came across a tree with crisp white petals, calyces covered in rust-coloured hairs. Its thick pods had fallen flush to the ground. The boys went forth with an empty sack and brought back a whole load to the campsite. They sat about chewing the ripe pods and discarding the others. They slipped the edge of the machete blade between the crevice and cranked them open, splitting them like oyster or mussel shells. There were plenty to go round. They came over and dropped so many before him his eyes could not digest the mound piled at his feet. His mouth filled with juices he had not known for some time. It may have been as good as gnawing at vegetables found unexpectedly in an abandoned patch.

They walk by day, rest mostly by night. They don't come across another living thing for some time. A stretch of days that may seem longer than it really is. The path leads on through this maze in the bush. It winds and forks and they wind and fork with it. The pain in his feet grows intolerable. His back hurts. They slap his backside or spine often with the flat of the machete. Soon the bow of his ribs begins to pout a cage round his chest. He is losing weight, getting weaker. There is a sore at his neck that oozes at night and dries to a sticky scab in the sun. It gets worse.

The woman veers between schizophrenic states like a chameleon. Her babe wedged inside her, clamped in its incubating cell. The lanky boys stoop along and the man too. The machetes and the rifle. The radio that once in a while they huddle round, surfing the airwaves in vain until finally the batteries die altogether and there is only silence. Their water is running out.

Two days later they are walking the same narrowed bush when the path begins to widen. Suddenly it opens up to a wide dirt road which cuts diagonally across it. They stop and the man looks up the road, right, left, right again. He withdraws his scrap of card from his trouser pocket and studies it. Glancing up at the far-off terrain his eyes settle on a distinct conical hill swabbed with the dark greens of trees. They turn onto the road and the cart straightens up on the level turf and goes careening forward with the ease of a locomotive skidding along iron rails. They move along swiftly, all prodding towards the inkling of some great twist of fortune around the bend.

A road this wide, smoothed and graded, must lead to some place that appears on a map, to some area accounted for in the known world. Beside them there are signs the virgin veld is thinning and then there is the sight of low rutted fields knitted into the land. The cart leaves a fine russet spray of bald soil in its wake. Eventually they come to a fork where a pole is pegged into the ground. Across its top is nailed a sheet of wavy tin pointing up the road and in faint ochre letters some legend is inscribed. They stop and scrutinize the lettering and run the words over their tongues. The man stares up the path of the road and trains his sight again on the distant landmark cone blaring like a hazy tower against the starched blueness. They press on up the road.

They rise some and then dip again and at times it's difficult to lug the cart uphill. He feels weaker and weaker. When they climb the slight ridges, the veld on the right thins and they are given a glimpse of the lands below. In the distance the square patches of fields stand out starkly against the yellowed flush of the bush. His eyes are blunt and he can't see well. Further on, the road angles sharply and the boys go scouting ahead. Soon the man leads them off at a tangent into the bush. The cart strains to part the dense grass; the boys have to heave from behind and lift it off its wheels. They plough through the scrub and the flange of grass and he almost stumbles over his own feet. They cut across a flush sector while the road skirts round them and after a time they come to an abrupt halt. There is a tall security fence, knotted atop with gnarled coils of barbed wire. The boys stagger forwards to part the grass and open up a window with a wide view onto a sprawl of farm buildings close before them.

The farmhouse nestles in the wattled shade of tall pouting trees, their fissured bark rough and grey, their pods flat and kidney shaped. They are exotic anomalies to this landscape and stand out more prominently than the house itself, which is long and low and flat with a red tin roof in places rusted brown in runs of flaky bronze. A veranda runs along its length with low squat Spanish arches. The windows are all closed, the curtains drawn, the dense mosquito gauzes ratcheted tight. Even from a distance a wide and uncompromising desertion of the place is tangible. A truck stands in the yard bricked up with its bonnet open, its oily innards stripped and heaped about. The browning lawn has grown thick and weedy, the tawny flowerbeds dry and drooping in the sun.

Adjacent to the house is a fenced courtyard and in it some dogs lie against the muddy soiled walls. Their tails whip tirelessly at the flies. One shakes its ears. Another hauls itself to its feet and limps over to the fence, staring half alert in their direction. The old habits that die hard. A quick shiver runs across his aching spine. It's a black dog, its rack of ribs moulded through its sleek coat. Skin and bone and barely alive. It glares at them and pricks its ears up and then trails off, flumping to the ground. The man watches the dogs for a while. Possibly he is thinking: what is keeping them alive? Or: who is keeping them alive?

The man reaches behind him, grips the butt of the rifle and swings it off his shoulder. The boys take their cue and unsheathe their machetes. They move off to the right, stalking along the bush like bandits, a pride behind a herd. This is a vain attempt to silence their progression when every roll of the cart's wheels over the scrub crackles and bristles. It makes them seem ludicrous. They creep along an arch of bush, along the hem of the fence until they have come almost full-circle. Again the boys part the grass and the man kneels down and trains the rifle barrel through the fencing. There is a huddle of outbuildings before them, at the back of the house. A workshop, then a series of coops and sties. In the coops a few fat hens wobble and flutter. In the sties lie some goats gazing out across the diamond-shaped wire and into the encroaching bush and the wild afield.

They stare in wonderment at the goats and hens for a long time. It seems like an illusion, or some cunning trap. They stay there, lowered and readied, the man looking through the scope of the rifle at every sector of the yard, probing every hollow, every deepening scar of shade. Then he sits up. Then they move off, back through the bush, trampling the pink-haired spikelets of the grass and clawing their way towards the yawning sight of a clearing that lies ahead, off to the right. They stoop down as they approach the bare pitted redness of the earth and then stop altogether. They cower and scan the openness. Beyond there are the thatched tops of huts, mulched grey and neatly fringed, almost swallowed by the spread of a stubby tree with dark corky bark and an umbrella spray of coral-red flowers. They look on intensely, every muscle stiff and straining.

The compound is deserted. They inch forwards and begin to delve into the huts one by one. They yield little of value: a few pots, some tatty fabric, some utensils. All else was cleared out when the occupants fled. There is a fire pit with cindered logs and a pool of cinder ash. Then, from round the back of the huts, one of the boys calls out. The man steadies his rifle and stalks forward. But the cry isn't one of fright or horror. They all shuffle round and ahead they see the boy waving at them, leaping up and down like a child at play. The wave of excitement hits them. They almost don't know how to respond. Away from the huts and a small way into the bush there is a clearing and in the centre of a clearing a black well plunges deep into the earth.

They work the hand pump eagerly. It squeaks and hisses. There is a running grumble that slurps deep from the guts of the well and water suddenly gushes from the tap. They each sate their thirst one by one and repeatedly.

He stands there looking on. His sore mouth salivating. He senses he will get his chance so he doesn't panic or grow impatient. At last they unhitch the cart and he goes stumbling forwards and begins to drink his fill, lapping at the tap for some minutes. His parched throat thaws and his stomach bloats until he is close to retching. The containers are filled to the brim and then they sit about and rest. The relief is so tangible it's as if each of them has shed ten years from their slack, wearied bodies.

A short while later the boys strip naked and wash themselves from head to toe, cupping water into their palms and dousing the grimy filth from them until once again their skins shimmer with that black slippery sleekness. They look like the oiled bodies of seals. The man follows them. The woman rinses their clothes in the water, scrubbing them in her hands before wringing them out and spreading them in the sun to dry. She strips too, unashamed of her fulsome breasts, the nipples swollen and gibbous, draped over the tight stretch of patchy brown skin pulled around the sphere of her belly. They wrap sacks round their waists as loincloths and bask in the eclipsing shade of the huts. Even the rifle stands cocked up against the mud wall, the belt of bullets draped on the ground, away from the man for the very first time.

So the afternoon lies supine before them, a long and languid lull that is alien to their lot. Here they are just five figures knit in a capsule of space and time, cocooned in the bliss of ignorance, spun out of nothing but the air on their breath, the water running through them. They curl in the sloping shadows and sleep away from the glazing sun. For this short time it's as if they are bereft of everything that has gone before. If any one of them were to wake now, stagger from their bedding and stand in the amber dusk light, they may fail to place the last hours and days of their ordeal at all. It would be like a benefaction, something they could never know and would hardly understand. In this momentary absence of blood and bullets, booms and bodies, all is a lucent space, something akin to the whiteness of the far sky or the fineness of pooling water that blinkers their vision. Even the rope that ties and binds him during this time becomes nothing but an illusionary figment. When the night comes they rouse themselves and sit under the spume of stars waiting for the encroaching spores of reality to catch up with them again.

Late in the night he hears the muffled whispers burning about him and movement and footsteps trailing off into the bush. He doesn't stir. He lies there listening to the night-time sounds: the close scrawl of a cricket sprouting a lone soliloquy accompanied by a dull faraway lowing.

The others return soon, pulling something through the bush. He can hear the thrush grass bending and the swish of a weight being dragged across the slippery stalks. He raises his head and focuses his eyes and sees them grouped round the grizzled remains of the dead fire. The boys are kneeling over some formless matter, hunks of black heaped on the ground. Then the form becomes the shape of stiff legs, tipped with the silhouetted cleft of hooves, and a neck arched back. It's the body of a goat lying slack before them. There are three in total and in a clutch beside the goats are some hens, the necks lopped, the heads tossed away. Speedily and quietly the boys work with their machetes and a small knife. They gut the goats, tearing at the inside of the skin, drawing it back to discard the innards. They heap the viscera aside and it sits there like some dark gelled accusation. The boys pool the black blood back and forth between the skin and the flesh and drain it into a pot. Meanwhile the man sits plucking the feathers from the hens and in no time at all their shiny pink skin glows plump under the deep night stars and the orbed moon that has now arisen.

They cannot see well but they make the progress of skilled butchers. They break apart the limbs of the goats, hack at the joints, splice the flesh. Soon the carcasses are nothing but hollowed-out shells, scaled down to naked bone and cartilage. They dump them aside in the bush. All that's left are the piles of meat – clean, odourless, fresh – which they sit before now in silence and at rest.

The man scoops up the pot and hands it to the boys and they drink from it in turn, sipping at the rich darkness of the blood which stains their lips and teeth and dribbles a bit down their chins before they lick at it or swipe it with a finger. Warrior boys at some ritual initiation, streaked and marked for battle. They stack the meat atop the sacks and in the metal bowls. Some of it they pierce with hooks shaped from a coil of wire and hang it from the trees to bleed out. Then he drifts off into his blanking detachments again.

In the morning there it is all about them in the quivering

grey of dawn like an excessive promotional display in a deli. There is something surreal about their luck and its sudden excesses. What will they do with such a bounty of meat before the sun rots it through and the flies suck it up?

The woman wobbles from her mat and cooks them up a feast for breakfast. The fire is restacked and lit and soon the hooks of meat dangle in the smoke and brown and blacken over the embers. They sit about and gorge themselves, chewing and slobbering at the meat, a pack of cannibals after a pre-dawn hunt. He has no taste for it. It repels him. The smell of it cooking sends him bilious, the sight of it makes him want to heave. He sticks with his own food and plain as it is he gets by on it. There is a lot more to their clutter this morning. In the night they have managed to loot an assorted bundle of clothes, a few pillows and blankets, some empty glass milk bottles and some Tupperware boxes from the farmhouse. Some cutlery too. After the meal they sit about salting the meat vigorously with a salt-shaker.

They drink their fill again from the well. Each one in turn and he last of all. They fill all the containers to the brim and stack them on the cart. The chassis slumps, the axle sags. Once they have finished luxuriating in the water the man sets about dismantling the well pump. He sits there bashing at the parts with the butt of a machete until bit by bit the pipes come loose and the nuts, bolts, springs, coils lie splayed in the sand about him. Meticulously he picks them up, shakes out a plastic shopping bag from one of the sacks and deposits the parts, wrapping them up tightly to store away.

They press the salted chicken into the Tupperware. They unhook the slips of goat meat from the trees, strip long thin branches and tag the hooks on each end to balance it out carefully. There are three altogether. The slices of meat are crammed on full until the sticks bulge and bend in the middle. Then they rip some sheeting and bundle the sticks across the backs of each of their necks, himself included. They look like cattle or oxen with braces fixed to them. The meat bobs about to and fro on the hooks still bleeding. When the sun rises full the salt will dry it out and preserve it and in this way they will have meat for a good few days to come.

They gather the rest of their wares. The man slings the rifle over his shoulder and straps on the belt of bullets. The woman is eased into the cart. They have to keep moving for her sake. They pull themselves away from this place and the well. It is not easy. He senses their reluctance. Perhaps he feels it most keenly, his legs heavy as they lead him off, rooted deep in some purling vein. His brain well stemmed in the emollience of it. They peel away and curve off from the compound and ease back onto the track.

They follow the road from the compound which weaves and arches, drawing near the tall security fence of the farmyard. With their bellies full and their bodies cooled, their minds may be doused in their good fortune, their guard lowered. As they curve onto the road leading them away from the farmyard a human call breaks over the morning thrum and a figure in blue overalls comes jogging up the road behind them, carrying a staff. He calls and signals them with his hand to slow and wait. His attempt to look urgent is pathetic.

They draw to a halt and the man slings the rifle from his shoulder and strides forward, calling back. The blue figure slows to a spindly walk, his hair steel-coloured, the wiry silver curls of his beard bristling starkly against his gaunt, puckered face. His eyes have sunk deep into his skull and through the unbuttoned overalls his bare chest, ribbed with a bow of bones, glares out. He grumbles between short gasps of breath and points with the staff at the farmyard and at the racks of meat they carry. He spits with rage and the man listens to his ranting for a time before stepping forward and slugging the butt of the rifle into the man's temple. It cracks against his skull like a whip. The farmhand falters back on his feet and keels over in a slight swell of dust. There is a moment of raw fright between them all. The rifle butt is still raised and they all look on at the body heaped on the ground. A neat rivulet of blood seeps in the silence down his temple, dripping into the soil and staining it.

The man shouts for them to move on and they walk forward, stiff with shock. There is little conversation from any of them after this; little that resembles their former ease. The boys stalk forward, weary on their feet. The ever-stoical face of the man shows no glimmer of remorse. He is, as ever, hardened, resolved. The woman slumps down in the cart, turning herself away from the day and its actions. She lies there quiet and petulant. All this is for her, in a way. The deeds of man and his desperation. They trudge on up the road and away from the farm, rejoining the narrow path that snakes them off into the thick smothering bush once again. They plough on, the heat notching up, a scourge breaking over them at midday.

So in the heat they wind away through the plush bush. When they are tired they stop and drink and when they are hungry they pick at the dangled railings of dried meat and gnaw on it. Often they stop because the woman is ill or she has been wailing in pain. There is now little shade out here: the trees are sparse, bare, whittled down, all staggered away from the line of the path. To compensate, the vlei grass grows tall and barbed, with sheaths that are keeled, awns that are spiked and tinctured a burnt gold. As they pass through its arching passages it itches and irritates them, stinging their eyes. They get tired of hacking at it. Sometimes the racks of meat get tangled and they have to dislodge them from their necks and carry them aloft. Other times they skim the tops of the tassels effortlessly.

But the passage each time is fraught with an edgy tension: they want to know what awaits them on the other side of the screen. Once he thinks he sees the brown bulk of some mammal streak the deep undergrowth beside them but he cannot be sure. Glimpsed above them all the while through the wreathed overhangs is the clear blue sky, the faceless dome under which they crawl. Some senseless depth the mind cannot reconcile. Seldom a cloud is posted in the sky. Never a hint of rain.

The further they go from the city – such a distant memory now – the more hostile, the more alien everything becomes. He has still to discover the purpose of their travels or why it is they ensnared him. All along the journey the gun has been a constant worry to him, a force of threat and terror. His instincts stretch to the vague understanding that once they have dispensed with his services they may dispense with him altogether. He fears this more than anything. He is aware that he is only a slave tied to his services. A thin thread that may be, the weakest of attachments. He may become a liability. He may have no further chore to undertake. Nothing more to pull. But how his mind will flinch when the AK47 is cocked at his temple or his neck at the end of all this, his ears anticipating the catastrophic blast.

Perhaps they will spare a bullet, but hack into him with the machete, slash at his chest till his heart gives way and his brain goes blank? Maybe they will strap a bomb to his back and send him walking into a crowded village or small town full of militants to clear the way? Or they may sell him or use him to barter when the food finally runs out. Then what will be his fate? Sold on to the next journeying terrorist, guerrilla soldier, rebel leader? So the ordeal can start again, this mind-swept hell. Escape has crossed his mind many times even though it's impossible. Where would he go? Out there? He would last a day. Maybe two. The sheer loneliness of the bush, the infinite solitude of freedom would probably finish him off. He would be a real captive then, tied to his heartbeat, chained to the slavish paranoia of his mind. The open plains would be his den. The wide savannah his prison cell.

The truth is that he's often too tired to think about it. Often he just wants to sleep, not caring sometimes whether he wakes again or not. Even the mosquitoes would struggle to keep him awake. Even the distant fear that hounds him, the contingency of fright frizzling on in the distant reaches of his dulled, sun-bashed brain. He presumes the rest of reality drones on in a hazy reel which he senses with a certain quivering dread may not be real at all. And one can't do much — not eat nor drink nor rest nor plan an escape — when one is forced to walk and walk as he's forced to, those long trudging miles with no end in sight.

The end of yet another day. Another day which may be one or many days, in which they may have travelled far or not at all. They come down the side of a kopje through a tall stagger of beige bush and into a clearing of sparse scrubland.

A red pool of dust. Clomps of weedy grass scattered in tufts like islands. They come to a halt and here it seems they will settle for the night. Here where the sun smashes into the sleek sides of a scarp and shards of copper light fall in steep decline down the sides of a ravine. The boys as usual are tasked with hacking down firewood and building the fire. The man maps out who is to sleep where and who is to stay on guard. They eat a little supper: half a tin of baked beans, slivers of relish, slivers of the meat.

In the distance the sun plunges and blazes a weakened red, then an intense orange. He couldn't say this evening that he is too downhearted or unhappy. Or even terribly afraid. Rather his fear has settled down into a blunt edginess. So the evening sits for a while, then night comes. The bonfire spits and roars and from the tree where he's tied he looks on in strange wonderment at the glowing embers for no other reason than to think they're dancing in his eyes. He beds down to the naked night where above them the spills of the firmament trawl and blinker. Births of some reckoning that are relations to them all, seeded from their inner selves, the ever deepening spawn. Out there labour is eternal. Slow, huge, cataclysmic. All things are atomic and evolutionary and universal. Out there a star is born and here a child will be its cosmic sibling. All is the purest iron.

The meat dries but the pieces that weren't salted through begin to turn grey and stink. Flies crust in on it. The airy stench is unbearable. He feels nauseous and his stomach is queasy. He grows weaker still. He can feel his bones decalcifying from the inside out; he can feel his muscles harden into knots, his skin slacken round his thinning torso.

Finally they resign themselves to the loss of the meat. They pull off the rotten pieces and throw them to the bushes, cursing the misfortune of it. The chicken they devour quickly, fearing the same outcome. They break it into pieces and skewer the flesh over the fire. The meat is scorched and blackened so there isn't a trace of moisture left swimming in it. When it is done they draw it off the skewers, pull it apart with their hands and bite into it. They turn it in on their tongues and chew on it.

Their bellies are full of poultry and they each have a dram of water. They set off early in the grey breaking glow and have made good progress by the time the sun is full over them. The air is cooler first thing and not so humid, not so sapping. There is an inkling of a westerly current strident above them, but by late morning there is no trace of it. The heat stalks back and they begin to tire. His feet hurt and his head pounds. Finally late in the afternoon they near a clearing in the veld. The bush thins to scrub and then to a bald clearing of smoothly polished sod circled with logs. Some gathering place. Some site of ritual and worship.

They crawl on through the flange and beyond the clearing the path winds a further distance until eventually the veld thins again and the tracts of cultivated land ease into the panorama. But the fields are bare and ropy with weeds dried crisp beneath the summer's scorn. He looks across the plains where there is an arc of low stubby trees and nestling just beyond them is a ring of huts fused with the rufous glow of the soils and the beige thatching of the bush. Their step quickens at the sight; the prospect of rest and shade edging them on.

When they get closer he begins to realize that something is amiss. At their helm he sees the man's breath deepen and caution enter into his step. They follow in his wake, slowing their pace. Even from a distance the silence and stillness of it throngs the stale day. From just beyond the hem of trees he sees the air quivering, sheets of blackness bending and billowing in the low altitudes. Then he registers the swarms of flies, the low seething hiss zapping the air like some electric surge. They hardly dare put one foot ahead of the next. Behind him he's aware of the woman listing sickly over the side of the cart, gripping onto the edges of the cab. The boys fall back. But the man pulls on the rope so it bites into his neck. His legs strain, the harness tautens and so their lolloping contraption gets jolted along regardless.

The smell. Another few paces onwards and it swamps them unawares on the back of a slight furl that sweeps down low over the compound and careens towards them. At first like some rotting fetor the brain knows no similarity to, some alchemy of the sun and the air combined. Then like the stench of offal thrown to the cesspit days ago. The others mask their faces with their hands but he is not so lucky. The reek hits his stomach; he belches and stumbles forward to the awaiting horror.

The dead lie littered over the clearing, like something in an epic poem of horror and damnation. It is a sight the eyes are almost unable to encounter or register. The forecourt is slaked with viscid blood, drying rivers of some quick and frenzied holocaust. They lie fallen to the laved earth; their skulls cloven grey and raw, the mutilations of their gutted bodies too incomprehensible to fathom, unravelled to the orgy of flies festering and sucking in a fevered pitch. There is no ground deprived of a corpse and no place the eye can land without visiting a slew of bodies. Like prized trophies dumped from a day's hunt in the wild. They stand there some time, seemingly fixed to the ground, to the aberrations that draw in their stares.

The reality is something that paralyses them, throwing off their sense of awareness of the known world. The sun has grown weaker in the moments they stand there, paler as if in its own solemnity. Soon it will go down over this death scene. Time will file the edges; the coming wind and heat and rain and the saprophytes will do their bidding, gnawing at the flesh, picking at the skin, bleaching the bones whiter, whiter than light.

Finally they pick their way around this cemetery and stagger off towards the nest of huts behind it and then onwards to the vacant kraal. The ghostliness of it. Each tub of a hut squatting in the stillness and the silences of the great vacancy that has sated them. Doors ajar to dark interiors. The disjointed function of their emptied states. Fragments of spirits hankered in the deeps. The man and the boys venture forward and probe each one. The woman and he remain stationary outside. As the sun slips away and the light mellows, he feels a shiver quake his body that is no ordinary coolness breaking in the air. He tries to ignore the line of bodies petrifying behind him, except for the roam of flies that quicken their erosion and the smell that sears the mind whenever there is the slightest shuffle of a breeze.

The scavenging men upturn little of value. There is no shame in rummaging amongst the relics of the dead when one is desperate. The village has been well and truly ransacked. Only some little bits of bedding and straw mats and a clattering of utensils has been spared by the rampaging militia. No food that he can see. He stands there as they excavate hut by hut and he is tired. Behind him the woman somehow manages to disembark the cart unaided. She stands stretching her bloated body and kneading her fingers into the base of her spine, a downcast look on her face. She wobbles off behind the nearest hut and he listens for the gush that accompanies her ablutions. He feels his mind drift off to some place where the grizzly tension that haunts his sight and scalds his brain doesn't goad him. The men come back clutching their finds, staring beyond him at the open cart. They look to one another. Evidently she has been gone for some time.

They scout the kraal and the huts and the fields. They are tired just as he is and mutter and curse the annoyance of it.

He is left standing there with the cart attached, unable to sink to the ground. He breathes hard into the curling air and waits there amongst such visions of the dead that he hardly knows. There are moments he would envy their restive poise, freed from drudgery and the shackles of existence.

Eventually they come trailing back, the boys dragging the woman between them, her feet carving a wake of dust behind her in which the grainy figure of the man strides, flailing her feet and legs at random with the butt of a branch he has hewn from a tree. He sees the streaming anguish run down her face, the clear channels of tears wash between the dust on her cheeks. Her mouth is wracked in the spasms of her screams that sour the declining day. They drag her towards him and he stands watching it all, a neutral spectator at some ancient ritual.

The man continues to lash her and she yammers and wails at each strike. They pull her into one of the huts and the boys fall away panting whilst the man goes into the darkness after her with the stick. He hears the thuds and shouts reverberate and his own heart quicken in his throat. The boys hang around peering on, each with the look of raw sickness. When the man breaks free from the hut he throws down the stick and comes striding towards him. He can smell the rage of this man. He ought to bolt now before his captor reaches for the

rifle and sticks a bullet in his skull. He shudders on his feet
and clenches his eyes but the man walks right past him and
fiddles with the sacks on the cart, rifling amongst the clutter
to unearth a stretch of the rolled wire. He walks back to the
hut and scrapes closed the door across the formless whimpering of the woman, wiring it shut so tight there is no beast
in the known world that would breach it. He stands before it
and looks on for some moments. He walks round the hut and
kneels against its baked walls and rests his head in his arms,
heaving breathlessly and looking up at the unheeding sky and
dropping his head again to his arms. The boys stand cowering. No one moves for a good time. Gradually the light falls
dimmer and greyer over this fractured scene.

The boys compose themselves and set about the business
of a camp. They undo the harness and the weight of the cart
falls from his shoulders. What a relief that is, as if a boulder
on his back has been dropped to its rightful place. He staggers off towards the walls of the nearest hut and breathes
deeply. His vision swims and the ground wavers beneath
him and the events of the day fluctuate, a gyre swivelling in
his mind. The boys clatter round him and move him off to
the far side of the kraal where they are screened from the
bodies which had been wilting away into the coming
darkness. No redness in the sky this dusk. Just the blinking

scar of the distant horizon beyond the fields and the bush stretch and the ruddy effluence of the day spilled skywards.

The man at last picks himself up and comes along to their station, busying himself with the boys. They unravel their wares and pile some kindling, striking a single match to light the fire which pulses dimly like some singular stroke of life out there, at the end of this day. They huddle about it wearily. The boys may as well be old cripples nursing the ills of time. The man is quiet except for the odd groan, perhaps in response to some perpetual haranguing of his tired, faltering mind. He presses his body against the coolness of the kraal fencing and lets the slated walls rub against his muscles and bones. He hunkers down and his aching limbs fall numb and his spine is very sore.

The woman is to remain locked up all night. Like a grounded child she gets no supper. She cannot be heard but he presumes she whoops still, coiled up in the dark confines of her vault. There are probably no rags or bedding for her to rest on. Such is her lot. They pick some meat off the racks and chew on it. They delve into the sacks and produce a couple of maize cobs. The boys skewer them and char them over the flame. The man chews through one and the boys share theirs sulkily. He gets nothing, just looks on disconsolately. The cobs are too precious for him. Perhaps in his own detached way he understands this too.

Once they have supped they rest against the walls of the hut, slumped there, three tramps at the slag end of a day without mercy. At a place where the small things matter so much, the very rub of existence. Finally, one of the boys slumps over to him and undoes the gag, loosening the ropes a fraction from his raw neck. He is given some water; they may not know the value of their lives but they know the value of an asset.

After this he sleeps well enough for a time. When the wind rises in the cool early hours the stench of the corpses circles through the air and wakes him with muddied thoughts that his overtired mind cannot at once dismiss. There are no waifs of the night stalking about him. No ghouls picking themselves up from the spent ground, staggering and staring out over the barren lunar greyness, but still he is adrift in some promontory of the mind. Seconds pass of an unplaced fear, a despondency and dullness more terrifying than any haunted land. He looks about but all is still. The men have quartered themselves in one of the huts. The woman is still locked up. He is alone out here.

Dawn quivers and he glimpses the coming light. The next time he looks the fullness of day is replete and one of the boys is kicking him and pulling on the rope. He shuffles to his feet and tries to compose his waking mind to the new day. His back hurts as never before but he doesn't wince or groan. They pull him along and station him in front of the cart. The harnesses are attached in their usual custom and then they all stand and watch as the man unfastens the wire on the door and pulls it open so that a shower of light shatters the darkness of her cell. The dust motes scramble, flies scatter. Somewhere beyond that gauzy fussing is the woman and the child in her womb and the question looms of whether or not they have survived the heat and hostilities of the night.

She is battered and bruised and has oozing welts on the backs of her calves and shins, a wide suppurating cut below her left eye. Her left cheek is swollen. She limps out aided underarm by the man. Her slotted eyes look glassed and embittered but she is supple enough in his grip to allow him to install her once again in the cab. The crusts of yesterday's tears lie on her face like scars; in the daytime glare they now unclot, slacking the dried blood of her wound into a fresh stream. She mewls softly, her head droops down across her chest. The welts on her shins and calves will bulge, ooze, puss over. Scabs will soon form hard, sealing her flesh. Her face will heal when the gash dries into her skin; the swollen cheek will recline to the bone. She will be okay.

They load up the sacks, wedge the water containers between her legs and off they trundle once again. The cart lolloping along as ever, its two fat wheels branding the fine soil with their tread, some mark at least that they have come and gone. Weaving past the kraal and through the huts, they move away from the line of corpses now surrounded again in the daylight by a clustering orgy of flies. They ease their way through the fields, back onto the path and walk the hard unending land again. They inch along it. Its rusted soil, the scabby tufts knotted to the turf. The vlei grass that is a weak green in the morning glow, sweet with dew, and livid at noon when the parching sun closes in, scorching everything.

The slog as ever is arduous in the unbending heat. The changing folds of land. The bush thinning; the outcrops rising; the kopjes saddled with stubby, reticulate trees. Then the semi-arid terrain. He has never in his life seen harshness like it. A drought has visited this land and the veld here is so dense and impenetrable it's as if iron spokes have been forged in the bowels of the earth and pushed through. He has never tread rocks as hard or brazen. Rocks cast from the same plutonic spurt as the vlei, metal-cased and glass-sharp. The distant scarp walls stagger round them like Gothic monoliths, rending a dull echo as they file through them bit by bit.

Out of the valley and across the plains they tramp. In the distance another low ridge rises, staggered against the frieze of blue. Conical, bulging, slowly sharpening. A row of dykes soon snakes before them. The path leads nowhere but onwards to its cobbled base. Upwards they go. They surge the scarps and he battles to keep his footing on the shards of rock, the narrowness of the passes. They unbundle the racks of meat and stack them in the cart and the woman is aided; the man takes her and helps her hobble on. It's impossible for the cart to wheel up such terrain so the boys unlatch the harness and take control. They have to steer the cart between them, one pulling, the other pushing. They angle the wheels and lift it, heaving at the chassis. Somehow they jangle forward. They toil like this for a while, like some great wounded beast lugging its dying hulk up into the caves to sleep. Then the right wheel lodges in a boulder. Both boys push and strain. From under them the boulder disintegrates and dust billows up. The cart topples sideways in a plume and veers down the ledge.

The sound is unnatural and jars the ear as the cart cascades downwards. The sacks and provisions splay far and wide. The man turns and roars in panic, the boys are already shimmying down the scarp after it. The cart smashes into a lean tree and bolts sideways and is caught amongst the claws of thick scrub. It rests there still and empty. The boys reach it in no time. It has not fallen from too far a height. The man picks his way down soon after, looks over the wreckage and falls back against the side of the ledge, burying his head in his hands. The boys look at one another. The cries of the man plummet down the spree and reverberate off the low boulders. A sad whimpering plaint bells out about them.

They spend the remaining hours of daylight scratching and clawing at the incline, its scars, hollows, lees. The cart is intact as far as he can see but its left wheel is severed and the axle looks bent. They dig the missing wheel up from the undergrowth and the man sits about the wreckage trying to fathom a way to repair it. Not easy without tools. Finally one of the boys combing the scrub unearths the coil of wire. The man sets about mending the wheel with wire and flint and some spokes of wood that they splice with the machetes.

He bashes at the bent axle with rocks. He needles the splints into the sockets and wires them tight to the undercarriage. How long it will last is anyone's guess.

The boys scrabble over every inch of the area and scoop together the remains of their wares. The pillows and blankets are salvaged, the racks of meat picked from the scrub and dusted, the grit picked off them with painstaking attention. But one of the sacks has burst and the millet has scattered amongst the soil; the mealie meal sifted off vaporously into the white hot air. The milk bottles filled with water have smashed against the rocks, their contents long ago leaked into the gravel. The Coke bottle too. The larger of the water containers toppled and rolled, but with luck its top held firm. The boys carry it back up the dyke like a holy relic.

Then one of them finds the shopping bag filled with the parts of the dismantled well pump. Meticulous as ever, the man undoes all his work on the cart and using bits and pieces he sets about fixing it all over again. He spends a good two hours hunched over this chore and not one of them speaks for this time.

They heave the cart back up the crag face. It isn't easy but they do it. They spend a stark night up there on the dyke. The cool air is not unwelcome but it's lined with a frigid edge. The man sits silent, brooding, phlegmatic. The boys know they are banished so they skulk off a further way up the dyke and he doesn't see them till dawn. A little sliver of the meat is all anyone eats. He wakes in the night to the woman crying softly. She doesn't stop. Like the mosquitoes she sobs in a low drone. The man lifts his head and crawls over to her. He runs his hand over her cheek. He kisses her neck. Then he moves a hand down to her bulging stomach and all he can hear is her heaving chest. The man crawls back to his bedding and lies down, covering his head with his arms.

They come down off the dykes sometime the following morning. The boys carry the battered cart the whole way. He just does as he's told and walks. The woman has to stop every few metres: she bends over, sucking at the air. They plumb the flatland sinks for a bit before they decide to test the cart. They lower it to the ground, attach the harness and lead him on. It lollops along ungraciously, a limping animal intent to outwalk its injury. Yet it seems stable enough. The man stands observing. A slight grunt. He gestures and the woman comes over and they ease her into the cab. The left side has cracked but the back seems firm. It sags but the wheel holds. They trundle forwards.

The sun is unforgiving down there in the lowlands. It is not long before they tire, start to sweat and pant. The man pulls them along, labouring hard. He is extra cautious with the water now, only allowing them small breaks every hour. Without the Coke bottle they must pour it into the metal dish and each sip at it in turn. The dish is slimy with the dried juices of the meat but he laps at it when they leave a little in it for him and is grateful for small mercies.

They stoop on, sapped of every store of energy their bodies had mustered. When they stop now they all bend over double. One of the boys is the first to break with a stitch. He holds the side of his stomach and grimaces. Tears bleed down his face. The man pulls them on, ignoring the moaning cries of the chorus behind him. He seems deaf sometimes to all suffering, all pain, all logic. Only when he presumes the next hour has passed does he allow the bowl to be half filled and handed around. By then the boy has fallen some way behind and can barely walk. His hands are crippled and stiff, his mouth frothing small bubbles as he pants and sucks and pants.

Further on, the wheel buckles. The woman is jolted; she grips her stomach in pain. It seems to pass. The man shouts and curses, ordering the boys out of the way. Without wasting a moment they haul the woman from her carriage and set about another maverick repair job, clanging and battering the undercarriage. The wire is bound tightly, the splints are hammered in.

Late in the afternoon they reach a spread of thick, dark trees with furrowed bark and the bush thickens again, huddling them in. By now each footstep is a strain across every muscle, every fibre in the body. He feels the pain over him completely. Then beyond that, a numb deadening. They all collapse at the finishing post of a tall forked tree they had sighted from afar. Its trunk is splayed like a cross, marked there in that desolate dusty boneyard of things that were living but are no longer, of souls that had lingered. Not yet in his whole life has he experienced such a thudding quake of relief.

The boy with the cramp sits shaking and vomiting the little he has to vomit. A rampant fear sits over his whole being in a grey shroud that is visible to all. The woman subdues her own afflictions this evening and tries to attend to him. She wobbles off to one of the trees, hacks at the dry bark with the knife, strips the soft pap from the inside and brings it over to the bowl where she mashes it with the butt of one of the machetes. She mixes a little water in and takes it to the boy, rolling it into tight balls in her fingers and feeding it to him. He takes it into his mouth, sucks on it and swallows; a moment later he retches it up. She kneads another ball and passes it to him. He takes it. It is some time before he can keep a mouthful down but eventually he manages to suck at all the pulp. A while later his hand falls away from his side and his eyes flicker again. His breathing calms.

That evening they strip some trees of their leaves. They gather a large bunch of them up and sit about using fine strips of bark and grass to knit the leaves together into basins the size of plates. Then they take up their machetes and slash an area of bush until they have carved out a few metres squared. The leaves are laid out atop the shorn ground and left overnight to catch the sweet dew that they hope will come by morning.

It is the worst night of all. They don't light a fire this evening, they barely eat. They just sprawl out as if dead, drifting off in the hard grass. The tree where they tie him is spindly and when he is finally allowed to crouch down to rest he finds it buckles when he tries to lean against it. His back pulses with pain. In the absence of a fire the insects move in and maul them. He hears the party tossing, murmuring, slapping at themselves but tonight he doesn't hear the woman wake up.

In the morning the dew has collected in the hollows of the plaited leaves. They tiptoe towards them and with all the concentration in the world they lift the plates from the ground, pooling the water and draining it into the container. He looks on in amazement. This little creation traps them half a cup of water. The boys are proud of their achievement but the man doesn't say a word. He's taken to sucking the dew off the vlei grass. The succulence of it his only luxury. Once sucked, the grass is not too bitter to be bitten into and chewed. In such a way he does fine without their ever dwindling strips of salted meat. What other food stuffs were lost to the dyke he cannot tell.

The only thing to do is move on. They can only press forward and not succumb to the slowly stalking menace of the wild. The land dips and the lolloping cart picks up speed as they go down into a broad plain. During the descent the wheel flops, the cart ditches into the alluvium and leans sideways. The woman is jerked violently in the cab; she clutches onto the sides to stop herself toppling out altogether. They all run to her assistance and she lies there humped uncomfortably amongst the clutter. Her hands are groping her stomach, spasms of pain zap across her face. They prize her out and right the cart.

There is a growing hum that breaks suddenly low in the sky, growing in volume until a tremendous roar foreshadows the quick jagged sprawl of blackness reeling over the land, enveloping them, careening past in a shudder. They cower down. He stands there as the mottled chopper blades low over them, listing slightly to the right and veering in an arch down over the flatness of the plain. Its growl follows in its wake and quakes through them until all is just a low battered buzz in the distance. The shape of some large bird swooping away into a speck.

The woman has stopped crying, stifled into a silent fright. The man looks on, tracking the flight of the chopper as it dissolves into the far pale hemisphere. A moment later there is another straining roar and this time a pair of choppers streak overhead to the right of them at an altitude higher than the first. The brown and grey fatigues mark them as military planes. The man looks on nervously, his eyes cast steadily to the sky. His mind is at work; doubts are rising; the fear is setting in. He swings the rifle from his shoulder, feeds in the bead of ammunition from his belt and stands there readied.

Then he orders them into action. Out here on the verge of the sparse plain he knows they are fully exposed to the next convoy that flies over. They hoist the woman off the cart and deposit her atop some of the bedding on the soil. They set about repairing the wheel once again. All three of them are fussing over it like bees about a honeycomb. They tip the packet of spare parts, unroll the coil of wire. He hammers and bangs to straighten the chassis. The splints are aligned to the sockets, threaded through the wheel and bound tight. No more choppers careen over them during this time but the air about them is still frigid in their aftermath.

They set off again. There is an urgency now that they all understand. They need to cross the plain and take refuge in the far outcrop of trees before they're sighted from the air.

The chopper could swoop low pumping shots at them, knocking them off as easy pickings. They trek hard. The cart swivels and bounces behind him but he's prepared to make the extra effort. The heat surrenders to the terror that quivers through them. Their ears are pricked for the slightest murmur of an intermittent drone across the wide drift of sky. The man walks with the rifle trained to the path ahead of him and the whole savannah is in his sights. They do not stop.

The sky remains still and taut and nothing other than those three choppers breaks the solemnity of the day. Eventually they cross the plain and begin the hard ascent of the hillock. The woman gets off the cart so it's easier for him to pull. He fears the long day's slog will be the final breaking point for his back, he feels something angular protruding from his spine as if some vertebrae have come dislodged. Still he lumbers on and finally they reach the summit. The land fans wide below, bristling greenly before them.

The hillock is dense with trees and their shelter up there is at least assured. They lay out a camp for the night. They unpack what little they have left and sit about haggard and exhausted. The boys just want to fall onto their bedding and sleep. A day's hard graft, heaving at the cart to get it up the hill; today they've worked more than he has. Certainly they look the product of their labours, listless and moody and filthy. When the dwindling slivers of meat are divided up between them they decline theirs, waving it off with a look of mild revulsion. The man scolds them, chastizing their lack of gratitude, and then eats their share, making an elaborate show to mock and tempt their regret. It doesn't work.

The pain tonight feels as if it flinches deeper into his body than it has before. He wants to spit and kick and lash at them. They bind him up; they drag him along; they tie him up at night. What right have they? He is sick of it, the misery of it. But such thought is senseless when here they all are — weary, sore, downcast, moody — still a band of five together at the top of a hill out here in the creaking dark and all of them alive, all teetering on. They have lasted this long. Perhaps they'll last a lot longer. Somehow they'll do it. They don't light a fire tonight. The night falls, a black mist about them up on this summit. Then the coolness of the air swishes around them and either eases the pain he feels or compliments it — he cannot be sure. Soon the faces of the others grow smudged and thick and are finally nothing more than blackness.

He wakes in the night. He thinks he hears a trail of footsteps attempting to ascend the hillock. His mind veers from the mugginess of sleep to a sharpness that is perhaps too real after all to be more than an illusion. But he hears footsteps thud against the cobbles and slash away against the vlei, the prickly trees. He tunes his ears and listens. He thinks he is wide awake now. This is no sole wayfarer, there are at least two pairs of feet, but then the rhythm of them grows more complex, the pattern of sound more heady. There are not two of them but three or more. He listens for a long time. The noises have stopped. He looks skywards and the moon has risen and sits like a toy dangled above a cot. His heart quickens. He lies looking at the moon and next to it the brightness of a single planet aloft in the throbbing sky.

When dawn thickens there is no sign of the intruders or evidence of their passing. They all sit about and the man takes out the last cut of meat and divides it up between them. A pitiful slice is all they get. The look on their faces is of some breaking desperation. No one talks: the only sound is the creaking of trees stretching, spreading themselves to the coming day. Something slips off a rock that may be a lizard or a snake but is probably neither. Everything is dead. Up here on the hill and amongst the trees is no different to the low flatness where all living things seem to have fled the revolution.

Their lack of energy sits over them, a dry scab full over the body. The man crawls across a ring of rocks and stations himself at the edge of an outcrop, looking out over the land. He sits for some time scrutinizing the panorama as if he were waiting for some mystic message or sign from the ancestors long strung in the ether. Maybe he is ruing his lack of planning, feeling baffled at how the path has led them so awry. Somewhere below them a military base crosses their path. It has three choppers crouched down on a crescent of ground. He is fairly certain of that.

They spend the whole day holed up there, listening all the time for another squadron of helicopters. But nothing breaks the stagnancy. They tie him up again and he looks at them with piercing bewilderment. As if he has the energy to break now and run off. But his stares go unchallenged so he lies against his tree and waits. Around noon it's steamy and humid and every breath brings a vapid warmth to his tongue. His mouth feels like a kiln. They siphon out a dish of water but he's offered none. He doesn't warrant even a slurp today. He watches them drink. Then he lowers his head, closes his eyes and tries to think of times when water was aplenty and he could stride into a lake or dam and weave his way down to the murk where the reeds stemmed and he knew for those moments while his breath

213

held out that this was the precipice of another world. The dark coolness of water took on the meaning of myth in his existence.

They next permit themselves water late in the afternoon. He watches how they pour the container and can deduce by the lightness in hand and the angle at which the man pours that the water is close to running out altogether.

His thirst turns into a pain at the back of his throat. Dry, scratchy, blistery. Late into the night he begins to feel feverish. An untraceable coldness spawns from the insides of his bones thawing outwards, gradually heating, hitting the inside of his skin in hot spasms. He lies there and waits for it to pass but when it doesn't he begins to feel an impenetrable despondency break deep inside him. Some lurching terror close at hand, the feeling that some malign force is watching over him in the darkness, bringing the cold and the heat that wracks his body and mind. Ahead of him he sees the hazy outline of three tall figures standing and watching over them all. They don't move, but they are looking. He stands up and tries to wrench himself free from the rope, moaning as the panic rises in him. He feels a sudden desire to leap from the ledge and roll floundering down into where he can't be seen. One of the boys wakes and throws something to keep him quiet. He grows more edgy. The boy comes over and kicks him in the shin. He is shocked into some instant awareness of his actions, stops moaning and stands still. The boy swaggers off to his pit of rags and falls onto them. He stands looking about him. The figures have gone, bled into the inky night. He sinks down again but his raw throat keeps him awake.

In the morning when he rises his mind is clear. Placed before him is one of the grass plates. He sees the beads of dew collected between the leaves and a sheer ecstasy blanks over him. He strains forward and licks at the juices, feeling it ooze down his raw throat. The rope has been untied so he gets up and moves at once to the tufts of grass, sucking out the sap from the blades, gnawing at them for their sweetness.

Today the others have also stripped the grass and they chew at it before scrounging in the bushes and the undergrowth, hacking at the roots of trees with the machetes. They collect a gathering of grass shoots, roots and bark. Kindling for a fire is found and a pyre stacked. The box of matches is brought out. The water from the grass plates has been drained into the dish – they pour a bit into the pot and set it to boil over the fire. The woman scrapes off the dirt from the roots, peels them and dices them; the blades of grass, too. Then some leaves she has mashed almost into a paste. The brew boils away and when it begins to bubble she scoops the pot off the heat. They let it cool, then take it in turn to spoon ladles of the soup into their mouths.

After the meal the man crawls out to the ledge again and sits there looking over the spooling promontory. He sits and gazes at the open spaces for a long time. Sometimes he rests his chin on his hands, like a monk at his meditation, out there on the ledge overlooking the world. Beneath the roof of the heavens, if there are heavens. Then he makes his way back and gives the order for them to pack the cart. The boys grab one end of it each and take charge of its safe passage down the kopje. The woman is held underarm by the man and his other arm trains the rifle ahead at the openness before them. He walks free as a bird. He contemplates seizing the opportunity to break away and plunge himself into the density of the plain they approach except that he is a slave to his nerves just as he is a slave to them.

The bush is thick and the spiky coral flange of trees pokes at him as they pass, stabbing him with thorns. If any choppers were to blade overhead now the man should be confident enough that they are completely screened by this wide shield of savannah staggered all around them. Barely an hour later and the first of the boys begins to spew up, reeling off into the bush and bending over double. A few seconds later another spate comes. They stop and look at the boy retching away. They look at one another. Before long they are all kneeling in the bushes and hugging their stomachs as the spasms grip them, throwing up their innards in a spray of muck and bile. The broth. So much for nature's gifts. They can barely move more than a few paces on before one of them has to turn to the bush. They are sweating, their skin has turned pasty. Then the cramp sets in. At one point they are all lying reeling in the dirt, holding their stomachs, clenching their faces as another bout of retching comes on or the pain of the cramp notches up and strikes.

The trees provide a little shade so they all crawl off to one and take refuge to nurse their ills as best they can. There is not much they can do but sit it out. They let their bowels run and their systems flush while they get more and more dehydrated. Then a fever begins to set in. They sit there against their trees shaking and sweating and bemoaning the sun and the cold, the dark patchy figments of their blazed brains, each alone and stricken with some shaky dread hammering down into the very core of them, the nerve roots of their souls. Even so he does not avail himself of the chance to run free. He hunkers down by the cart and pants miserably. Pain quakes through him too.

The fevers don't break easily. The boys cry and moan, at times as if their bodies are possessed by the unclaimed spirits that shackle through them, throwing their innards to the bush. They call out for help but are on their own. The woman can barely open her eyes. She lies on her side in the grasses, hugging her stomach. The man has managed to pull some of her bedding from the cart and drape it over her legs. He puts some water on his finger and tries to get her to suck on it. Her sour tongue slips through her yellowing teeth but she barely has the strength to lick. The man lifts her by the arms and cradles her in his lap, stroking her shivering limbs, her flushed skin. Sometime in the late afternoon, he calls out to her, shakes her by the arm, slaps her cheeks. He prizes open her eyes which roll back white in their sockets. He lifts her limp, azoic body in his arms and draws her close and cries out in an anguished howl that shatters the spaces all about them.

Dread slips into the air. It is electric. He can feel his limbs go numb; his heart starts a slow pounding in his chest. He stands up; some force comes from beneath him and rocks him to his feet.

The man's anguish exorcises the fevers from the boys who sit up at once wide-eyed, sober, startled. They look on, fright masked across their faces. The man chides them into action:

they jump up dizzily, gather their belongings, throw them into the cart. Together the three of them lift the woman's sagging body and lay her in the cab and they stagger onwards as if their souls have conjoined in this one moment to bring them all the energy they need. He senses the duty falls on him to be the strongest now. He falters on along the unfailing path; the others limping alongside him; the man slapping her cold cheeks, trying to rouse her from the depths to which she's plummeted. When one of the boys falls away sick and breathless, unable to keep pace with even the slow trudge, the man shouts after him and wills him on. He straightens, flexes his limbs again, catches up. Not for an instant does anyone allow themselves a moment to consider the possible fate of the woman and the infant quivered up inside her. How they manage to get as far as they do after all they have been through is a miracle brought forth from the deepest well.

She lies slumped and lifeless. What is the point of this mad surge if it's all in vain, if the inevitable has occurred, here at the end of the world and the freakish history that's gone before them? Her hooded eyes stay shut for long periods of time without a flicker or blink. At such moments he begins to think that indeed she lies there as dead as anything that has come and gone in this world.

The path forks and without warning the man veers them sharply to the right and they canter along almost at a right angle to the path they have taken all this while. There is an uneasy shifting alignment in the journey; a pull on the body's compass, its magnetic field that perhaps directs the instinctive route towards safety. They had been so committed to their path. He doesn't like it but he bears it. Then the man's intentions become apparent: the rusty trees thin suddenly, there is a screed of crisp, golden veld, columns of tall beige vlei grass that they press forward through and rapidly break into a clearing that takes them all by surprise. They lurch to a stop. The four of them, the cart, the woman in it. All standing there on the lip of a wide tarred road, white strips of paint streaked along its centre, curving out of sight. He looks right and left. The road is empty.

They quickly reel back, shielding themselves again in the bushes. It's not easy turning the cart around. They sit down panting, resting their heads in their arms, sweat beaded on their drawn faces. They clutch their stomachs again: one of the boys quickly disappears into the bush and they hear the familiar sound of heaving and spitting. The man is crouched by the woman, dripping the last of the water from the container into the dish. He lifts her head, parts her dry mouth with his fingers. He runs a line of water round her lips. She doesn't respond. They watch the water evaporate from her skin. The man slams his fists in frustration onto the side of the cab. He looks into the white-hot air with a rage that would sear a man at a thousand paces. He dribbles a bit more water onto her mouth, slaps her. Briefly her eyes seem to roll but they can't be sure. Silence for a while. The expectant dredge of time. Then there is movement in her mouth, though it may just be the flicker of her tongue against the dryness of her lips.

They cannot sit in the bush like this waiting for her to die. The boys position themselves some distance from the front and back of the cart. They inch it out of the bush, start trawling along the rim of the road. The boys continually signal the road is clear either way. No vehicles come by for some time. It may be that no vehicles travel this road now. All the better. They could never trust a car or a truck to stop for them now. Their slim chance of help is to reach one of the small towns pitched along the route, find some water, some food. The road begins to dip and beyond its falling curve the sun is already set low in the distant horizon; the filmy light begins to wane and weaken. A few minutes later the boy at the rear of the convoy starts waving and shouting. Immediately they trail off into the bushes and hide themselves behind the ledge of bush. They wait though they cannot afford to.

They hear a low rumble growing but they can't see anything. The roar gets louder: a congregated clatter, the straining chug of diesel engines. Then the first of the battery swoops past them. A grey-brown lorry mounted on tall fat wheels; they see the clutter of the chassis; the engine mounted below and the dark massive underbelly of it. They cower down. It's not easy for him. Fortunately the bush is tall and they have managed to duck down in a small ditch.

Another lorry trails past. Then another. He sees a curious cargo on the back of them: two soldiers are stationed at each end of the carriage, sitting there in the breeze, the barrels of their AK47s pointed to the sky. Huddled beneath their watch are the packed bodies of a cluster of bare-chested boys. There are at least fifty of them, staring at the lone bush they pass, the unyielding sky, sewn together at the necks by yards of steel wire. Their tonsured heads are polished slabs of blackness refracting the dimmest orange glow of the falling sun.

The trucks thunder past. There are three of them altogether. They watch each one loll by with its terror-crazed cargo: boys looking outwards on an unknown destiny. The boys in the bushes are looking back at them. When they have trailed off into the distance they creep out of the veld and begin their trek again. The boys at each side, watching the road. The man walks beside the cart, talks to the woman, pleads with her to open her eyes, gather some strength. *We have no water left,* he is perhaps saying to her in breathless pants, *no food either. We are all sick and weak and sore but we have come a long way. We have come a long way for you and as long as there is a tremor of a heartbeat in you and as long as the baby lies there we'll walk on.*

They walk on. They will walk that darkening slip of road until they happen on some instance of hope and salvation.

The evening comes over them, furling and thickening around them like a gas, miasmic and toxic. There is some portentous reckoning in the air. Their lives poised on a knife edge. The night falls soon after and the insects come out along the road. They don't hear another car coming. They don't see in the distance the stark fusion of headlamps specked into darkness and so they carry on all the while. Straining and limping, each one of them haunted by pain, withered with weakness. The moon rises low and yellow; the slate-black air cools and for a while it gives them some momentum. Then a star appears beside the moon as it always does and always will while the living have eyes to see it. An icon of the vastness and smallness of being. He registers it briefly and they carry on walking.

Up ahead in the darkness there is a furling blackness that gradually takes the shape of something squat and solid. At first he thinks it's a figment born of the dark, the tired, stolid mind. But the others register it too. They stop and wheel the cart into the bush and crouch down to scan the area. They can see nothing: just a shape hooded in black, stencilled against the night. They crawl on, tracking the tall grass. Slowly the angular form of a building takes shape. Then they see some more beyond it. There is nothing else they can gauge. Everything is quiet, formless, looming. Static and stagnant in space and time. There is not a light up on the stoep of the building, or those beyond it. No wan candlelit pulse or the blur of hurricane lamps. They creep closer, stop and look. The man is thinking hard, his eyes steeled on the prospects of what this clutch of civilization has to offer. He mouths instructions to the boys. They ease the empty water container off the cart and draw their machetes and skulk forward. Two slim beings slip from the silence and slowly steal into the broadness.

They leak out of sight. The man looks on with atavistic tension. A long time passes in which they see nothing and hear nothing. The only movement is the slow lithic fracturing of the air. His tired eyes strain to glimpse what is real against his doleful mind. The woman is still, silent in her cot. He's sure she has not uttered or grimaced since the night fell. The man holds her flaccid hand and squeezes it and doesn't let go. There is nothing he can do now. All his energies are invested in the boys and their mission.

After a while the man slides the rifle from the cart and trains it over the dark blobs of the buildings. They hear something shatter in the distance. It may be the glass of a windowpane the boys have smashed or it may be nothing other than the climatic shriek of the stillness that has finally splintered over them. He looks on and the man looks on too, his body erect and readied.

Nothing happens for a long time. Then ahead of them there comes a shuttle of lights and a dark vehicle sweeps by and skids to a stop outside the building. Grey dust unravels around the headlamps and all is blanketed in a lunar haze which hangs thick for a while over their stunned minds and over the night before atomizing into the metallic shape of an army jeep. Three soldiers get out brandishing torches that probe the stark brick of the building in fidgety beams.

They start forward. He can see their lank bodies and the rifles slung on their shoulders.

The man lurches forward in the bushes and trains his rifle, his heartbeat thudding against the torpid earth. The soldiers scan the area. The torchlight spearing the sides of the buildings, mining stretches of sand and gravel. They edge onto the stoep and scour their lights against the chromed, webby windows, leaning inwards to search the interior. One of them stills his torch and gestures to the other two and says something. They come together and in unison shine their torches at a designated area inside the building. The man veers forward a bit, plants the rifle and coils down to look through the scope. His hand sits flush against the trigger. His skin and muscle flinching. But he breaks his sight and looks up. He is breathing heavily. He sets his sights again and lies there trained on a soldier's chest of mottled grey and green that he can barely see. It is no good. He'd probably miss. And then what?

He pulls away altogether and sits up breathing hard. He has to muzzle his mouth with his hands his breath is so loud, so punctured with fright. He sits there and looks back at the cart where the woman lies. He closes his eyes for a second so tight the world – its evils, its sacrifices – must vanish entirely. He looks over at the buildings again but does not re-engage the scope.

The soldiers bash in the door with one short kick. They storm in and there is only the briefest sound of a scuffle. One last stand. Soon the boys are shunted out and behind them come their three assailants. The rifle pointed at them will stop them fleeing. They are kicked in the calves and they fall to the stone stoep and lie there weak and helpless. One of them manages a gibbered cry before he is kicked in the back and in the stomach with the sharp hard end of a soldier's boots. The butts of the rifles are pounded into them. They squirm on the ground. Twitching as something severed of its nerves, sliced deep down the spinal column. Soon the jeep starts up and skids away down the road and when the billowing dust settles in its vacancy there is nothing left there but the cloistered dark.

The man is stone-faced now. This is what he has to be. He raises himself and turns to the woman and wipes her brow with the edge of the bedding. He takes her arm and feels for a pulse. Then the man gets up and walks forward, leading him on. No expression passes between them. Nothing between captor and captive that indicates an easing of their union, a final acknowledgement of their dual martyrdom. That they are after all both victims of one and the same system. He pulls on the rope with one hand, the other gripping the rifle, and they go staggering forward out of the bushes.

The man leads them to the buildings. He follows, afraid of the electric chill that still zaps the silent throes of the air. He tries to halt in his tracks and buckle but the man turns in an instant and leers at him. He stands still and calms himself. They move on slowly. The man brings them to a halt outside the stoep and here he looks down briefly at the spot where the boys were kicked and beaten, their absent bodies still somehow scorched into the ground.

The man tiptoes onto the stoep and looks about. Then he stands dead still. Rigid as a wildcat poised to strike. He cocks his head slightly. To the side of the building there is a faint hissing sound. Something static, intermittent. The man grips the rifle firmly and stalks forward, edging his way to the side of the stoep. He lines himself flush against the wall and peers round it. They all know to be absolutely still. The hissing strains, weakens, strains. Then they hear the voice of a man calling out something, slow and repeated.

A pool of light inches over the gravel and grows stronger. There is the crunch of footsteps. The light breaks from beyond the wall and a figure stops dead in his tracks, raising his torch. He stands there with the cart behind him, ready to flee. The light piercing, intrusive. The blurred figure frozen behind it. There is a short catastrophic blast and another and the rifle jolts in the man's arm each time and the light shudders and wobbles and the figure hits the ground. He stands there still, waiting for the horror of the sound to reconcile itself to the reality of the night.

The man staggers forwards and looks out over the ledge of the stoep and down at the body of a man spreadeagled on the ground. Two rings of red blubber from his gut. In his hand there is a radio transmitter which still hisses and crackles in his dead clutch.

The man shuffles towards the body and kicks the transmitter from the upturned hand. He bends and picks it up: not once does the barrel of the gun leave the man's gut, dead as he is. He thumbs at it, turning the dials but the sound only hisses, dies, hisses again. He backs away from the body and brings the radio over to the cart and puts it next to the woman. He goes back to the dead man and leans down to pick up the torch that's rolled away, shining its beam tangentially into the night.

With the rifle jutting from his midriff he makes his way back to the stoep and enters the building. All he sees from the outside is the torch flare up the concrete grey walls with an orangey glow, the man's tall shadow reeling against it. There is some ransacking, a discordant din. Finally he comes out. He lugs the container the boys took with them: it is at least half full. He stacks it on the cart and moves back inside with one of the empty sacks. He comes out again with the sack dragging behind him, bulging full with something.

He stashes it next to the woman and leads them on with haste. Away from the store and the sprawled body on the ground.

They move down the road, beyond the hazy unravelling of the town, and ditch into the bushes again. The man hauls the container from the cart and fumbles in the dark for the tin sheen of the dish. He tilts the container and a slush of thick dark liquid comes pooling into the dish. He sniffs it and dips a finger in to taste it. He crawls round the side of the cart and cradles the woman's head in his arms. Gently he drips the brew into her gaping mouth. The first bit dribbles away, sliding down her chin, down her neck and cupping in the hollow of her throat. He re-angles her head in his arms and talks to her, urging her to consciousness, shaking her awake. This time she manages to gurgle and swallow. Her throat bulges; the brew sidles down slowly. He repeats the process several times. He makes sure she has as much as she can take. The whole time he is whispering in her ear and chattering to himself. He rocks back on his feet, swaying her loose, swollen head in his grasp. He sways and he whispers and in whatever language his utterances are universal. A prayer in the night, some calling to a higher being.

After a while the man rummages in the sack the boys had filled in the store and brings out some lumps of food. It looks like dried figs, dried tomatoes, dried relish. The woman is too weak to eat them whole. He looks at her, longing for the taste of what she disregards, feeling it sit on his tongue and slip down his raw throat. The man sits there breaking some pieces of it up in his hands and mashing it between his palms. He mixes it in with some of the brew and feeds her some pulp. He slumps beside her on the turf and rests her head in the hollow of his neck and they remain motionless for a good while.

Over all of this he stands in his usual role of observer, seer of everything, bystander. He struggles to make sense of all that is happening to them, in the frosty vagueness of what his life is. It's as if he is always a step away from the immediate action of their saga. He is pulled along their path, shunted about in a never-ending skein of confusion, in the urgency of someone else's fate. He is no interloper; too much separates them. Too much that can't be overcome. If the woman dies this night he'll think nothing of it. If the man then takes the rifle, props it up to his chest, leans forward and blows a hole in his gullet only the sound will shatter through him and then dissipate into ripples of nothingness. The boys are gone: so be it. He never could care for them. He, in his state, who knows nothing of empathy.

While they remain still he nestles down as best he can and as much as the harness will allow him. He lies there and lets the shock and exhaustion of the day fester over him. The mosquitoes are virulent out here. They swarm in and suck on them. He is sure there must be dampness or moisture close at hand.

His thirst is insatiable. When the shudder of the night's events wears off he registers a deathly, painful thirst wedge into his throat and dry him up from the inside. It frightens him. He looks over at the container and then at the bowl lying at the man's feet and wonders if there's anything left there he could lick. He stands and looks down on them, still and silent, their coupled breaths deep and shallow in a strange altruistic pairing. He nudges forward, shuffling in the catch of the harness, and leans down to the bowl. The sides are laved with a moistness, the odd scrape of tomato flesh, relish tassel. He brings his tongue to it and noses round the bowl, licking at the juice, the coolness of the steel.

Something elevates in his misdemeanour that he can't place; a faint surge of life lisping into his nerve-ends. Then the pain rockets at his head: a flat blast judders in his ears and he stumbles away. The man has kicked him in the side of the head. There is a sharp sting that burns at his cheek; his ears are imploding. He is up and from the corner of his eye he sees the man come for him again, fists bared. In the confusion and panic he lashes out and kicks back, stamping forward and trying to trample on the man's legs, crush his shins, his ankles. Only the weight of the cart and the restriction of the harness stop him going for his chest, his neck, his skull. He lurches forward: this could be his one chance. The man has fallen and cowers and cries out. But there is another cry that halts them both. He holds back, breathing deeply. They both look at the woman who is sitting up and clutching her stomach and screaming in pain. There is wetness puddled on the soil beneath her dress, burst waters from her womb.

The spasm of pain that jabs her does not come again for some while. They are up and spurred into action and ploughing their way along the road. She lies in the cart, her legs sprawled over the rims. Fear and shock are etched through her.

They pace the night-time glower of the road but even now there is paleness fusing itself gradually into the distant dark; the womb of the moon has sunk already; a first yolk of brazen light drifts absently into the horizon. The man is a flutter of nerves. He keeps looking up and down the road. He must be wondering who or what will save them now the hour has come.

After a while they see a small metallic blob astride the road, a slip of white which soon lengthens into the shape of a car. They press on towards it. There is a tall white man standing at the rear, his back towards them. He is busy funnelling fuel from a jerrycan. A few yards before they reach him he is alerted to their presence and staggers back in panic.

The man is waving his arms to catch his attention, but the white man is fumbling at his boot lock and stuffing the jerrycan and funnel in. He rushes round to the driver's door and gets in. Beside them now, the man begins to call and plead. He cups his hands in a manner that is deplorable; he kneels beside the driver's window and begs, pointing all the while to the woman, miming the globe of her belly in the air against his stomach.

But the white man has started the car, its revs abrasive against the morning solemnity. In a flash it is gone, a streak dimming in the distance, the man still knelt on the ground, praying for a miracle.

He gets himself together and they move on.

Finally, just left of the road, they see a rickety sign posted into the gravelly soil and propped up with rocks. Snaking behind it is the sandy slip of a road. The man draws them to a halt. He bends over double, panting with visible exhalations of relief. There may be half a smile that breaks from his lips, blankets his face, shimmers in his eyes. The sign has a slender white cross painted on it and beneath it a name. They turn onto the dirt road and trundle on. Something about the man's attitude, his bearing, indicates a real shift in his demeanour. He chats to the woman; he comforts her. He points ahead up the winding stretch of dust as if to indicate to her the expected loom of some providential happening, some act of salvation at hand. Faith that ahead lies the end of the journey, the final destination, the route the mysterious path was always leading to. He can't be sure, but something about the inexplicable and sudden lightness of the man's gait conveys this to him. That help is at hand, that they'll make it after all.

Another contraction rips through her just before the road levels out and leads them to a low fence. Signposted at the entrance to the rusted gates is the same emblem of the cross in washed-out white, this time pasted in the centre of a rusted old plough disc. Beyond they can see the metal casing of a water tank atop a tripod, hard and ferrous in the early glinting sun. Beyond that, past another hem of bush, a cluster of low prefabricated buildings set flush against the khaki sprawl. The man fiddles with the gate, unravelling the springs of barbed wire that lock it. He pushes it ajar.

They enter and wind along the road, passing another cross, this one wooden, staked into the ground, surrounded by a bed of dead, ashen daisies. The water tank sizes into proportion and they walk on underneath its sheen. All is quiet, unmoving. The weight of stillness gravitates through him, a staleness to the place, a vacancy so palpable it thrums the morning air. The first row of buildings are completely deserted. Some stand open, others are shuttered. Inside there are glimpses of iron bed frames, low and sprung. The man begins to slow. He exchanges glances with the woman. He looks over the desolation. This is not what he expected.

They edge on in a shrill silence along the red-brick and concrete buildings, asbestos sheeting across the roofs. They come to the end of the first row and stop in their tracks. Beyond them they see mounds of earth dumped in conical piles; to the left the ground falls steeply into a pit. They step forward and a huge crater opens up on them like a quarry. They can't see the bottom. Levelled to a foot beneath the lip of the pit are piles of bodies: naked, slim, sleek and black. Boys or adolescents. Each one with a slack, twisted neck. Bloodless welts across their throats. A savage mangle of limbs, torsos, heads.

The man staggers back, his mouth agape, his wide eyes scalded. He eventually turns from the gravesite and begins to scan the far tangle of buildings beyond them. He looks too. Then things fall into focus. Stationed behind a frieze of low, hobbled trees they can make out the shape of an army truck. They track their line: three of them, the last with its cab jutting out into a clearing, like the head of some car-nivorous beast. Then they pick up the sight of a jeep parked outside a building. There may well be three helicopters sitting in a cleared arc round the back. Just then he sees something move along the line of the buildings. Three shapes, three men dressed in fatigues. They may be coming towards them.

The man kneels and lurches for the rifle off the cart, hauling them back along the route they came. They run across the first row of buildings; back along the path by the water tank; fast towards the gate. The woman is jolted back and forth; she cries out in pain, and lists over, gripping her stomach, the labour contractions biting into her. The man pulls them on. They exit the gate and veer sharply onto the gravel track that winds back to the main road. The jagged bush reels past them; the trees blur; the sky above them shudders. All he knows is the sound of desperation their failing feet make as they crunch the gravel. The cart has never sped so fast. The right wheel is joined only tenuously. He can feel that it isn't going to hold long.

They have no idea what or who is coming for them. They don't look back. He can't bear to think what will come roving up behind them, purling a wake of dust as high as the trees. There is a moment when he senses the notion of being hunted. Of being quarry fleeing the gathering, rollicking pace of a wild cat ranging in on him at a pace he can't assimilate, with a lust he'll never know. It is a moment of abject

241

fright, of the purest lucidity he has ever had. He doesn't think of it for long.

They reach the main road and turn onto the smooth, soft tar and continue up along it. They cannot go at this pace for long. They'll all be in a heap on the road in no time at all. They slow to a hurried walk and the world steadies and resizes around them. There is blood drumming in his ears. His throat is tight. The woman cries out in anguished pain, retching and screaming. Her fists are knotted, her arms wrapped round her stomach, her head thrown back in a spasm. The man stands and watches. He scrunches his face against the pale ebbing heat, raging against the hopelessness of it all.

The contractions come quicker now, racking up against her every few minutes. They try to carry on but it's becoming impossible. The man drags them into the bushes; he kneels by her and talks to her. She is gasping, struggling for breath. He takes one of the empty sacks and holds it aloft over her to gift her some shade. He unscrews the lid on the container and dribbles some of the brew onto his fingers to dapple round her lips. Her brow is sluiced in sweat.

A bluish streak shoots past them on the road, the sound sucked into a vacuous rush. The man leaps up with the rifle and runs into the middle of the road. The back of a blue sedan: he takes aim as if he is some thoughtless automaton and slugs a few rounds into it from behind. Its rear windscreen shatters and it swerves from left to right in the road and back again. Fright zaps through him and his muscles flinch. He hears the skid of brakes and the car comes to an abrupt halt in a ditch beside the road. The man trails after it. The doors spring open and the blobs of beings in the distance can be seen trying to flee into the camouflage of the bush but he is quick to tag them down with the spray of rifle bullets he pumps into them. They fall in various attitudes, quick and soundless. One of them tries to pull himself up on his legs and crawl into the bushes but he is already tracking him, putting another bullet into his spine. The figure slumps forward and is still.

The man looks once to make sure none of them is moving and then runs back down the road. Watching the man, something notches up in him and tells him to run. The gun and its associations. The man and his madness. He tries to rear up and kick forward but already his old foe has him by the harness and is kicking his shins and slamming the butt of the rifle into his ribs. The blow is so hard he thinks his skin has been sliced clean open. It has: blood wells instantly. His insides reverberate in the aftermath. He stumbles on his feet, the pain blistering through him.

The man drags him by the rope and pulls him down the asphalt towards the car. There is rage in his blood now; his whole body arched and flexed; his jaw an obsidian arch of some primal determination. They go stumbling down the track, the cart and the woman behind him as always. He shambles along and when they close in on the car he sees the full spree of bodies lying beside it. The stark redness of blood against white tanned skin. A man has been hit in the head; a lobe of his grey brain sizzles across the tarmac.

The man lifts the woman from the cart, mustering all the strength he can, the adrenaline still sidling through him. He lays her on the back seat of the car, atop the crystalline scatter of broken glass that lies across it like big globules, like hail stones. Stripping the cart of the container, the sacks, the bedding, he bundles it all into the passenger seat in a mad and furious rush. He closes the passenger door, comes round the rear of the car. He brushes right past him and stops. The man looks at him, his hand clutching the rifle, his breathing stunted. His eyes are filmed over with an opaqueness that can't be forded. But the thought he was grappling with obviously fails him.

He climbs into the driver's seat and slams the door and attempts to start the engine. The car jolts forward. He tries again. It stutters and jerks. Twisting at the ignition; the car chokes but won't turn over. He tries again, sitting there bashing the steering wheel with his fists and screaming to himself. He looks out of the window, up ahead at the road. Then he twists the key again; the engine strains and turns over; he revs it hard; black smoke billows from the exhaust and scatters into vapours. Through the back window he can see the woman's face flushed in pain but he doesn't hear her screams above the commotion. The car goes shunting forward, down the road, away from him and the empty cart.

He stands there and watches them disappear into the distance and then he looks down at the bodies lying across the road and dead in the ditch. The pain in his side comes back at him. He looks down and sees the blood weeping. He closes his eyes and feels his feet quake beneath him, his mind mildly fracture. There is nothing to do but carry on. The cart is now light and empty; it feels strange. Its presence has crudely shifted: the car already a far dash winding away from him all the while. He can feel its pull on his body, the phantom presence of the woman. He walks the trampled earth alongside the road for a while and he doesn't really know what he intends to do. Everything is suddenly aimless. Just an endless scrawl of yellowish grass streaking all about him and he doesn't know where to place his feet, where to sink his heart.

The cart is a burden without a purpose. It must be disposed of. The ropes are bound too tightly round his shoulders to simply slip off. If he walked on and on at some point – in a week, a month, a year – they may simply fray or unravel, the cart may bit by bit fall apart. The wheels will come off sooner or later; all he'll drag behind him is a raft of wood, a crank of iron. That too will slowly break up into planks and a pole.

He paces on until the road veers again and dips. Appearing in the near distance is a coned kopje standing green, hazed over and saturated with a darkness of trees. The prospect of shade that'll fall over him, a cool cascade. A trunk to lean on and rest. The ineffable notion of being lost in the vastness of himself. He plunges into the bush, the cart lagging behind. It's an effort to pull it through the flange. He lumbers and pulls: his sights set on the dark rising mound before him. The trees are narrow and stubbly with weak, pendulous branches and the first few attempts he has at ramming the cart between them is futile. The trees bend or snap; a hammer of shocks splinters up his spine. He staggers along.

A short way up the slope there are two granitic outcrops covered in a coat of scabrous moss, streaked with bronzed stains of rust and water drip. Lying beneath them is a cluster of boulders, small as cannon balls, large as monoliths. He looks over them. He thinks hard about what he's going to do. Then he charges against the ledge sideways. Behind him the cart smashes against the ledge of stone. He hears the cab crack and splinter; the right wheel bounces off down the ridge; the cart sags behind him. He braces himself and charges at the next cluster of boulders. This time an intense pain surges up his spine and he yammers loudly but already the weight has snapped away from him and he falls freely amongst the rocks. The cart tilts and angles down the scarp crashing into the trees below.

Next he tries to unbundle himself from the clutch of ropes. Lying against the stones and rocks he begins to slide his back up and down, trying to hook the thickness of the rope against a sharp nook or ledge. He edges against the rocks and pushes himself hard against the rutted surface and tries to rip or fray the thread. He feels a sharp pain claw into him and then a cold sting at his flesh and he knows he's cut himself badly beneath his coat. He carries on struggling even though he is tired and thirsty and sore. At last he feels the rope catch on a claw and he pulls down hard against it and drags the tassel of rope up and down his body. The tension of the binding eases. He stands up and the straggles of rope fall away from his body. Soon it lies in a heap round his feet. He pants in relief. He lies down to rest.

He lies there and lets the pain wax up and down his spine. His ribcage is throbbing; the wound is bleeding again. But he is free at last of his burden. The sun can't entirely penetrate

the wash of trees and only filters down in shafts. He realizes
he is bathed in a dappling of shade. The stone he rests against
is cool beneath him and doesn't cause much discomfort.
Those slabs are dipped into the earth and cooled by the soil
and at their core there is some mineral as cold and as dense
as ice. He lies there lank against that earthly solace for some
time.

A while later he is roaming the inclines and steps of the
scarps and weaving his way through the trees where his
senses take him. He climbs and then dips a long way. His
footing by no means secure. The shards of stone beneath his
feet are like quarry stone chipped and smashed by some
great drill bit or crusher. Still he manages to pick his way
along it. He comes down off the far side of the kopje. The
vlei here is emerald-glazed, the grass rooted in short tufts
which grow more prominent and there is the occasional wild
flower pinned to a shoot or buttoned to a branch. He is tired
and he is thirsty and he doesn't know what time of day it is.

He is looking for water. He may just happen across a
stream, the same way he happened across a flowering vegetable patch in the middle of a wasteland. He goes deeper,
deeper. There is a dank, lemony glow around him; he can see
the fine motes of dust flaking down from the infinite tops
of the trees. At last he stops and takes a rest. There is plenty

of rich vlei grass here for him to feed on. If he's still here in the morning he'll suck the sweet dew from the stalks. He comes across to a small clearing covered in a carpet of thick dried leaves which crunch underfoot and will make as good a resting place as any other. He stands amidst it for a while. He looks out and down across the kopje and over the stretch of savannah quickly receding into the lapping waft of blueness. Just beyond the clearing the bush runs thick again, and beyond that is the lip of the road.

He looks up. He looks out across the plain beneath him and sees the dark patches where some clouds overhead stencil their shadows over the earth. It hasn't rained for a long time. He can't recall when it rained last.

He plods away off down the kopje, away from the trees. His wound is seeping into his grey matted hide, his spine aches. His four tired hooves are bruised and gorged and raw. He trawls through the bush towards the road. It's far easier now without the cart and the ropes. If his memory were better he may remember the days when he fled the noise of the revolution and took the quiet back roads to avoid the mayhem streaming from the city; fleeing the brash, blaring voices of the men who broadcast warnings and threats in a strange grumble. He would remember that he came across a plantation up in the hills on the city's out-skirts and he lay low there for some days, rummaging around for food. He stood on the hillocks and watched in the distance the sky glaze over with weakening yellow pulses and then the settlement in the air of great towering belches of black smoke. He would remember the last time he walked free.

He crosses the bridge of veld between the kopje and the roadside and then he walks in the bush along the course of the road itself. He ambles for some time and makes good progress and with the cart unhinged he walks a great deal further than he imagined he could under that blistering sun. No cars pass, or trucks. No choppers blade overhead. Around a bend in the road he spots something heaped half in the bushes, half jutting into the road. He can't see it clearly to begin with. He takes a few more steps forward till his vision clears and he is able to see the shell of a sedan scorched black across its bonnet. Its rear is a pale blue that glimmers in the daytime glow.

He walks on in the bushes towards the wreckage. The shell of the car is smooth, the paint singed, the crisp black steel shining through in places like a mirror so that the formless stagger of bush is almost reflected in the panels of the doors. The front windscreen is intact. Heaped over the steering wheel is the body of the man, a bullet-hole wound in the side of his temple, his eyes glaring out stiff and static as ever on some distant goal. The tyres have been shot out and the rear door lies open, exposing a vacancy of space in which his mind can almost place the limp figure of the woman, lying there in the throes of childbirth.

4

19 November

Got a call from Veronica, wailing down the phone. 'Have ecstatic news, darling – we have an offer!' At once the dread ran through me. Oh God, I thought, the Chinese man, the Greek man.

'No no, from another gentleman. He's offering a lump sum transfer, but wants the deal settled quickly.'

'But no one else has seen the place,' I said.

'That's the beauty of it, darling – he doesn't want to. He's buying purely on spec & location. This is the best thing we could have hoped for.'

After I'd hung up, I sat thinking. Half relief, half sadness. A great deal of puzzlement. Still can't take it in. I'm debating whether I should pry into it a little more or just take the money & run.

20 November

Phoned Veronica back after a sleepless night. 'Look, can you give me a bit more info on the buyer?' I asked.

'Also the terms of the deal. It all sounded a little hazy yesterday.'

For once she sounded a little distant. 'I'm drawing up the contracts now, darling. Will have them over for you to sign in a flash.'

'No, look, that's taking it a bit too quickly. I'd really like to know more about who's buying it, maybe even meet them before I go signing anything away. After all, this is my family home we're talking about.'

There was a pause on the other end of the line. 'Ian, we have a deal. No fuss, no haggling. I can assure you it doesn't come much better than this. But he does want a quick deal. The offer's on the table. You know it's a bad market right now. What does it matter who the buyer is? He's good for the cash – direct US dollar transfer – you're leaving the country & you need your house sold.' Then: 'Plus, we need to make this sale, Ian, you & I both.'

I thought for a second. 'Okay. Go ahead.'

By four o'clock I had the papers in front of me. So quick, so processed, so neat. Me, Veronica & a very smart black lady, who arrived in a silver Mercedes & introduced herself as the buyer's lawyer. Lots of exchanging documents, signing on dotted lines, Veronica standing over us, fretting till the last.

'When does your client want to move in?' I asked the lawyer.

'Oh, he doesn't. This is part of an investment portfolio.'

'Right, I see. Can you tell me a bit about him?'

'I'm afraid I cannot. He wishes to remain discreet.'

'So what becomes of the house?'

'The property will become an asset to a holding company. That's all I'm at liberty to say.'

'Does this company have a name?'

'Darlings, let's just sign up & be done,' Veronica chipped in. I could see how rigid her body had become. I looked at her, then back at the lawyer.

'Right. Can I stay until the end of January?'

They looked at one another.

'I don't see why not,' she said.

Do I have it in me to care? I have the asking price sitting neatly in an offshore account. I'll be gone in two months. I'll cross the border & be out of this place for good. Do I really care who takes over my house? Whether it just sits in the name of some vague shelf company for the next five years possibly gaining value, possibly not?

I'm undecided on all the above. I'm undecided on everything all of a sudden.

21 November

Another brick dismantled, another part of the hem unpicked. My last day at school. Final assembly was bearable until we all stood to sing the school anthem, accompanied by the pipers. Wrench in the heart. Then on to the end of year staff lunch. Subdued affair. Everyone on a knife edge about the future of the school, the future of the country. Not a good year all round. Muller especially down in the dumps. He bid us farewell with a subtle hint of embitterment towards us. Loaded sarcastic comments like, 'Many of us who've tried to stretch our wings know that the grass isn't always greener on the other side.' As there were seven of us leaving not one of us felt particularly moved, I don't think. When it came my turn to say a few words I had been standing there thinking what to say. I wanted to say, 'I have no reason to be leaving you all, I've admired this school, it's been my second home, but these are unsettling times & unfortunately I can't see that I'll have a future here, being what I am, being a young white male.' Instead I just said thanks & good luck. They gave me a nice edition of *The Great Treasury of Western Thought*. It'll probably end up at Auction Express like everything else in my life.

22 November

Am trying not to think of school. Or the sale. Slept late & didn't surface until near noon. Thumbed through the shelves & spent the afternoon reading in bed. Read in snatches & dozed off for a while in languid oblivion, quite lost in those quaint & ageless worlds I'd transported myself into. Victorian London, the roaring Twenties, the frozen wastes of Russia. Finally got up around 4 a.m. Sat about in my boxers & tinkled on the piano (in bad need of tuning before it's sold). Dug out my old scores & set about trying to get my fingers to remember the patterns of the runs & chords & melodies. Have fixed myself on relearning the first movement of the Waldstein sonata. Why, I don't know. Some dive into escapism? Hit the right notes, but nowhere near up to tempo. Couldn't get a very pleasing tonal quality on the high passages either. V. impatient.

23 November

Interesting turn of events. Had a sudden unexpected text from Alicia asking me to go along with her to a recital by a Czech cellist & I could think of no reason not to. The whole way through the programme flashes of our previous relationship came to me. Has it really been four years since we parted company? Since her impatience with me snapped &

she left for brighter prospects in London? Maybe it was the proximity of our bodies, side by side again after all these years. Maybe it was the familiar scent of the perfume she still wears. I recalled the almost formulaic pattern of our affair – sitting around arguing endlessly about art, politics, philosophy, rapidly getting through a bottle of red wine, sometimes a pasta dish, then always ending up in bed having urgent, animalistic sex which wasn't always entirely satisfactory, but was nonetheless a welcome outlet. The relationship in many ways more a union of souls & minds than a coupling of bodies.

The recital was something of a disappointment. A paltry fifty or so people, mostly rather elderly, scattered around that huge, cold auditorium. Hardly an electric ambiance. The poor guy went through the motions well enough & played a piece by Ravel I'd not heard before. Afterwards, Alicia said, 'Come back to my place for a bite to eat.'

I followed her home – a garden flat in one of those secure complexes. Modern, stylish, cosy atmosphere. As soon as I walked in I sensed the lashings of class & taste the girl has. A slight ache settled over me when I thought for the briefest of moments what I'd missed all these years. (What could have been?)

It turns out she has been back for some months, in fact

the better part of the year. She has obviously come into some money. Didn't really enquire too much, but I know she's not into teaching art anymore. Something about starting up a ceramics studio, designing elaborate frescos & tiled floors & fittings. I got the impression she's a tad ashamed of her clientele – bound to be the fat cats & cronies building their new palaces in the hills. The flat is v. well decorated. She's invested in some fine works of local art. Hung them well too. Impressive: the eye for arrangement, the overall aestheticism of the place. I felt as if I'd entered a pleasure dome, out from the wastes of a desert.

She'd pre-cooked an Italian chicken dish, reheated it on the stove & tossed together a salad. I cracked open a bottle of Simonsvlei Pinotage, 2002. We drank & ate & in the background a CD of rustic Spanish folk music played. We talked of everything & nothing. The usual. Then she let out a measured sigh & said, 'Ian, don't you sometimes think all of this is totally unreal?'

The comment threw me somewhat. I looked at her & thought about what she meant, but words failed me.

She continued, 'I mean, this life we live here, doesn't it seem totally divorced from reality?'

I considered. 'I suppose it's unique all right. We're certainly living a life few people overseas could ever imagine.'

She sipped her wine but looked a little downcast all of a sudden, as if something was weighing down on her.

'But that's just where you're wrong,' she said. 'We're not living it are we? We're just fuckers on the sideline, bystanders, even worse than that, totally oblivious saprophytes who just plod along in our little world of perceived hardships we so selfishly claim to be our own.'

I was quite taken aback by her tone of voice. 'What do you mean?'

She sat back in the couch & gave a half smile. 'Oh I don't know. Nothing really I suppose. It just makes me wonder if we have the right to claim we're part of an experience we're actually 99 per cent removed from & untouched by, that's all.'

I thought long about this & something of a protracted silence fell between us as we finished the chicken & the bottle of wine. I knew what she meant, but somehow I didn't want to accept the biting way she put it. I've always been self-obsessed to a degree I know alienates people – it boiled down to our initial split – but I've always been content to believe that I'm at the centre of my own world & by extension that world revolves around me. To think that conception is inaccurate, that Alicia is perfectly correct in saying us whites are actually living in a fool's paradise, that we don't know an iota of what's really going on out there, left me feeling unsettled.

A little later we made love tenderly & without forewarning. I laid her out along the wide cream couch & peeled down her panties & ran an eager finger across her moistening clitoris & then rolling on a condom from my wallet I pulled my body up against hers & eased myself into her. Utter bliss.

I left late. After sex we lay together for some time, dozing on & off, I think both succumbed to some indolent mood. Then finally I whispered to her that I had best make a move. I told her the power was out & that I was apprehensive about the house being left in the dark. That may have been the truth, or it may have been an excuse to slip away from a situation that had gradually become awkward. I had noticed a subtle frigidness sidle into her body & I presume she noticed the same in me, for we parted with an unstated but mutual understanding that perhaps the events of the night best be considered a random undertaking & not the start of a fresh entanglement. We were subject to all the typical post-coital indecisions & reservations I suppose.

24 November

Am deeply perturbed. After thinking yesterday was a one-off, Alicia began texting during the afternoon & by evening I was back at her place & events repeated themselves.

When I left it had begun to drizzle. The windscreen had misted over & I had some problems navigating my way down the potholed roads in the dark. Large tracts of the neighbourhoods I drove through were completely black. I stopped at the intersection by the Catholic church where the traffic lights were off. I looked right & left but before I could accelerate, the oddest thing happened – a man pushing a wheelbarrow veered in front of my headlights. He stopped & put his hands up to signal my attention & then started walking towards the car.

My gut instinct was to put my foot down hard & either drive through him or else try to skirt round him. But in the panic my foot slipped on the accelerator & the car jerked forwards & stalled. By then he was at my side window, tapping vigorously. The fright I got. I didn't know what to do or think, & was only aware of the need to be compliant. I kept telling myself, 'If you antagonize this man he's going to pull out a pistol or a knife.' I inched down my window & he leered in at me.

'Please,' I began to say, 'I don't want any trouble, okay. We can talk.'

But it wasn't what I expected at all. He began to plead with me desperately, saying, 'Ah, baas, please help me, baas, please.'

Tried to smell if he was drunk or high on weed but it didn't seem so. Then I thought perhaps he was just a beggar trying his luck.

'I can't help you,' I said, waving him off, 'I don't have any money on me.'

He said, 'No, baas, I don't want money.'

'What then? What do you want?'

'My wife, she is having baby,' & he pointed to the barrow still sitting blurred & bulging in my headlights. I looked at it & registered through the stark slats of drizzle the figure of a woman lying squat on her back with her legs spread across the handlebars, clutching her swollen stomach. A most bizarre sight. V. surreal moment.

I started to do up the side window, saying, 'No no, what do you think I am, hey?' Part of me still thinking it was an ambush, a hijacking.

He said, 'Please, baas, we just need lift to clinic, please, please.'

But by then the window was up & I had started the ignition & pulled away, passing the barrow with the woman & him rushing towards her in the rain. This was all I could see of them from my rear-view mirror before they vanished almost instantly in the folds of darkness.

Drove the rest of the way home v. disturbed. Kept playing

the scene over in my mind. The cold, hard, reality of it. Something grainy, pared, raw. It's late now & I'm tired. But I can't seem to get it out of my mind.

25 November
Morning

How did they proceed on in the dark after me? How did they make it with the rain falling over them like a scourge over the plagued? How did they navigate the unseen potholes? What if the wheel of that barrow got wedged in a crater in the road? What if she was thrown off? What if the man, already tired, exhausted, spent, had to heave with all his might to lift it? To deliver it from the ground? Did they make it in the end, just him, his wife & the barrow trundling those slimy hellish roads all the way to the clinic? Or did they encounter someone else, someone with a little compassion & humanity to finally help them? How many others did he try & plead with – how often was he left crying in anguish as another car sped quickly from their midst? And after all that, what of the clinic? Did they get all the way there? If they got all the way there, she most likely being hit with labour contractions closer & closer together, what were they then confronted with? A building deserted of unpaid, striking staff? The gates shut, bolted, pad-locked? What if there was no room for them there? If the beds were full of cholera victims & AIDS sufferers? What if they turned them away? What then? An unseemly birth in the first dry place they could find? Under a tree or a bus shelter or in an alleyway littered with snoozing drunks, rats, rancid garbage, excrement? Would he know what to do? Would he know to tell her to breathe at the right times, to push when needed, to hold her hand & let her squeeze it through? Should the miracle occur & the baby be born despite all this adversity, against all the odds that the cruel world has thrown at its first weak & wistful breath, will it then survive at all? Given they would have nothing dry to wrap it in & little chance they could incubate it if the rain continued to fall, as it did all night, at times in torrential gusts.

Noon

I can't exorcize it. Something beyond an image is pinned to my mind. Something about that wheelbarrow. Something about the sight of it there on the asphalt. Something about the sight of its heaped human cargo, dumped in it. So grotesque & wretched. Something about the image that furls in me, the image that makes me associate her with visions incarnate of every evil blight beset on man. Something about the weight she carries like a burden into the world. Something about the inventiveness of it too. Something startling, wonderful. To resort to such measures – such an indictment yet a testimony too. Something signalling the allotment of one man's entire desperation.

Later

Why can't I just shrug it off, internally, as I do every other savage tragedy that unfolds about me every day? Like when I'm driving & stop at intersections & tatty, filthy, balding, belly-swollen children tap at the windscreen & look at me pleadingly & cup their hands for money? Why can't I just roll the window up on this one, cut off the sound of his breathing, his pleas, as I do with all the others? Why is it my fault another tyrant in this world has chosen to cling to power? Why am I the one left now to weigh that cost?

Evening

Tell yourself you're being ridiculous. I'm being ridiculous. Any person in that position, given the times we live in, times of lawlessness, violence, crime (yes, spell it out to yourself – lawlessness, violence, crime) would have done exactly what you did. Now realize this sovereign point: it's your God-given right to protect yourself first & foremost, even your natural right to act as you did, out of precaution, out of trepidation, out of rank fear. Call it what you will. It's the nature of man, the nature of the beast in us all. Try to think of this instead: Alicia's cunt slick & wet before you, waiting to be eaten. Waiting to be parted & fucked.

26 November

Slept badly. A glumness has descended over me. My existence is banal. Moped about. Tried to read but my eyes just scanned the pages. Sat hunched at the piano, fingers dead & heavy on the keyboard. The Waldstein just seems too difficult now. I'm bored with the mistakes I make & the disjointedness of the sound I produce. Staggered for a while, around the house which is no longer mine. The gardens that belong to a holding company. All the furniture & clutter I haven't got the energy to start packing up & getting rid of. Not really sure of my existence at all today. Odd remark to record. Everything a fraction removed, my mind seems half shut to the reality of things. Did some chores. Not in the mood for Alicia today. Ignored her texts. Power still off. Going to sleep & draw a curtain over the world.

27 November

Morning

Bad dreams. Hot, restless night. Images roving at me, sounds of the fractured Waldstein. The pulverizing sight of the woman on the barrow; the man at my window; Alicia's strange pronouncements the night of the recital; the whole saga of Tobias's leg; leaving school; selling the house; the darkness. All morphed into one image. At one point thought my head was going to explode. Got up this morning & shoved four Disprin down my throat but I've got a feeling this is no ordinary headache.

Later

Thought: I've been living here, in the country of my birth, in the land of my parentage, all this time – haven't left at all – & I've experienced everything: the whole journey of a fledgling country, from birth to now, thirty years later. I was just a small boy when this country came into being. I was tiny when they signed the charter & Dad came back from the bush & put aside his fatigues & pledged allegiance to the new republic. It was a new beginning for everyone. A fresh slate. So we've been side by side, siblings in infancy, in childhood, in adolescence, as adults.

Realization: I've been a willing participant, a screw in its machinery, its mechanisms. A component part to every little thing.

Question: am I to blame?

Later

The admission ought to come now that I've sunk into something of a depression. Perhaps this has been coming on for a time & I should have seen the signs but didn't. Have just become used to how life is here, how every little stress gets notched up on the psyche & becomes the new benchmark for normality. The ever-shifting sands of sanity. I thought I had become immune to it. I thought it was branded into my mind, absorbed into my pink skin. Yet peel away the top layer & we have a nation of psychotics hankered down there in the muck. Maybe Alicia's on the verge too? Maybe we're more susceptible, us 'types'. I fear that the proverbial great wave is coming. Everyone standing in its surge.

Addendum

Going back to that previous thought – is it not too easy to surmise I am to blame because I am part of the country? Isn't it more pertinent to say the country & I are actually divorced & therefore, because of the separation, we are both to blame? To allegorize: in our parallel growths, a great divide was drawn on the day of our births. It was drawn in the sand. (In fact it was never erased from days gone before.) It was drawn there between this nation & me. A divide separating race from race, man from fellow man. In that disjointed state we have grown up deformed, autistic, simple-minded, unable to reach maturity. Or conversely, we are both fully fledged beasts, both alike in brawn & breast & brainlessness. We bash one another with the clubs of our tongues, the boots of our contempt. Or further yet, we were both stillborn & only our vengeful infant souls waft the mythic air, circling one another like weary tramps in the night. Or we are nothing at all. We were not born, in that sense of the word. We're a miscarriage of ideals. And nothing can come of us that is any good. The body has rejected us, aborted us unseemly twins. Where then is the new conception, the new birth?

1 December

In between snatches of sleep & a raft of ponderous thoughts, I slip a notepad & a blunt pencil into bed with me & I jot down ideas, observations, questions I have of myself. I write a screed of notes, scribbling sometimes out of what seems an automation, driven on by some force within me. I have to keep doing this to keep the dark fear out.

3 December

Have been writing almost constantly. Lots of it I tear up, having started a train of thought & then discarded it. Other stuff I keep prodding at, nudging the idea, the notion a little further, seeing if it will snap. Between sloth & slumber thus I levitate. Am beginning to sketch in my mind an idea of how, if anything, I can make up for that night in the rain when I failed to help that man & his wife. For I believe that's the catalyst, the genesis of my decline. Everything else is a building block towards this juncture, this point in time where I hurtle along that dark rainswept road & at that intersection, from the crossroads, there comes a man wheeling a barrow with a woman atop & an infant clawing to be born & where our paths cross something *happens*, some interconnection is formed which is fate-ordained & can't be undone.

4 December

This venture has to born out of a desperate need to come clean, to make up for my failings as a human being, as a participator in the suffering of my own kinsmen. Alicia summed it up best when she said that we – the whites – don't have the right to claim we're part of an experience we're removed almost entirely from. How can a white man in Africa ever know what it means to suffer at the hand of the oppressor when by our very lineage we are often the oppressor ourselves? Even by default, even unwittingly, even now, when we all squeal the cries of the victim, we cannot extradite ourselves from guilt. We may not be the tyrant incarnate, but we're nonetheless the silent, serpentine collaborators in a vast, encompassing crime against people on our own land, of our own soil – our fellow human beings.

There – it's said. Can I bear to look over this entry again, to look it in the face?

Later

What is the best way to pay due recompense for my role in this crime? To atone for my failure to help that man & his wife in their moment of need? What is to be my punishment? How will I suffer, as they have suffered at my hands?

Surely the only way would be for the event to occur all over again & for me to place myself at their disposal until we reach the clinic & the baby is delivered. I'd be of service to them, one man to another. But then, given that I own a vehicle & they don't, or given that I belong to the privileged & they to the peasantry, or that I am white & they are black – in short, that my *status* is one exalted over theirs – such an act would be one of charity only & while that in itself is a worthy notion, it would mean I was a willing participant, I was merely tolerating their intersection into my life, *pitying* them,

& as such I would be achieving nothing. While I may be inconvenienced, I wouldn't be part of the *experience* of suffering, of hardship.

What then if that man had pulled out a pistol or a knife & hijacked me & forced me to drive him & his wife to the clinic? In that instant, surely, the roles would've reversed beyond my control & I'd have become his victim & he my aggressor & his status, given the bearing of a weapon, would exceed mine, meaning I would have no choice but to obey his every command in fear for my life. In effect, his aggression would *enslave* me. By force he'd have entered my space & taken possession of me.

And is this not the heart of the matter? Is this not what I am ultimately guilty of? Oppression, enslavement? It's the colonial blood that surges through my veins, the history that constructs me, the attitude I adopt. It has defined me all along, has made me complicit. A hundred years ago on the spot where I write this now, it is no secret at all that my forefathers enacted the heinous misdeeds that constitute human bondage, ranging about the plains with shotguns & sjamboks, coercing men to their labour by fear & oppression, demeaning them by stripping away every right a human being ought to own by birth & now, a century on, the only evident change is a physical one. We have substituted the whippings & beatings & the barrel of a gun with something equally extortionate; we have refined our methods but continue the abuse. We have substituted the loss of our status with an attitude equal to it. In short, we continue.

But returning to the man & his gun, & to my quest for punishment – it would be pointless undergoing such a brief & painless submission. I'd succumb to his threat & open the back door to let them hustle in & then drive while he pointed the knife or the gun at my neck. The fear may be punishment itself, but the hardship would be trite. A ten-minute ordeal & afterwards I'd just drive away, a little shaken, a little numb with nausea, but none the worse for wear.

No. It's no good just being a slave in the theoretical sense. I'd have to enact it too. I'd need to endure the toiling, the physical pain, the abject suffering. I'd need to withstand this over a lengthy period of time, to be brought to my knees, to be ill-treated, to be whipped if I fall behind in my labours or the ordeal overcomes me.

Moreover, to be a slave, to be punished as a slave, I'd need to be silenced. I'd need to be rendered voiceless, speechless, whether my tongue is cut from my mouth or my lips bound with a gag, so that I'd be deprived of the ability to beg, plead, reason with my master. In the same way I roll up the window on the calls of the beggars, my white ears deaf to their anguished black lips.

Later

I ponder this: is the act, *could* the act – of writing, of sitting down & chaining myself slavishly to my desk & writing page after page after page until my fingers stiffen (or even blister & bleed) & my back aches & my eyes strain & my head dizzies with tiredness, be in any way an act of recompense? The discourse a form of labour; every page my servitude, its completion my liberty, the whole ordeal my catharsis?

5 December

Early morning

During the night I sketched this in my head: I have my protagonist captured & enslaved at the very beginning. Taken against his will. Tied up & shackled off. He's traded for some reason, as lowly as he is he has value to some-one. Or someone needs him for something, some task a slave undertakes, carrying or hauling or digging. Perhaps carrying something on a long journey. A primitive land where everything is apocalyptic dust & ruin, in the after-math of some war, some famine. Something to make it all the more taxing, all the more gruesome. The pain must be the thing. I want to feel it through him, every step.

Later

To add: would it not be preferable if I was another being altogether? An animal, a beast of burden perhaps, so that my master would not need to be lumbered with the prospect of feeling an iota of compassion for my suffering? It would be easier for him if he didn't. I'd have to obey his every command for fear of my life. Then I'd be a slave, punished as a slave, true to the word. I'd be at his beck & call, subject to his every whim, his every command. I'd need to live off every word he said, wait with bated breath for my next instruction. In the end I'd be so conditioned to my lot that the very notion of freedom would slip from me like a coat & I'd lose my identity, my sense of self in the raw, naked service of another.

17 December

When the notes & scraps & questions became page-long ramblings I found myself sitting up in bed & writing for hours at a time. It got uncomfortable. I migrated to my desk, installed myself one morning with a ream of newsprint I dug out of a box of school papers & a blue biro & my notebooks beside me & I've been continuing to scribble & scrawl my musings

& imaginings ever since, page after page, hour upon hour, day after day. A strange compulsion. The house is in a mess. Sometimes I'm disturbed by calls & people asking to come round & look at what's for sale. They do come. They must think me odd. I haven't shaved for a week. They pick around & offer me money & I rarely think about it, just accept it. Off they trundle, parts of my existence wedged in the boots of their cars. The lounge suite already gone, the dining-room table, the garden set, lots of stuff from the kitchen. Have given up aspirations of the Waldstein. Had to when the piano was sold. Am not eating v. well. Power off. Have ignored Alicia's texts & been curt with her on the phone. She quipped something like: 'Leopards never change their spots.' Take it the whole dalliance is off. Not fazed. All is writing. My life is the desk, the paper, the pen.

5 January

Here I have remained almost ever since, in my den all hours of the day & night. My eye droops across the page, my hand scribbles on & even when the light of day fades & the night comes up, I do not put a halt to this streaming narrative. I just stagger my way into the bare kitchen & probe the windowsill & find there the shaft of a candle I light with a box of matches & carry it back to my little desk where now all this paper lies heaped in an unmitigated mess. Here I'll sit all hours of the night & not think a thing of it. But sometimes the stub of the candle goes dead & I do sneak off to bed.

7 January

I write of blood & violence & untold misery. Of hacked corpses littered on the ground, lifeless terrains & starvation. It comes to me from an imagined horror, of what could be, of the potential of human depravity. Sometimes it makes me feel sick. Sometimes I want to recoil from the page until I realize, with an equal numbing dread, that all my prophecies are real.

8 January

When I surface from the malaise of writing that I can't seem to stop, I sometimes wonder about Tobias & his poor leg. About the pain sunk there, the sore that wouldn't go away because it had, at last, after years of being held in abeyance, lingering beneath his black skin, broken through to the surface, manifested itself as a mark on him, a mark of the abuse he'd suffered. Then I think about his cries & his pleading to me. How he came to me in pain & how I fobbed him off time & time again with the white pills I tossed him, like a bone tossed to a begging dog to shut it up. It's nothing new, my crime. It stretches back to the day I could talk, to the day I learnt to utter commands from my chattering toddler tongue & realized that out of the shadows someone soon came running, a vague but eager black figure, smiling always, keen to impress, to ingratiate, to pick up the toys I left strewn across the carpet, clean the green juice I'd spilt on the floor, wipe my snotty nose, my stinking arse.

Did he get home? Did he make it there? Or was he stopped along the way & beaten & intimidated? Did militia youths pounce on him & attack him for no reason save the impunity they've been granted in their tyrant's name? His bowler hat knocked off, his little cane snapped in half. His proud checked suit torn, his knapsack snatched. I'm given to thinking the worst. I hope I'm wrong. But wherever he may be meandering, homewards to his village, or rested up there, glad to be rid of his uncaring, demanding boss for a while, if I could say anything to him, it would be: Tobias, you served me & my family for all these years uncomplainingly. What makes a man serve & yet in the end, at the final counting, not seem at all like a servant? Please share your secret.

9 January

Restless. The pace of my all-consuming pursuit has waned in the past few days. Can't think why, can't place it. Went for a sleep this afternoon. (Barely have a bed left to sleep in the rate everything is being snatched up.) Suddenly I awoke knowing a dreadful truth. I got on the phone to Veronica straight away.

'Tell me the man who bought my house isn't who I think he is?'

'Darling, what do you mean?'

'The man who bought my house – my family home – he's not, he's not one of *them* is he? The anonymity, the shady holding company, the cash in hand – who has access to that kind of money these days? Hey? Who's going around buying up property without even stepping foot in the place? Hey, tell me that?'

But the phone line had already gone dead.

And so it's confirmed: I am embroiled to the neck in the corruption of this place. Wedged neatly in place in a system I help feed & fatten.

10 January

I don't know how to end my story. I'm trapped, enslaved here, true as the word. I keep fearing that if I don't end my chore, if I don't see my narrative to its conclusion, then the text is going to kill me – metaphorically, psychologically – will at some point lunge out & deal the death blow. But now

I see that is not going to happen. Instead it is left to me, as a final cruel irony, to kill the story. I will have to find a way. I'll have to do it sometime soon.

11 January

Why has my narrative faltered? Why has my tale come to a grinding halt? I haven't been able to write for some time now. Have not been able to resolve it, to get to the end, to a place where I can say, enough, let the child at last be born, let this painful journey be over. It was going so well. All those days it came spinning out of me in a deluge. My beast was suffering well enough. How he's laboured for the purposes of the narrative. He's tired & aching. One can't decry the need now for an end to it all, some well-earned respite. I'm exhausted sitting here. My back is killing me, my neck stiff from the poise I keep, huddled over this stack of papers all day. Why have I complicated matters, why have I let them wander from me – those boys first of all, then the pair of them driving off in a blue sedan, then the man getting himself shot, the woman disappearing – why has it all gone so awry? They were never supposed to go near that road: I knew the temptations.

If only he had had a voice from the beginning & I could have had him say: *Enough, this was a false move. My sole purpose, my sole existence even, is in the immediate service of that woman and her unborn child. Let me take a step back & undo my last few paces & put back the ropes & rebuild the cart & move with haste down the kopje & back across the veld & to the road & catch them in their folly as they try the ridiculous notion of attempting to drive a car off into the unseen distances where utter doom is their only fate!* 'Wait for me,' he'd call out. '*I'll keep walking for you, I'll do what I can.*'

12 January

No one to blame but myself. Terrible night. Giddy with thoughts that kept coming to me, over & over. Finally arrived at a horrid, pertinent truth.

Out there my donkey stands beside a gunned-down sedan, while somewhere, breezing along the firmament, hovers my authorial hand of God, the ultimate hand of fate. I should have been able to stop that lot disappearing one by one from my narrative. A writer is supposed to be the most omnipotent god-voice in existence: I'm supposed to be in charge & my characters are supposed to obey me. Why have they deserted me like this, fled me just before the grand climax?

This is what I now believe: I have come to suspect that they have acted in unison against me. I truly thought that by undertaking this mammoth task, subjecting myself to the pain of this cognitive exercise, I was atoning for my failure to act that night, or on any other occasion, or for being nothing more than a passive bystander in the collapse of a system, rather than share my load, pay my dues. I thought I was stepping inside the experience. I perceived my metamorphosis, my reduction to the most lowly of beasts, to be an act of homage to those people, an offering. But now I see I have done nothing but re-enact my crime. I have done it again. I kick them when they are down, writhing on the road, & I put a boot into their backs.

I – the donkey – we – were never their slaves. Paradoxically, by the mere fact that I controlled their every move, their every facet of being, by the instance that I plucked them out of my imaginings & held them forcibly in this narrative, I enslaved *them*. As author I am *their* master, they my slaves. I have been controlling their destiny, their fate was in my hands; just as it was that night when our paths crossed at that intersection & in my position of omnipotence – by the mere designation of my status as someone who had the cards in his hand, who could *choose* a path of action & not be subjected to it – I became the author of that man & his wife's destiny. I *enslaved* them to my choice.

Is it any wonder that the subconscious realization of this caused the fracturing of the story? Is it any wonder they conspired to break free from me, *their* master, just as my beast had longed to break free from them? It is any wonder when they were nothing more than stereotypes from the beginning, picked to represent a principle in motion as opposed to the reality of the human experience?

Even their hellish post-war surroundings I merely gleaned from my memory, from international newsfeeds documenting the blight of the warlord across Africa, the genocides, the massacres, the ethnic cleansing. It was a landscape pre-painted for me, a template of numerous composites. And the descriptions of the wild they trod across? Who would know that I sit here at my pine desk & lying beside me are a series of reference books which I plunder with regularity? *The Bundu Book 1: Trees, Flowers and Grasses of the Veld. The Bundu Book 2: Geology, Gemmology and Archaeology.* For the truth is I haven't been into the heart of the country for some time. I haven't experienced it.

I sit here in shame. Perhaps it's from this understanding I know I need to leave. That I can never be reconciled to this place. Maybe I have found my reason.

13 January

I think about them in this vein a lot now. I know I haven't done them justice, given them a real voice, made them real human beings. I didn't see them beyond significations of what they stood for & hence they never stood a chance. In this admission alone I find the entire weight of my failure come down on me. I had never stopped to think what tribe they belonged to, what their origins were, their genesis, of which chiefdom they called themselves. And where is the kraal that is their motherland? Take the boys. I perceived them to be well conditioned. Their physiques are of men of the land. True men, in any sense, in any culture. Dare I imagine their communion with the hoe & the budza & the panga from an early age? Each bundled tight to his mother's back (whoever she may be) & she all day in the fields labouring in the full scorn of the sun. Those lean black chests bare to the elements all boyhood, splicing wood, ploughing troughs, clubbing samp, in ways that would be their daily ceremonial.

All I chose to depict of the woman was her condition. I chose to make her the product of her pain & discomfort. The continual sourness of her character. But what I failed to do is look beyond type, look at the person, the race she is descended from. Had I done this I would have realized my gross misrepresentation. Isn't it well known in their myths that the mother-to-be labours on undeterred & when the time comes she drops the hoe in the field & births there

astride it & is handed the hoe again when the grisly umbili-
cal cord is snipped (yes indeed — snipped — with that same
blade that breaks the soil!).

I suspect I've made too much of her complaining, her
weakness, understandable as it is. If the journey was to
take place again tomorrow, if I were to wake up & take to
my desk & everything were to fracture around me (& if he
were to saunter off from the plantation & by some miracle
find a patch of vegetables & there be captured), I'm convinced the woman, in light of my new reflections, would
be a far tougher, far more co-operative soul. Perhaps then
our paths would never need to cross & that's as it should
be?

Later

I'm disheartened that I can't do more for them. But maybe
I can. Maybe the least I can do is finally give them names,
baptize them in my mind? Knowing them as well as I do, I
expect I should. So enough of 'the man' & 'the woman' & 'the
boys' as if they're just Everyman pieces in a medieval miracle play. The man I think I'll call Baba. Baba — father. It's
obvious I'll call the woman Amai. Amai — mother. What to
call the two boys? How about: the one Farai, the other
Kudzai?

14 January

Perhaps, in my mind, at least I feel as if I've set them free. Even in death – if I can't resurrect Baba, Farai & Kudzai – if, in some way, their deaths are a sacrifice for the greater good, then perhaps they are free on their own terms. Free from my tyranny. Up there in the spirit world, or cast adrift on a crisp white piece of paper, a kind of heaven for dead characters. I don't have time to indulge in this any more. Not now, anyway.

The lady from Auction Express arrived today & behind her a huge lorry. Away went the last of my life. Talk about leaving it late. All I have now is a suitcase, a few shackles, a few books. They took my desk from under me, almost. I had to lift the cluster of papers, & this journal, as they carted it away from where I sat. So much to do.

Even as ruthless as I've been in stripping away my life of late, I haven't been entirely successful. Can one ever be? Have heaps of boxes sitting around filled with bric-a-brac that I don't know what to do with. Amazing the junk one can acquire in a lifetime. The baggage of one's existence. Piles & piles of stuff I've turfed out to Sixpence. Must think Christmas has come all over again. He brims from ear to ear & goes off down to his kia laden with boxes & packets & bundles. Later on I'll square up with him as there won't be time tomorrow morning before I leave. (Intend to get away at six on the dot: optimistic?) He's staying on & in many ways I'm relieved about that. I'll look him squarely in the eye – well I intend to – & say, 'Sixpence, look after the garden, hey – nice, nice.'

The house is empty & in every room there is an echo that trails after you. Feels like a sad lament, as if it's mourning my departure already. Ridiculous assumption. But how many months will she stand empty, stocking up value but losing the essence of a home? Something deep down tells me all this has been a colossal fuck up. Yet I suppose last-minute reservations are not an uncommon affliction.

I have not spoken to Mom & Dad for some months now. Doubtless they tried to phone at Christmas only to find the line dead, disconnected weeks ago. Alex & James may have sent e-mails. I guess I'll find out when I reach South Africa & plug in a cable to reconnect with reality.

I'll be sleeping in a sleeping bag on the floor tonight. Not looking forward to it. Anticipate I'll be stiff as hell tomorrow & rue the decision, the whole trip to the border. I could have gone to stay with friends. People have offered. Linda & Ron for one. I played with the idea of sneaking back to Alicia's, one last night, one last romp. Not that I think she'd have me now. I don't think I'm fickle with other people's emotions but I keep my distance. I don't know why. I read & I suspect someday a book will tell me. Books & writing have been my anchor.

Muss es sein? Es muss sein.

Later

Shuffled everything into the few boxes that will fit into the car, rolled out the petrol containers. One I funnelled into the tank, the other I'll need about an hour before the border if everything goes according to plan. Have checked passport, car documents. Have a flask of water, some packets of crisps.

Now what? Deathly hollowness in the house. I'm sitting on the floor in the study, my sleeping bag next to me. It's a hot night. Turns out there is about half a candle left. The power will never come back, I believe. Not real power. When the candles across the city & then further across the country all finally burn into nothingness, & the paraffin stocks for the hurricane lamps dry up, is this the point when darkness will finally come forever to these people? When the anarchy will at last break & 'be loosed upon the earth'?

Is there no way to avert this? Is there no way the story can end, the child can be born of a new generation, free from the seeds of the past?

What if we – my donkey & I – embark upon a journey, a long journey to an unspecified destination, far away? What if we begin it tomorrow? We will be trotting along, or driving along quite pleasantly, having shed our burdens & the ropes that bound us one way or another. It'll be a hot, cloudless day. Then ahead we'll see, perhaps round a bend, a car parked on the side of the road, a blue car, a small sedan. We'll see this car & at first our instincts won't be particularly aroused because there isn't anything uncommon about a car stationed by the roadside. So we'll think nothing of it, nothing, that is until we are almost alongside it. Then we'll see something which piques our attention. Nothing immediately alarming, nothing that shudders through the brain. Yet at once we'll sense a certain neediness emanating from the figure who stands beside it clutching her stomach. A certain look of distress, or discomfort. Enough to make us feel that we have a duty to stop & reverse, or turn around, & offer our assistance.

We'll pull up alongside this woman – we won't even register the colour of her skin – & see with shock the state of her condition, the urgency of her need. In a language all three of us will understand, whether it be English, or a traditional language or even the silent transferral of meaning between man & beast, between beings of different yet equal distinctions, we will say, 'Are you okay? Do you need our assistance?'

At this point she'll look up, hardly aware, because of her distress, that we have come to aid her, & she'll smile & we'll see relief & gratitude break over her face & flush away the panic that held her, the panic of being out here alone with a baby on the way.

With that smile she'll say, 'Oh thank you, thank you, how I've been waiting for someone to stop & help.'

She may break away in a convulsion of pain, a labour contraction & we who are not so familiar with the inflictions of childbirth will panic, perhaps even more than she, & without hesitation we will be jolted into action.

We'll take her underarm & support her to the car, or perhaps we'll even crouch down low on the ground & she'll ease herself onto our back & grip our neck or our ears & we'll rise gently & go staggering off. We'll make haste, trotting if we can, or streaming along the roads at great speeds & we'll keep telling her that it's all going to be fine, that we'll make it in time. We'll say, 'Don't worry, amai,' or, 'Don't worry, mother, it won't be long.' She'll be breathing deeply now, the contractions coming closer, the pain intensifying. But at least she'll know she's in good hands. She'll lie there & know she doesn't have to worry because in the end her fears were appeased, someone has stopped, someone has given her a helping hand.

Speeding along as quickly as we know how, our charge clinging on behind, we'll finally see a sign ahead, just left off the road, a rickety silver-sheeted sign posted into the soil with a slender white cross painted on. Streaking behind it is a sandy slip of a road which we'll turn down & hurry along, kicking up dust in our path. The road straightens & will lead us to a low fence where there's a plough-disc with the same white cross. The gates will be open. We'll see a water tank on stilts & around a wisp of bush there'll be a modest clutch of buildings. We'll race up & stop & at once there'll be three nurses who come rushing out to meet us. They'll be wearing pale blue uniforms with crisp white wimples. We'll be relieved to see them, women who know what to do in these circumstances.

They will aid her out of the car & she'll hobble in their clutch & just before she disappears into the ambient coolness of the wards she will look back & say, or mouth, in the language which is universal to us all, 'Thank you.'

There will be nothing more we can do. We won't know what happens. We won't know how long it will be until that baby is delivered. Until it is brought into this world, until its first screams break out over the labour ward & one of the nurses bundles it in swaddling & lays it close to the bosom of its mother.

There'll be nothing more we can do but we'll have done enough. We will leave, driving away or walking on in the sun. We'll go on with our lives.

It's late. Better stop. Long day ahead tomorrow. It's hard to fathom that in two days I start at the new school. There is only a tiny flicker of the candle left. It dances in the last pool of wax, the last thread of string it clings to. I'm going to stop writing now & when I put the last full stop on the page I'm going to shut this journal & wait a moment & then blow the candle out.

Acknowledgements

I am indebted to a reading of Michel Foucault's essay, 'Qu'est-ce que l'auteur?', translated from the French by Jouse V. Harari, in *Textual Strategies: Perspectives in Post-Structuralist Criticism*, edited by J. Harari, pp. 141–160 (Methuen & Co. Ltd).

I am extremely grateful to Mrs Drue Heinz for providing me with a residential Hawthornden Fellowship in May 2009 which allowed me to complete work on a draft of this novel.

I am likewise grateful to my editor, Francesca Main, and publisher, Suzanne Baboneau, at Simon & Schuster, and to my agent, Bruce Hunter, at David Higham Associates.

An exclusive interview with Ian Holding, author of this novel

What inspired you to write *Of Beasts and Beings*?

Three things happened to me that formed the genesis of this novel.

1) I came across images in a *Time* magazine article about the post-election violence in Kenya. The images were horrific, but somehow epic – biblical, even.

2) A friend of mine sent me an email containing a photograph of a makeshift cart being hauled by this thin donkey, taken somewhere in the African bush. On the side of the cart was painted a red cross and lying in the centre was a patient in the throes of an illness. Crazily, it was meant to be a joke, entitled 'African Ambulance' or something, but it hit a very definite nerve for me. My immediate thoughts were: how far have they come and how far do they need to go? This,

combined with the Kenya pictures, triggered off the idea of writing a perverse kind of nativity tale.

3) Driving down the road one day I actually saw a man pushing a woman sprawled in a wheelbarrow. I don't know whether she was pregnant or if they even needed assistance, but the image stuck with me.

But beyond that, my role, or status, or existence as a citizen of my country, had been bothering me for some time. We have a scourge in Zimbabwe that needs dealing with – colonial baggage. It's been at the forefront of our national social consciousness for a long time now and it isn't going away. Quite frankly, black people use it as political capital and white people ignore it. I wondered: how many of us think that by being white we are somehow exonerated from blame for what has gone on in Zimbabwe in recent years? The typically ignorant answer is: we aren't a cause of the problem, but its victims. I realised that is a shallow, easy, pathetic response. I thought: if we really examine ourselves and our attitudes then we'll see that we have a great deal more to consider. I was eager to confront these issues of white denial and white mentality.

The premise that got me thinking was this: what would you do if you were placed in a situation where someone needed your urgent help? A life or death situation, perhaps. And because you thought for your own safety first, or because you felt it wasn't your problem to deal with, you declined. How would you feel, how would you cope, when you came to realise the consequences of that decision?

What made you choose this particular structure for your story?

I have always been intrigued by the idea of how writing can be a powerful reflective mirror for the ways in which society functions – more specifically, the *act* of writing, or the process of it. In other words, what role does the author play above and beyond the narrative he writes or creates? Is the author the omnipotent God controlling destiny? More specifically in this case, are characters beholden to their author and does the author *enslave* his characters to their choices, their settings, their scenarios? I realised that this idea could be a perfect vehicle for an allegory on colonialism or enslavement. I know it's metafictional, and some people might label it as nothing but a trick, but its possibilities fascinated me.

I also had this idea about writing a nativity tale of sorts. I'm not religious, but something about the journey under-taken to achieve such a symbolic event, overcoming all the hardships and obstacles along the way, felt like a powerful metaphor for what I was trying to convey. In the end, the two opposing forces, so to speak – the guilty writer and his troubled narrative – reconcile, and so the ending is retold, is made *possible*, by his new understanding or approach. The child can be born; hope can have a chance. The transformation of the writer over the course of his diary entries was of course the whole point.

Did you face any challenges whilst writing the book?

I always thought the expression, 'a second novel is the hardest to write' was just a cliché, but it's not. After the ease of writing my first novel, *Unfeeling*, (which I wrote in six weeks flat), I did struggle to write this book. Part of the problem was a lack of time and the pressure to write a follow-up. Stress and time constraints aren't exactly a writer's best friends. A lot of this was my own fault, for one reason or another. Also, I think part of the challenge came from the fact that as a previously published author, I now knew the bar was raised somewhat and the task was made a little more complex by knowing so much more about writing. That may seem like a contradiction in terms, but with *Unfeeling* I just wrote with this raw energy, not knowing whether what I was writing was any good or not, and now I found I was writing far more consciously, obeying too many rules and thinking way too much. So a few drafts really didn't work and were abandoned early on. Fortunately, the more time passed, the more I sort of forgot about this infliction and so the process became a lot easier.

I didn't face physical challenges of any consequence, not of the kind that I know some writers or people who want to write in the world, and particularly in developing countries, face on a day to day basis. I had a roof over my head and food in my belly and I don't take that for granted for a second. Yes, the electricity went out frequently, but I've learned that writers don't need luxuries and writing doesn't rely on mechanical infrastructure. This is a great plus. Just light a few candles, whip out some paper and a biro, and you're good to go.

How does this novel relate to your own experience of life in contemporary Zimbabwe?

It does and it doesn't. Yes, there are sections of it which will be familiar to Zimbabweans who face the same annoying challenges of life here, now or in the near past – the inconstancy of electricity, water and certain commodities, the hassles of bureaucracy and corruption, the endless vacuum or stalemate between the two political parties, the poverty of the people – but as with anything I write, I don't see these as curses particular to Zimbabwe. This is why I made the journey sections purposefully *not* specific to Zimbabwe. In fact not Zimbabwean in the real sense at all. They could, in effect, be anywhere in Africa, or indeed anywhere in the world where lawlessness has completely broken down and the result is that people are denied the protection of the state and must fight for themselves. What baffles me is that we – the common bond of mankind – still allow this to happen, given all we know about the inclinations of human nature and the savagery of past history. Nonetheless, the old adage about power corrupting absolutely is unfortunately apt to several of the world's leaders; that a blind obsession with power can lead to such a scenario as I have written about is what I wanted to explore.

Despite similarities with my own life in Zimbabwe, the character who writes the diary entries is not me. But I can easily see myself in his shoes and so I suppose I wrote him with the feeling that his dilemma was only a theoretical step removed from what could so easily have been pure autobiography. Whenever I get into the car now and drive anywhere – day or night – I wonder what the chances are that events might unfold as they did for my character and whether I will be faced with a situation where I might need to act where he failed to do so. If anything, I suppose writing this novel has heightened my awareness to that very real possibility and it's definitely made me adjust my mindset.

What would you most like your readers to take from *Of Beasts and Beings*?

This is going to be an unsatisfactory answer, I'm afraid. I don't necessarily feel it's a writer's place to come between a narrative and its reader. Essentially, once I've written the book and it's in print, it really belongs to each individual reader and obviously everyone reads differently and takes different things from every book. I know I often read a book and gain something from the experience which someone else who read the same book didn't. Or vice versa. So I wouldn't want to dictate any terms or play any authoritative role over my own narrative. I just hope I have managed to write a story which invites people to think about what has just been presented to them on the page.

Did you always want to be a writer?

Yes – a writer or a concert pianist! But I would never have had the nerves needed to perform in public. By nature I'm an introvert, and of course to be a performer, to share or express something like music, I think one has to be something of an extrovert. So I was never very good in public, not that I ever reached any great heights as a performing pianist, mind you. I don't have any problem with being an introvert. The nature of writing really is introspection, to inquire *within*, whether it's yourself or the characters you write about. Writing is also a very selfish occupation. It's solitary and it's not collaborative. Not like some of the other arts. You're preoccupied with what interests you at that particular time and nothing else really needs to matter; everyone else can more or less go to hell.

When I was growing up in Zimbabwe in the 90's as an adolescent, I had this impression that I was living in a wonderland of sorts. The country was thriving economically; it was eclectic, multicultural and safe. If there were problems brewing I was happily naïve to them. At this stage I went through a phase where I idolised P.G. Wodehouse and thought that writing could be just such a form of escapism into a bygone era, which actually resembled the Zimbabwe of the 90's a great deal. Everything was socially comforting and in a way very quaint, and often extremely funny. A lot of this came from my mother too, who can tell hilarious stories about any number of everyday occurrences. But by the time I was twenty and the new millennium came, this innocence was lost.

Since then I have looked at writing as a process of confrontation. Issues concern me, grate with my conscience or otherwise seem inexplicable to me, and I set about to tackle them through writing, to try and work *through* them, and hopefully to a point where I feel some kind of resolution, some kind of catharsis. It's a very personal thing, which is why I go back to the notion that to me writing is an introspective act. Whether or not other people see things the way I do or are troubled by the same issues would be impossible for me to say. Which is why, I suppose, writers really have to write for themselves first and foremost, to satisfy some inner need.

This, of course, is not to say that someday I won't be able to readdress the way I see writing and maybe reach a place where I can write the kind of escapist humour I wanted to growing up – perhaps once the angst I currently feel has been let from my veins or I find myself in an alien country where there's nothing to incite me, where the roots aren't so strong. But at the moment I'm engaged with the society I inhabit, for better or worse, and feel compelled to explore it, seeing as I don't have a voice in any other capacity.

How did your first novel get published?

The combination of a wonderful literary agent and a great editor. I had a fantastic team behind me who allowed me to realise my dreams, who made me believe in myself and promoted me to the hilt. I am very lucky to be a Simon & Schuster author!

Who are the writers that inspire you?

There are several, and obviously not nearly enough time or space here to talk about them all. I read widely, across a number of genres, although not nearly enough modern fiction as I'd like to. I go through periods when certain writers don't appeal to me; then, suddenly, they do. However, there are authors who seem to have a constant allure and whom I admire greatly because their work seems to tap into something *different* – I know that's a hopeless descriptor – but somehow it seems they have their finger on a different pulse to everyone else and being different – in anything – is what attracts me.

The Polish poet Wislawa Szymborska has an eye and an intelligence that I can't help but revel in. In the space of a short, seemingly simplistic poem, she can often encapsulate the breadth of an entire novel. She has wonderful, often painfully solemn, cadences, too, and a terrific sardonic irony. But for sheer beauty of language, I love Seamus Heaney. He has that wonderful Irish ear which can make words sing. I think the best lines of poetry I've ever read come from his poem *Oysters*. He starts: 'Our shells clacked on the plates/My tongue was a filling estuary/My palate hung with starlight . . .' The more you read that, the more you realise how brilliant it is.

Arthur Miller is America's Shakespeare – I have little doubt about that. I think Miller understood what the great Greek tragedians and Shakespeare did – which is that an audience loves to empathise, that it's part of our core humanity to do so, and Miller's plays are brilliant modern day tragedies about Everyman characters we can *feel* for. Harold Pinter totally rewrote the rules on what the dramatic form can achieve: unexplained, unplaced menace that ripples through the unuttered angst of his characters, which is a landmark device of modern literature. And it says so much about modern man and the modern world, too, without really seeming to say it at all.

As far as prose writers go, Thomas Pynchon fascinates and annoys me intensely. I have been trying to decode *Gravity's Rainbow* since I was a teenager and I am still none the wiser. But there are passages in that book which must rank Pynchon as one of the greatest modern prose writers. The same could be said for Samuel Beckett, though I haven't got a clue what any of his prose means, except that it *sounds* great to read and it's hypnotic, it keeps drawing you further and further into this indecipherable space and often you find yourself terrified to be there, which is quite a thrill.

I have huge respect for the South African novelist Damon Galgut because I feel that with every novel he is trying to push the boundaries a little bit, test the form, take his narrative to new and unique directions. Yet he never feels contrived or self-conscious and he writes so subtly about far-reaching issues. Leonard Michaels is my favourite short story writer and his grasp of the dimensions of language and his sense of phrasing is often very musical; he wrote in rhythms which take the ear by surprise and often evoke alarming responses. Evelyn Waugh is a sentimental favourite of mine and a grossly underrated giant of the modern novel. On that, I consider Virginia Woolf's contribution far more significant than Joyce's, even though I like what Joyce tried to do with prose.

But I think J. M. Coetzee has had the most formative influence on me as a writer. He is a master novelist who is also a towering intellectual and his achievement has been to marry the two into seamless narratives of often devastating power and reflection. Coetzee uses the novel form to *question*, to *probe* society and the individuals who inhabit it, especially those on the fringes who somehow, paradoxically, seem to represent us all. He is also a remarkable essayist and polemicist and a first rate linguist: he knows what words mean and stand for and his fiction shows time and time again how a whole encounter or scenario can turn on a single word. This is what I covet most about him.

Which book would you most like to have written?

Sophocles' *Antigone*. Two thousand years later and it is still as resonant now as it was then. To me, it's the great political and social allegory in the canon of Western literature. And almost every line, certainly every speech, is studded with those Sophoclean jewels of wisdom. Lines like, 'To think your own the only wisdom, and yours the only word, the only will, betrays a shallow spirit, an empty heart,' really resonate with me, particularly as a Zimbabwean. I mean, take this exchange in a modern context:

Creon: Since when do I take my orders from the people of Thebes?

Haemon: Isn't that rather a childish thing to say?

Creon: No, I am king and responsible only to myself.

Haemon: A one-man state! What sort of state is that?

Creon: Why, does not every state belong to its ruler?

Haemon: You'd be an excellent king – on a desert island!

What's your writing regime?

One of the great luxuries of writing is that it is incredibly portable and requires you to have no specialist equipment. A great deal of my work is simply cerebral. I would say 75% of the time I spend writing is just thinking, coming up with ideas, imagining scenes, devising character traits, plotting mentally. I hardly ever make notes and do little research – it's fiction, after all! The great thing is I can do this anywhere and normally the best ideas for narratives come to me when I'm doing one of three things: listening to a piece of loud music, driving very fast or standing in the shower. I think it's something to do with motion and how it connects or stimulates the rhythms of the mind, the areas that deal with the creative flow of ideas. Or at least this is my theory.

Music is a huge influence on how I write. I cannot write *and* listen to music at the same time – the music always wins me over – but before I write I like to get into the mood of a particular scene or episode by listening to a specific piece. Sometimes I think my subconscious directs me to choose the piece I do, because I have a knack of selecting something at random without intending to write and then finding that the piece very quickly gets me thinking about a scene or an interaction between characters. When I was writing the journey sections of this novel, *Of Beasts and Beings*, I recall listening to lots of Shostakovich's string quartets, especially the slow adagios. To some people that may seem a weird choice for a novel set in Africa, but of course really great music has a transcendental universalism about it – it's a language which speaks across cultures and boundaries – and there is something in those quartets which speaks of a force, an entity, something which is trying to 'flee the system', to break free or escape the mechanics of totalitarianism, and so I suppose there was a bridge to what I was thinking about.

When it comes to actual writing, I tend to write very quickly, within a matter of months or weeks, and I stay up very late into the night. I can seldom write during daylight and never early in the morning. What I write initially I hardly edit or correct. I like to get the first draft down raw and unhindered. Then comes the slow process of redrafting and self-correction and the painful exercise of staring yourself long and hard in the face, trying to convince yourself you're not the biggest fraud out there.

Music seems to be a big influence on you. Is there a musical performer or performance that is a particular favourite of yours?

Martha Argerich playing Prokofiev's Piano Concerto No. 3 in C, Op. 26. Specifically, a performance she gave in Turin in 2008 with the RAI Orchestra, conducted by Tugan Sokhiev. Check it out on YouTube –

http://www.youtube.com/watch?v=yL-HA4Heu2M

The greatest living pianist playing one of the great works in symphonic piano literature: sublime.

Can you tell us anything about your next book?

Only that it is very different to this one. Every book needs to be.

Excerpt from *Unfeeling*

by Ian Holding

The boy with emerald eyes everyone calls Davey sits on the veranda of Aunt Marsha's farmhouse, hugging his knees in the searing morning sun. He is shaking, his mind restless, thinking of Edenfields – the Cape Dutch house clutching the hill, just above the cathedral-like tobacco barns and the cluttered chemical-smelling sheds, then down to the brown Broadlands Dam lying beneath the hill, and the fields rutted and rugged, spreading beyond. From the hill's summit at Eden's View he could stand squinting and know that everything he could see belonged to Edenfields Farm.

Aunt Marsha's veranda is a smooth stretch of glazed red granite. The rich stench of floor polish makes the boy queasy as he stares at his reflection, still on the stone floor. Looking up to steady the spinning in his head he is lost in a blurred haze of khaki: branches, twigs, leaves, moss. The landscape won't settle, something in the air seems to reject him, the sudden wild squall of a bird perched high in a dry tree.

Up, out and beyond, he can feel the heavy silence, the flustered settling of the wild.

But in his head strange noises trouble him, grating and scratching about like the snorting of a pig. His hands, stiff and skeletal, shake continually. Sporadically, he claws at his skin with filthy nails, scraping grooves through days of dirt and grime. His body is battered and bruised. His guts shift and stir – he leans forward, grips his stomach, throws up on the steps below.

From the deep shadows of the veranda, Aunt Marsha rises from her wicker chair and moves forward to put a cool hand to his shoulder.

'There, there,' she whispers.

Nothing brings him relief. He cannot focus on a thought, hold an image still long enough to recognize what it is or means. Sudden snatches of memory swim across his vision, cancelling out the blotted garden. Sitting back against the cream pillar, his teeth chattering, his hands shaking, he is aware that Aunt Marsha stands, mutters something, withdraws. It feels like the removal of a gag. Alone, his body exhales. A convulsion follows, the breaking of a fresh sweat and a coldness creeping on him, a bone chill.

Only when he finds himself clutching a cold glass and glimpses again the haze of Aunt Marsha above him does he surface to feel the dull throb of pain at his temple, the roller coaster wobble of nausea. He lifts the rim of the glass to his soured mouth. He tastes the sweetness of the Coke, then the rush of rum and throws up again. He sits back, clutching his tender stomach, hearing the bird complain at him invisible in its tree, and then, a moment later, the sun's heat escalates.

He had taken a bottle of Captain Morgan's as he left Edenfields, the shotgun tucked under his arm. He'd planned to retrieve the gun from its hiding place, kick down the living-room door, blow away everyone who moved. Instead, he'd inched down the passage, utterly exhausted, battling to hold the heavy gun steady, the barrel constantly bearing towards the floor.

Being back in the house had done nothing to appease him. Its life-force had gone: he felt no slow pulse rise from its foundations, no current move through the sunken pipes and trusses. There was nothing to suggest what it had been. He'd thought the house would have spurred him on, that being there inside its walls, under its roof, would have filled him with family memories, steeped him in the essence of what he'd lost, if just for a moment. Instead, the place seemed sterile, or, worse, indifferent to him. She had spread her terminal gloom to it. The evening was still, the air warm and stale and hard on his lungs as he moved deeper inside – to his left a crescent-shaped table bearing the brass bulldogs he'd once given Ma for a birthday present, on his right a series of teak-framed lion photographs he remembered her hanging on the wall. Ahead: the bedroom, drawing him in like a vortex, for the next act. But in the end he took no delight in pulling the trigger.

Thinking about it now, he realizes he should have expected this anticlimax. He had long ago learnt that death is a strangely quiet thing, even for people. On that night a couple of months before, as he reeled against the cupboard in his parents' bedroom, the bed red and soaked, a pool of blood edging towards him along the beige carpet like a snake across stone, it had been pure silence pounding in his ears.

Being back in the house disturbed him in other ways he didn't anticipate. The memories that he had cherished since that night soured and after a while he withdrew as quietly as he'd come, taking only the bottle of rum from the bar counter in the lounge. Purposeless now, he wandered down the hill, through the cream-pillared gate, and didn't look back at the tight grip of the house, fort-like on the kopje, betraying him with its stubborn stillness. Even though the woman was now dead, Edenfields didn't seem cleansed or redeemed. Nothing had been restored, nothing replaced. He wanted to get far away.

He walked over the red soil, along the dusty road that cut through the scorched fields. The sky darkened; shrill insects seemed to berate him. The wind shifted every now and then, washing him in the evening's coolness. There was not another soul about, but in any case, the last couple of days had left him far beyond caring whether he was seen or not. He walked steadily through the quick fall of night, climbed to the peak of the high kopje, to the sacred place his great-grandfather had named Eden's View – a place he knew the fat woman would never have invaded – and there he leant against a rock face, exhausted, delirious, drained of will or reason.

With darkness blurring the edges of the tobacco barns, swallowing up the blue hills, there was nothing between him and the murderers. The militia had appeared from nowhere, caught them unawares, permeated the farmhouse like vapours. And now they were beginning to come again, this time through his ears, his eyes, the soles of his feet, the hardness of the rocks, from out of Edenfields itself, a shroud of killers, a shimmer of raised pangas, just when he should have defeated them.

Then the haunting sound of a boar rose again, sticking hard in his skull like a razor-edged arrow splintering the bone, slicing cleanly into his brain. In pain, he drove his body hard against the boulder, bruising his spine, cutting his shoulder blades on stone shards sharp as glass. The blood welled through his skin, dampening the grime on his shirt.

But there was no boar. Insects buzzed in his ears, nestled in the dampness of his sweaty arms. Below him the land stretched black and boundless, fold upon fold, dale upon dale, burnt and barren. When the wind blew, he pictured ash rising in a great grey gust across the vast wastelands of the farm, his Edenfields.

So in fact he hadn't taken the farm back, hadn't achieved what he wanted to. He couldn't raise the dead after all.

He broke the gold bottle-top seal with a quick turn of his hand and lifted the liquor to his lips. He left the gun by his side, waiting.

Then the night condensed into a black shadow, surrounded by sunlight, and the shadow took his head on to its shoulder. It was Aunt Marsha: a featureless angel etched in gold, her words distant, incomprehensible, but calm and caring. She moved forward, peered into him. He saw there – he can't remember – something soft, motherly in the spark of her eyes, a connection.

Then she shook, spun away. A shatter of glass as the emptied rum bottle smashed against rock, a shudder within him, a fall again into darkness.

Ian Holding
Unfeeling

SHORTLISTED FOR THE DYLAN THOMAS PRIZE

Davey is in the attic when the gang comes. At sixteen, he's almost the man his father wants him to be, and almost the child he was. But something from beyond the ages keeps him above, locked in shock, as beneath him his parents are murdered and his family's farm is 'reclaimed'.

The neighbouring farmers – his parents' closest friends – take him in and try to care for him, try to bring him back into their community of normality – the club, the church, and, after a few weeks, his boarding school. They look to cope, like their people have always done.

But Davey is on a different path. One night he escapes from his school and embarks on a harrowing, terrifying journey across Africa, coming home to Edenfields, looking for redemption.

'Shows us one corner of this tragic landscape with a raw intensity . . . Compels attention'
Independent

ISBN 978-1-41652-248-5
PRICE £7.99

'An evocative, compelling and ultimately moving mystery with a captivating central character'
Brian McGilloway, author of _Little Girl Lost_

'Amazing. I was hooked from the first page... A brilliant, must-read story, all the more powerful because it's told through the bewildered logic of a child. I read it with an ache in my chest for all the Lesleys and Jonesys out there'
Anna Smith, author of _Until I Find You_

'A serial-killer mystery and a whodunnit, but so much more. Tragic, gritty and haunting, yet brims with bittersweet humour and a main character who will steal your heart away'
Janice Hallett, author of _The Twyford Code_

'Conveying her intelligence and courage while still passing convincingly as that of a smart 12-year-old girl, Mylet balances the whodunnit aspects with the painful lessons Lesley is learning about life... It's a testament to the strength of Mylet's characterisation, and his ability to make us care about her, that by the end of this excellent debut the real question is not so much "Who committed the murders?" but "Where does Lesley go from here?"'
Herald

'Tense yet tender, as moving as it is gripping... Set to be one of the Scottish crime books of the year. I loved it'
Chris Brookmyre, author of *The Cut*

'An extraordinary story quite brilliantly told. Lesley is a wonderful character, and J.B. Mylet catches her voice perfectly. I found myself staying up long after lights out reading "just another chapter". And then another, and another'
James Oswald, author of *All That Lives*

'The most authentic child's voice I have read in a long time. Heart-warming, heart-breaking and utterly compelling. I could not put this beautiful book down and it stayed with me long after I finished it'
Marion Todd, author of *Old Bones Lie*

THE
HOMES

THE HOMES

J.B. MYLET

This paperback edition first published in 2023

First published in Great Britain in 2022 by
VIPER, part of Serpent's Tail,
an imprint of Profile Books Ltd
29 Cloth Fair
London
ECIA 7JQ
www.serpentstail.com

1 3 5 7 9 10 8 6 4 2

Typeset in Garamond by MacGuru Ltd
Printed and bound in Great Britain by
CPI Group (UK) Ltd, Croydon CR0 4YY

A CIP catalogue record for this book is available from the British Library.

ISBN 978 1 78816 705 5
eISBN 978 1 78283 805 0
Audio ISBN 978 1 80081 057 0

For Alice and her gran

1

'*Les!*' whispers Jonesy from her bed. 'Lesley, you awake? I cannae sleep.' This time louder.

'*You* cannae sleep? I'm the one whit's got to fight her.'

'I know, I cannae sleep, you're gonnae gub her.'

'Nuh-uh, I'm deid, I'm so deid.'

I haven't opened my eyes yet. I know if I open my eyes I will have to be awake and if I am awake it's morning, and if it's morning I'm going to have to fight her before school starts and she's twice my size.

She is Glenda McAdam. I hate her. I didn't start hating her. She's always hated me. I did nothing to make her hate me; I wasn't horrible to her, I didn't say nothing about her, but she just always hated me. I think it's because when I was in the same class as her, I was always top. She didn't like that. I'm not in the same class as her now, I've not even been in the same school as her since last August. There's one school at the Homes for most of the kids, but me and three others – one girl and two boys, all of them older than me – have to get the bus and train every morning to the grammar school.

The fight is at 7.30 a.m. My bus comes at 8 a.m. The fight is outside the front gates, where the paths meet the road into the Homes. Glenda's cottage is only fifty yards from the gate. The cottage me and Jonesy live in is on the hill and looks down towards the gate. You can see Glenda's home from ours. When I finally make myself open my eyes, I see Jonesy has her head at the window. She's watching, staring at Glenda's cottage for signs of action.

Glenda McAdam is a bully. She's my bully, but she bullies everyone else too. She's got friends, but they are only her friends because they are scared of her. I am scared of her, but I'm not willing to be her friend to avoid it.

I shouldn't have agreed to the fight, but I was the one that suggested it. Glenda's always picking on me, has done for years. So I told Jonesy I was going to fight her, and that I thought if I fought her it would make her stop picking on me. Now I think I'd rather she just continued picking on me.

'She's gonnae bust my heid, Jonesy. She could kill me.'

'She's no gonnae bust your heid. She's gonnae hit you a bit and make you say you give up, but then it will be done. And if you're lucky she'll leave you alone. Mibbie let her hit you a bit and start greetin'.'

'I'm no greetin, I'm gonnae get a knife.'

'You're no gonnae get a knife.'

'I am, too.'

'If you stab her, her brothers will get you. If you just let her win then she'll leave you alone. Pretend to try at the start, then let her win. She's gonnae win anyway, so just let her. You're making a sacrifice. It's a smart move, Lesley, and you're the smart one. Lose the fight and the big hippo will leave you alone for ever. If you're lucky, you could get in there and smash her one before she gets hold of you. Just don't let her sit on you. She's a beastie, that one; if she sits on you, you're definitely deid. I've seen her sit on her friend before and her friend went blue.'

'Can't I say sorry?'

'Nah, you can't back out now, everyone's coming. You back out now and everyone will hate you. You said fight, and if there was no fight they'll all want to fight you for denying them a fight. Those are the rules.'

'I feel sick.'

'Course you do, I would too. Still, it'll be over soon and then you'll be fine.' She looks at the clothes I laid out on my chair last night. 'Do you want to pack another school shirt?'

'Why?'

'Cos that one's gonnae get blood on it and they're no going to let you get away with that in your school.'

'Aw no, I like this shirt. I'll wear something else for the fight, a rubbish one.'

'Are you really going to do it?' comes the voice from the bunk at the end. It belongs to Shona. We share the room with her, Eldrey, Pam and Mary. Eldrey and Shona have the bunk beds at the end. Shona's bed is the one on top. She says as she's the oldest she should get it. She's the eldest by three days.

'Aye,' I say, trying to sound confident.

'She's gonnae gub yuh,' Shona says.

'Aye,' I say, fully aware of what is going to happen.

'Good luck,' she says. 'And if you can, kick her in the fanny, if you can find it on the big monster.'

Jonesy laughs.

I would laugh too if I wasn't so scared.

*

We wash our faces in the sinks and I get dressed. I wear my normal skirt but I wear my shirt from yesterday as it's going to need a wash anyway.

I wonder what Glenda McAdam is doing now. I bet she's punching the walls in preparation, eating raw eggs and getting into a pure rage.

Jonesy goes down to get some breakfast, but I go back to my bed and lie on it. I can't eat, there's no point, plus everyone else in the house is going to be staring at me, they all know about the fight. I think our houseparents, Mr and Mrs Paterson, know about it too. They are not going to stop it, either. She'll be helping Cook lay out the plates for breakfast; he'll be sat reading the paper with everyone tiptoeing around trying not to annoy him.

Jonesy comes up after her breakfast. She's brought me toast. She leaves it on the floor by my bed.

'It'll be all right, Lesley, you'll see.'

It won't. But it will be over, and all I care about is it being over. I've just got to get through it, and I don't want to greet. Not in front of Glenda or in front of anybody.

'Right,' I say, 'I'm ready.'

I don't feel ready. I'm never going to be ready for this. I feel so sick. It's time to leave the cottage. No amount of wishing is going to get me out of this. I've got to just do it.

I get up, leave our bedroom, and walk down the stairs, Jonesy following behind me. Everyone is watching. Everyone knows this fight is going to happen.

As I leave, no one says any words of encouragement. They know there's no point. They know I'm finished.

Mr and Mrs Paterson don't try to stop me. Fights are going to happen, they can't do anything to stop them, so they don't.

Is this what boys have to go through every time they have a fight? Then again, they just start fighting, they're not stupid enough to pre-arrange it and make themselves sick with worry waiting for it to happen.

I walk down the path and I'm shaking. I've never felt so ill.

I see Mr Sharples, the caretaker. He sees me, he probably knows what's going on, too. He's not going to stop it either. I can tell by the way he is looking at me that he knows I am in for a beating and is just going to let it happen.

There's twenty kids at the gate already, boys and girls together, all excited to see me get hurt, and I realise it's not just Jonesy who's followed me out of the house – all of them are here, joining the crowd. I've done nothing to them, but then sometimes anything here that's a break from the normal is what gets them excited.

People like seeing other people get hurt. Humans are cruel.

I pace back and forth by the entrance gate; if I stand still they will see me shaking. I want to cry. I am not going to cry. I want to run away. I want to be anywhere on this planet apart from here and now.

I can see Glenda McAdam's house, Cottage 8; there's people waiting outside it. I keep looking to see if she's coming.

Her brothers are waiting; her brothers are even worse than her. Her whole family is Gorbals feral, her older brothers are some of the maddest people in here, they're pure crazy.

I could get out of it by begging. As long as I'm humiliated, this can be over. But I'm tired of her, I'm tired of the grief.

'There she is,' says someone behind me, and a surge of nausea sweeps over me. I thought I was feeling sick before, but this is worse.

Glenda is coming out of her cottage. I want to run away and never come back.

'Be calm, Les,' says Jonesy.

I could charge at her? Take the fight to her, go on the attack?

But I don't, I can't. I stand on the spot, frozen.

She's coming. She's big. She's so big. And ugly. Oh, Christ.

I feel the blood rush to my face. My muscles lock up. I clench my jaw.

I keep my spot, by the gate.

The gate.

I can see her face. I can see her nostrils flaring.

She's coming.

She's saying something. She's shouting at me.

I can't hear what she's saying.

The gate!

Ready?

BANG!

Just as Glenda gets to me I grab the gate and swing it, swing it with everything I've got, and it hits her.

She goes down.

She's down and she's groaning, and I don't know what to do.

I'm standing over her.

'HIT HER!' they're shouting.

'HIT HER! KICK HER!'

I grab Glenda's hair and pull her head back, but I don't hit her. She looks stunned.

I lean down, my hands still shaking, and I say, 'Please leave me alone.'

There's blood on her head. Some runs into her eye. She's confused. 'All right,' she says.

'Promise?'

'I promise,' she says.

I let go, and then walk off towards the bus stop. There's a groan of disappointment from the crowd. The kids wanted more fighting. They wanted more pain. Some of them are following me. Someone shouts, 'Wooooo!' It's Jonesy. Others are cheering too.

Jonesy jumps on my back. I glance back and Glenda's still on the floor; her little cronies are trying to help her up.

I still feel sick. I'm still shaking. Oh God, I hope it's over now.

I start to cry. I didn't want to cry but I can't help it.

Jonesy holds me tight while I sob. Some of the others around me start patting my back. I want them to leave me alone, I just want to get on the bus. I pull away from Jonesy, then I'm sick on the grass. The kids around me are laughing. This is their entertainment for the day.

'Can you leave me alone now, please?' I ask.

'Yeah, leave her alone,' echoes Jonesy.

They do what she says.

She walks with me to the bus stop, holding my hand and squeezing it tight.

'You knew you were going to do that, didn't you? The gate. You knew all along. God, you're so clever. You lured her to that spot and then *bam*!'

I don't say anything. I don't because I don't want to lie.

I didn't have any plan for the gate. I didn't have any idea what I was going to do. It wasn't until she was stood in front of me that second that the idea came to me.

I get to the bus stop to see the bus coming down the hill.

'Hey,' Jonesy says, squeezing my hand again. 'Hey.'

I look up at her. She wipes some of the tears from my face.

'Lesley Beaton,' she says, 'you're my hero.'

2

I was put in the Homes when I was three weeks old.

The Homes is an orphans' village. It was built at the end of the last century as a place to put all the homeless children from Glasgow. There are about thirty cottages and nearly eight hundred children, and each cottage has a housemother and housefather, plus a cook. It's a self-contained place with its own school, church, shops and even a small hospital.

Us kids aren't necessarily here because our parents have died. Lots of children are like me, put here because we couldn't be raised by our families.

Some of us were taken from our parents for our own safety, as they weren't capable of looking after us. If the mother died sometimes the father couldn't raise the children on his own, and if there were no relatives to take the kids, then they would come here.

You don't get so many in here whose fathers have died, or aren't around. It seems mothers are mostly able to look after their kids, but dads aren't. But my mother couldn't care for me and she thought it would be best for me to go here when I was a baby. I don't miss her as I've never had her to miss.

She does come to see me sometimes, but never more than two or three times a year. Her mother, my gran, comes to see me more; she seems to like me. She brings me sweets and clothes and sometimes takes me out for tea.

Maybe my mother genuinely doesn't like me or maybe she is embarrassed to see me living where I do and not with her. She's never said as much but it's something I think about.

I never knew kids lived with their parents until I was six. I just thought all kids lived like us. I'd never really met kids who weren't from the Homes until I was about eight or nine on a trip to the seaside. The kids on the beach teased us until one of our boys hit one of their boys and they all ran away.

After that, I asked why I was here – I asked my gran, not my mum. Gran told me it was for the best, that my mum wasn't ready to be a mum back then and that she herself was too old to take me.

Then I tried to ask more and she just changed the subject.

3

I come back on the bus from school that afternoon still sick with nerves. Will Glenda be waiting for me, after revenge? She knows – and I know – that I got lucky, and that if she fought me again she would teach me a lesson.

As I get off the bus there's a crowd of kids by the gate. Just girls this time, though. The boys are off playing football; last year everyone was football mad because it was the World Cup, even though Scotland weren't even in it, but this year it's back to being only the boys who are interested. I don't know much about football, but I hear what the boys on the bus talk about and some of it sticks. So if a boy wants to talk to me it means I know something to say back to them.

Jonesy is on the edge of the crowd; she sees me and comes running. I think I'm in trouble and she's going to tell me something bad, but the fight between me and Glenda is old news.

'You've no seen Jane Denton, have you?' says Jonesy.

'Nuh, what's happened?'

'She's done a runner, nobody's seen her. Reckon she's gone off with a fella. She's a good-looking girl. Bet she's shacked up and getting it off some young stud, huh?'

We walk back towards the group of girls. I can see Glenda is in the group and I feel sick again, but we keep walking towards them.

'Who told you?' I ask.

'Rose in her house. Says they are proper jumpin' today in Cottage 12. Says that they've called Jane's family and they've no seen her, but they're going to put polis outside their home in case she turns up.'

As we get to the group, Rose Millar is there answering questions from everyone. The police have been to Cottage 12 and the car is parked near the front steps. They've spoken to all the girls in the cottage about Jane and about where she might have gone and if any of us knew anything.

Glenda is looking at me. I stare straight back at her; she holds my gaze for a second, maybe two, then she nods. *We are not enemies any more*, I think.

After a while Jonesy pulls me away and we walk arm in arm back to Cottage 5.

'She's gettin' a shaftin', that's all it is. She'll be back tomorrow unable to walk, the dirty one. She's going to be so embarrassed when she walks in. But who cares about her? Let's talk about you, you crazy nutter. You're the girl that done Glenda McAdam; ding dong the witch is deid, unreal.'

'Get away.'

'Get away? You're the top dog now, Lesley, I'm gonnae have to be your skivvy. But that's all right, I know I'm safe now. Don't mess with me, or my pal Les is gonnae get yous.'

She pats me on the back several times just as we are getting to Cottage 5. As we come in, Mrs Paterson, our housemother, is there. I like her. I don't know if she likes me. Sometimes she's nice to me, but other times she can be cruel. She has a pretty face. Her hair is always perfectly set every morning before we come down; I never know how she does it. It is jet black and shaped like a crash helmet that men with motorcycles wear. She has a fringe that's level as a ruler and at the back it just touches her collar. She always makes sure us girls have brushed our hair before we leave the cottage each morning. She's said before she doesn't want other houseparents to see the kids from our cottage and think, *They don't have standards in that house.*

She likes to dress smart, too; I suppose she thinks if she looks good it will make us want to look good. Jonesy doesn't really care but I try to do my best.

'Whit's going on, you two?'

'Jane Denton's done a runner, miss,' says Jonesy. 'Gone off with a fella.'

'How do you know this?' says Mrs Paterson.

'Everyone says so.'

'Well, everyone might not be right, you know.'

'Yes, miss.'

Mrs Paterson opens the door to see what's going on outside, before shutting it again.

'Right then, Jonesy, upstairs and git your hands washed, they're a mess.'

I go to go up with her, but Mrs Paterson grabs my arm. 'Not you.'

'Miss?'

She moves me round to look straight into my eyes. 'I will not have young ladies of this house fighting. Do I make myself clear?'

'Yes, miss.'

'And, Lesley ...'

'Yes, miss?'

'Well done, you.' She squeezes my arm. 'You're a brave wee girl, but don't ever do that again, you hear? Now, have you had your tea? I think Cook has left it out for you.'

I smile at her and she smiles back. She does like me. I feel warm all over and safe for the first time today.

*

In the evening all the talk is of Jane Denton. Jonesy is telling everyone just what she thinks she's getting up to while we're all stuck here. I don't know where she's learnt all this stuff, not from me. She can be quite crude when she puts her mind to it.

Everyone's buzzing about it. My fight is forgotten. It was only this morning, but it's old news. I am so tired after not sleeping last night, and not eating breakfast or hardly any dinner. I hope Jonesy doesn't keep me up tonight with her tales.

I know Jane. She used to live in our cottage a few years ago, though she's fifteen or so – three years older than me – so I've not really spoken to her since she left. She's pretty; she's got this scarf and she knows all the boys like her.

I'm not surprised she's got a boyfriend. When she walks down the pathways all the boys watch her. I wonder if she even knows they're doing it – they pretend that they haven't seen her and then as soon as she's gone past they all turn round and nudge each other.

Maybe one day the boys will do that when I walk

past. They don't at the moment. I'm not ugly, but I'm not one of the ones they go crazy for. It doesn't matter anyway as none of the boys our age are interested in girls; they're only interested in football and hitting each other, and I can't tell which one of these things they like more.

If people say anything about me when I go past it's something about being stuck up or a swot. I'm not stuck up. I might be a bit of a swot compared to them, but that's only because I like the schoolwork. They just hate me cos they hate all school, they can't understand how anyone can like it. Besides, I don't care what they think, I'm going to leave here one day, and if I can leave with qualifications, it means I have a better chance of never having to see them again.

I lie on my bed and do my homework while Jonesy, Pam, Mary and Shona look out the window. They're watching people going past, and squeaking whenever they see another police car.

Pam thinks Jane Denton will be fine, she's just 'done a runner', which is a common occurrence in the Homes. Jonesy, of course, thinks she's off with a man. Mary and Shona think she's been kidnapped. I wish they would go downstairs while I'm trying to work. I don't say anything, though, I just let them get on with it.

At lights out they are still talking about it. Mr Paterson

comes in specifically to tell them to shut up. I think of saying, 'And so say all of us,' but I don't, I just lie there in the dark thinking how much I love that gate.

4

My first memory is of falling down the steps at the Homes and cutting my arm. I must have been three or four at the time. I was running out of the cottage with some of the others when I stumbled. I put my arm out to break the fall but the speed I was going I missed getting it down on the top step so I went down the two steps and landed on my arm and shoulder.

I was wearing short sleeves so I got badly grazed and blood started to come out. I remember lying there calling for help and crying. Someone came, an adult, though I don't remember who, and they took me to the infirmary over the other side of the Homes.

Jonesy was there then. I remember her trying to hug

me as I cried, as if she was trying to squeeze the pain out of me.

Jonesy is Morag Jones. She is my best friend. She has been in my cottage as long as I can remember and always has the bed next to mine. Even when we have to move beds, which we are made to do each year, she will somehow arrange it so that within a few days we are sleeping next to each other again.

They did once try to have us permanently on different sides of the room, but Jonesy just talked non-stop, and she would talk over the other beds to me, until the people in between moved so she could be next to me.

Jonesy has always been a bit scrawny. She eats anything that comes near her, but she's built like a skinny dog, all bones and excited energy.

We are going to be friends for ever and when we leave the Homes we are going to go and live in Glasgow and get a flat and get boyfriends who will buy us nice dresses.

She sometimes gets us into trouble with her never-ending talking, and she gets the odd belt for it. She will cry and be quiet for the day afterwards, but then she will start again. You can't stop her talking. In science we have learnt about an unstoppable force and an immovable object. Jonesy's talking is an unstoppable force.

We are both twelve. She is obsessed with boys and when we will get boobs and how we can make ourselves pretty. She wants to marry a soldier when she is older. She says they get regular money and they are away a lot so she can have the place to herself. Her dream husband isn't such a dream that she wants him around all the time.

I don't know who I want to marry. I certainly don't know what job he will have, but I want him to be kind, and I want him to be smart, and have a nice suit that he will wear to take me out, and I will have a nice dress, and when we walk past people they will think, *She looks nice, I bet they have some money.*

Jonesy and I always look out for each other. The Homes is a dangerous place and you need people to look out for you, your 'team'. The adults aren't always that bothered so unless you have people who can back you up, you are in trouble.

There are a couple of little gangs that the boys are part of. I think that some of them are part of it so the other gangs can't pick them off. The older girls in our cottage look out for us, which I am grateful for, but then they can be nasty sometimes if they are bored and want someone to pick on. It's like they won't allow other people to pick on us, but they will pick on us if they want. Like we are their toys to play with.

Me and Jonesy, for ever joined at the hip. 'The Chatter Twins', Mrs Paterson calls us. We look so different, we act so different, but we are definitely twins who are lost when we are separated for too long.

Having a friend like her makes it bearable to get up in the morning. You need someone like Jonesy in a place like this. She can be a bit annoying sometimes but everything else about her more than makes up for it.

5

The next morning there's a scrambling up the stairs then the door is kicked open.

'She's deid!' comes the cry from Jonesy. 'She's deid!'

'Who's deid?' asks Shona as she jumps off her bed.

The other girls crowd round Jonesy; she's bent over panting. 'Jane ... Denton ... deid ... the woods.'

'Jesus bloody Mary and Joseph,' says Pam.

'Holy shit,' says Shona.

'Oh Jesus,' says Mary.

Eldrey says nothing. She doesn't talk much.

The room is lit up with excitement, we've never heard news so bad. I don't say anything either; I'm stunned. We all thought Jane was going to be with that fella she was supposed to be seeing.

Jonesy recovers her breath a little. 'I saw her body, there was blood everywhere, it was disgusting.'

'Where was it?'

'The woods over the back, behind Cottage 12. I was going to get the post and I heard all this shouting and screaming and some people were running away from it and others were running to it. When I got there everyone was just stood round her staring.'

'Didn't anyone try to save her?' I say.

'They couldn't, she was too deid. It was obvious she was deid, her eyes were bulging out and everything. I've never seen a deid body before, it was horrible.'

'Eurgh,' says Pam.

'Do you want to go and see it?' Jonesy asks.

'No,' says Pam.

'Yes,' say Shona and Mary.

Eldrey still says nothing.

I say, 'I dunno, it's wrong, isn't it?'

Outside we hear sirens.

Everyone looks out the window as police cars and ambulances go up the path. Kids are standing in the porches of their cottages, trying to find out what's going on.

We see Mr Gordon, the Superintendent, storm down the path to a police car. He looks so angry. Someone is going to get it really bad today.

Mr Gordon is a bastard. It's funny that so many of the children here really are bastards, but the Homes are run by another sort of bastard. Jonesy calls him the 'Bastard of the Bastards' but never when adults are around.

If you get on the wrong side of him, you are going to have a very hard time at the Homes. He likes me because I work hard, but I am still so scared of him that sometimes I think I will wee myself if he looks at me badly. I just try to keep out of his way. I've heard the stories of what he's done when he's angry; I don't know if they're true, but I don't want to find out.

He is a bald man who always wears a suit, and he constantly looks like he has been stung by a bee, but is trying not to show you how much pain he is in. It seems like his body is trying to burst out of his clothes. I don't know if he got big after he bought them or if he bought them small so it showed up his size; either way, when he is walking you get out of his way.

'Back in your houses!' he barks. 'Back in your houses or it's the belt!' Other grown-ups are issuing the same orders as they follow in his wake.

We run down the stairs and stand on the porch of Cottage 5. Mr Gordon is talking to a policeman and Jonesy is edging nearer to hear what they are saying. *You're gonnae get killed next if the Super catches you*, I think. And he does catch her. While listening to the policeman talk, he gives Jonesy a stare that could stop a tree falling.

Jonesy comes back to us and we go back into the house. Everyone is listening to her as she has all the information. She has seen the body. She describes it over and over again: the stab marks all over Jane's chest, in her neck and even her cheek.

'Her knickers were off, just sort of on one leg by her ankles,' said Jonesy.

'Why would you take your knickers off unless you were having a wee in the woods or a grown-up told you to? Why would someone stab you for that?' says Eldrey.

'You're an idiot, Eldrey. Someone's done something to her. Raped her,' says Jonesy.

'What's raping?' says Eldrey.

'It's when they stick it in you but you don't want them to.'

Eldrey looks thoughtful. No one asks any more questions.

By the time she has finished, I can see the body every time I close my eyes and all I can think of is Jane. Why would someone do that? How could they do something like that here? The woods are only three hundred yards away; the killer could have walked past our front door.

'Didn't she use to live here?' says Shona.

'Aye,' says Mary. 'Left about six years ago to go to a cottage where she had more friends.'

'You can move to be with your friends?' asks Pam.

'You have to have friends first.' Jonesy gives her a look, then carries on with more of the details. When Jonesy finally stops talking, we don't know what to do next. We are supposed to have breakfast and then go off to school. How can we go on as normal after what has just happened?

Mrs Paterson walks in and says, 'Right, you lot, I want you to have eaten your breakfast and have your school uniform on in the next fifteen minutes or there'll be trouble.'

No one moves until she says, 'Don't make me get Mr Paterson, because then you'll be in real trouble.'

Mr Paterson is not just a threat; he is the punishment. I am not sure what Mrs Paterson sees in him. He's quite grumpy, and for a man who has to work with kids he doesn't seem to like kids very much. Perhaps he thinks that it is Mrs Paterson's job to care about them, and his is just to dish out the punishments.

I wouldn't say he was handsome – Mrs Paterson is definitely the better-looking of the two – but she does like him, even if he is a little shorter than her. She never wears heels as he would look even shorter still. If you mention that he's short, you are for it. And not a one-off, you are going to get it loads. Jonesy did once and she gets it loads off him. That said, there are some girls he just takes against in here. I am usually fine unless I have done something really bad, which I rarely do.

6

Each cottage has children of all different ages, but the same sex, so as to keep us apart. Not that it always works. Some of the older girls in our cottage have come back with the remnants of the woodland floor on their backs, and everyone knows what they have been up to.

The price of ever being caught is that you take such a beating you'll think twice about doing it again.

The Patersons are quite strict houseparents compared to some of the others. When you go to other cottages their houseparents do seem kinder, but then maybe that is because we are guests and they are as strict as Mr and Mrs Paterson once we have gone.

There is also a cook for each cottage. They sometimes change, so we just call ours 'Cook'. Our cook has been with us for many years, but we still call her Cook. We get three meals a day, which is much better than many children in 'normal' families get, so we are told.

Religion is strong in the Homes, which you can tell as the names of the roads in the village are things like Patience Avenue, Holy Road and Spirit Street. The founder of the Homes is buried along with his wife in the church cemetery. He has a strange presence here. When I was very young I would often confuse the image of him and God, and to me he was like a god in that he was around us at all times, and I often had a feeling he was watching over us. There were many paintings of him in and around the village and there is a picture of him in every cottage. I wonder whether he would have wanted that. He doesn't sound like the sort of man who would appreciate pictures of himself everywhere.

There's also a lie that this is a happy place. It's not. When people come to visit – important people like mayors and politicians and famous people – we all have to pretend that everything is lots of fun and we spend our whole days smiling. All the grown-ups get scared that one of us will misbehave and tell them what it is really like. If important people think it is fun, fun, fun here, they will never do anything to make it better.

There are around twenty-five children living in Cottage 5. I think we have a good cottage. The sort of 'middle' girls live in our room. Then there's a room for the 'big' girls, who we are all a little scared of but look up to at the same time, and a larger room for the younger girls, who we can get to do what we want. Finally there are a couple of babies that we help to look after.

Some other cottages are much less nice – Glenda McAdam's, for one – and some of the boys' ones are pretty rough. Cottage 14 is bad as their housefather, Mr Roberts, really likes to dish it out. You can tell boys from that house as someone has always got a black eye or a limp.

We've got two little two-year-olds. I suppose they're not really babies, but they are in terms of the house. Everyone calls them 'the babies'. Some nights we have to help prepare the tea, sometimes we have to lay the dining-room table, sometimes we have to bathe the babies. Their names are Betsy and Alvin. They are usually quite fun to bathe, but they get really excited and you can end up soaked.

They are jolly, though, all smiles, although Betsy bites if you are not careful and Alvin can scratch, but other than that they are good fun. When we get bored we race them. Alvin wins if he's not distracted. Betsy's probably my favourite, but Jonesy likes her too and we often try to be the ones to bathe her.

Jonesy sometimes points out that there are only two

willies in the house, Alvin's and Mr Paterson's. Some-times Alvin pees in the bath. I think he does it on purpose. He looks so happy when he does it that he can't not be doing it intentionally. Jonesy once held him up and pointed him at me when he did it. She's gross.

The babies sleep down at the far end of the landing. We're lucky to be up our end as we are quite far away from them and they can really greet sometimes. I think they put them near the big girls' room so they know how much hard work little children are and don't get pregnant.

7

After breakfast I leave for the bus. I don't want to go; I want to stay to find out more news about Jane Denton. All day at school I think about nothing else. I don't really have any friends at the grammar so I don't have anyone I can talk to. I think of mentioning it to a teacher, but even though this is a good school, and not full of dafties, if they see you trying to suck up to the teacher they can give you hell for it, so I don't do or say anything.

At dinner I sit on the wall where I usually sit, wondering what is happening back at the Homes. I tend to just sit by myself at dinnertime. No one really bothers me, but then I don't really play with the others much. They all have their own groups that they keep to. I speak to them in class and sometimes when we are eating but mostly I just keep to myself.

Usually I am delighted to be away from the Homes; today I am missing it, everything is going on and I am stuck here desperate to get back.

When the bell goes, I rush to the train station and make an earlier train than usual. At the bus stop by the station I see one of the older boys who also comes from the Homes. Usually he travels with his friend, Ronnie – I have never seen him alone before, and that makes me brave. I ask him if he knows anything about Jane. It turns out I know a little more than him, so he is interested. I tell him Jane Denton used to live in our house but left when I was about six and she must have been nine. I have never spoken to him before but because of this we have a reason to talk.

His name is Daniel and he is fifteen. I've always thought him and Ronnie are super smart. I try not to bother them, and stay out of their way when we are on the bus, but this is different now; this is an emergency.

We talk on the bus on the way back and when we get off he says, 'Bye'. He's never said 'hi' or 'bye' to me in my life, but it seems normal because of the situation.

I sprint to my cottage and he to his. It has been the most exciting day the Homes has ever seen and I've missed most of it.

I get into the house and I can't see Jonesy. I rush upstairs and she isn't in our bedroom and neither are the other girls. I go down to the kitchen and Cook says they are away over near the church so I turn and run there as fast as I can.

*

When I find them, they are in a huddle by the small group of trees at the bottom of the path that leads up the hill to the church. I am out of breath when I get there.

'What do you know?' I say, panting like crazy.

But they don't seem to know any more than they did this morning, though Jonesy was happy to recite it again, that Jane Denton's body was found in the woods behind Cottage 12. She had been stabbed in the face, in the throat, the legs, the chest. Her hands and fingers were also cut, showing that she had put up a fight to protect herself.

'Whit was she doing in the woods?' I ask.

'I dinnae know?' says Jonesy, as if I have offended her.

'Just askin',' I say. 'Do they know how long she had been deid, like when she was killed?'

'I dinnae know, but the last time anyone saw her was yesterday dinnertime, so it could have been anytime between then and this morning.'

37

'Well it wouldnae have been this morning, would it?' says Shona. 'No one gets up and stabs someone before breakfast. It would have had to have been last night.'

'Why'd you say that?' says Pam.

'Cos if it was in the afternoon someone would have found her body before, right? If it'd been in the evening or at night, that's why she's been there a bit.'

'So where was she all afternoon, then?'

'I dinnae know, I'm no a psychic,' she says, as if we're blaming her.

I keep thinking of more questions but there is no one to ask. Did Jane know the person who killed her or was it a stranger? I don't know about the others, but I feel scared and at the same time excited.

We don't know where we should go. Should we go back to the cottage, or go to the woods where the body was? They have taken the body away but apparently there are police still up there. Someone said there were journalists at the front gates of the Homes trying to get kids to speak to them.

There are other groups of kids dotted around the grounds: groups of four or five, all doing the same as us and speculating. There are no boys playing football any-where. The boys always play football until they are told to come in but Jane's death seems to have stopped them.

The minister, Mr Samson, comes out of the church to

talk to Mr Sharples, who is pushing a wheelbarrow. We watch them talk for a while, then Mr Sharples leaves. We look up the hill to see what Mr Samson is going to do, whether he is going to invite us into the church to offer some words of wisdom or try to explain it to us, which he usually does if something bad happens. In the end he tells us all to go back to our cottages as standing around gossiping won't help anyone.

This isn't gossiping. Gossiping is talking about if this girl likes that boy. Someone is dead at the Homes. I don't say that, of course. He may be a man of God, but the minister is not averse to someone getting the belt. Not that he does it himself. He tells the Super or your housefather and you get it a day or two later. 'A belting from God,' Jonesy calls it. Once I came home and Jonesy was walking funny. 'Whit's wrong with you?' I said.

'Got a message from God,' she said.

'Oh aye, what's he say?'

'No talking in the pews,' she said, and pulled down her skirt to show me her red raw behind.

8

The following morning all the children in the Homes are called to the Central Hall.

The whole Homes only ever gets together once a year, for Christmas. The Central Hall is the only place big enough for us all to fit at the same time, and even there there's so many of us you can't sit down, so we all have to stand.

We get told this is happening at breakfast, and get led across to Central Hall by Mrs Paterson.

It means me and the others who go to the grammar school will be late.

Me and Jonesy walk hand in hand. 'It's about Jane, it's got to be about Jane,' she says.

'Of course it's about her,' I reply. I squeeze her hand. I feel bad again that this is exciting.

We get in the Central Hall and some of the adults are shouting, 'Wee yins at the front, big yins at the back.'

Me and Jonesy are sort of middle yins, so we pick a spot in the centre. Jonesy spots Kelly McDowell, who comes and joins us with a new girl who looks dead scraggy. Jonesy hangs out with Kelly at school as they are in the same class and she is probably her best school friend, not best house friend or best friend-friend like I am. Kelly's in Cottage 2 and the messy girl is probably from there too. I'm glad she's not in Cottage 5 as she looks like she might have fleas because she keeps scratching.

There's a lot of chat going on. Everyone is talking when Mr Gordon gets up on stage. The Superintendent says nothing, and then, in a second, the room goes quiet. He need do nothing up there. Eight hundred kids and silence, it's amazing. They are as scared of him as I am.

Jonesy squeezes my hand again and I squeeze back.

He doesn't shout, he just talks, but he talks loudly and clearly, so everyone in the hall can hear.

'Right, I am sure you are all aware of what happened yesterday. It is a sad, sad day for everyone here, and I am sure for you, and those who knew Jane closely. Our number-one aim here at the Homes is to keep you safe, to get you a good education and learn the teachings of the Lord. But keeping you safe is first, second and third on our list of things to do.

'This is our responsibility, but we also need your help. We need you to look out for each other, and we need you to tell us, and in particular to tell your houseparents, when you suspect someone may be in trouble.

'With this in mind, I have brought Eadie Schaffer to come and talk to you. Many of you may know her—'

Jonesy gives me another squeeze. 'You know her, you know her!'

'She works as a psychologist to the Homes so if any of you have any problems, she is here for you to talk to should you need it. And she wants to talk to you this morning, so be quiet while I bring her up on stage.'

There's a murmur in the hall. The Super turns to look at everyone and the murmuring stops.

Eadie comes on stage wearing a dark blue jacket and blue skirt with a cream blouse. Her hair is tied back. She's quite young to be so important.

I have to go to see her every once in a while. They like to keep track of me. They never tell me why, but Jonesy says it's because I'm freakishly clever and they have to keep an extra special eye on the freaks. I've never asked why she does it, but it's really nice to talk to her, she's super-super smart.

I go on Saturday mornings, or in the week after I get back from school. My school only does Monday to Friday. The one at the Homes has religious education on Saturday morning, so when everyone goes to that, I go and see Eadie. I can call her Eadie and she doesn't mind; actually, she says she prefers it.

We talk about anything. There's nothing I am not allowed to talk about, which is great as if there's anyone annoying me I can just complain to her for half an hour, or longer if there's no one to follow afterwards. In fact I don't even have to talk. One time I was having trouble with my homework and it was worrying me, and she said to run home and get it and we would go through it together. It was great. She is great.

'Good morning, children. Some of you may know me, some of you may not. I am the psychologist dedicated to the Homes. My job here is to help you if there is anything bothering you, particularly in relation to your thoughts or feelings. I wanted to talk to you this morning about what happened here yesterday. Now obviously what happened to Jane Denton will have been a terrible shock to you all. It was a cruel and devastating act that is very hard to come to terms with.

'Many of you will be having strange feelings that you may never have had before, feelings of loss and of sadness. This was a tragic event that happened to someone we know and where we live. What I wanted to say to you is that if you need to talk to me, or any of the houseparents, we are here to help you, all you need to do is ask. We are here to listen, and we are here to support you.

'My office is on the second floor of the hospital building, about a hundred yards up from the front entrance for those who have never been. If you want to just turn up you are welcome to do so; you may have to wait, but I *will* see you. Or you can ask your houseparents to make an appointment for you.'

'*She's so nice*,' whispers Jonesy. Others start whispering too, and the murmuring gets increasingly loud.

The Super gets back up on the stage. His face is twitching with menace, he looks at us like we are small insects that he hates, but even though he hates us it's his job to protect us, so that is what he has to do.

This time he doesn't use his powers. 'QUIET!' he calls out.

We go quiet again.

'Now remember what has been said. Keep safe, keep vigilant, and most importantly, keep together. An incident like this is terrible but it is also incredibly rare and whilst I do not wish you to be scared, I do need you to be careful. We will leave the hall two rows at a time. Mr Reynolds will let you out from the back. No pushing – I SAID, NO PUSHING.'

We wait our turn to get let out. It takes about ten minutes until we are all outside.

'So you talk to her every week? She seems amazing,' says Jonesy.

'She is. You should talk to her. You go in there, talk to her and then come out feelin' so much better.'

'Aye, I might,' she says, 'even if it is just to get out of RE.'

'I've told her all about you.'

'She knows about me?'

'Aye, of course she does, you're mah best pal so we often talk about you.'

'What does she say?'

'Nuthin', she just listens.'

'She doesn't tell you what to do?'

'Nuh, we work out what to do together.'

Jonesy and I walk back to Cottage 5. We walk in silence until Jonesy says, 'I can't get the sight of her out of my heid. Every time I close my eyes I see her body covered in blood. I'm scared, Les.'

I squeeze her and tell her it will be all right, but it's not what I think. I'm scared too, and I just want to feel safe. Why would someone kill Jane? I bet she never hurt anyone.

I say goodbye and Jonesy goes off to the school and I walk towards the bus stop to wait for the next bus.

The other three grammar school kids come and stand with me. I don't talk to them, but I do listen in to their conversation to see if they know anything that I haven't heard. Ronnie says to Daniel, 'Why did they have to kill a pretty girl? There's plenty of ugly girls round here we wouldn't have missed.'

Amanda Bell, the other girl who gets the bus, tuts. She looks at me as if to say, 'These two are idiots.' I nod in agreement, but we don't say anything – she's fourteen, so I'm usually too scared to talk to her.

When the bus comes, we all get on and sit in our separate areas. Daniel doesn't even look at me. It's like yesterday's conversation never happened.

9

I go to the grammar school in town. I go because I passed
my qualifying exam, or qualy as we call it, last year. I was
so happy to pass it I could have cried. I studied hard for
it and it was worth it. The others in my room took it too
but didn't pass. Jonesy didn't expect to pass, but she was
still happy for me.

Shona was less happy for me. The school told her she
had passed her exam, then a week later they told her
they had made a mistake and that she hadn't. She was
so angry. She blamed me for it. It wasn't my fault she
didn't pass or that they mucked up the marking but
that didn't matter to her. They wouldn't let her take the
exam again either, they said their decision was final. For

47

months she wouldn't speak to me and she tried to turn the others against me. It was awful.

In the end I was the only one in my year who did pass the exam. I knew what it would mean; I knew I would have to go to a different school, but I knew it would be a better school, for brighter kids, with fewer dafties and people who didn't want to be there.

I never told anyone, but I didn't find the exams that hard. I pretended it was impossible, as did all the others. They wouldn't like it if they knew. If anything, I like exams, I like the questions, figuring them out and getting to the answers is just the best feeling. Like when you think it's impossible, then you look at it again and it all becomes clear.

Sometimes I can't get an answer, and when that happens the question just sticks in my head. Sometimes I will be doing something totally different and the answer will pop in. It's too late by then but it's nice that my brain carries on trying to work it out while I have moved onto something else.

Going to the grammar school means I have to work a lot harder, I have more homework and I have to travel for an hour there and back. I am fine with all these things as I know why I am doing it. I am getting smarter, learning more and I'm enjoying it, though again I would never let anyone know that.

On Sundays we sometimes have religious quizzes at the Homes. Everyone has to work together as a cottage. If you get an answer right, you get a point. If you win you get lots of sweets for the cottage. I study hard for the quizzes too. I get lots of the questions right even though there are much older girls in our cottage. When we win Shona is happy enough to eat the sweets but deep down I think she still doesn't like me.

Because I go to the grammar school, my day is different to the others in my cottage. My school is ten miles away, and when I get up I am the only one who has to put on a school uniform. No one else has to, as they go to the school in the grounds.

My uniform is a white blouse with a tie that is black, red and yellow. I have to wear a grey skirt and a black blazer. It's hard wearing the uniform at the Homes as you stand out and it makes you a target for kids to shout at when you walk past.

I have to get downstairs and have my breakfast quick. My job in the morning is to make the porridge for the house, so I get in the kitchen early with Cook and get that going as soon as I can. I eat mine, then get my bag and head off to the bus stop.

The bus is a Garner's bus, cream on top with the bottom half cherry red. You can see the top cream half above the hedges as it makes its way down to our bus stop. If you miss it you might have to wait another half-hour for the next one so I always make sure I'm early.

We are the last and first stop on the bus route so when we get on there are no other people. They get on later, but when we get on it's just us four Homes kids and the driver. The driver is often the same man who will say hello to us. He doesn't say hello to other passengers, so I wonder if he feels sorry for us because of where we come from. The bus takes us to the railway station and then we get the train to town, and walk on to the school.

School finishes at 3.40 p.m., then it's train and bus back, and I get back to the Homes about 6.15. Everyone in our house eats at 5 p.m. so Cook usually puts some food aside for me. It's a long day but it's worth it and even when it's tough I am still grateful that I get to go there every day instead of the Homes school.

Jonesy can't believe some of the stuff they teach us at the grammar school. The chemistry stuff is amazing; they never teach anything like that at the Homes school. It's fascinating and you come back with your head full of facts and ideas. Maths is my favourite; I absolutely love it. If I had my way I would do maths all day every day. If I have maths homework I do it on the train as I can't wait to get home to do it. There's something so complete about it, when you get it right, you are right, and there's that feeling when you land upon the answer and you just know you've cracked it.

But more than that, there's a moment when you are doing a maths problem and you are so involved in it, and concentrating so hard, that there's nothing else in the world except the problem; no bullies at the Homes, no mum who abandoned you, no girls gossiping or saying things about you, no people judging you because you come from where you come from, just you and the problem and for a wonderful moment nothing else exists.

We are doing quadratic equations at the moment. I love algebra. When you crack the challenge there's a moment of joy that you've got it, you solved it, you beat it, but it's also followed by a moment of sadness that you are back in the real world, but that's all right because there's always another problem to solve.

10

I am in the cottage kitchen after school eating my tea, whilst Jonesy is running through her thoughts out loud.

'Why would someone kill her?' she says.

'Whit?'

'That Jane girl, why would anyone want her deid?'

'I dunno. Any number of reasons.'

'Well what are they? Come on, Les, you're the brain.'

'They hate her. They're jealous of her. They want her deid or need her deid.'

'Why would anyone need her deid?'

'I dunno, I'm just giving you possible reasons, I didn't say it was *the* reason. Mibbie she saw something she shouldn't, or mibbie she knew somethin' they didn't want people knowing about.'

'Like whit, like a spy?'

'I'm just giving examples.'

'What if the person just liked killin' people?'

'Yeah, that could be a reason.'

'Yeah, they just liked killin' people and they wanted to kill some more people, more people like us ...'

'Don't be daft, Jonesy, people don't get killed for fun.'

'What about those Montrose murders?'

The murders happened seven years ago. A man from Lanarkshire called Peter Montrose killed a lot of women, eight, they think. But they caught him and he went to Barlinnie jail, then they hanged him. Jonesy is obsessed with him. She will bring him up at any time.

'They caught him.'

'Aye, but whit if there's someone else like him, someone else going round killing girls.'

'They've no killed *girls*, they've killed *a* girl. They couldae done it for all sorts of reasons, as I've said.'

'They've only killed one girl *so far*. Even that Montrose had to start with one—'

'Jonesy, if you don't shut up I'm going upstairs to read.'

'I'll shut up.'

'Thank you.'

'Makes you think, though, doesn't it?'

'Shut it.'

*

Later in the evening we hang out at the top of the stairs to eavesdrop on the big girls. The rumour is that Jane was pregnant by the man she was seeing and that's why he killed her, so she didn't have his baby.

At this Jonesy and me share a look but don't say a thing.

At bedtime that night Jonesy whispers, 'I don't want to go to sleep, Lesley, just in case.'

'Sssshhhh!'

'Aye, you shush me, girl, but you wait.'

'Night, Jonesy.'

'Night, Les.'

Jonesy is often quite scared to go to sleep, usually because of ghost stories. We have this thing in our bedroom where we tell each other ghost stories. They don't scare me, and the reason they don't scare me is because I know they are made up, and the reason I know they are made up is because when I tell my stories I just make them up.

Shona is the other one who is good at telling stories. I enjoy hers, but I know she makes them up too, as I asked her. The other girls get genuinely scared, it's a bit pathetic, but then it is also a bit funny. Jonesy is the worst for it. It's as if the story comes out your mouth and happens straight in her brain, there is no questioning or calling it for what it is, which is a giant made-up fib. I feel sorry for her sometimes, how she takes everything so literally.

*

'Leeeessssss!' A whisper from the next bed.

'Whit?'

'You awake?'

'Naw.'

'Aye, you are.'

'So?'

'Can I come in with you?'

'Naw.'

'Why no?'

'Go to sleep.'

'I can't.'

'You can. Just shut up and it will happen.'

'I did shut up, but my head won't shut up.'

'I'm going to sleep now.'

'I bet you don't.'

'...'

'Les?'

This conversation happens about three times a week,

always after the ghost stories, and I stay silent until she goes quiet.

I have got willpower when I try, and tonight I have to really try.

11

Jonesy and I have the beds by the window as we got in the room first and called them. Once we called them, that was that. We also dived on them so they immediately became ours. Shona and Eldrey are on the far side of the room. Mary and Pam are in the middle. It has been the six of us in this room for the last two years.

Shona and Eldrey came from Cottage 11 when the houseparents left and they thought there were too many kids in there for their replacements. At first we didn't like them because we didn't know them, it had just been Pam, Mary, me and Jonesy before that, but after a while we found out they were friendly.

Out of the six of us obviously Jonesy is the chatty one, but Shona can be quite chatty and bossy too. She can be argumentative and she won't back down if she thinks she's right. If Jonesy isn't about, she's the first one to say something.

Her family situation is quite strange. Her sister and her were taken away from their family for their own safety. Apparently, the dad was very, very bad and used to beat them but also used to interfere with them. She never really talks about it, but she has once mentioned it to me. Her sister is two years older, but she didn't come here, she went to another home, which doesn't make sense. There are a lot of siblings in the Homes. I wish I had a sibling in the Homes; it would give me someone special.

Eldrey was Shona's friend from Cottage 11. She is very quiet. Jonesy and me come as a two, and so do Eldrey and Shona. Eldrey seems to follow Shona round wherever she goes. Shona bosses her about all the time. I've asked Eldrey before when we've been alone why she lets Shona talk to her like that, and she says that she doesn't mind and that Shona is a lot nicer when other people aren't around. I just think it's all a bit unfair.

Eldrey is a proper orphan. Her mum died when she was six months old and her dad tried to look after her, but when she was eighteen months he was hit by the hook from a crane at the docks and it killed him stone dead. She was with neighbours when it happened; they cared for her during the day, but that day he never came back to pick her up. Eventually someone came round in the evening to tell them what had happened.

She got some money out of it. All the dockers put in for a fund and it's being held until she is sixteen.

She got brought here at two years old and always thought, like me, that this is how kids grow up. It wasn't until a relative came to check in on her one time that they explained what had happened to her parents.

I don't know what is worse, her situation or mine. At least she had parents who wanted her, but then they were taken away. I had a mother who didn't want me, but then I have a chance to get back with her as she is still here. Eldrey has no hope of that. To make things worse, Mr Paterson doesn't like her and gets angry with her all the time; she's always getting called into his study for a beating. It's unfair as Eldrey doesn't speak enough to make most people angry. It's awful to say but occasionally you can see why Jonesy gets a belt, but Eldrey is so quiet, and after everything she's been through it seems doubly unfair.

Pam and Mary are a bit of a double act too, in fact the whole six of us get along. We say that we are quite lucky that we all get along and are in the same room. Some of the older girls in their rooms don't get on. They're always falling out and having to switch rooms as one girl doesn't like another. Mrs Paterson says we are much easier to look after than they are. She can lose her temper with them really badly when she has to, but she doesn't with us.

Pam is probably the baby of the lot of us. Although Eldrey is quiet, Pam is small, so we sometimes treat her as being younger, even though she's in the same year. She's got a bit of toughness in her; her family was from Calton and it's rough as anything around there. That's not to say that she's trouble or dangerous. I often thought they put us six together as we are not the rough ones, unlike the McAdam kids. They put them all together – the boys in Cottage 13, and the girls in Cottage 8 – and they put us nice ones all together so we wouldn't have to get caught up with them. Only problem is, sometimes it creates a bit of an 'us and them' thing but I suppose that's better than us becoming one of them.

Mary is the tall one, she's a beanpole. That's what they sometimes call her. She's as thin as a rake. Eats everything but stays really thin. It's strange as she has a younger brother in Cottage 21 and he's really short. Jonesy says it was different dads but I don't dare ask.

Mary has never said why she's here. It will be one of the five reasons: her parents are dead, dangerous, on drink, in prison; or she's unwanted/unable to be looked after. None are better or worse than the other.

Mary is quite clever. I think if she worked hard she could go to my school, but the thing is I don't think she wants to work that hard, as she hears the names I get called for going to a different school and I think she'd rather not stand out.

When Jonesy sees me getting called a swot, or stuck up, she is more likely to do something than I am, even though she has said to me that when they call me stuff it makes her feel proud because it means they can see that I'm better than them. I am not better than them, I am just different and like school more, but she seems to see it that way.

That's our room, I'm quite proud of it, we all get along, we are nice and I like them all. I am lucky, I suppose.

12

On Saturday morning I go to see Eadie. I like talking to her. I think the reason I went to her originally was down to the maths tests. We used to get a test on a Friday, either in maths or English. I was good at English but not great, but the maths tests I loved. I used to get 49 out of 50, every time, 49, 49, 49. I would always get one wrong, but then one time I got 50, then again and again. That's when they told me I should go to see Eadie.

Talking to her, you're not being judged, you can say anything to her, anything that is worrying you, any problems you have. I love the hour that I get with her every other week.

She also deals with the epileptic kids. There are two cottages for them, one for those under fifteen and the other for over fifteens. They get teased mercilessly. The house for those over fifteen is called The House that Shakes, the one for under fifteens is The Little House that Shakes. No one knows what causes epilepsy. Some people say it is the devil inside them trying to get out.

I even like the smell of Eadie's room. The hospital area smells of disinfectant all the time and I associate that smell with going to see her, but her room itself doesn't. It seems strange to say, but it smells of books. There are books all over the room, on shelves, stacked on her desk, on a chair. I don't read much other than for homework. I should read more but it's hard to with Jonesy about, talking all the time. It's almost like I'd have to find somewhere to hide to read in peace, and that wouldn't be very kind to her.

Eadie's are all serious books: psychology books, medical books. I asked her how she got into her job and what she was like at school, trying to work out how she found a way to this. She avoids talking about her personal life; when I ask about her mum and dad or if she has a husband or boyfriend she will always say, 'Now, Lesley, we are here to talk about you, not me.' This always leaves me feeling as if I don't really know her, even though after an hour with her I feel like she is the best adult I have ever met, or more accurately that she really knows me and that someone finally understands me.

That office is the one place in the world I feel safe, where I can just be myself. If I am having a bad day, if I can just hold on until I get to see her, everything will be all right.

I hope she feels the same way about me, that she likes me more than the other kids she sees, as I like her more than all the other grown-ups. I might just be another kid to her, but I never feel like that.

'How are you, Lesley?' she asks as she leans forward in her chair.

'I'm scared. Jane Denton got killed. Someone came into the village and stabbed her until she was deid. Why would someone do that?'

'We don't know Lesley. They are clearly a very bad person, but fortunately there are very few people that bad in the world.'

'Well there's one around here and I cannae sleep properly since it happened. I keep havin' bad dreams, like I am in the woods and there is someone trying to kill me and I have to get back to the cottage but I cannae because the floor of the woods is muddy and my feet keep getting stuck.'

'There, there Lesley, that's normal, that's just your brain working through something shocking.'

'I don't like it.'

'Of course you don't, that's natural. Something

shocking has happened. I haven't been sleeping well since Jane died either.'

'Will they catch whoever did it?'

'I am sure they will. This is a small village and the police are going to speak to everyone. I am sure it won't take long. Just remember, if you get scared again you always have me here to come and see, all right?'

*

Me and Jonesy sneak out of the cottage before dinner and walk fast round the back of the houses to the woods. It is now two days since Jane was killed.

Up ahead we see the roped-off area. There's a policeman standing there, hands in pockets. 'Whit are yous two doing?' he says as we walk up to the rope.

'Nothin',' I say, 'just looking at where, y'know ...'

He laughs at us. 'Oh aye, come to stare like all the others?'

'No, we're gonnae find out who did it,' blurts out Jonesy. I am stunned by this news. We didn't agree to this. 'No one is cleverer than Lesley, she'll work out what happened.'

'I'm sure she will,' the policeman says with a smile.

He doesn't let us go any further, but we can see the poor girl's blood still there. There is a lot of it. If she'd been murdered inside, they would have cleared the blood up, but you can't really clear up blood from a forest floor. It has seeped into the pine needles on the ground and looks like the remains of an old brown puddle.

'Aye, she was lying right there,' says Jonesy, pointing to the bloodstains. 'Her body was all laid out like this ... awful pale n'all.' She does an impression, flopping forward like a puppet with its strings cut.

'Do you think she lay there for long?' I ask.

'Alive or deid?'

'Both.'

'Awww, imagine that, lying there and feeling all the blood coming out of you knowing you are going to die. Do you think she screamed?'

'Aye, course she screamed. Wouldn't you scream if someone stabbed you?'

'Aye, but then why did nobody come?'

'They must have covered her mouth? Or mibbie killed her straight away with the first stab. Who d'you think done it?' I say.

'Some sick bastard, that's who. Why don't they just round up all the sick bastards and say, "Right, which one of yous did it?"'

'It dinnae work like that, Jonesy.'

'It should.'

We walk further round the rope.

'Hey! Careful where you're walking,' says the policeman.

'Awright yerself,' says Jonesy. 'Don't know why he's so chippy,' she mutters to me, 'she's deid, we cannae make it worse.'

'Evidence, Jonesy, there's evidence in there that'll tell you who done it.'

'Righto, I've had enough,' says the policeman. 'You twos, you've done your looky-looky, time to git away or I'll call someone to *take* you away.'

'Yes, sir,' says Jonesy. 'Right away, sir.'

We walk back to our cottage and sneak in the back door so the Patersons don't know that we were out.

'They really must have hurt her,' says Jonesy, as we're going up the stairs. 'See when I cut my finger, that hurts, but see how much it must hurt if someone sticks a knife in you, and again and again. Aww man that's gonnae be brutal.'

'I know. Poor girl must have suffered.'

'And she must have seen who done it cos the knife wounds were all on her front so the person has come towards her.'

'Aye you're right, like if you were running away they would have been in your back, but if they're in your front you knew them and you were fighting them.'

'Fighting them? Like another girl here? Like a square-go but one of them has a knife?'

'Mibbie?'

'Naw, if there's a square-go there's a hundred people here to watch it. First talk of it and everyone would be there.'

'Mibbie she met someone secretly?'

'Aye?'

'Or mibbie a surprise intruder, and she's tried to talk them into no doing it?'

'It's doing my heid in, Les.'

'Mine an' all.'

'Dinnae tell the other girls we were there tonight.'

'Why no?'

'Just dinnae.'

You can tell when Jonesy is thinking. It looks like her face is trying to squeeze her eyes out, they squint off into the distance. She's working through it all, she doesn't know when she's doing it but she can't stop it.

We go up to our bedroom. There's homework I have to do but I can't concentrate. In the end we lie on my bed gazing at the ceiling with Jonesy starting every sentence with the words, 'Hey, what if ...'

13

In the afternoon, Gran comes to the Homes to see me. The sun's out, so we sit on a bench in the gardens, sort of watching the boys playing football. Enough time has passed since Jane was killed for them to think it's acceptable again. Gran says she's heard the news about what happened to Jane. It hasn't been in the newspapers yet, but she'd heard from a friend who knows someone who works here, so she wanted to come and see me.

She says her first worry was that it was me. I tell her not to be so daft, no one wants to kill me. She then warns me that there are bad people in the world and that you need to keep the good people close to you and safe.

She changes the topic and starts asking me about school and how it's going. She asks what my favourite day is. It's Wednesday when I do double maths and we have started to learn French. Everyone seems to hate French, but I like it. I want Jonesy to learn French so we can talk in secret to each other in a language no one knows. They don't do languages at the Homes school, so I have been trying to teach her.

Gran has been to the village tearoom before coming to our cottage and has brought me two small cakes. I eat one right away and stick the other in my pocket for later.

She's starting to look older. She doesn't have a stick but she might need one soon as her walking is slowing and she rests her hand on things to make sure she's stable. She's sixty-two. She's worked all her life on her feet in textile factories in Paisley. She sometimes brings me scarves made out of amazing fabrics. I love them, but I have to keep them hidden in my box as folk will nick them here. The only person I show is Jonesy and we sometimes wear them when no one else is about. I would never wear them outside; people get jealous of anything they think is a bit flash.

We talk more about how I'm doing at the grammar school, but Gran keeps going back to the stuff about Jane. I tell her all about the Central Hall meeting and being late for school. I don't tell Gran that me and Jonesy went up to the woods where it happened.

Gran is good to me, but she doesn't talk about my mum

much. When I've tried to ask, she always changes the subject. Occasionally I will ask just to see if things have changed. They haven't. She always just says, 'Your mum says hi,' but I'm sure she hasn't. I'm not sure Mum always knows that Gran comes to visit, or that she comes so often.

She tells me about this film called *Dr No* that has this man from Scotland called Sean Connery in it. She says he used to be a milkman to her friend's aunt away in Edinburgh. In the film he plays a secret agent. I say it's not fair as we never get to go out of the Homes to the cinema. We get films some Sunday afternoons but they are always really old. I like seeing them, escaping for an hour or so, but what I really, really want is to go to a cinema in a town. Gran says if she can take me out one Saturday, she'll take me to the cinema and we'll see a film together. I get super-excited about this.

She says Grandad hasn't been so well. I've never met Grandad. She talks about him a lot but he's never come to see me. I've asked her to bring me a photo of him but she never does. She says he's got a cough that won't go away and it's causing him to stop working. If he's not working, he's not earning, so things are a little tough for them. She wants him to get out of the city and have a break, and says the air of the Highlands would do him the world of good. He says they can't afford it, but she is saying that he can't afford not to.

She lights up a cigarette and blows the smoke out the side of her mouth. I tell her about my chats with Eadie and she says it's nice that there's someone here looking out for me.

She writes down the phone number of her house. She tells me to keep it safe and that if I get scared I am to go to Mrs Paterson and get her to let me call her. I tell her I will keep it in my secret hiding stash, underneath the big chest of drawers. No one knows about it, not even Jonesy.

She tells me to keep safe, then gives me a big hug. When I hug her I do it too hard and she ends up blowing the smoke into my hair and coughing.

'Sorry, Gran,' I say.

'Don't ever apologise for a hug, my girl,' she says, and then off she walks to the bus stop.

I go back to the cottage to find out if there's any fresh news from Jonesy.

14

Jonesy has always been in my life. Apparently, we used to walk around hand in hand everywhere as toddlers, and while other children our age wouldn't share with each other we would always share, though not with others, we would only share between ourselves. They called us 'the twins' even though she had ginger hair and was much thinner than me. I had blonde hair at the time but it's since gone darker.

There are one or two photos of us from when we were really little but not many. In the two that I've seen we look happy together, and in both we are holding hands, but Jonesy looks as though she was up to something, even back then.

People say I'm the clever one and she's not, but that's

not strictly true, we are just different in the things we are clever in. She will see things that I would never notice; she will see socks that don't match on a girl from twenty yards, she'll notice a teacher is not wearing a wedding ring, or alcohol on a grown-up's breath. She's paying attention all the time; her mind doesn't switch off. It isn't always paying attention to what it *should* be aware of as she's too busy watching everything else, but it's never not switched on.

I really like school but it's never suited Jonesy. They used to separate us in the lessons as I would work and she would want to talk to me, then I would give in and talk. 'See her hair?' she would say, pointing at another girl. 'Never washes it, that one.' I would start laughing and then we would both be in trouble. At ten we ended up getting separated as they moved me and a few others up a year and I ended up taking my qualification exam a year early with Shona.

Her family background is a little clearer than mine but no less bad. She has a mum and dad, she must have to be born, but she's never met them. She was taken away from them in the first three months; she has been told they were 'incapable of responsibly looking after her'. She heard that her mum has tried to get her back but that they won't let her. Her mum doesn't know where Jonesy is, so she shouldn't be able to turn up here, but there's always a chance. I think her mum has been locked up before, there was a rumour about that, but in the loony bin rather than prison.

Sometimes Jonesy wonders aloud about her mum, wondering what she does for a job, what she's like, if she talks as much as she does. I've never heard her talk about her dad.

I don't know if it's better to have a family that don't want you, but which you occasionally get to see and a grandmother who likes you, or one that can't have you and never gets to see you. Neither is great. After a while you don't worry about it, you just get on with your life. I've never heard Jonesy really complain about it. I might sometimes complain but Jonesy never does, she just endlessly wonders. She doesn't even complain when she gets a thrashing. Perhaps she should wonder about the thrashings; maybe she should wonder why she gets so many.

Here's a few things to know about Jonesy:

I've never woken before her.

I've never said the last word before we go to sleep.

I've never beat her into the bathroom in the morning.

I've never seen her go a day without smiling.

She is a joy to be with. The first thing she ever does in the morning is come over to my bed to wake me. I usually tell her to get away, then I'll check the time and if I don't have to get up I'll tell her to go back to sleep. Sometimes she wakes at 4 a.m. and is ready to go; when that happens she goes back to bed and stares at the ceiling until it's acceptable for her to get up again. The other girls in our room sometimes complain, but deep down they love her – she's Jonesy. They'd miss her if she wasn't in the room.

In *The House at Pooh Corner*, there's a character called Tigger, and that is who Jonesy is, she's our Tigger, always up and raring to go, nothing gets her down.

We have to worry about her around Christmas. She's always so excited we have to be careful her head doesn't go pop. From December the first she just has this look in her eyes that we are all living in a wonderland and everything will be perfect as Christmas is nearly here.

Anyway, me and Jonesy, we are a team, we are one. Some people say to me, especially some of the teachers back when we were at school together, 'Why do you hang round with her?' They don't know her like I do, and how great she is, and, yes, she can be a bit annoying at times but I wouldn't swap her for the world.

15

Sunday morning and Jonesy and I are in church, and I can't stop thinking about dinner. I saw the joint of beef that Cook was preparing when I loaded the big stove up with coal before church. I had to scrape out the rubble and ash of the previous batch and put in fresh coal, then light it, but it was hard to concentrate after I'd seen the beef.

Cook was rubbing it with lard and throwing salt and pepper over it. Beef is my favourite roast. We get the best gravy with it; it goes over everything. I just want to lick the plate clean.

In church, Jonesy tries so hard to be good, but she just can't manage it. Jonesy is scared of God. It's usually Jonesy who will try to make *me* laugh in the wrong situation, but in church it's the other way round, it just all feels so silly. Sometimes she turns into someone with a broom handle up her bum, and it seems like she is trying really hard to behave and listen and that will be when I decide I want to make *her* laugh.

The minister holds up some bread and says, 'The body of Christ!' I rub my belly and let out a quiet, 'Hhmmm, tasty.' Then the minister holds up a goblet with wine in it and says, 'The blood of Christ!' and I say, 'Hhhmmm.'

Jonesy squeezes her eyes shut as tight as possible to stop herself laughing. Eldrey and Shona look down the pew to see what's going on. Jonesy is twitching, trying to control herself, and I'm holding my face still as an angel who would never dream of making a noise in church.

When we get out of church, Jonesy pushes me, smiling. 'You're a rotter, whit'd you do that for?'

'I'm so hungry, Jonesy, I cannae stop thinking of dinner.'

We get back to the cottage and it smells wonderful. So often I miss eating with everyone in the week, so Sunday dinner is a real treat for me. All twenty-five of us and the Patersons sit at the big table in the kitchen. Cook puts the meat on the table, and there's roast veg and roast potatoes and gravy and you can see the steam coming off it.

It's Mr Paterson's job to carve the meat, and it's like

we are a big normal family for one meal of the week, like all the other families around the country sitting down to their Sunday roast. He makes us bow our heads and says grace. I bow my head and close my eyes. Halfway through I open my right eye to see Jonesy with both eyes open, scanning the room. I shut my eye again in case she sees me, makes a face, and then I end up laughing and getting the belt.

Grace ends and Mr Paterson takes out the big carving knife and the metal thing he sharpens it on. Swish, swish he goes, five or six times. All I can think is, *Get on with it and give us our food*, but he draws it out like he knows we are craving. He then dishes up the meat, Mrs Paterson does the potatoes, Cook does the vegetables, and the plates all get passed down the table, and Cook hands out the jugs of gravy.

When we all have our plates, Mr Paterson gives us a nod and we start to eat. There is no talking as we are busy enjoying the best meal of our week. Even Jonesy shuts up for the five minutes it takes her to eat the meal.

God, I love Sunday dinner.

16

It's the following Saturday and Mum has come to the Homes. I don't know if Gran spoke to her, but she turns up when I am expecting to see Gran instead. I don't know if she has seen the news; we don't get newspapers in the Homes shops, but I see them when I go to school and back. Maybe she is worried about me. It would be nice to think she *does* worry about me; it would be nice to think she thinks of me sometimes.

Mum tends to come once every few months, probably to check that I am still alive. She looks really sad today, but then she often looks sad when she comes. It could be that she's sad all the time, or that seeing me makes her sad. Eadie said once that she may feel embarrassed that she can't bring me up herself, maybe it breaks her heart to see me. Eadie says I should try to show her compassion as Mum probably finds this hard too.

She shouldn't find it hard, she's my mother, she should find it easy. Other people's mums love them. I don't know why Mum doesn't love me.

She tells me she has been let go at her job and that she's taken to cleaning two pubs in the morning, and a doctor's place in the evening. She says she is very tired. She talks about herself pretty much, she doesn't ask much about me, other than to ask what I know about the murder. I tell her that Jonesy and I went to the place where it happened and saw the blood.

I should be grateful that she comes at all and that I've got a mum.

The conversation isn't a good one. I don't know how she is related to Gran, as Gran is so much more fun. Maybe fun skips a generation in our family; hopefully I've got it, but then I wouldn't want my kids not to be fun too.

Eventually she says she has to go and pick up Lynn.

'Who's Lynn?' I ask.

'My daught—'

'Daughter?' I say. 'You've got another daughter?'

She looks down at her feet, then up at me as if she is going to say something, then down again.

'Forget it,' she eventually says.

'No, Mum, I cannae forget it. I've got a sister? Mum,

where is she? Where does she live? Does she live here? Is she at another children's home?'

'No.'

'Well, where is she?'

She won't answer. More silence.

'Mum, can I meet her?'

'No.'

'Well, where is she?'

'At home.'

'Whose home?'

'My home.'

'Your home? But—'

She mumbles something.

'But why does she live at your home wit you? Why cannae I live at home wit you?'

'Because ...'

'Because what, Mum?'

'Just be quiet.'

We sit in silence. I look down. I am breathing hard through my nose. I don't want to break the silence, but I just can't understand ...

'Ah hate you, Mum, Ah hate you! I wish I could have had any other mum in the world as they would have been better than you!' I shout as I run back to my house.

And as I am running, I decide for certain that I am never going to speak to that woman again.

17

When I get back to the house I go straight to my bed, hide under the sheets and start crying.

The problem living where we do is that there are six of us in the room, so you are never alone and you can never cry in peace. Eldrey is lying on her front on her bed looking sore, probably thanks to another belting from Mr Paterson, but she kindly goes to get Jonesy, who comes up to see me. Mrs Paterson also comes up after a while.

I can't tell them for a long time, I just cry and cry, and then when I try to tell them what happened I start to cry again.

Eventually I tell them what Mum accidentally said. How the reason she probably never came was that she was at home with her other daughter, the one she chose to keep.

'At least you have a mum,' Jonesy says. It doesn't help.

Mrs Paterson just rubs my back while I cry. I've got snot all over the bed and in my hair so she goes to get a towel and rubs my face clean. She tells me it will be all right.

Mrs Paterson has to be strict because there are so many of us, but sometimes she will sit and listen to you and hold your hand. I say some horrible things about my mum and she lets me. I've often wondered why Mr and Mrs Paterson don't have children of their own. Maybe they can't, or maybe they think they can help more children by working here. It has to have been her idea if that's the case.

The anger passes and I start to breathe normally again. I take out a hankie and blow my nose. Every day I understand a little bit more about myself and why I am here. They should just change the name of this place from 'the Homes' to 'the Unwanted', cos that's what we are, unwanted by our families and unwanted by God.

I ask Mrs Paterson, 'If God didnae want us, why did he have us, or why did we get born to people who didn't want us?'

Mrs Paterson says, 'God wants us all, Lesley. He wants and loves us. Sometimes the path he chooses for us is obscure, but it all becomes clear in the end.'

'But what if that's too late, miss? What about Jane? What if she didn't find out her path before she died?'

'I don't know, Lesley, I can't answer for God. Would you like to speak to the minister?'

'I want to speak to Eadie.'

'I'll see what I can do,' Mrs Paterson says.

I look at her, and I think I have started to see a pattern. Mrs Paterson doesn't mention God much, it's Mr Paterson who says grace, and neither of them goes to church on the weekend, but the moment I ask a difficult question it's 'God loves us all' and 'God has his plan', like it's a giant excuse for the unexplainable.

*

I don't go down for tea. Jonesy doesn't go down either, she just stays with me and we lie together in my bed. I sometimes feel the only person I've got in this world is Jonesy. She tells me I am the only person she has really loved, other than Tim Fitzgerald who's two years older than her, brilliant at football and 'a pure dream', but that if she has to choose between the two of us she will choose me. That makes me smile for a while. Then I am sad again.

I just want my mum to explain why she didn't want me. I will ask Gran when she comes again, but I think she might be in on it too. She must know I have a sister, but then why didn't she tell me? Why are these people lying to me? Do all grown-ups lie?

Today I have gained a sister and lost a mother and probably a grandmother all in one day. Nothing has changed, but what I know now I can't un-know, and it makes me so sick. It's just so unfair.

By the time I fall asleep my head hurts with all the crying. I decide that I am never going to cry again over my mum, she isn't worth it. My tears will only be for people I love and she will never be in that category. I will never expect anything from her so she can never let me down.

18

Sunday morning and after church Jonesy suggests we go for a walk out the grounds to some fields she knows. I know she is only doing it to try to get me to not think about my mum. I appreciate it but my mind keeps drifting off to thoughts about who my sister is, what she looks like and why *she* gets to live with Mum. In church I hardly sang anything.

We walk up Faith Avenue towards the Homes entrance and there are three men by the road. They come towards us, so Jonesy and I turn right instead of the way we were going. One of them gestures to me and waves as I try to walk off.

'No, hen, no, wait.' He pulls out a notepad and a card of some kind. 'I'm a reporter with the *Glasgow Herald*. I just want to talk to you.'

'To me?' says Jonesy. 'Why do you want to talk to me?'

Quick as a swallow he changes direction and is talking to her instead.

'Well you see it's very important we find out all the information we can about the murder as it is big news.'

'It is, isn't it? We saw the body. Well, me and some other people – no Lesley here, Lesley didnae see the body, but she did come up the woods with me a couple of days after to see where the body was and there was a policeman, but there's probably clues where she was found, and—'

'Jonesy, shut it,' I say, as quietly as I can so she can hear it and he can't.

'And what is your name, hen?' asks one of the other men. They are all listening to Jonesy, which is making her happy, but I don't like the way they are writing down everything she says.

'It's Morag Jones, people call me Jonesy, but Morag Jones is my full name. Don't have a middle name, posh kids get middle names, I didnae get one, I might give myself one when I'm allowed to do that. How old do you have to be to do that? Sixteen, I would think – I'm twelve now and I live in number five. This is Lesley, she lives in five with me.'

'And what is "five"?' he asks.

'Cottage 5, it's a girls' cottage. They all have numbers. Ours is five.'

'HEY YOU!' comes a roaring voice behind us. It's the Superintendent.

'I THOUGHT I TOLD YOU TO GET TO—'

'Yes Mr Gordon, you told us to get off the grounds and that is what we did.' The reporter sounds scared. It's good to know that Mr Gordon can scare adults as much as he scares us. 'We are not on the grounds. We are outside.'

'Girls, get inside now.'

We walk as fast as we can back through the main gates without it becoming a run. We can hear the Super growling at the journalists behind us, but we daren't turn back to look.

I realise as we walk back that it's taken my mind off my mum, but also it made me realise that the murder isn't just big news at the Homes. It is big news everywhere.

*

Mrs Paterson got word to Eadie Schaffer that she needed to see me. Mrs Paterson's sometimes good like that. It's hard for her, it must be even harder for her husband, in a house with nearly thirty girls, all screeching around all the time. I think that's why he gets angry sometimes and tells everyone to shut up, but it's to be expected. If Mrs Paterson was in a house with all boys I think it would drive *her* crazy. She's said that before to explain when he does get angry. He blows his top and it's scary as anything. I would say he has favourites and girls he doesn't like, but that wouldn't be true. There's definitely ones he doesn't like and has got it in for, and the rest of us he just tolerates.

The key with Mr Paterson is to work out what annoys him – that's where Jonesy goes wrong. She has no sense of what she does that annoys him, and then she gets the belt. If you are too noisy around him, instant belt, but also if you are too meek and mild like Eldrey he doesn't seem to like that either. He also hates running in the house, but all grown-ups seem to hate that.

On Monday morning Mrs Paterson tells me that when I come back from school I should go and see Miss Schaffer and she will stay late to talk to me. At dinner-time I just read a book on my own to eat up time and distract myself. It's a good book, called *Kidnapped* by Robert Stevenson, so I think about the character Davie's troubles instead of mine.

*

When the bus home drops us off, I walk back towards Cottage 5 before realising that I should be going to the hospital building to see Eadie. She's with some other kid, so I wait outside her room. If you go to the doctor you wait your turn but you are never in there more than five minutes; with Eadie, a person can be five minutes or they can be an hour, you never know. She never rushes you and she always listens completely until you are done.

This time, I have to wait half an hour and spend the time reading my book. It means my tea will be cold, but if I am her last visitor of the day I don't have to worry about others waiting for me to leave.

It's worth it.

The smile she gives me when I come in feels so nice that I nearly start crying straight away but I don't. She must have had a good chat with Mrs Paterson, because she knows everything that has happened.

She lets me talk and talk about how unfair it is, and what a terrible person my mum is. She doesn't tell me I mustn't say that, she just lets me talk and talk. It is gone half seven by the time we are done.

When we are finished I feel so much better. I could have said nothing – just being in the room with Eadie makes me feel better – but getting it all out is a relief.

*

Back at the cottage, a bowl of thick vegetable soup and some bread have been left out for me. Cook has put it aside in the kitchen and covered it with a plate. The bread is hard and the soup is cold, with a skin on it that I use a spoon to scoop off, but it tastes good, and I drink some milk with it.

Jonesy comes down and finds me in the kitchen eating. I tell her that Eadie is so great, that she's the only adult who's ever nice to me all the time.

Jonesy says no adult has been nice to her all the time. She says she likes the ones who just don't belt her too often and that is good enough for her. We agree that kids are nicer than adults and hope that we don't become horrible people when we get older.

We talk all evening. It's getting to be summer and it's lighter for longer. When it's time to go to bed it's still light outside. We pretend to sleep for a while, then Jonesy joins me in my bed.

19

'Les?'

'Whit?'

'Leeesss?'

'Whit?'

'Leesssssssss!'

'Whit is it!?'

Jonesy is jerking her head as if her ear has been caught with a hook and is being yanked by a fisherman.

Shona and Eldrey are with us in the kitchen, and I am eating my tea after school. They turn to look at Jonesy to try to work out what she's doing. It's not hard, she wants to talk to me and she wants them not to be there, but I am tired and hungry and whatever it is can wait.

Except it can't. Jonesy is clearly going to burst if she's

not able to tell me something. She's staring at me from behind the other girls, eyes popping out of her face. Shona is in the middle of a story about a boy who spoke to her today. Me and Jonesy don't care. Eldrey will listen to anything to keep the peace, and Shona will keep talking until she's told to shut up, or there's no one there to listen to her.

There's this cruel thing the girls in the cottage sometimes do; I say the girls, but it's Jonesy, mainly. It's like a choo-choo train, and it starts off slowly, as if the train is far away. It goes, 'Dinnae-care, dinnae-care, dinnae dinnae care,' and then it gets louder: 'Dinnae-care, dinnae-care, dinnae dinnae care,' until eventually it becomes, 'DIN-NAE-CARE, DINNAE-CARE, DINNAE DINNAE CARE!' and everyone is joining in and whatever you were talking about you can't carry on with it any longer. It's cruel and unfair and Jonesy starts doing it now.

Shona knows what it is and knows what's coming so she stops her sentence, declares, 'You lot can all get stuffed,' and storms out of the kitchen. Eldrey looks at us two as if she doesn't know whether to stay or go with Shona; if she stays, she'll be lumped in with us. Jonesy solves the problem by twitching her head to imply Eldrey should get away, and she does.

So now we're left alone. I'm just finishing the last of my carrots and tatties.

'God, I thought they'd never go,' she says.

'Really?' I say with a look.

'I've got to tell you something, something big.'

'Aye.'

'No it's big, I mean big, big.'

'Aye.'

'Les, I think I might have done something bad, but it might be good. I found something, and you have to promise not to tell anyone what I found. And I mean *promise*, promise.'

'Jonesy, come on, just spit it out.'

'Promise?'

'Jonesy,' I say in my stern voice.

'All right, all right, but this is ... oh this is ... Right. You know Jane, deid Jane, stabbed Jane, stabbed deid Jane ... I found her diary.'

'Whit?'

'I did, when you were at school. Nobody knows I've got it. I found it – well, retrieved it.'

She's right, this is big; this is enormous. Ordinarily I would say, 'You're lying,' but I know Jonesy better than anyone and I know when she's lying, and the pure excitement in her eyes means there's only one answer.

'Where did you find it?'

'Well, you know how I'm friends with Brenda who's in Jane's cottage? She took me to Jane's room to show me

95

it, like where she slept and everything. The polis have all been in there and been through everything, her box and all. But like, where do you keep stuff that is top-top secret that you don't want anyone to find ever?'

'In my box and locked.'

'No, the secret stuff, the stuff you don't want anyone to find.'

'I don't know what you're talking about.'

'Les, quit messing, I know where you keep your stash. You hide it under the chest of drawers and wedged in the corner.'

'How did you know about that?'

'I'm no as daft as you lot think I am. So I thought, if that's where Les hides things, I wonder if Jane does the same? So when Brenda goes out the room I lie on the floor and reach underneath just to see if anything's there, and it's like the pools coupons times a hundred – jackpot! She's only got this tiny wee diary. Small, like the size of your hand.'

'Well, where is it?'

'I put it with your stash. When the girls are out the room we can go get it. I need your help, though; it disnae make sense, all weird letters and stuff.'

*

'Beat it.'

'*I want to use the lavvy*,' comes the shout from the other side of the door.

'I said beat it.'

They leave, but then there's a louder banging on the door from Mrs Paterson. 'Whit's going on in there?'

'Just doing our teeth, miss,' says Jonesy. We were smart in that we'd brought our toothbrushes into the bathroom so we would have an excuse if anyone caught us.

'Well get out now, you've been in there long enough,' she says.

There's not a lot we can do but come out, first making sure our toothbrushes are wet in case she checks. We go back to our room.

'Whit were you two doing?' Shona asks.

'None of your business,' says Jonesy.

We're not going to get a chance to look at the diary tonight as the lights go out soon and we've not got torches. Jonesy hops straight into my bed and whispers, 'Whit we gonnae do?'

'Wait till tomorrow.'

'I cannae wait that long.'

'You're gonnae have to.'

'But Les—'

'Shut it.'

'Les—'

'Shut!'

That night is one of the longest in my life. Night of a thousand twitches. Like sleeping next to a puppy with the hiccups.

20

Jonesy is waiting for me when I get off the bus in the evening. She tells me that she tried to read the diary on her own at dinnertime.

'Les, I still couldn't make any sense of it. It's full of initials.'

'You've read it all?'

'The lot. I don't understand it. Are you going to get your tea?'

'Naw, let's go somewhere and read it.'

We scurry to the nearest bench, me carrying my schoolbag and her carrying the diary inside her top so no one can see. We sit down and she shows me. The pages are very small and the writing is cramped. It's in pencil and you can see bits have been rubbed out. But the paper is thin and sometimes the writing has gone through it. Not every day is written on; it seems to be a mixture of the mundane and exciting.

15 March
Met T aft schl by gym. Said I diff frm oth grls. Kssd, nrly sn.

19 March
Grls tkng abt me. Thy nd 2 kp mth sht

22 March
T ddnt lk at me at all tdy, think smth wrng

25 March
T kssd me gnst wll.

'What do you think it means, Les?'

'Well, the first one looks like it says, "Met T after school by the gym. He said I was different from the other girls. We kissed, nearly seen."'

'God, I know that, Les, that's obvious, I'm no an eejit. What I meant was, who is T?'

'I don't know.'

'Well how do we find out?'

I read some more. Lots of mentions of T. Jane seemed

to like T more and more. But after the 8th of May there's nothing. The last entry says '*mtg T tmrw, gttg thgs strt*' and that's it, her life over. It's hard seeing her life no longer on paper.

A life that stopped when she had so many empty pages to be filled. I feel a sadness for Jane Denton that I didn't the day she died. Then, it was just shock; I didn't know her well so I didn't feel sad, just scared. Now, seeing the life she had taken away, I feel the loss.

Jonesy and I try to guess who T might be, who we know with that initial. Maybe it stands for something else. Maybe it's a code?

I tell Jonesy this but then say that I don't think Jane was the sort of girl who would have used a cipher. I have to explain what a cipher is. Once Jonesy gets her head round it, she agrees that it doesn't sound like Jane.

My mind is racing. We go back to the cottage and spend the rest of the evening trying out our theories on one another.

'So who is T?' says Jonesy for the tenth time.

'Dunno, but it's got to be one of the boys or men at the Homes. She definitely likes T but mibbie T forces her to do somethin' and she fights back and T kills her. Or what if T sees her with another boy and kills her? Or, or she doesnae like T any more and splits with him and *then* he kills her?'

'It's got to be one of them. Jealous as hell, I reckon, jealous and he's gone, like, "If I can't have you no one can," and he's killed her cos he cannae handle her with anyone else. But who is it?'

'Well they're gonnae be older than her, right? She's no going to be going with a boy younger than her, is she?'

'Who's her housefather?'

'Mr Calder? The fella's a cripple, he's got arthritis up to his eyeballs. Has to use a stick. *I* could take him.'

'Les, if you can take Glenda McAdam, you can take anyone. Could be you, Les? Did you go in one of your rages? Has your new power gone to your heid?'

'Get off, will you? This is serious. Who do we know whose name starts with a T? Tim Fitzgerald?'

'My Tim?' She snorts. 'Naw, no my Tim, he's too nice, wouldnae be him. Besides, he's fourteen and Jane was fifteen, there's no way she'd be going with him, girls that good-looking don't go with boys younger than them.'

'Tommy McAdam, Glenda's brother? He's her age.'

'Aye, he's a wild one, proper daftie.'

'Right, so Tommy McAdam. There's got to be more Ts.'

'We talkin' first names or surnames?'

'I dunno.'

'Cos probably dozens of kids in the village have got Ts for surnames.'

'Ah, Jonesy, I dunno.'

This goes on for another hour and by the end we have a list of twelve boys of the right age with first names that start with T and fourteen with surnames that start with T. But no one who we think Jane Denton would have wanted to kiss.

21

'Your dog's here,' says Amanda as we get off the bus together.

'Hey?'

'Your dog – your wee pal. She waits for you by the gate wagging her tail. I've seen her do it before.' She's nodding towards Jonesy, waiting at the front gate again, and shouts, 'You wait for her like a wee doggy waiting for its master, don't you?'

'Shut it, curly.'

'Dinnae tell me to shut it, little thing, I'll batter ye.'

'You will not.'

'Jonesy, stop it,' I say.

'Aye, good dog, sit,' says Amanda, staring at Jonesy as she walks off to her cottage.

'Whit you doing talking to her?'

'She's nice.'

'She's a spod.'

'She's no.'

'Aye she is, but it disnae matter, more important things, Lesley, more important things. I have a question for you. It's a simple question. Are you ready for your question?'

'Aye ...'

'Lesley, am I or am I not a genius?'

'I suspect the answer might be that you are, in fact, a genius.'

'Correct, well done. Now, for an extra point, would you like to know why I am a genius?'

'Yes, Morag Jones, I would very much like to know why you are a genius.'

She's started skipping with excitement. 'What lesson did I have today?'

'No idea.'

'Geography, I had geography. And who did I have it with?'

'Everyone else in your class?'

'Incorrect. Well, correct, but that's not the right answer.'

'So ...'

'Mr Taylor. Better known as the Gorgeous Mr Taylor.'

'And ... are you in love again?'

'Again? I was never not in love with him but I wasnae the only one – and I know something you don't.'

I don't answer or prod her. I wait for her to do it herself.

'Wanna know?'

'Of course I wanna know. Just get on with telling me.'

'T. T in Jane's diary. She's only been going with the teacher!'

'Naw.'

'Aye.'

'Naaaw.'

'Ayyyyyye, I'm telling you. It's got to be T that Jane would be kissing round the back of the school.'

'But it could be anyone.'

'It could, but it isnae. C'mon Les, we went through every boy with the initial T and couldn't think of any that Jane Denton would kiss. Him – she would definitely kiss.'

'Aawwww Jesus, Jonesy, what if you're right?'

'I am right and I've been waiting all day to tell you.'

We've just about got to the cottage by this time, and I stop her. 'Whit do we do now?'

'I don't know. We could tell him we know it's him?'

'No ... no, we tell the polis.'

'How? How do we do that?'

We go inside. Cook has left out a piece and ham for me. I eat it while Jonesy continues to yabber. I don't listen as I am concentrating on my thoughts.

When she's done with her talking and I'm done with my eating I tell her, 'There's four people we can tell: the polis, Mr Gordon the Superintendent, and Mr and Mrs Paterson.'

'I'm no telling the Super, and we don't know anyone at the polis to tell. Let's go for the Patersons. But how do we tell them about the diary, that I took it?'

'Christ, I didnae think about that. Forget the Patersons. What about telling the polis anonymously?'

'Whit's anonymously?'

'When you send something but you don't tell them who you are.'

'Like a letter without writing your name?'

'Exactly. Let's write a letter and send it to the polis to tell them that Mr Taylor was going with Jane and he probably killed her.'

'He couldn't have done it, though.'

'Why not?'

'He's too beautiful. Nobody that beautiful could do a thing like that.'

'He is beautiful, isn't he? Doesn't mean he didnae do it.'

'It disnae seem fair. They'll have to send a beautiful

man to prison. Why couldn't it be an ugly man? That way you get rid of a killer and an ugly person at the same time.'

'You're terrible, Jonesy. I hope you never become a judge.'

'Yes you do, you'll want friends like me in high places one day.'

22

'She's here again,' says Amanda as we get off the school bus.

Jonesy ignores her, comes rushing up and grabs my arm and walks me, firm and fast, into the Homes.

'They came, Les, the polis came and they took Mr Taylor away. They came this afternoon. Everyone saw it, EVERYONE. We saw them take him in the car and drive him away.'

'Christ, Jonesy. Did we do the right thing?'

'Of course we did. He was going with her, she probably wanted to end it or tell someone which means he's in trouble, so he's killed her.'

'But did he? All we know is he was going with her. Doesn't mean he killed her.'

'That's for the polis. We just poked them in the right direction with your letter.'

'My letter? It was *our* letter. We both decided to do it.'

'Aye, of course, I just meant you wrote it and posted it. That's got to be why, yeah?'

'Aye, definitely. Why else would they have been here?'

'They could have worked it out for themselves.'

'Nah, they didnae have the diary.'

'What did he look like when they took him away?'

'Like he was gonnae cry. He wouldn't look at anyone, just stared at the ground. He didnae seem like him, like he wisnae gorgeous like usual.'

'Jonesy, it's hard to be gorgeous when they're putting you in a polis car.'

'Aye, but you know what I mean; it looked like him but it didnae.'

'You haven't told anyone about the diary and the letter have ye?'

'No, no, no, cross my heart and hope to die. I widnae do that. You can trust me.'

'I know I can, Jonesy, I just know you get excited sometimes.'

'Nah, I've got this, hen. You and me, putting bad and beautiful men in jail.'

I laughed at this.

'We should write a book, Les – *The Bad and the*

Beautiful, about this gang of men who are like unbeliev-
ably beautiful, but they are also secret killers and they
go around the world seducing women and killing their
husbands.'

'You're nuts, Jonesy.'

'I'm a genius, Les, people just don't know it yet.'

23

Another girl has gone missing.

It's been more than two weeks since Jane Denton was killed and now Sally Ward has disappeared. She's not been seen since after school on Friday. That's twenty-four hours and the adults are going crazy. Some of the kids are saying that she was a friend of Jane's, though some say that's not true, and no one really knows what to think.

Earlier today I saw the Superintendent marching across the grounds. Mr Gordon always looks angry, but this time he looked like he was going to kill someone himself.

Mr Paterson is suddenly being protective of us for a change. Just before we sit down to eat, he sticks out his chin and says no one is allowed out of the house after tea, even if we have finished our chores, and that there is going to be a curfew from now on. Other than going to school and back, if we leave the house we must get permission from him or Mrs Paterson.

Sally Ward is fourteen or fifteen, just like Jane Denton was. I don't think there are any rumours of boys. I have never heard of her; she's not one of the ones we know. She's not from a cottage near ours – I think she's in 29 over the other side of the village – and she's probably not pretty. You tend to know who the pretty ones are, and you tend to know the people in the cottages around yours as we are in and out of each other's.

Everyone is so excited at tea. I'm not sure I mean excited, maybe agitated, even more so than when Jane went missing. We are all talking at the same time and the noise is really loud. After saying those things about us being safe Mr Paterson gets angry and starts shouting over us to make himself heard. He tells us we all have to eat in silence and anyone who speaks will be sent to bed without any food.

So we are silent. Jonesy can't bear that; she keeps pulling a face at me. Mr Paterson sees her and makes her stand outside and wait until everyone has finished their tea before she is allowed back in to eat on her own. She hadn't spoken so he couldn't send her to her room.

Jonesy doesn't care, which is her problem. She never cares when she's told off. I don't know how she does it. I hate it when they shout at me.

When we get back to our bedroom all the girls are round Jonesy's bed as she tells them that if Sally is dead too, then that means there's a mass murderer on the loose killing girls at the Homes and we could be next.

'It's like you said, Jonesy, it's like the Montrose murderer, isn't it?' I say.

'Exactly,' said Jonesy. 'He's out killing and raping again.'

'What, you think he's escaped?' says Mary.

'No, I told you, he cannae have escaped cos they hanged him in Barlinnie,' I say.

'What if they hanged the wrong fella?' says Jonesy.

'Naw, they hanged the right fella. No more murders once he was hanged.'

'Aye, until now, that is. Mibbie it was someone else and they've just been lying low. And why do they always want to kill young girls? Can't they kill old men or something, or is it more fun for them to kill kids like us?'

'Whit's going on?' says Mrs Paterson, entering the room.

'Why do they always wanna kill young girls?' Jonesy asks her.

'What on earth are yous talking about?'

'There's a killer on the loose and they are killing young girls.'

Mrs Paterson rubs her face, then fixes Jonesy with a look. 'One unfortunate girl was killed, that's true. But today's event is different. A girl has gone missing – it's happened before; it will happen again. Sally will turn up and you'll see what nonsense you're talking. Now, lights out and go to bed. And if there's any more chat there'll be no film tomorrow.'

A collective cry of 'MIIIISSSSS!' goes up at the threat.

She turns the light out and I know Jonesy is going to say something. I know it.

But she doesn't, she doesn't say anything. For a whole two minutes, and then she says, 'Well, she would say that, wouldn't she? She's just jealous that they dinnae want to kill and rape her because she's too old.'

I lie there shaking my head in the dark.

24

The police have brought sniffer dogs in. They did it while we were all at school so they thought we wouldn't notice, but there are always kids about, and kids always notice.

Dogs' noses are supposed to be a thousand times more powerful than human noses, so they can find where you've been by the smell. The dog handlers got some of Sally Ward's clothes, rubbed them in the dogs' faces and let them try to find her. The dogs went crazy apparently. Ran everywhere but found nothing.

Mrs Paterson watched it from the front of the cottage. She was the one telling us not to gossip, and now she is the one telling us what happened.

*

At breakfast the next day, Mrs Paterson taps her glass with a knife and everyone goes quiet.

'I want everyone's attention, please. Quiet, quiet. I need to talk to you young ladies and I need you to pay close attention.

'You're aware that there was a tragedy with Jane Denton, and it was very, very shocking and very, very sad. Now Sally Ward has gone missing, which is again very sad. We don't know whit's happened to her, and speculation doesn't really help the situation, but the polis are worried so we should be worried.

'What I am saying is delicate. I don't want you to be scared, but I do want you to be careful; I want you to be extra careful. As you know, you are to come home straight after school, and from now on I would like you to travel everywhere in pairs.'

'Is Sally deid?' asks Jonesy.

'Morag, what did I just say about speculating? It doesnae help. The polis are worried that she is, aye. We just don't know. But I do know this: life is in many ways harder for us ladies. Sometimes people – men – target young women. This could happen to you at some point, and you need to be careful. Keep your wits about you, keep an eye out for each other. Life isnae fair for a young woman, and you need to be aware of that. Don't be naive, don't be complacent. Be alert and have each other's backs; there is a thing called the sisterhood that we all belong to.'

I look around to see if Mr Paterson is there as I am worried that Jonesy will point out that he isn't part of the sisterhood. He isn't there; maybe Mrs Paterson asked him not to be so she could say this.

'I'm just sayin', be careful out there. Out there,' she says, pointing at the door, 'and in the world.'

A tear rolls down her nose.

'Now, let's pray. Heavenly Father, thank you for the food you put before us, and thank you for our health. Please look over us and protect us and keep us in your heart, as you are in ours. Amen.'

'Amen,' we all say.

'Let's eat.'

And we do, in silence. I don't want to break it by talking, and it seems like neither does anyone else.

25

After breakfast I go get my bus. We don't have to be in till ten thirty today as they are showing around the new students for August's intake. Perhaps they don't want us students about to scare them too much. I was so scared when I first went to the grammar school, but I needn't have been; the pupils are much less dangerous than the kids in the Homes.

On the bus, we all discuss what we know about what's happened. I usually sit near Amanda but not near enough to talk. As there are only four of us, we get a double seat each.

Daniel and Ronnie tend to sit at the back and Amanda tends to sit in the middle, although sometimes with them. I did sit at the front on my own but have recently started moving backwards nearer to them. This time all four of us sit near each other in the middle; after Jane's death and the news about Sally it has meant a break in the established social rules.

It's strange that normally we don't usually travel together as a group. We all go from the same place to the same place, at the same time, on the same buses and trains, yet I wouldn't say we travelled together. Today we do.

Ronnie, who is tall and skinny and has a lot of spots on his face, says that he's heard it was a minister who took Sally because she was impure, as a warning to all other girls. Daniel says he thinks it might have been a werewolf. He is just trying to scare us; he's too smart to believe in werewolves. Amanda says that she has spoken to Sally before – she knows a girl in her cottage a bit. She's been over to Cottage 29 since Sally disappeared and the atmosphere in there is Baltic – all the girls were all crying and are convinced she's dead. They think she had a boyfriend as she had been sneaking out in the weeks before, but no one knew who it was.

None of us really know Sally. We all think she must have been killed, too, like Jane was.

At the grammar school we are the centre of attention; now Sally's gone missing, the newspapers have gone crazy again and all the children want to know what's going on at the Homes. Sometimes they tease us about having no parents and living in the Homes, and are snooty about us, but today we are the most important people at the school. Had I seen anyone suspicious hanging around? Who do I think did it? Are there many policemen about searching for Sally?

Even a teacher asks me what's happening. I tell her what I know, but not that Jonesy saw Jane's body when she had been killed, nor that we went to look in the woods where she was found. As for Sally, I just say that people run away sometimes, but obviously they think she's been murdered too. I feel bad guessing about what's happened but that is all everyone's doing, we know so little – especially why it's happened.

By the end of the school day I am so tired of talking and saying the same things. On the train and bus none of us says anything, we all just stare out of the windows at the fields as they go past.

26

Gran is waiting for me when I get off the bus. Usually you are only supposed to have visitors at weekends, so she must have got special permission, or she didn't ask and just turned up.

I had managed to forget Mum for a bit.

The tearoom is shut so we go and have a seat on a bench. Gran tells me the truth about my mum. She had wanted to tell me before, but Mum had forbidden her from speaking to me about it.

I have two sisters and a brother. The girls are six and four and the boy is two. She tells me their names but it is too quick for me to remember them. I think one was Ann or Annie.

She then explains everything to me. Everything. She

tells me who my dad is. Not his name, but where he was from and what his job was. He was from Donegal, in Ireland. Mum was a young shop worker, nineteen, when she met him. She only went out with him a couple of times but that second time she got pregnant and he disappeared shortly after, presumably back to Ireland. She knew his name and where he was from but nothing more.

Mum had me, but she was on her own, and they all decided that the best thing to do was to put me into care. They heard about the Homes and agreed it would be a good place for me. She gave me up at three weeks old and Gran said Mum became ever so sad; for long afterwards she wouldn't speak to anyone.

Eventually she met a man and they got married and had a baby girl. Gran says that Mum's intention was to bring me back into the family once she had a family of her own, and that's what she still wants to do, but the time isn't right as the children are so young and I am doing well here.

She also says that the reason Mum is how she is when she comes to visit me is that she finds it very hard, as she wants me back, but she can never tell me that as she doesn't want to get my hopes up in case she can't make it happen.

I don't cry. I want to cry again but I don't. But it is

nice to hear Gran say that Mum actually does want me back.

It's good of Gran to finally explain things; she says she feels I am old enough to know the facts. She says that she had thought I was old enough to know for a while now, but she didn't want to go behind Mum's back. But after the last time I saw Mum, she told Gran that it was time to tell me the truth.

Gran says it is a huge relief to finally be able to tell me and she says how sorry she is not to have been able to speak about it before and that she hated having to keep it from me.

She is such a nice lady, my gran. She has a kind face, and her eyes are warm and caring. When I fell out with Mum my only worry was that I wouldn't get to see Gran again.

I think you can tell that she is my gran. She looks a little like me even though she is much, much older and her face has more lines on it. Jonesy has met her and she says I look like her. Actually, she says I would look like her if I had been in the bath too long.

Gran asks me about Jane's murder, whether I've heard anything. She didn't know about Sally Ward going missing and that she is still missing. It's been four days now. She's got to be dead; everyone is assuming she's dead. Someone would have seen her by now if she wasn't. Gran is horrified at the thought of it. I tell her about Mrs Paterson's speech at breakfast and about her saying that life is much harder for women than for men.

When I say this, Gran looks at me for a long time. I think she is trying to work out how to reply.

Eventually she says, 'Life is different for women. It's not necessarily worse, just different.'

She pauses. 'No, it is sometimes worse, but only in some ways. Some ways it is definitely worse to be a woman, there is no doubt about that, but in other ways it is better, and I think that when you are a woman it will be a better time to be a woman than it has ever been before. But it is never easy, and it is often hard.'

'Was it hard for you, Gran?' I ask.

'Yes, Lesley, it was hard for me, but life is hard for all of us. There's no getting away from it.'

'What about for film stars?' I ask.

'It's hard for them, too. Just because they're famous doesn't make their life perfect.'

'So what should I do, Gran?'

'Just be you, my girl, and if you stick to being you, I am sure you'll be fine.'

I don't know what she means by that, but it seems nice and I feel good when she says it.

I tell her a little more about Eadie and she is happy that I have someone like her here for me. Then she has to go. Her bus is coming soon and she has to get home.

'Is your husband a good man?' I ask before she leaves.

'Who, Francis?' she says, then breaks into a smile. 'Yes, he is a good man; he's not perfect, but then no one is, and I think I made the right choice in marrying him. I'll tell you all about it one day.'

With that, she gives me a big hug.

She waves goodbye and I go back to the cottage with too many thoughts chasing each other round my head.

27

Jonesy has got in trouble. I worry as she can't help getting into trouble sometimes. She tries really hard to stay away from it, but then she will find some way despite herself to slip up.

I've tried to help her but you can't. She's a good person, there's not an ounce of nastiness in her. I worry that there's a part of her that can't help pulling her in the wrong direction, even if she wants to go the other way. I don't get in trouble that often, and when we are together it doesn't happen that much because if I can stop her I will.

She got caught with a bag of sweets. Got a dozen off the belt.

It wasn't her who stole them. She was given them.

The Homes has a general store to buy things from. It sells supplies for the cottages like food and milk and we regularly get sent there by Cook to get her things. It also has sweets we can buy, as we get a small amount of pocket money each week, plus I occasionally have money from Gran. She is not supposed to give me money as some children don't have grans or visitors so it's unfair, but many times after she has visited I will find some coins in my pocket that she has slipped in when I wasn't looking.

Some of the older boys worked out a way to get into the shop when it was closed. They climbed up a pipe, stepped onto a ledge and got in through one of the back windows. They were going in every night for the last week; they waited until lights out, sneaked out of their cottages then climbed in and took some sweets. They were clever about it; they only took a few so that the adults wouldn't notice. If they had taken all the sweets in one go an adult would have figured it out straight away.

It was the McAdam brothers who did it – well, definitely one of the McAdams was involved. They are in Cottage 13, or unlucky-for-all if you live with them. It's away over the other side of the Homes. They have another sister besides Glenda, Angela, who is in Jonesy's class; she's less big and less crazy than the rest of them. She gave Jonesy some of her share of the sweets, as they are sometimes friends, so it's not even like she stole them herself.

Eventually someone realised that kids had been stealing from the shop so the houseparents were told to search everyone's bags after school and anyone with more than two sweets was going to get the belt.

Jonesy had far more than two sweets. It was obvious. Mr Paterson gave her a dozen.

When I come home from school she is crying in our bedroom. She tells me what a bastard she thinks Mr Paterson is and how he really whacked her. She shows me her bum and it's beaming red. There is blood in two parts. Jonesy never really swears, none of us girls do, but she's right, he's a real bastard when he's got that belt.

Jonesy's lying on the bed on her front so she doesn't have to sit down. She says she thinks Mr Paterson enjoys doing it. Mrs Paterson could have done it, but she didn't.

I often think he hates us littler ones, especially Jonesy and Eldrey. Perhaps that's why the Patersons never had kids, as they can't handle them. He can deal with them when they are bigger; maybe they are not as annoying then. Mrs Paterson doesn't like the bigger ones and their 'teenage drama', as she calls it.

I know what Jonesy is talking about. He's used the belt on me before. I got back from school late for tea. It wasn't even my fault; the bus had broken down. We had to wait by the side of the road for an hour for another bus to come.

I had chores I was supposed to do that day, to help with the washing, and I missed them. When I got in the kitchen he just said, 'Beaton – THREE.' That means you are getting three lashes with the belt. He then wrote it down in his notebook. He writes it down like a to-do list of who needs to get them and how many. He will either do it on a Saturday all at once, or if it's really serious, like it was with Jonesy today, he calls you into his study and does it straight away.

I had to wait three days until the Saturday. I tried to tell him that it wasn't my fault, but he didn't want excuses. He said if he let me off then it wasn't fair on others, which means he *did* know it wasn't my fault and he was going to do it anyway.

I told Mrs Paterson and she said not to complain about her husband and that it's harder than you think to keep the house in line, so just accept it. I did accept it, I didn't complain, doesn't mean it wasn't wrong. He didn't even give me light stripes, but big whacks, ONE-TWO-THREE.

I can't bear to think how bad twelve must hurt.

Jonesy's face changes. 'I'm gonnae get him one day,' she says. 'I'm gonnae get him and then he'll be sorry. I don't know how, but I'm gonnae get him back.'

Sometimes her face gets so serious that she looks crazy. When she goes like that there's nothing you can do but agree with her. I've tried arguing before but if her face is like that there's nothing that's going to get to her.

'Aye, sure you will,' I say, nodding.

'You don't understand, Les. If I says I'm gonnae do it, I'm gonnae do it.'

Shona and Eldrey come into the room. They see Jonesy with her bum in the air lying over the bed and they can see she's been crying. They had been talking on their way in but as soon as they see her they go quiet.

Then Eldrey says, 'Belt?'

'Uh huh.'

'Whit for?'

'Sweets.'

'From the shop?'

'Uh huh.'

'The stolen ones?'

'Uh huh.'

'Angela McAdam got it too.'

'How d'you know?'

'Moira Campbell told us.'

Moira Campbell is in Angela's cottage.

'Aye, she got ten,' says Eldrey.

'Ten?' asks Jonesy. 'But I got twelve.'

'Aye, but no off the Superintendent ye didnae.'

Jonesy's right, Mr Paterson's a bastard. The Superintendent is a bastard and he's a bastard. Mr Paterson *can* be nice to you, though he tries his hardest not to be. Mr Gordon isn't nice to anyone ever; I don't think there's a nice bone in his body.

Jonesy lets out an 'oooooffff' sound and she starts to smile. Which makes me, Shona and Eldrey smile.

That might be the one lesson I've learnt in the Homes; no matter how bad it gets, there's probably someone getting it worse.

28

They've found Sally Ward.

She's dead.

Two boys found her in a river about two miles from the Homes. She was wearing a summer dress. The boys had been fishing when they spotted her, tangled up in the reeds and lifeless.

Mr Paterson announces this news at breakfast. I know something is up as he held me back from leaving for school at my usual time and told me to get a later bus. We are all eating and he's been standing by the door waiting for everyone to come in before he taps an egg cup with a spoon to get us to be quiet. We know it is something bad. He only ever does something like this if it's bad news.

His head is bowed and his voice is shaking when he starts talking. I've never seen him so upset. 'I'm sorry to have to tell you all this, but Sally Ward's body has been found by the river. It was found yesterday afternoon and it appears that she may – and I repeat *may* – have been murdered. The police will have to confirm this.'

There is a big intake of breath. Even though that's what we had thought had happened, we still get a big shock that she is actually dead.

Jonesy says something like, 'Oh God.' I can't say anything. I feel dizzy. I didn't know the girl, but for a moment I think I might vomit on the floor.

Mr Paterson then says, 'Now, obviously this is a very disturbing thing to happen; we wanted you to know the facts before any rumours start. We are going to keep the curfew in place. Don't be afraid, but be careful.'

There is more silence. No one wants to be the first person to start talking, and no one wants to be the person to start eating or pick up their cutlery. How can you have breakfast when you have just heard something like that? We all sit trying to work out what to do next.

Eventually Mrs Paterson breaks the silence. 'Eat up,' she says. 'This is terrible news, but you've all got to have breakfast or you won't make it through the day. Come on, now.'

We slowly begin to eat, and kids start speaking, but

only in a whisper. Most look stunned. One of the older girls is crying and another is comforting her.

*

After we finish, we run up to our bedroom. 'Jesus. Jesus. Jesus,' is all Jonesy keeps saying.

It is too shocking. Sally has definitely, definitely been killed. Why else are you dead by a river unless you've been for a swim – but why would anyone swim in that mucky cold river? No, she's definitely been killed. We all agree about that.

Two dead girls in a month. It is the most scared I have ever been. Also – and I don't know why – but I am excited, I think it's just that the news is exciting. It is massive, massive news, the second most shocking thing that has ever happened here after Jane being killed.

I have to get ready for school and catch the bus. I usually like to go to school but right now I want to go to the Homes school with everyone else and talk all about what has happened.

'Tell me anything you find out,' I say to Jonesy as we say goodbye. 'And stay safe.'

'You too, Les.'

*

When we get back to the Homes in the evening, Jonesy is waiting for me on the porch of the cottage. She isn't allowed out to wait for me by the gates any more.

It turns out that the Homes school was cancelled for the day, which Jonesy said drove Mr and Mrs Paterson crazy as the kids were all in the cottage and not allowed to go out. Mr Paterson gave numbers to four girls and put them in his book, for doing nothing. He's going to have a whole morning of whacking them this Saturday. Surprisingly, Jonesy wasn't one of them.

They can't cancel school again tomorrow. They can't have no school and no one allowed out of their cottages, it just makes the houseparents angry.

Jonesy says she heard that Sally had been strangled. Apparently, her neck was really red and her eyes were bulging out when they found her. She doesn't tell me who told her this, so I don't know if she knows this is true or if someone told someone who told someone who told Jonesy.

'D'you think someone had sex with her?' she says.

'How can you tell?' I ask.

'The polis will know; they can just tell.'

'How?'

'They look in their fannies.'

'Eugh.'

I eat in the kitchen while Jonesy fills me in on what's

been happening. At tea they had a minute's silence for Sally, then they weren't allowed to talk during the meal.

After I eat, we run upstairs to our room. Everyone is on Jonesy's bed again. I sit on my bed and listen to them talk about Sally.

By the time the lights go out we are convinced there is a madman out there who wants to kill the girls from the Homes, and if we aren't careful we will be next. We don't tell ghost stories as we are all terrified enough as it is.

We ask Mrs Paterson if we can sleep with the light on. She says no. We all wail and she says she will leave the door open and the landing light on and if anyone is scared they can come and see her.

I have never known the Homes to be this collectively scared. The older girls are really worried, as whoever it is seems to be targeting girls their age. There is a lot of noise coming from their room and Mrs Paterson tells them to shut up. The truth is the killer could be after anyone. But as Gran said, life is harder for girls. I decide to go and see Eadie tomorrow, even though it's not my normal day. I don't think she'll mind after what has happened; she will probably have a queue out the building.

29

The next day kids at school still want to speak to us Homes kids because of the murders. It's terrible, but it means more people are talking to me and I think I have a new friend – Clara Dee. I knew who she was before, but she never spoke to me at break time as I kind of stood on my own in the playground, or did my homework in a classroom so I wouldn't have to do it back at the Homes.

She invites me to come talk to her and her friends to tell them all I know. I feel really bad because they are all listening to me and I make out that I knew Jane really well and that she was a proper friend of mine and that I am upset, so they put their arms round me to comfort me.

I know what I am doing is wrong, but they just seem to want to know more and more, so I just kept telling them things. They ask a question and I answer it with something, even if I don't know the real answer. The more I say the more they keep talking to me and the nicer it feels.

I have never been that bothered about being popular as I am just happy to be at the grammar school, but to have them be so interested in me gives me a feeling I like. To have a group of friends is the most wonderful thing.

*

On the bus on the way home Amanda tells me that Mr Taylor has been released by the police as they don't think he did it. He couldn't have murdered Sally Ward as he was in a cell when she was killed. She says she heard her houseparents talking and apparently they had ruled him out as Jane's killer already but Sally's death confirmed it.

She says he's not going to be coming back to the Homes, and that a lot of girls are disappointed. Turns out it wasn't just Jonesy who had a big crush on him.

I walk back to Cottage 5 to drop off my things before going to the hospital, and find Jonesy sat on the steps. She looks happy to see me and comes running up. I tell her I am going to see Eadie, and she looks sad, so I say,

'I'll come and find you as soon as I am done,' which cheers her up a little.

'What do you talk about?' she asks.

'Anything.'

'Anything? But you can talk to *me* about anything.'

'Aye, but this is different. She's just really nice to talk to.'

'Can she tell you who killed Jane and Sally?'

'I hope so, then I can stop being scared.'

'Scared? You don't have to be scared, Les. If you can beat that beast Glenda, you can beat anyone. You smash them with the gate and I'll kick them in the peanuts.'

30

When I get to the hospital building, I walk past a boy from Cottage 14 who has clearly taken a beating, and up the stairs, and take a seat outside Eadie's room. There are two boys there ahead of me, but they don't take long. I have spent a great deal of time sitting outside Eadie's room and I can tell you that boys take far less time than girls in there. I don't know if they have fewer problems, or if they tell her their problems quicker.

After half an hour the second boy comes out and Eadie appears in the doorway and beckons me into her office.

'Ahhh, the lovely Miss Lesley Beaton,' she says. She is wearing a twinset. I never knew what a twinset was until I met her ('How come your jumper and cardigan are both the same colour, miss?'). She's the only person I've ever seen wear one. This one is fawn with black trim. Her skirt is black, her shoes are black. You can see, like everything else in her life, she thinks about it.

'Miss—'

'It's Eadie, Lesley, you know that.'

'Those deid girls, Eadie, is someone tryin' to kill us? Does someone want all the girls deid, Eadie? Does someone want to rape us an' kill us? Why do they want to kill us and rape us? Do they rape us then kill us or kill us first? I would rather be killed first before I am raped, but I dinnae want either to happen.'

'Calm down, calm down,' she says. 'Now take a deep breath.'

'I wee'd my bed last night. No one knows because I took off the sheet and hid it in the cupboard then turned the mattress over. I never wee the bed. I don't want to be killed, Eadie.'

She gets up out of her chair and puts both her hands on my upper arms and holds me. She looks at me until I look back.

'Breathe slowly, Lesley, breathe slowly and calm down.'

I didn't realise how scared I was until I started speaking.

'Something shocking has happened, and it's natural to be scared, but let's look at things rationally. What has happened is rare – very rare. There is every chance no one else will be hurt. The deaths might not even be connected, it could just be a terrible, terrible coincidence.'

'Miss – sorry, Eadie – it cannae be a coincidence. Even I know that.'

'Maybe not, but it is rare. And you are safe and you are well and your friends are well, so let's not be afraid of things that we needn't be afraid of.'

'So there *is* a mass murderer? Like Peter Montrose?'

'We don't know, but you can't go around spreading panic, understand? I am talking to you as if you were an adult. You are a bright girl, Lesley, so I am going to treat you as such. Yes, it looks as though both girls were murdered. Yes, you should be careful, but no, you should not be scared. You can't spend your life being scared.'

'Yes, Eadie.'

'Now I want you to know that there are going to be police officers patrolling the Homes to make sure everyone is safe. People take your safety very, very seriously, so we won't let anything happen to you.'

'Yes, Eadie.'

'So what have I just told you?'

'Dinnae say nuthin' to no one, miss.'

'Now it's time for my question.'

'Yes, miss?'

'Is everything all right with you, Lesley? How have you been feeling about your family situation?'

'Oh yes, I ... I sorta forgot about it. I was angry but then my gran explained some of it, and with everything happening with Jane and Sally, I've been forgetting to be upset about it.'

'Well that's one good thing to come out of this.'

'Miss, that's naughty, you shouldnae say that.'

'You're right, Lesley, I shouldn't make jokes, sorry. But what I will say is, if you do get upset about it, you come and tell me. Yes?'

'I will.'

'Right, on you go.'

With that I get out of my chair and smile as I wave goodbye. Then I leap down the stairs and run back to the cottage to Jonesy.

When I leave Eadie I always feel like I have a new coat of paint on me. I go in feeling tatty and run down and I come out feeling ready to face the world with my bright new colours.

31

We are to be interviewed by the police today. They have come to our cottage. Mrs Paterson told us at breakfast they would be coming and before we had finished eating there was a knock. Shortly after, one of the officers put his head round the kitchen door to get a look at us. As soon as he did we all went silent. When he pulled his head back we all started talking again.

There are four policemen in all. They each take a different room in the house and we have to go to one of them and have him ask us questions. We all line up, then Mr Paterson tells us which room we have to go to.

I line up with Jonesy in front of me. She gets all excited while we wait. Four other girls get spoken to first, then it's our turn. Jonesy's policeman is in uniform, quite young, a little bit handsome. When she is told to go to the reading room where he's asking girls questions, she lets out a muffled, 'Yus!'

I go to the kitchen for my interview. My policeman is the only one not in a uniform. He is older than the others, maybe forty or fifty. His hair is parted on the left; it is slick and combed back and to the side. When I walk in, he points to the chair I am to sit in, then he lights a cigarette and starts another page on his notepad. He goes through a series of initial questions, like name, age, how long I've been here. He writes all my answers down with a super-fast scribble.

I'm not sure why he wants the last one. I was going to ask him how he thinks that might help, but when I look in his eyes, I can see he is someone I'm not going to help by asking questions, so I keep quiet.

He takes a big draw on the cigarette and on the exhale says, 'Right, my name is Detective Boyle. You know why we are here: to find out what you might know about these two incidents and where you were at the time they happened.'

'I will help any way I can, sir,' I say, making an effort to talk posh. I tell him I will help in any way I can, but I am not telling him about the diary or that it was us that sent the letter. That would get us in trouble and I don't want us in trouble, and I don't want us getting the belt.

'Did you know Jane Denton or Sally Ward?'

'No. Well, I knew who they were, but I didn't know-know them. I mean, Jane lived here years ago, but I mean *years* ago and she wouldn't remember who I was as I was only wee then.'

'Have you seen either of them with anyone they wouldn't normally have associated with?'

'No,' I say. 'Can I ask a question?'

'Aye.'

'Is it a mass murderer?'

'I can't answer that.'

'Cos me an' Morag Jones think there's a madman on the loose. Like Peter Montrose.'

'And why is that?'

'What if they hanged the wrong man?'

'They didn't.'

'But how do you know?'

'Trust me.'

'Why?'

'Because I'm a policeman.'

'And?'

'And because, young lady, I saw the evidence. I saw the evidence, I saw the man's eyes, and I saw them hang him by his neck. He killed those women, and he's dead, and I'm glad he is. Do you understand?'

'Aye, sir. But, sir ...'

'Yes?'

'Was it no Mr Taylor then, sir?'

'What do you mean?'

'They took Mr Taylor away a few days ago. Then Sally Ward died and now Mr Taylor is free, so you must think it's no Mr Taylor who did it?'

'No, it's not Mr Taylor who did it.'

'Not even Jane Denton?'

'No.'

'How d'you know?'

'Because we eliminated him as a suspect. Now, this is supposed to be me asking the questions, not you.'

'Sorry, sir. We're just scared thinking that someone's trying to kill all the girls in the Homes. So if it's not Mr Taylor, then there's someone free to do it again.'

He pauses for a moment. 'I think there might be an extremely disturbed individual who we need to catch. We can't confirm whether the two deaths are linked; all we can do at the moment is investigate what has happened.'

'Can we help?' I ask.

He seems to decide that I have nothing more to tell him. 'You can help, young lady, by keeping yourself safe and making sure your friends stay safe. Now, send the next girl in.'

As I come out Jonesy is already waiting for me. We go

upstairs to our bedroom to find out what the other girls were asked. It turns out Jonesy can't remember what she was asked because she was too busy staring into the eyes of the policeman, who is, according to her, 'beautiful'.

I tell her what my one said about Mr Taylor, and what he said about Peter Montrose, and how he'd seen him hanged.

'Aww ... gross,' she says.

'I think we need knives,' I say.

'Do you think?'

'Aye, we need to protect ourselves if we get caught by the madman. We need sharp ones. We'll steal them from the kitchen.'

'When?'

'The sooner the better. Tonight.'

'Deal.'

32

First, I feel the breathing on my face, then I hear the whisper.

'Les, you awake?' says Jonesy.

I am warm under my sheets. I don't want to come out, but unfortunately this was my idea. 'What time is it?' I ask.

'Dunno. Too dark to see. It's late or early.'

I slip out from under the bedcovers. I have my pyjamas on and I went to sleep with my socks on so I wouldn't have to put them on in the dark.

'C'mon, let's do it,' Jonesy says.

We walk softly across the bedroom and she opens the door. It creaks, so she nudges it just a little bit more. The landing is dark and the house is in complete silence.

We go down the stairs, sticking to the side so the steps don't creak. We cross the hallway and I feel the cold of the tiles through my socks, then we open the door to the kitchen. Again there is a small creak from the hinge when the door is pushed. We slip inside.

We can see a little clearer in the kitchen as the light from the streetlamp outside bathes the room in a slight yellow glow. The drawers in the kitchen dresser are big, so if you are going to ease one out quietly you need two people to do it. I point to Jonesy to go to one handle and I take the other.

I am just about to tell her to pull when we hear someone exhale, a sudden, 'Urrrrrrrgggghhhhh,' from behind us. Jonesy and I freeze. Mr Paterson is sat with his head resting on the table, with an empty bottle of whisky in front of him. He is fast asleep.

Jonesy looks at me and I look back at her. She must be thinking the same as me, which is, if he wakes up and catches us we are beyond dead, but also, we've come this far, do we go through with it and try to get the knives?

Mr Paterson breathes out again. He is silent for maybe fifteen seconds then lets out a huge breath. I am not sure how he is breathing in, as he only seems to be breathing out.

Jonesy nods at the drawer; she thinks we should go

for it. I shake my head and point towards the door. She shakes her head and nods at the drawer again. I try to do my angriest face; there's no way I am going to get the belt again.

She shrugs and agrees. We look at Mr Paterson. Jonesy holds her hands up as if to say, 'Why?'

We reverse out of the room and go up the side of the stairs again and I slip back into bed. Jonesy slides in next to me. 'Whit was he doing?' I whisper.

'He's a drunk,' she replies.

'But the grown-ups aren't allowed alcohol in the houses.'

'He hides it. I've seen it in cupboards before. Some of the boxes under the sink have bottles in them. He must wait until everyone has gone to bed before he drinks it.'

'D'you think he heard us? D'you think he opened an eye?'

'Naw, he looked blootered. It's what grown-ups do.'

'Whit about Mrs Paterson?'

'Whit about her? She must know.'

I don't know how long we kept talking but Jonesy stayed in my bed for the rest of the night.

*

When it's time to get up and go down to breakfast on Sunday morning, Mr Paterson is there eating his toast as if nothing has happened.

We both watch him, because he doesn't know what we know. Jonesy smiles and shakes her head and we both turn to Mrs Paterson to see if we can tell if she knows what her husband has been up to. But we can't tell.

33

Mum comes to see me in the afternoon. I don't want to see her. I don't want to be anywhere near her.

We usually sit in the tearoom and talk when she comes, but this time we go for a walk around the grounds. She is wearing her long dark coat, and her hair looks greasy and a mess. I don't think she is taking care of herself.

She doesn't try to hug me when she sees me. She just coldly says, 'Hello.' I reply with the same and try to put as little niceness in it as possible.

We set off walking down Faith Avenue, then go up Praise Road and around, via Love Avenue and Church Road back again – the full loop. We just walk together in silence. I am not going to break it, I refuse to. I don't have anything to say and I don't want to try to make her feel better.

We keep walking the damp roads until Mum finally says, 'I'm sorry, Lesley.'

I wasn't expecting her to say it, so I don't know what to say back. So I don't say anything.

'I'm sorry. I'm sorry I wasn't in a situation to be able to bring you up myself, but you being here is the best thing that could have happened to you.

'I really want you to come and live with us, I really do, and I will make it happen, just not right now. I've always wanted to be able to have you with us. When you were born, I couldn't bring you up, but now I have a proper home for you. I just need it to be the right time.'

I stay quiet. I can't seem to think of anything to say that would seem right, so rather than say anything wrong I say nothing. At least she said sorry, at least I know she wants me. She's never seemed like she wanted me before. She is not very warm or how you would think a mother should be with their child.

'Would you want to come and live with us if I could get my husband to agree to it?'

'Of course, but only if *you* want me.'

'Want you? Of course I want you. I've always wanted you, Lesley.'

She turns me round and holds my hands. There are tears in her eyes as she tries to speak. I am still determined not to cry; I am not going to show her I care. I can't, I can't care, I can't let her in.

'Lesley, I want you so much, I want you to come and live with us and be the big sister to your brother and two sisters. It might take time, but never think that I don't want you to be with us.' She squeezes my hands. 'It's just we can't right now, but one day.'

With Mum there's always an, 'It's just ...' I believed her up until she said that. But now I remember everything else she's ever said that has never come true. Things she's promised in the past, times she's said she'd come see me and not turned up.

If Gran says she'll come, she comes. If she says she'll bring something, then she brings something. If she says she'll do something, she does it.

I'm not sure how she could have given birth to Mum, nor how I can be related to Mum. I'm like Gran – I always do what I say I'm going to do.

When Mum was saying sorry, I had started to believe her. I really wanted to. But those two words make me think of all the times she's let me down. I stop listening to her for a while. I realise I don't look like her, so I must look like my father, whoever he is. I don't act like her, so I wonder if I act like my father too. I wonder if he even knows I exist?

I start listening to her again, but I realise they are just words. Only words.

'I was so worried when I heard about that second girl getting killed. I couldn't stop thinking about you. Are you kids scared? I saw the polis at the entrance. How is your friend? Are you looking out for each other?'

I stop listening again.

We walk some more. I let her ramble on.

When it's time to go she gives me a squeeze and says, 'We'll be together soon.'

It means nothing.

When I walk up the steps to Cottage 5, I don't turn back to look at her before I go inside.

34

Seeing Mum always makes me feel worse. I never feel happier after she's been, unlike when Gran comes. *She* never fails to make me feel better. The next time I see Eadie Schaffer I'll ask if she can arrange it so I don't have to see my mum for a while. She can do that and put a block on visits if I need it.

After my chores I go upstairs, get into bed and pull the blankets over my head so I am hidden. I don't cry. Mum can't make me cry any more. If I don't believe her promises, then she can't let me down or hurt me. You can only be hurt by people you care about. The only person I care about is Jonesy and that's how I am going to keep it. The smaller the number of people you love the smaller the number who can let you down.

The other girls come into the bedroom and start talking. They don't see me under the bedclothes. They're talking about a boy at the Homes school. Does he like one of the girls, does he not, does he like someone else? I don't know the boy they're on about.

One day I am going to escape this place. When I am seventeen I will get a home of my own, probably with Jonesy. We will get jobs, we will get money, we will have a life where people don't give you the belt for doing nothing wrong, where people don't try to fight you because you are cleverer than they are.

I think we will move to Paisley or Glasgow. Maybe Glasgow, as it is bigger. One thing for sure is that when I leave here I will never come back. Or if I do come back it will be in a big black car with a driver. I will drive through the Homes but I will not get out of the car. I might wind the window down a little but not too much.

The call for tea goes up. I can't face talking to anyone else today so I stay in bed. Jonesy pops up to see if everything is all right. I tell her I'm fine but that I just want to be alone. She says she'll bring up some bread rolls for me.

Then Mrs Paterson comes up. She's obviously asked where I am. I tell her I am fine and that I didn't enjoy seeing my mum, so I want to stay in bed for the rest of the evening. She seems all right with this, but says she will bring up a plate of food as I need to eat.

She also says that this is a one-off and I am not to do it again; if I agree to eat my tea and not do it again then she will leave me alone.

35

That night Jonesy gets out of her bed, crawls across the floor and gets into mine.

'Budge up,' she whispers. I move over and she gets under the blankets. 'Know what I've been thinking, Les?'

'Usually never.'

'We can sort this. And we *have* to sort this, find out who killed Jane and Sally, otherwise we might be next. The polis dinnae know whit goes on round here, not really. That means we've got a head start. You could work out who did it. You just work out who knows them both and it's probably them, right?'

'Not necessarily.'

'No, not necessarily, but still probably, aye? If we

found out who could have done it, Lesley? If we found that out, we could work it out?'

'Mibbie.'

'Aye, mibbie. And mibbie I could sleep in here with you tonight?'

'Away yerself.'

'But I'm scared, Les, I'm s-s-s-scared and you can keep me safe.'

I know she's joking but I let her stay. Sometimes I let her stay, sometimes I don't. The benefit of her staying is that it's nice and warm and there's someone to hold. The problem is it's a bit squashed and she gets 'the jumps' in the night. This is when for no reason she suddenly starts to jerk in a dream, and it wakes you up, but never her, and it drives me crazy.

She falls asleep quickly. I lie awake for a while wondering who knew both girls, and that if they struck again it would be bad for the Homes but easier to work out. That is a horrible thought; the more girls die, the easier it should be to find out who killed them.

Are we bait? Is that what the police do, wait for something like this to solve itself by letting more people die and getting more clues?

This is my last thought as I fall asleep.

36

Bedlam this morning. Shelley McDade – one of the big girls from our house – has gone missing.

We are woken up, as always, at 6.30 a.m. by Mrs Paterson ringing the bell. I hate that bloody bell. I was having a dream and she ruined it. We all get dressed in our room while Mrs Paterson gets the babies up, then the next thing there's a panic from the big girls' room.

The big girls' room is down the end of the hallway. There are six of them in there and they are aged fourteen to sixteen. They give us so much trouble if we ever go into their room, but they can come into ours whenever they like. They often take things and threaten us with a 'doing' if we tell on them.

Anyway, Shelley McDade is gone. Her bed isn't made;

she has just *gone*. She went to bed last night, then when everyone woke up in the morning she wasn't there. It doesn't seem as if any of her clothes are missing.

I go cold. The thought that anyone could come into our house and take one of us without anyone noticing makes me pure terrified.

Mrs Paterson and Mr Paterson are frantic, they're looking everywhere they can in the house. Cook comes up to help. They keep searching in the same places, as if Shelley might come back in the time since they last looked. We just stand on the landing watching them racing about.

'Stay in your rooms!' shouts Mr Paterson.

We go back to our bedroom and Jonesy sits on my bed with me. Shona and Pam sit with us. Eldrey is on her bed, silently looking at the floor and shaking. Mary is as scared as anything. She keeps walking backwards and forwards repeating, 'Oh no, oh my God, oh no, oh my God ...'

Mary really likes Shelley. We all seem to have one of the big girls who we like. Mine is Fiona Manning. She always keeps an eye out for me. She's a wee bit cannier than the others, which is why I think she likes me.

'Whit have they done with her, whit have they done?'

Pam gets up and peers out the window. 'Shit, it's the Superintendent,' she says.

We all rush to the window.

'Oh my God, he looks like he's gonnae murder someone,' says Jonesy.

'He does an' all,' says Pam.

Mr Gordon storms up the cottage path and bangs on the door. Someone lets him in, and we go to the bedroom door to see what's happening. We open it a little so we can just see down the stairs.

'What the fuck is going on?' he shouts.

Mr Paterson is trying to calm him down and tell him what has happened. It's strange seeing Mr Paterson – who can be a bastard – be intimidated by an even bigger bastard.

We hear bits of their conversation. Mr Paterson says when they last saw Shelley, what happened when they went into her room this morning, who her friends are.

The Super asks if the police have been called. When Mr Paterson says no, the Super shouts, 'Well, why the fuck not?'

Mr Paterson gets on the phone, then the Superintendent starts to march up the stairs. We shut our door but can hear his boots coming up. He opens our door and looks in. We all hold our breath, then he shuts the door. He goes on, opening every door on our floor.

'Holy shit,' says Jonesy.

'I know,' says Pam.

'Look! Look!' shouts Mary. 'It's her, it's her, it's Shelley!'

We go to the window and it *is* her. She's walking up to the cottage carrying a towel.

'Oh, she is so deid,' says Pam.

We don't have a chance to go and tell anyone before Shelley opens the front door and walks inside. We all run to the top of the stairs again. Mr Paterson turns around and puts the phone down. He sees Shelley, walks up to her and before she knows it – SMACK – she's on the floor – sparko.

None of us says a word. Mr Gordon comes out from the last bedroom on the landing. He walks through us and down the stairs.

'That her?' he asks Mr Paterson, pointing at Shelley on the floor.

'Aye,' says Mr Paterson.

'She all right?' the Super asks.

'She won't be when I'm done with her,' says Mr Paterson.

The Super doesn't say anything, just nods and steps over her body and leaves the house.

Mr Paterson sees us all at the top of the stairs. 'GET BACK IN YOUR ROOMS AND STAY THERE TILL WE CALL BREAKFAST!' he shouts.

We do as we are told.

I had been feeling very sorry for myself. If Shelley has done nothing else, she has managed to make me stop feeling so bad. But I worry for her. She's in for an awful day.

37

At breakfast we are told that we all have to go to the Central Hall again. I tell Mrs Paterson that I will miss the bus and miss school. She says I have to go and that she will try to get Mr Paterson to drive me to the school afterwards to make up time, but if that isn't possible I will have to work on my own in the cottage. She says that missing one day of school won't kill me.

Jonesy and I walk hand in hand from the cottage to the hall. Standing room only again, although this time it is only the girls who are here. The other girls are scared, I am scared, Jonesy is beyond scared. She's been having nightmares for weeks now. That's probably why she's been coming into my bed more than ever. It is as if she thinks I am going to be able to protect her from them.

In the hall everyone is trying to work out what we have been called here for. Is it about Shelley? Has another girl been killed? Have the police caught whoever murdered Jane and Sally?

The hall is bare when we walk in. It's used for lots of different activities, but when there's one of these meetings everything is cleared to the side and the chairs and tables are stacked. It's a cold morning – especially for this time of year – so most of us have our coats on and we don't know how long we are going to be in here so we don't take them off.

Mr Gordon walks onto the stage. Jonesy squeezes my hand.

'Ladies,' he says, then a moment later, 'LADIES!' until we are finally silent. 'Thank you.' He looks around the hall. 'You all know what has happened here over the last few weeks, and I understand that you are alarmed by this situation. That is natural.'

Him trying to be kind and compassionate is even more unnerving than when he is a straight-out psycho.

'What I want you all to know is that you are very safe at the Homes. There are many responsible adults here, so if you are at all worried, speak to a grown-up.'

This is just what he said before, when Jane died. I feel suddenly cold. If he is just saying the same things, then he doesn't know any more than he did and we are not any safer. He is supposed to be in charge of the Homes, so if he is just saying words with no meaning then we are helpless.

I see Eadie Schaffer at the side of the hall. She doesn't see me as she is facing the stage.

'This is a tough time,' Mr Gordon goes on, 'but the police are on the grounds and the Chief of Police has called me personally and told me that they will catch this person. That said, we can do more to protect ourselves, so for now, I want you all to continue to go about in pairs at all times. Plus we are going to be handing out whistles to all of you girls. These will be delivered to your cottages this afternoon. Most importantly, be alert; if you spot something you think is suspicious, tell an adult. There is no harm in being wrong. It's better to be safe than sorry. Together as a community we will get through this and things will return to normal.'

'What, beatings and beltings?' whispers Jonesy.

No one else hears her but I nudge her anyway.

I want to ask Mr Gordon if there are any suspects, or who the police think might have done the murders, but the Superintendent doesn't ask for questions. I think of putting my hand up to ask anyway, but I don't want to draw attention to myself.

He ends with, 'Dismissed.' There is a scrum at the

door at the back of the hall as we all try to file out at the same time.

'They havenae got a clue who's done it, have they Les?' says Jonesy, as we get into the fresh air. 'If they did, they would give us some idea that they were close to catching them.'

I think she is right, but I want to calm her so I say, 'They might no want to alert the person they think did it.'

'Nah, garbage, Les. They don't have a clue. Like I've been saying, it's up to us to find out who did it. Not for them, for us, so we can be safe. If we find out who did it, I'll be able to sleep normally again.'

'You might be right, Jonesy.'

'You know I'm right, Les. The polis have got their job to do catching bad guys. I've got my job to do stopping people raping and killing me. It's gonnae be my number one priority.'

'You off to school now?' I ask.

'Aye, you?'

'Going back to the cottage. I've missed the bus but Mrs Paterson says Mr Paterson will run me over to the school and if he doesn't I'll have to stay at home.'

'Oh, you lucky bleeder. I wish I could have a day at home.'

'Really? I like school, I'd rather be at school than at the cottage.'

'Aye mibbie at your school, no ours, no way.'

Jonesy is convinced my school is some wondrous happy place and everyone is a brainiac. Neither of these things is true. Even at a school like mine there are people who are cleverer than others. I just try to keep up. Some of them are super-clever, though. There's a boy in the year above me who is a certified genius. He walks strange, like he's walking up a hill and leaning into it at an acute angle. That's my favourite angle, by the way. I like an obtuse angle, but the acute angle is my favourite. I like the look of it, I think it's a cute angle. That is my best maths joke. Jonesy has never got it, but I like it all the same.

38

The cottage is always quiet when everyone has gone to school. The babies usually make a bit of a racket, except when it's their morning nap. Then there's a numb silence. But as I get closer to the house, I hear Mr and Mrs Paterson shouting inside. They don't tend to shout that much at each other, at least not compared to some houseparents. Over in Amanda's house, Cottage 9, apparently they row all the time, and sometimes one of them goes away for a few days.

Mr Paterson comes out of the house. He looks angry and is breathing through his nose.

'Get in the car,' he says shortly. I haven't done anything wrong but he clearly doesn't want to take me to school.

The car is a dark green. It has two doors and the seats

fold forward if you need to get in the back. I don't know the type of car, I'm not that interested in them. Some of the boys my age are; they still play with toy cars like they are children, even though they are twelve. Football and cars occupy their minds; they make them happy. Like a dog playing with a ball. I think in a couple of years they will wake up and realise there are girls all around them, and pay attention to us, but at the moment a lot of them don't even know we exist. *We* know *they* exist; they don't see us.

I get in the front seat. I've never been in Mr Paterson's car. In fact, I haven't been in many cars – I get buses or trains or walk – so getting in one is a treat, or it would be if someone more cheerful were driving. And I've never been in the *front* seat of a car before. I am excited and scared.

Mr Paterson starts the engine and we drive out of the Homes. I am not going to say anything to him, it will probably only make him angrier, so I just look out of the window at the passing fields and hope he doesn't start shouting at me. It's not my fault the Superintendent called the assembly and made me miss the bus.

After five minutes he actually speaks. 'So how are you feeling, Lesley? I hope you're not too scared with what's been going on?'

'It's no nice, Mr Paterson,' I say. 'Why would someone do something like that to Jane and Sally?'

He stares at the road ahead. 'Unfortunately, Lesley, there are some bad, bad people in the world.'

'Like Peter Montrose?'

'Aye, like him. He was a very bad man, and that's why they hanged him. How do you know about him?'

'I heard what he did. He raped and murdered women, didn't he?'

'Yes he did, but he's gone now.'

'Whit if they got the wrong person, Mr Paterson? Whit if Montrose wasn't the killer?'

'They didn't hang the wrong person, Lesley.'

'But whit if—'

'Lesley!'

I look down at my shoes. They are black lace-ups. I try to keep them as clean as I can because the teachers can pull you up on them if they are scruffy. The sole on the left one is starting to wear away near my big toe and sometimes water seeps in if it is a wet day.

'You do feel safe, don't you, Lesley? You know you have grown-ups around you that you can trust. We won't let anything happen to you.'

'Aye, Mr Paterson.'

We carry on driving. I thought he was just going to drive me to the train station, but we go all the way into the town.

We are about two minutes away from the school when

I say, 'Mr Paterson, me and Jonesy are going to find out who did it. We'll work it out and then we'll all be safe.'

'You do that, Lesley, you do that,' he says, but he doesn't sound convinced.

I get out of the car and Mr Paterson drives off. I try to open the school gates but they are locked. I don't know if they lock them to stop people getting in or to stop kids getting out. Luckily after ten minutes it is first break and a teacher comes into the playground and lets me in.

My new friend Clara Dee wants to know why I am late, and wants all the latest news about what's going on at the Homes. I tell her, and I make it sound as exciting as I can. We go to the spot in the playground where we hang out now, dodging the rampaging boys.

When the bell rings we have to go to separate classes, but we agree to wait for each other in the dinner hall so we can sit together. I feel terrible for a moment, for thinking *I hope this excitement continues*, as it will mean Clara will still want to be my friend. I know I shouldn't think this, but sometimes it's hard when you have been on your own in the playground so often.

39

When I get back in the evening all the girls have been given whistles and are standing outside the cottage on the grass. Jonesy had got one for me and rushes up to hand it over. We are not to blow them under any circumstances – except if we are in danger, of course – so after about half an hour everyone starts blowing them. Some of the boys have made it a game to steal them off the girls and run around blowing them.

I can see why we have been given whistles; the grown-ups weren't to know how silly the boys would be. I'm sure they'll get bored of it and they'll be used properly by tomorrow.

I tell Jonesy about the car trip with Mr Paterson. I tell her what he said about Peter Montrose, how he's definitely dead and that the policeman had said that too.

'They *would* say that,' says Jonesy. 'They just want us not to be scared.'

'Aye, but if it's no him, then who is it? It could be anyone.'

We walk back to the cottage. Mr Paterson is stood in the doorway, but he doesn't say hello or acknowledge us, so we just walk past him into the kitchen. I sit down to eat the tea that Cook has left out for me. Cook is still there, tidying up.

'Get yer whistles?' she asks.

'Aye,' we both say.

'You keep them with you, aye?'

'Aye,' we both say again.

You don't want to mess with Cook, she has knives and a temper. We always do whatever she tells us. Jonesy isn't scared of many people, but she is scared of Cook. Cook's forearms are like the giant hams we get at Christmas. Sometimes when you budge past her you can feel how strong she is. If she were a man, she'd be a soldier.

I eat my tea while Jonesy talks to Cook. I realise if someone else is going to be next it's not going to be Cook. No one would stand a chance with her. I need to be more like her, but people are never going to fear me, I just don't have it in me.

40

After I've eaten, Jonesy and I sit on the steps and look over towards the duck pond. I don't know why it's called the duck pond because no ducks ever come to it. Boys occasionally get thrown in it especially if it is their birthday. 'Dunked pond' would be better.

'We need to catch him. We need him to be put in jail or, better still, hanged,' I say.

'Could you do it?' asks Jonesy.

'Do what?'

'Hang him. If you knew it was him and you had to pull the lever, could you do it?'

'Aye.'

'Aye, me an' all. Would that make us killers?'

'Not until we've done it.'

'Aye, so we're potential killers.'

'We're all potential killers, Jonesy.'

'I think you are more of a potential killer, Les. I think you would do it and no give it a second thought. I think you would be reading your book, reach up, pull the lever and then go back to reading.'

'Give off.'

'You would, Les, you're a stone-cold killer, so you are. I'm keeping one eye open at night from now on.'

'I could never kill you, Jonesy,' I say. 'I need the sound of you talking to get to sleep every night.'

'You'd still hear me talking. I'd come back and haunt you and widnae ever let you sleep again.'

41

I tell Jonesy I'll see her back at the cottage and head for the Homes library. One of the things the founder believed in – apart from the sanctity of the word of the Lord, which would bring salvation to us children of sin – was that education would be another saviour. So the library is huge.

I love the library. I'm not a big one for stories, but I love facts, and books have lots of facts. I can read the encyclopaedias from cover to cover. I'll read anything that I can learn from. They also have old newspapers. Other children have used the newspapers to find out why someone's dad is really in prison. Today I want to read about the Peter Montrose murders. They scare me, but I need to know all the details.

I ask the librarian where the papers from ten years ago are. She asks what I am looking for and I say I am looking up articles from around the time my little brother was born. From then it is just a case of forwards and backwards with the papers. There was nothing at the end of the year, but at the start they mention Peter Montrose had been caught. In the middle of the year they hanged him, but I want the reports from the trial so I can find out what exactly he did.

He murdered eight people. It's a relief to find out that it wasn't just young girls he murdered; he murdered older women too. Reading the transcripts from the court it seems pretty certain that they got the right man. The doctors said he was a psychopath, he had no compassion, and if he hadn't been caught he would have killed again.

*

I go back to the cottage. Jonesy is upset that I didn't tell her where I was going. I only went without her because she would have got too excited in the library and would have been unable to keep her mouth shut. Libraries are supposed to be quiet and she wouldn't have been able to cope.

She seems disappointed that it really couldn't be Peter

Montrose killing Homes girls. I love Jonesy so, but sometimes she's a bit too crazy to keep up with.

We do our chores and then go to our room. Jonesy gets out an exercise book and shows it to me. She's already started to put together a list of suspects. She points at Suspect 1.

'It's the da of Glenda McAdam.'

'Away,' I say.

'No, true. You look at it, Lesley, look at it. You add the bits together and it comes back to him. You've seen him, aye?'

'Aye.'

'He's an evil-looking man.'

He is an evil-looking man. He's been in Barlinnie countless times. When he turns up at Cottage 13, you know about it. He has four kids in the Homes. Their mam is rumoured to be a drunk or a whore or both, but no one ever dares say it to them. Maybe that's why Glenda and the brothers are like they are. It can't be nice having parents like that.

'Well guess whit, Les, I heard the big girls talking yesterday and Jane Denton had a run-in with Glenda McAdam two months ago. Lots of kids at school are saying that Jane and Sally were friends, though no close like you and me, more like me and Brenda, so mibbie Glenda hated Sally too. And more, Sally Ward went out with one of the brothers, but then just split up with him, and then like two days later she's deid.'

'So why would it be the dad? Why wouldn't it be the brother?'

'Aye, right enough, Les, but anyway the brother doesn't look evil enough. The da would, though, he'd strangle a puppy for eating a sausage.'

'Away, Jonesy.'

'It's true, Lesley, and you could be next. You duffed Glenda, it could be you that's going to get done now.'

'Dinnae say that, Jonesy.'

I feel sick. It could be Mr McAdam. He is a bad man. He has a reason, even if it is not a good one. The bad parents, the really rotten ones, are not supposed to come to the Homes, they are banned. But no one can stop him from turning up when he wants to see his kids. There aren't any adults strong enough to kick him out and usually one of the houseparents has to call the police, but by the time they arrive he is already gone.

Some people hate the police, but imagine if that is your job, you turn up and you've got to get rid of someone like him. I wouldn't want to do it.

Even though I doubt it is him, he is someone to keep an eye on. After all, Jonesy has a point – he *is* capable of it.

42

I have had an amazing day at school today. I get pupil of the week. I've never got it before. The pupil of the week gets to wipe down the blackboard at the end of Friday's lessons. Mrs Andrews says I have been working incredibly hard. I *have* been working hard, but no harder than I usually do. I don't know why she chose me this week in particular, but things seem to be going better for me now that I am friends with Clara and we have our own set of friends. I would have felt awkward being pupil of the week if I wasn't friends with them, as I could have been teased, but now that I am it makes things a lot easier.

For dinner we have jam sponge and custard, which I love, and Richard Metting smiles at me as we walk down the corridor. Some days it just all goes for you, and some days it goes against you. Sometimes I think it doesn't matter what you do, it just happens like that, but mostly I think the harder you work, the more likely it is to work out for you.

Life's funny like that. I might have not worked hard and all three of these things could still have happened.

When I get on the bus to go back to the Homes I almost don't want to. I don't want it to be the weekend, because that means it is two days until I get to come back here. Still, I am happy.

Ever since the time us four Homes pupils sat together, I've been sitting in the middle of the bus, where I can hear what the older ones are talking about. And I was right that as boys get older they get more into girls. Today Daniel and Ronnie are talking about a girl with breasts at school; they are trying to use better and better words to describe them: 'amazing', 'immense', 'science-defying'.

Amanda is saying how pathetic they are. Ronnie says that jealousy is a lousy trait in a woman, which makes Daniel laugh. Amanda looks hurt, but she tries to pretend she isn't. If I've learnt anything at the Homes, it's not to let them know when something they say affects you. If they spot it, they can get at you, and that will make it worse. It's hard to do and if even Amanda

Bell can't do it, and she's one of the most impressive girls around, then the rest of us have got no hope.

The boys continue to tease her until she shouts, 'Oh, grow up,' and turns around to face the front. I am peeping back through the seats to see her and she catches my eye. She shakes her head, not at me, but at what she has to put up with. One day I would like to be her friend.

The bus stops at the Homes. As Ronnie walks past Amanda he has his fists up his jumper to make it look like he has giant breasts, and he says, in a high-pitched voice, 'Oh, bye, Mandy, have a nice weekend,' and walks away like a girl. As we get up to leave the bus I almost speak to Amanda; we have a moment, a look, but I don't, I am too shy, and she's too old for me to really talk to.

I walk towards my cottage, regretting that I didn't take the chance to say something, when I see a big crowd standing outside. I walk through the crowd, trying to get to the front steps.

As I do, I hear Kelly McDowell say, 'She's here,' and I see Eadie Schaffer is stood on the porch. She rushes towards me and gives me an almighty hug, repeating over and over again, 'I'm so sorry, I'm so sorry.'

'What is it?' I say. 'Why are you so sorry?'

'It's Morag,' she says. 'She's been killed.'

43

I don't speak to anyone for a week. I can't get any sound out. I shut down.

At times my body won't move, and I can't make it move. I am no longer there. I watch people talking to me but can't hear them. I can't eat. I sit in my room a lot.

They talk about putting me in the hospital but Eadie argues that I need my home environment. It is decided I will stay at the cottage and that Eadie will visit me in the morning and evening and sometimes at dinner as well.

They keep me off school for a couple of days, but that doesn't help, I have nothing to do, I sit frozen, with people asking me if I am all right and do I want tea. I have never been offered as much tea in my life, as if tea will help bring Morag back.

Jonesy was strangled. They didn't tell me at the time, just that she had been killed. I hear later that she was strangled. She was found on the back steps of our cottage. I can't go round the back of our cottage as I worry that if I see the steps I will see her body.

Cook found her. Cook is also too distraught to talk. She will cook food but she won't speak. They offer her time off, but she shakes her head and points to the kitchen.

From what they have said it sounds like Jonesy fought and fought. I know she would have. She had so much life in her and she wasn't going to give that up without a struggle. No one has said if she was raped. I don't want to know if she was.

44

The days go by as if I weigh two tonnes; it feels so hard to move my body anywhere. I wake up every morning and my first thought is, *I am awake*, and then there's five seconds before I remember what has happened. I think, *I wonder if Jonesy is awake, or if she's going to come into my bed*, and that's when I remember and that is when the sadness comes. It's so heavy, and I can feel it all over my body. And I just want to go back to sleep because when I am asleep I don't know she is dead, but when I am awake I do know, and I know I will never see her again and then I start to cry.

I don't know what to say to anyone. The only thing I can think is that it's so unfair. I could think of a hundred people more deserving than her to die.

Eventually I start to talk to people again. At first to Eadie, then to the girls in my room. The girls in my room are sad too, but they hug me and hold me tight. Mrs Paterson often comes up to check how I am doing.

At breakfast one morning Mrs Paterson comes and sits next to me. I'm eating my porridge and trying to avoid eye contact with anyone.

'How are you today, Lesley?' she asks.

'Alive,' I mumble.

'The police would like to talk to you this morning, if that's all right with you? They've talked to everyone else in the house but they'd really like to talk to you as you were Morag's best friend.'

'Fine.'

'It doesn't have to be now if you don't want, you can take your time.'

'Right.'

'You don't have to do it on your own. I can come with you, or Mr Paterson, or Eadie—'

'Eadie,' I say.

'Right, I think she will be on her way over anyway so if you go to your room after breakfast, I will let you know when she and the policeman get here. If you want to go to school afterwards, Malcolm – I mean Mr Paterson – can run you up there in the car, but by no means do you *have* to go to school.'

I don't tell her that I want to go to school; I like it at school, when I am in the house I have nothing to do and can't stop thinking about Morag and crying again, which makes them think I am still not ready to go back to school.

I haven't been in my room long when there is a knock at the door and Mrs Paterson comes in.

'Eadie and the policeman are here now,' she tells me. 'If at any time you want to stop talking to them you just let Eadie know, and I will be about if you need me.'

'All right,' I say.

I walk down the stairs and Eadie is stood by the front door with a man. He's much smarter than the other policeman; he's wearing a long brown coat, a hat and shiny shoes. As I get to the bottom of the stairs he takes off his hat and smiles at me. His face is very thin, and his parted brown hair is a bit of a mess from the hat so he smooths it down.

Eadie gives me a big hug. It feels good. She makes me feel safe.

'Lesley, this is Detective Walker,' says Eadie. 'He's come to ask you some questions about Morag, to get a better picture of her, as no one knew her better than you did. If you could help him by answering them, I am sure it would be really appreciated.'

He crouches down and looks at me eye-to-eye.

'I know this is going to be really hard for you, Lesley
– is it all right if I call you Lesley?'

I nod.

'I should introduce myself. As Miss Schaffer says, my
name is Detective Walker. I'm thirty-seven years old.
That's very old, isn't it? How old are you?'

'Twelve.'

'Twelve? So I am three times as old as you.'

'And remainder one.'

'I'm sorry?'

'You are three times as old as me with a remainder of
one.'

'You like maths?'

I nod.

'It sounds like you might be better than me at it.' He
looks at Eadie who nods as if to say, 'You are probably
right.'

'Anyway, I am Detective Walker, and if you want to
remember that, it's because in this job I have to do a lot
of walking. See my shoes?'

He shows me the bottom of his shoes and they are
nearly worn through on the soles.

I smile a little. I don't mean to, but I can't help it. He's
talking to me as if I am a baby, but I don't mind. He's just
trying to be friendly, I can see that.

'So I am thirty-seven and I have been a policeman for

seventeen years, which, knowing you, you will already have worked out how long I was *not* a policeman for.'

'Twenty years,' I say.

He nods. 'All right, Lesley. I know it will be hard, but it would really help me and the other policemen trying to find who did this if we get as much information about Morag as we can.'

Eadie suggests we go sit at the dining table. As we go through, the detective takes his coat off, then the suit jacket he has on underneath. He puts them on a chair as Cook comes to see if she can get us any drinks.

Eadie and the detective ask for a coffee. I ask for an orange squash.

Detective Walker sits down, gets out his notepad and pen and says, 'What we are looking for, Lesley, is background. Anything you can tell us about Morag would be useful, any detail you can think of. How long you've known her, was she happy, did she have any enemies, who were her friends, all this information could be vital.'

I nod understanding, and Eadie suggests I start by telling him how long I have known Jonesy, and what room she was in.

'I've always known Morag. We call her Jonesy as that is her surname, Jones.' I realise straight away I said 'is' instead of 'was'.

'We've both been in Cottage 5 since we were three

194

and I dinnae remember before then, so as far as I can remember I've always known her. She slept in the junior girls' room in the bed next to me. She was always my friend, my best friend, we did everythin' together, other than school as I go to a different school. Even then she would sometimes come and wait for me to get off the bus when I came back in the afternoon.

'She was a fidget, a real fidget, quite often she would go to bed in my bed and it was always really hard to get to sleep because she would twitch when dropping off and she was even worse when she went to sleep. She would go still, and then suddenly jump like she was being attacked.

'She loved her doll, Maggie. It's so manky, but she always had it with her when she went to sleep. She would bring it into my bed. It's in my bed now. She hated having it cleaned, but it had to be sometimes, as it got horrible. She left it in my bed the night before she died and I will be able to keep it, won't I?'

'I'm sure you will,' says Eadie.

'Good. So she was lovely and bubbly and she had lots of energy, and she wanted to do everythin'. And she was so nice and why would anyone want to do anything to her?'

'Did she have any enemies?' Detective Walker asks.

'Naw. I mean, not really. There were people who

didnae understand her, thought she was a bit out there, a bit crazy, but not anyone that properly didn't like her. Not like me. People don't like me cos I go to the grammar school. If anything, they'd ask her why she was hanging out with *me*. No, people liked her even if they found her a bit much.'

'Sure, sure,' the detective says.

I look at him. I really look at him. What is he thinking? Is he trying to work out if someone thought she deserved it?

'And what did she think of the other incidents?' he says.

'You mean the murders?'

'The other deaths; was Morag scared?'

'She was scared, we all were, but also excited.'

'Excited?'

'I know, she was a bit crazy, but any big news made her excited. She wasnae perfect but why would anyone want to kill her?'

At that point I catch Eadie's eye. 'Why would anyone want to kill her, Eadie?'

And then I start to cry. Eadie gets up and puts her arm around me.

'It doesnae make sense,' I say between sobs.

'I know,' says Eadie, 'I know.'

'I'm so sorry,' says Detective Walker. 'When I was your

age, I had a best friend called William. We were inseparable. But he caught pneumonia and died, and I just
couldn't understand it, how someone who was always
there wasn't there any more. I knew old people died,
but I had never known anyone young die, and he was
only ten. And I couldn't help thinking how and why,
and I had to fall back on my faith that God would have
a plan—'

'But if God has a plan,' I say, 'why would he have a
plan to kill Jonesy? That's just rubbish, that's a rubbish
plan.'

'We may not know why he does what he does,' the
detective says.

'Well if he does know then I hate him and I don't
want anythin' to do with him.'

'Don't say that,' says Detective Walker.

'Why not? Whit's he going to do, kill me too?'

'All right, I think we'll leave it there,' says the detective, and he gets up and puts his jacket and coat on. He
tears off a piece of paper from his notepad and writes a
number on it next to the name 'Frank Walker'.

'If you can think of anything that might help us, feel
free to call us any time at the incident room. Ask for me
and if I'm not there leave your name and number and
I'll call you back.'

He squats down again, puts a hand on my arm and

looks me straight in the eye. 'Lesley, we are going to do everything we can to get whoever hurt Morag. We have many people working on this, and we are going to find that person and they are going to be punished. I am not going to rest until they are caught. You have my word on that.'

I thank him and he gets up and leaves. I am left in the dining room with Eadie. After a few minutes of silence she leans over and says, 'You did well, Lesley, you did really well.'

I force a little smile. 'Why *would* God do that, though?' I ask her. 'No one will explain why. If I ask the minister, whit will he say?'

'I don't know, Lesley, everyone has their own opinion when it comes to religion.'

'And whit's yours?'

'It's not for me to say, my view is personal.'

'Why won't anyone give me a proper answer?'

'Because the answer is different for everyone, Lesley; the answer depends on what you believe.'

'All right, so I am asking what do *you* believe?'

'I don't.'

'Don't what?'

'Believe ... in the whole God thing.'

'You think it's made up?'

'Yes. I'm more science- and fact-minded.'

'But that's whit I sometimes think. I thought that before, and that's whit I was thinking now, cos, like, why would God do something like that and anyway how would he do it, and like, no one has ever seen him? It must be made up.'

'Who's to say what's right? But listen to me, Lesley, this is very important: you must not tell anyone what I've just said. Religion is very important at the Homes and I would be out of a job, immediately, if anyone found out. Do you understand?'

'I understand.'

Mrs Paterson comes into the room and I go a little red as it feels like Eadie and I are talking about something top secret and I think Mrs Paterson can tell.

'Let's go for a walk,' Eadie suggests, and we go off round the grounds and have the most amazing talk, like she is talking to me as if I am a grown-up, which no one ever does. If it were possible it only makes me think more of her. She doesn't think what people tell her to think, she thinks for herself. I vow to myself that from now on I will do that too.

45

In the afternoon I'm told to go to see the minister. Mrs Paterson says that as I have so many questions about religion and why God let Jonesy get murdered, perhaps I should go and talk to him. The minister, not God. I guess that Detective Walker must have told Mrs Paterson what I said about God. I wish he hadn't.

I walk up to the church on the hill. The clouds are a muted grey and the drizzle lands lightly on me. Not enough for a full coat but enough that when I arrive there is a gentle covering on my cardigan.

I push the church door open. It's heavy and it takes both hands and all my weight to push it open far enough for me to squeeze through.

Candles are lit at the front and as I walk up the aisle I

see Mr Samson stacking Bibles. He must have heard the door but it isn't until I am within a few yards of him that he turns round. He has a bald head like a chess pawn and a long black cloak. He greets me by taking my hands and clasping them in his, putting his forehead against them.

He gives me the creeps. He's been to the cottage a couple of times to console me and I have tried to avoid him each time. I didn't want to come, but Mrs Paterson insisted.

He invites me to sit with him in the front pew.

'I gather you have some questions,' he says, bending his head down as if to get a proper look at me.

'Naw, no really,' I say, hoping I can make this encounter as short as possible.

'Now come on, Lesley, there's no need to be shy. Mrs Paterson has told me about your questions, about God and so on. It's good to ask questions.'

I don't answer. I have become better lately at holding silences. I never used to be able to, but if Jonesy's death has taught me anything it's that I don't have to talk to anyone. They can't make me.

'My child, do not be afraid to share your thoughts. It shows you have an inquisitive mind. God values that.'

'Does he?'

'Of course he does. He wants all his creatures to think about the wonder of the world.'

'Does he want us to question whether he exists?'

'He knows people will question their faith at times.'

'He does? And what does he say to them when they do, because I'm thinking that he doesnae actually exist. For one, if he were to exist and control everythin' then why let whit happened, happen to Jonesy?'

'Our faith will be tested many times in our lives.'

'So you're saying God has decided to test my faith by killing my best friend? That's no right, is it? I don't think he's sat about and said, "I know whose faith needs testing, Lesley Beaton's. And the best way to test her faith is not by doing a miracle, or making a vision appear, but by having Morag Jones murdered." That doesn't seem like a test a normal person would set, and if it *is* a test God would set, then he's clearly some sort of crazy.

'By my reckoning there are two options: he does exist and he's a brutal, unhinged murderer, or he doesnae exist, and all this is just made up like Father Christmas and there really is no one in charge, so we are all just fending for ourselves. But then if he doesnae exist why would everyone go to all the trouble of building big churches to worship someone imaginary? They can't be lying to everyone, can they?'

The minister takes my hands in his again. I just want to scream, 'LET GO OF ME!'

He speaks in a calm, low tone. 'God has many paths

for us all, and we do not know why he chooses each path, but we have faith that the path he has chosen is the right one. And though we may question his ways, or even his existence, we know that he loves every one of us.'

I pull my hands from his. 'That doesnae answer my question; that also suggests he loves the person whit killed Jonesy, which goes back to my first point about him being crazy.'

'You have been through a lot, and it is only natural for you to question, but know that God will be there for you when you need him.'

'All right,' I say, giving up. I think if I sat here for a week he still would not be able to give me a straight answer. I decide to be polite. 'Thank you for your help.' I get up and walk back down the aisle.

As the sound of my footsteps echoes round the church he calls out after me, 'The Church is always here for you.' I lift up my arm as if to say thank you, but as I walk out I think the truth is, there is nothing for me here and I have just learnt the biggest secret of my life, that grown-ups lie, a lot, and the Church is the biggest lie of all. Father Christmas multiplied by a hundred.

The thing I can't figure out is, why would they do that? What's in it for them?

46

The next day is the day I have been dreading. I have to finally say goodbye to Jonesy.

This is the first funeral I have ever been to; only Jane and Sally's housemates went to theirs. I have never known anyone die, even old people. I am in a fog. I feel like I am walking in a giant balloon and everyone is looking at me to see how I am, and I don't *know* how I am.

They won't let me be on my own. If I go for a walk someone always walks with me and asks me how I am, and they keep saying I should talk about it, I should say what I feel, but I don't know what I feel and I don't know how to say it, and so I don't say anything. At mealtimes I feel everyone watching me. I want them to stop but I can't bring myself to say anything, so I just keep my head down so they can't see my face.

It feels like when you've been slapped hard on the ear and there's a ringing sound that goes all over your head for about ten seconds. I feel like that ringing is going on all the time. I physically feel as if I've been hit and am struggling to stand up.

And now it is the day of Jonesy's funeral, and there is no one here from her family. I don't know if they've even been told that she has died.

The whole house gets up in silence this morning. Even breakfast is eaten in silence. Everyone is dressed in black. It's Saturday so the others from Cottage 5 are held off school for the funeral. Everyone in our house is going, as well as her classmates.

The girls in our room keep crying. We all keep crying, and when two people are crying another person will join the group and cry, and others will join in and it never seems to stop.

For the last week I have had her doll Maggie in my bed. I gave it away last night so they can put it in the coffin with her. I wrote a letter for her and sealed it and asked them to put it in too. I will not tell anyone what was in the letter, it was personal, and when it's my turn to go I hope I meet up with her and we can discuss it.

'It's here,' comes the call from downstairs. Not 'she's

here', but 'it's here'. That means that the hearse has pulled up outside our cottage. I don't look out the window to see it.

'C'mon,' says Shona, and she takes my hand and leads me downstairs. The front door is open and it's at that point that I see the car and the coffin in the back. I think for a moment that it would be nice for Jonesy to be able to come inside for one last time, but she can't.

Mr and Mrs Paterson are stood behind the car and there are others standing behind them, all dressed in black. Mrs Paterson holds out a hand for me to join them and I walk along the path to the road. I try not to cry but I can't stop myself. I get to Mrs Paterson and she holds me close to her. Mr Paterson rubs my head, and my tears and snot go all over Mrs Paterson's black coat.

I try to wipe off the mess I've made. 'It doesn't matter,' says Mrs Paterson, and I grab hold of her gloved hand.

Mr Paterson gives a nod to one of the undertakers, who gets in the car and starts driving very slowly. We walk behind it down Faith Avenue and then right onto Church Road all the way up to the church.

Everyone is silent; the only sounds are the low rumble of the car, and feet on the tarmac.

When we get to the church we don't know if we are supposed to go in first, or the coffin. Eventually Mr Paterson tells us all to go in. Mrs Paterson walks in with me still holding my hand and we sit in the front pew. Mr Paterson comes and joins us. I cry some more. I want Shona, Mary, Eldrey and Pam to join us but they sit in the row behind me. Shona and Mary are white in the face, and Pam looks a bit sick. Eldrey has her eyes closed and is praying hard. She is the most interested in God out of all of us. Maybe she thinks he'll stop her getting the belt so much. I put my head down, alone between the two adults.

When everyone has sat down, they bring in the coffin and put it up on a stand. It's level with us, *she* is level with us. She is in that box, dead.

That thought stops me crying.

The minister gets up to his lectern and starts to speak. I can't hear what he's saying. After our talk I have little interest in what he has to say anyway, it's all just lies.

I think about Jonesy. Our bedroom is so quiet without her. I think of how the space her personality used to take up is now not being taken up by anything, nothing fills it, it is just empty space. I think about how it is all so unfair. She didn't get to grow old; someone took that from her.

The one thing I don't feel and haven't felt is scared. When Jane Denton and Sally Ward were killed, I was scared, but now I just don't care. If someone is going to kill me, then let them kill me.

Mr Paterson gets up to speak. I try to listen to him but cry some more. I hear some bits about 'being there for each other', and, 'Morag loved life, and we must hurt but then heal.' Neither bit makes much sense to me. Then he looks directly at me and says something about 'the twins', meaning me and Jonesy.

When it's over we stand around outside. Pam, Shona, Eldrey and Mary join me and we wait for them to bring out the coffin and put it in the car to take it to the graveyard.

She is getting buried in Paisley as Renfrewshire Council have requested she be put there and they are the ones paying for it. There's not enough space at the cemetery of the Homes church, not unless you're very important, and apparently Jonesy isn't important enough.

Mr and Mrs Paterson and I get in the back of a black car. There is a bus laid on to take the others to the grave-yard which is about twenty minutes' drive away.

We ride in silence. I stare out of the window and see grey clouds hovering above us all.

When we get to the graveyard we walk up to the hole in the ground. This is where Jonesy is now going to stay for ever, all on her own.

Mr Samson says prayers as they lower Morag into the grave.

We stand around until it's time to go back to the Homes. I decide to ride on the bus. I sit with Pam and Shona and they cuddle me all the way.

Back at the cottage there is food laid on. The Superintendent is there, and Mr Paterson introduces me to him. Mr Gordon already knows who I am, though he has never spoken to me before. He shakes my hand with both of his; the light comes off his shiny bald head and he smiles at me. His smile looks sinister. He might be trying to be nice, but I can't feel the kindness; he's always terrified me and him being nice is just as bad. His teeth are yellow and his skin is red and stretched, like he has been boiled.

'I understand you were good friends with Morag Jones.'

'Aye, sir, we were best friends.'

'I'm sorry for your loss,' he says as he rubs my shoulder with his shovel-like hand.

'Thank you, sir,' I say. I am determined not to cry in front of him. In fact I am determined to get away from him as soon as I can.

'We will find who did this, Lesley, and we will punish them.'

He fixes me with a stare, like he is staring *into* me, like the inside of me must know that he is going to be true to his word.

I don't doubt it. If he finds the person who did it, he will punish them with his giant arms and giant hands. But then, the police didn't find the murderer after Jane or Sally died. How is this any different?

*

Around about two o' clock the mourners start leaving the cottage. Outside, boys are playing football as if nothing has happened. How can they still do that?

I go to my room and start to read. I am reading a book called *What Katy Did* at the moment. Someone bought it for me in the hope it would make me feel better. It's about an American girl who is a bit of a rebel. I like it but I find it hard to concentrate on the words as I drift off easily.

At tea that evening we have sausage and mash and thick gravy, which is my favourite. I think Cook might have made it especially for me. Mr Paterson says grace in the same way he has done every night since Jonesy died. He asks the Lord to look after her up in heaven and to look after us down here.

He doesn't know that I know that there is no Lord. And if there is no Lord there is no heaven. So Jonesy isn't in heaven, she's just dead. No happy place in the sky, just lying underground in the graveyard in Paisley, surrounded by other dead people in boxes.

I am glad the funeral is over because I couldn't do it again. It was a day I needed to get through. Now is the next chapter of my life, but I don't know how I am going to do it without Jonesy. I stop listening to Mr Paterson and eat in silence. A few of the other girls talk, but it's still very quiet. It's always quiet since Jonesy died.

47

I go back to school on Monday. Clara Dee is very nice to me. All of her friends are now nice to me too. They wait for me to arrive in the morning, and they save me a space at dinnertime.

At the Homes I just want people to leave me alone; at school I am glad people are being friendly. Even the teachers are really nice to me, they check how I am, and smile at me when I come into the class. I am not stupid, I know that they know, and I know why they are doing it, but I don't mind. No one treats me like the poor kid any more. It's almost as if I was just like one of them. It's horrible that it has taken something like this to happen for them to notice me.

Now I'm back at school I'm happier than I have

been since Jonesy died and I think I know why. Jonesy was never here; she was never at the grammar school. There is nothing that reminds me of her. At the Homes everything I see reminds me of her. *That is where we sat together after she fell and cut her leg. That is where she had a wee behind the bush when she was desperate.*

The worst place is our bedroom. Being in there just reminds me of her non-stop. I've thought about asking Mr and Mrs Paterson if I could sleep in another room, maybe with the big girls, but then I realised I don't want to be away from Jonesy's bed.

Mrs Paterson's talked about them taking Jonesy's bed away. I said no straight away. I even slept in her bed one night when I couldn't get to sleep as I wanted to smell her.

They've given me a teddy bear, as if that would make up for the loss of Jonesy. He's called Albert. I am twelve years old and for some reason they think a teddy will help me. The strange thing is it really does help. I hug him when I go to sleep, and I like the feeling of him next to me, I feel like he will protect me. I shouldn't need a teddy bear but I can't help how I feel.

At school I work as hard as ever. At ten to three I know I only have sixty minutes left and I start to feel sick as I know I will soon have to get the train and bus back to the Homes.

I wonder if I should join a sports team so I can stay longer. There are teams that practise after school some days, but then I wouldn't be able to go back with the other Homes kids. I could ask Mr Paterson if he would come and pick me up, but I know what the answer would be. People are being nice to me now but that would be pushing things.

48

I come to a decision when I wake up. I decide not to be sad any more. I decide that I have a choice: I can either be sad about Jonesy for the rest of my life or I can do something about it. I can find the person who killed her, and I can make sure that they spend the rest of their life in jail or, even better, dead.

Every day that they are not caught is a day they are free and walking around, and I don't want them to be free, I want them to be in a prison cell feeling terrible for hurting Jonesy, or I want them to be waiting to be hanged and wishing they hadn't done what they did to her. I know you shouldn't want someone dead but I don't care. This person deserves to die for what they did to Jonesy and the other girls. If I can make that happen,

I will. I am closest to all of this; the clues must be closest to me. If a man killed Jane and Sally, why would he kill Jonesy too? She had nothing to do with those girls. The older girls seem to have been friends, so that might be a connection between them, but they definitely weren't friends with Jonesy. I just need to work it all out. Jonesy thought I could.

I'll speak to Detective Walker again and find out what he knows. I didn't say much last time, but if I get him to come back to the Homes I can tell him what I know and he can tell me what he knows, and together we can work out who did this.

When I get to school, I go to the stationery cupboard and take a notepad, then I start writing down what I know about the murders. When Detective Walker comes I'll put down what he knows too.

I have a purpose. The fog has lifted and it is time for action.

49

'She's called Petal.'

'I know,' I say.

'Wannae stroke her?'

'Aye.'

I walk up to the caretaker and the horse and pat her on the side. Her coat is matted. It is a dirty brown colour with a splodge of white on her face.

Mr Sharples watches me pat her. 'Aye she's a biggie, sixteen hands,' he says.

'She smells a bit,' I say.

'Well, wouldn't you if you'd been pulling round this cart all day?' He points to the wooden trailer behind her, filled with hedge clippings. 'New here?' he asks. 'I havenae seen you afore.'

He has, he saw me before the fight with Glenda McAdam, but maybe I am just forgettable.

'Nah, been here since a wean. I dinnae go to the school, though, I go to the grammar school, so am not about as much as the others.'

'Wannae help me walk Petal back to the stables?'

'Aye, all right,' I say.

Mr Sharples is wearing dungarees with a stained light green shirt underneath. He looks dirty, like his face needs a proper wash. His grey hair is brushed forward like some men do when their hair is going thin. I don't know why they do it, Mr Paterson doesn't. His is trimmed but you are not to mention his lack of hair, as he can get angry about it.

'She's a great friend,' he says, 'and do you know the best thing about her?'

'Whit?'

'You can tell her all your secrets and she won't tell a soul. And we've all got secrets, haven't we?'

I nod.

We walk down Love Avenue and he lets me hold the lead-rope.

'She's sixteen years old, is Petal. Old enough to start courting, aye? You're still a bit young for that, aren't you?'

'Aye.'

'Give it time, 'fore you know it you'll be fighting them off, eh?'

I don't want to talk about boys. I stroke Petal's nose some more, and change the subject. 'What does she eat?'

'Mainly oats. It's nearly time for her tea so you can help me feed her.'

'All right,' I say.

We turned onto Church Road.

'I havenae even asked your name, young lady. What is it?'

'Lesley.'

'Aww, that's a lovely name. My name is Mr Sharples.'

'I know. You live over at the farmhouse just outside the main gate.'

'Aye I do, I do. And Petal here lives in the field out behind it. She has a lovely field to wander around in.'

'Is she lonely out there all on her own?'

'D'you know, I've never asked her that. Hey, Petal, do you get lonely in that field all on your own? I bet you dinnae; I bet you've got lots of other animals you are friends with.'

'How long have you worked here?'

'Twenty years now. I've seen them all come and go. So many of you youngsters, you're everywhere, and all growing up so fast.'

We walk to the farmhouse. He uncouples the cart and pulls it around the side, then comes back and says, 'I'm just going to get a bucket of feed from inside, you two stay here.'

'Whit if she runs off?' I say.

'Look inta her eyes, Lesley. She's tired, she dinnae want to run off. She just wants a bit of food and a chance to stop pulling this cart.' He goes inside.

I turn to talk to Petal. 'You wouldnae run off, will you? You are a nice horse, and a nice horse wouldnae run off.'

She lowers her head to me and I rub the top of her nose and her cheeks. He was right, she does look tired. Her head jolts up when Mr Sharples comes back out with her tea and she shuffles a little with her feet.

'Bring her round the back, there's a place where I hook up the bucket.'

I lead Petal round the back of the farmhouse and he fixes the bucket to a fence pole. Petal goes straight in with her nose and starts crunching away.

I think, *Here I am with Mr Sharples and Petal and no one knows where I am, and I am always supposed to tell someone where I am going and to be in a pair.* I feel a sudden slash of fear.

'I expect you've been pretty scared with all the goings-on around here of late?' he says.

'They killed my best friend.'

'Who was that?'

'Jonesy. Morag Jones, they killed her.'

He is silent for a moment and then says, 'I'm very sorry.'

'I'm gonnae catch them. I'm gonnae make them pay for whit they did.'

'I'm sure you will,' he replies.

'You dinnae believe me, do you? No one believes me, but I will catch them. No one does that to Jonesy and gets away with it.'

'It must be really hard.'

'It is.'

'D'you want a piece of chocolate?'

'I should be getting back to the house.'

'It's just inside. It would cheer you up.'

'Naw, I have to go, I have to get back, but thank you.'

'S'all right,' Mr Sharples says. 'Any time you want to come and say hello to Petal just come on over, she's great at helping you not feel so sad. She's saved me from feeling sad many a time.'

I wave goodbye to him and to Petal and walk back to Cottage 5.

*

When I get back, Pam is on the front steps with Shona.

'Where *you* been?' asks Pam.

'I walked Petal the horse back to the farmhouse with Mr Sharples.'

'The caretaker?'

'Uh huh.'

'Oh God, Leeeesssss, whit did you do that for? He's a weirdy.'

'He seemed nice.'

'Les, he's a creep, he whistles at girls when they go past, did you no know?'

'Yeah, the way he looks at you is gross,' adds Shona.

'He was nice to me, let me feed the horse and offered me some chocolate.'

'Oh God, Lesley. It couldae been dangerous. He's strange, I wouldn't put it past him being the one whit's been doing it all. Jesus, Les, you had a lucky escape.'

'Getaway.'

'Think about it, Les. Who has keys to all the houses? Who can go anywhere in the grounds? Who would be the best person to hide a murder weapon?' says Pam.

'But—'

'He's no married, is he?'

'I dunno.'

'He's not. He's over forty and he's no married. Why not? Cos he likes young girls, doesn't he?'

'I saw the polis talking to him two weeks ago, before Jonesy.'

'They spoke to everyone.'

'I'm telling you, Lesley, be very careful.'

I feel bad. He was really nice to me, but they are right. Mr Sharples is a bit strange, I think, and I worry about him for the rest of the day.

50

Gran came to see me today. Eadie told me my mum knows about Jonesy. I'm angry that she hasn't come to see me herself. Neither her nor Gran came to the funeral.

Gran gives me the biggest hug when she sees me and she doesn't let go.

We go to the tearoom and she buys me chocolate cake and fizzy pop and tells me about when her brother died. He had a heart attack and just died in the back garden one day. She was doing the washing up with his wife when she saw him fall into the fence and then into the plants. They rushed over but he was face down in the soil. He had been turning over onions with the garden fork and his heart just gave out.

She talks about the days after he died. She says she

felt numb and confused. She says there's no set time for grieving and in a way it never ends, you just get used to it.

Then she starts telling me a funny story about a lady who lives on her street who people thought was carrying on with someone who wasn't her husband. She has never really told me stories like this before, but I think she is trying to treat me like more of a grown-up. The woman was seen leaving her house at strange times and people had started to talk about her. Anyway, it turns out she was seen in Glasgow city centre, in a bar, and she was kissing another woman, and now everyone on the street knows this apart from the husband and no one will tell him.

The gossip makes a tingle go through me. My first thought is to go back to the cottage and tell Jonesy. I finish the cake and Gran orders another pop for me and another tea for her.

After that we go for a walk around the village. I have never walked so much in my life as I have since Jonesy died. Everyone wants to take me for a walk. I think it might be so they don't have to look at me while they talk to me.

We walk up to the bridge over the stream at the front of the Homes and stand there watching the water flow underneath.

'There are some very bad people in this world, Lesley, but don't ever forget there are some very good people too.'

I say, 'I think you were born a good person, Gran, and my mum wasnae.'

She looks at me, horrified. 'I'll pretend I didn't hear that,' she says.

'Why?'

'Because you don't know whit your mother has had to go through.'

'Well, why do you come to see me and no her? If she loves me, surely she would want to see me. You do, but she doesnae.'

'Your mother loves you very much, so much you'd never know.'

'I don't know because she's never told me.'

'Lesley, your mother loves you even if she's never said so.'

'That's the thing, Gran, I don't think she does. I can tell *you* love me. But I think a lot of talk about love is a way for grown-ups to keep kids quiet.'

Since Jonesy died I've begun to realise that grown-ups lie, a lot. They lie to try to make you feel better, they lie to stop you asking questions. They say, 'It will be fine,' when it most definitely won't be fine.

Gran's face changes and she fixes me with a glare.

'Now you listen to me, Lesley. I know you're having a hard time, but I will not listen to you talk like this about your mother. You have no idea how hard it is for your mum to not be able to be with you. Now, let's get you back to your cottage.'

We walk to Cottage 5 in silence. I feel so alive having said out loud what I have thought all this time. I have never said anything before, to keep people happy. Well now I don't care about keeping people happy. I am going to say what I think, and no one is going to stop me.

51

I haven't seen so many policemen about the Homes in the last few days. I wonder if they think we're safe now as nobody's been killed for a while. But that doesn't make any sense. They should only have fewer policemen about once they capture the murderer. I don't know why they haven't arrested anyone. Maybe they don't care about us because we are kids without parents, so they aren't bothered that we are being murdered. If it was outside they would care; someone's parents would make the police do something. But in here, nothing. They send some police around for a few days, ask a few questions and then go back about their business. How many more of us have to die before someone is arrested?

After school, I decide to go and see Eadie. There's no

one waiting for her and no one in her office so I just walk in. She looks happy to see me. She's reading some papers but puts them aside when I appear and gives me a hug. She asks if I'd like a cup of tea and I seem to be getting a taste for it so I say yes. She says she was hoping I would come by as there was something she wanted to talk to me about.

I freeze. I immediately think it's something bad and I can't take any more bad news. She sees this and tells me it's nothing to be afraid of and she'll explain all shortly.

We go to the small kitchen near her office and while we wait for the kettle to boil she asks how my day was. I tell her about Clara Dee. I say I am becoming good friends with her – not best friends, as I will never have a best friend again, but definitely good friends. I tell her about what we are working on at school and the marks I've been getting.

She offers me a biscuit, which I take, and we go back to her office. When we sit down, she fixes me with a look and I know what she is about to say will be serious.

'How do you feel about adoption?' she asks.

I don't know. I don't know how I feel about adoption, so I smile and shrug.

'Because there is a couple who might be interested in adopting you. They seem like lovely people. Would you like to meet them?'

'I think so,' I say.

'You don't have to, you know.'

'I know. Well … aye, if you say they're nice.'

'They are. I think you will like them. I think they could be great for you.'

'I didnae think anyone would want to adopt a twelve-year-old. People want to adopt babies, not kids my age, once we've already gone wrong.'

'You haven't gone wrong.'

'Naw, that wasn't what I meant, I meant before we've got personalities.'

'Maybe that's true, but maybe there are people out there who don't want the trouble of bringing up a baby. Maybe there are people who think, *We don't have children, perhaps we could help someone who can be helped, who deserves to be helped*.'

'You think I deserve to be helped?'

'Lesley, I can't tell you anything, I can only guess at someone's motivations, and I can only suggest the child that would benefit most. I haven't put forward any other children to the couple. Do you see what I am saying, Lesley?'

'Aye … I think so.'

'Good. Now, this isn't straightforward, adoption never is, but the first step is that you are interested. The second is whether your natural mother is agreeable.

I hope you don't mind, but I have already talked to her and told her how good this could be for you and fortunately she has agreed in principle.

'The next step would be to arrange a meeting for you with the couple to see if you still want to go forward with it.'

By the time I leave to go back to the cottage I am excited by the idea. I am also scared; what if they don't like me? What if they are strange, or religious, or strict? Still, it'd probably not be any worse than being in here. Maybe something good will finally come of this summer.

52

On Saturday I am still thinking about what the girls in my room said about Mr Sharples. I decide to write down the facts.

Mr Sharples

- He is weird.
- He can get anywhere in these grounds without anyone suspecting him.
- He can carry tools that can hurt people and it not be suspicious.
- He could have been in the woods where they found Jane and just said he was after kindling.
- He could have driven Sally Ward's body to the river on the back of his tractor and no one would have noticed.

- Jonesy never liked him. Maybe she told him she thought he was a suspect?
- Being weird isn't a reason to be a suspect, you can be weird and not be dangerous, but he is weird.
- He was nice to me the other day, but maybe he was doing that for a reason, maybe he was trying to appear normal, because of what he did to Jonesy.
- No one seems to be doing anything about the killer. Why don't we matter?
- The police say they need evidence and if they aren't going to get it then I will. I will not sit around and let this happen to another girl. That girl could be me.

The murderer might not be Mr Sharples, but then again it might be, and anything I can learn about him will help, even if it means I can rule him out. I've never spoken to him before the other day, and he's never spoken to me before. But Pam said he whistles at girls when they go past. Maybe I'm too young so he *wouldn't* say anything to me; maybe it's just girls who have boobs he says things to.

Jonesy and I used to pretend we had boobs; we'd stick stuff in our jumpers and walk round the room like we were older. We even stole a bra from the big girls' room once, tying a knot in the back to make it fit properly. Then Jonesy pretended to be a boy talking to me who couldn't stop looking at my boobs. I smile at the memory of it, but as soon as I do I feel sad.

It makes me determined to do something. I'm going to go to Mr Sharples's farm buildings to see if I can find out anything about him.

Yesterday was the last day of school and it's now the summer holidays, so I have plenty of time to investigate him. I leave the cottage and walk around the village until I spot Mr Sharples, cutting the big patch of grass that runs along Praise Road. I know what I have to do. I walk fast through the gate and across to the farmhouse. I go straight round the back so no one can see me. I see Petal standing there in her pen, and wave at her. I remember what Mr Sharples said: 'The horse can't tell anyone,' so she can't let him know I've been here.

There's a large garage filled with tools and machines. I try the rusted red metal door and it opens straight away, but with a loud creak. Inside it is dusty and dark and the only light comes in through one dirty, dusty window. It smells of dried grass, mud and oil, and everywhere you turn there is equipment – a small tractor, a little motorbike; along one wall is a saw, a rack that has all sorts of screwdrivers and spanners on it, and some mallets.

If you wanted to kill someone there is plenty of stuff here you could do it with.

Along the same wall is a desk with a noticeboard above

it, which has letters pinned to it. There's a wooden chair in front of it with a brown overall draped over the back.

On the desk are a radio, a light, and what looks like a small engine of some sort that Mr Sharples might be repairing. There are also some letters and envelopes spread out.

The desk has two drawers, which I open; in one is a pair of battered shoes, in the other is a folder, but it's just filled with receipts. I open one of the letters. It's from Renfrewshire Council, saying that 'after consideration' his job would be continued.

I open another; this one's from the Dykebar Hospital.

Dear Mr Sharples,

I note with disappointment that you have missed your last two appointments.

It is vital that you continue your treatment with us. To miss further appointments would not only jeopardise your health but also your employment as we would be duty bound to inform your employer.

Please contact my office as soon as possible to reschedule an appointment.

Yours sincerely,

Dr H. Talbot

I can feel the heat in my face as I read the letter.

Shona and Pam were right – he's a mental.

The Dykebar is where the mentally wrong go. Some of the parents of Homes kids are in there; that's why they can't look after their children. And one of the older boys was sent there after he went crazy and started trying to attack everyone with a hammer.

I have to tell the girls. I have to get out of here.

Outside, I hear whistling and the sound of metal being rolled on the path. I drop the letter, run to the back of the garage and duck behind the tractor.

The door creaks loudly as Mr Sharples pushes it fully open. He's talking, but it seems to be to himself. I peep over the tractor wheel and see that his back is to me. He is stood at the desk, mumbling.

A bead of sweat comes down my forehead and rolls down my nose. I'm trying to breathe as quietly as possible. I watch as Mr Sharples pulls open one drawer, then pulls open the other one, then tuts.

My legs are starting to hurt. I'm crouched down and my thighs are cramping. He has to leave soon – I can't stay in this position much longer. Mr Sharples looks in the first drawer again and lets out a big sigh and then walks out, shutting the door behind him. The garage is now dark apart from the small patch of light coming through the dirty window.

I breathe out. I wait for what I think is five minutes,

to be sure he's left, and then climb out from behind the tractor. I try the door handle but it's shut tight and won't open. I didn't hear Mr Sharples lock it. I lean against the door but I can't get it to move.

I look around for another way out and realise that the window is my only chance. I put a small stool underneath it, open it up and squeeze through. It's so tight the metal frame scrapes my leg as I lower myself down. I have to go head first and end up doing a handstand to reach the ground. Luckily, I'm good at handstands at gym, and I take a few steps forward on my hands before flipping over to land, a little stunned, in a crab position.

I get up and brush myself down. I shut the window as much as I can, then creep to the side of the building to make sure I can't see Mr Sharples. He's not there, so I walk as fast as I can back to Cottage 5.

When I get there, Shona looks me up and down. 'Where've yous been?' she demands.

'Nowheres,' I reply.

'Then why is your shin bleeding?'

'Fell over, didn't I?'

She thinks about it. 'You fall over on your knees, not your shin, you liar.'

I have no response. I think about telling her what I saw, the letter, but I can't. It could be what Jonesy knew that got her killed.

'Got to go clean it up,' I say and run inside, up to the bathroom, and use toilet paper to clean up the blood.

I'm going to tell the police. I'm going to tell Detective Walker. I'm going to make sure that bastard gets what's coming to him.

53

The next morning I ask Mrs Paterson if it would be all right if I used her phone to call Detective Walker. He told me that if there was anything I could help them with I should call, so that is what I am doing.

Mrs Paterson takes me into her and Mr Paterson's living room. They have their own private space that we are not allowed into. I have only ever been in here once or twice. It smells different to the rest of the house, like stale air that doesn't move around much.

The phone is kept on the windowsill and she takes it down and moves it over to the table so I can dial the number. I haven't used a phone much before so when I try to dial I get it wrong the first two times. Eventually Mrs Paterson takes the number, dials it, checks it is ringing and gives the handset to me. It rings a couple more times, then a female voice says, 'Grant Street Police Station, how can I help you?'

Mrs Paterson stays, which is fine with me as she needs to know what is going on to keep the other girls safe. I ask to speak to Detective Walker and the voice says he isn't at work today, so I tell her that my name is Lesley Beaton, that I live at Cottage 5 at the Homes, and that I want to talk to him, so could he either call the Homes, or if he is going past he could come and visit as I have some important information that could help him.

I'm bursting to tell someone about Mr Sharples. I would talk to Jonesy if she were here. I would talk to Clara if it weren't the school holidays, but I can't trust the girls in my room to keep it to themselves and I don't trust most of the adults around here. They talk to each other so it could get out that way. I want to tell Eadie but it's a Sunday and she's not here. In the end I decide to tell Mrs Paterson. If anything happens to me I need at least one other person to know what I know.

'Mrs Paterson,' I say, 'if the polis call back can you come get me? I think Mr Sharples might be the one killing girls. Please don't tell anyone else yet as I can't prove it, but I found something that might mean it is him.'

She promises to keep quiet about it and I feel a sense

of relief to have told someone, although I can tell from her expression that she thinks I'm half cracked.

I go outside to meet up with the girls. I can feel Shona watching me. I know she knows something is up, but she doesn't ask what it is, so I don't tell her.

I'll just wait for Detective Walker to get back to me.

54

The next day I am drying the dishes after tea. They think I'm better now, so I have to join in with the chores again. I don't mind really. I was sick of sitting doing nothing and it was making me feel guilty.

There's a knock at the door, then Pam comes into the kitchen and says there's a man to see me. The girls let out an, 'Oooooohh.' I ignore them, put down the tea towel and go to the front door where Detective Walker is stood waiting for me. I see behind him that his car is parked at the end of our path.

'Hullo, Detective,' I say.

'Hi, Lesley,' he says, 'I got your message, and we were driving home when I suddenly remembered, so ...'

He gestures to the car as he says 'we', so I ask who's in the car.

'Oh that's my fiancée, Lizzie.' He waves at the car and a woman waves back. 'D'you want me to come in, or …?'

'They'll all listen to us if you come in.'

'We could sit here?'

'They'll listen to us here, too. Chores are just about to finish so they'll be out in a minute. Shall we go for a wee walk?' I suggest.

He looks at the car then back to me. 'Yes, yes that sounds like a good idea, I'll just tell Lizzie.'

'You could tell her where the tearoom is – we could meet her there,' I suggest.

'Yes, yes, another good idea, that's what I'll do.'

He goes to the car window and Lizzie rolls it down and I get a good look at her. She's pretty. She's wearing a light brown cardigan and her hair is dark and tied back.

When he speaks to her she nods and gets out of the car. He gives her some money and points her in the direction of the tearoom.

He watches her walk away, then comes back to me. 'So, how can I help you?' he asks, as we set off walking.

'Lizzie's very pretty. Is she a lot younger than you? Have you been married before?'

'What's this got to do with Morag?'

'Nothing, sorry, she just seems a lot younger than you.'

'Can we stick to why I'm here, please?'

'Aye, sorry. I was thinking, whoever killed Jane and Sally and Jonesy, they have to live here. They have to be on the grounds.'

'And why is that?'

'Because if someone was on the grounds all three times, who's no usually here, it would be obvious because people would want to know whit they were doin'.'

'Good point.'

'So it's someone who's always around. And it's someone who hates women.'

'Why do you say that?'

'Well, why else would you do it if you didnae hate women?'

'I see.'

'So who lives on the grounds and hates women?'

'I don't know.'

'The caretaker.'

I feel bad saying this as Mr Sharples was very nice to me. I feel like I am betraying him but it's more important that we are safe.

'I see, and why do you say that?'

'He's no married, is he? Who's no married at that age? And why is he no married?'

'I don't know.'

'Cos he's ugly. He's ugly and there are all these young girls around and none of them will look at him because he's so hideous and he gets angry and he thinks, *I'll teach them a lesson*. That could be what happened with Jane and Sally.'

'Right ...' Detective Walker's gaze is fixed on the trees. 'You think he had a different reason for killing Morag Jones, then?'

'Jonesy was younger than the others. But mibbie she told him how ugly he was, or, or mibbie she worked out it was him whit done it and confronted him, and he saw her behind the cottage and took the opportunity to keep her quiet for good. Think about it. He can go anywhere in the grounds and it wouldn't be suspicious, he's strong enough to have done it.'

I look at Detective Walker to see if he thinks I might be right. I don't think he does, as he grimaces and rubs his cheek.

'I'm sure we interviewed Mr Sharples quite early on, Lesley. But I'll go through the notes.'

'Mibbie he lied?'

'Yes, maybe, maybe.'

'He's got a reason, and he's got the chance to do it. How many people have the reason *and* the chance?'

'Hmmm ...'

I've held back the last bit of information, but Detective

Walker still doesn't seem convinced, so I hit him with it. 'And he's a mental.'

'A mental?'

'Aye, he's a lunatic, getting treated at Dykebar, that's where all the lunatics go.'

'And how do you know this?

'Saw it, didn't I. In his garage, I saw a letter.'

'You've been going through his private property?'

'Had to, sir. They havenae found who did it yet; someone's got to do it.'

'Lesley, I can assure you we have many men investigating this back at the station.'

'Aye, you've got many men, but none of them have found anyone, so mibbie someone else should try. After all, the next person he's gonnae kill isnae going to be one of yous lot, is it? It'll be someone like me, or even me. I cannae just sit about and wait for it to happen, I've got to do something.'

The detective looks at me for a moment. 'It's a good point, Lesley, I can't argue with it, but you shouldn't have done that. There are rules.'

'Aye, but what good are rules if we are all deid?'

'I understand what you are saying, but we have spoken to all the men who live and work at the Homes, they were the first people we looked at, and if there was anything suspicious we would have investigated further.'

'Right ...'

'But I'll tell you what,' he says, 'when I'm back at the station tomorrow morning I will read the file on Mr Sharples and see if there is anything in what you have said, a new angle.'

'Angle?'

'Yes, you know, a different way of looking at it.'

'Why is that an angle?'

'Well, Lesley, when you have a problem like the one we have here it pays to look at things from a number of different positions, or angles, to see if it looks different when viewed from another place. See that bush over there?'

'Aye.'

'Well that bush will look different to us when we're standing here to if we were over there,' he said, pointing at the junction, 'and it's the same with a problem or a case.'

'I see. All right. Thank you, sir.'

'And I'll come back and let you know what I find.'

Our walk is now leading us towards the tearoom.

'Detective Walker,' I say.

'Yes?'

'Why did you no get engaged until now?'

'I guess I hadn't met the right woman.'

'And is Lizzie the right woman?

'I think so, yes.'

'She's very pretty.'

'I think she is, yes.'

'Does she like going out with a policeman?'

'I hope so.'

'Are you having a baby, sir?'

'I'm sorry?'

'Are you havin' a baby, is that why you're getting married?'

'Why do you say that?'

'Because that's why a lot of people get married. And she touched her stomach when she got out of the car.'

'You are a perceptive girl, Lesley, if a nosey one. You will make a fine detective one day, I think.'

'Oh, I don't want to be a detective; I want to be a scientist.'

'Well, good for you, Lesley, good for you. You'll need to study hard to be one of those.'

'I will, sir, and congratulations.'

'I think it's time you went back, don't you?'

'Are you going to walk me back?'

'Err ...'

'There's a dangerous man on the loose.'

'All right, then yes, and I'll pick up the car.'

He walks me back to Cottage 5 and I ask him how long he has been a detective and if he likes it. His answers are: three years, after being a normal policeman for two years; and yes, he does like it. But he says sometimes it isn't very nice, you see some very unpleasant things, and sometimes have to give people very bad news.

When we get to his car I say goodbye and walk up to the cottage. I sit on the step to watch him drive off to pick up Lizzie from the tearoom.

I don't tell the girls what I have told Detective Walker; if they know they might let it slip and Mr Sharples would find out. But I start to worry that I don't want them to go anywhere near him or his hut, so when the lights go out and we're all lying in bed, I tell them I think Mr Sharples is creepy, and I'm not going to go anywhere near him until they have caught the murderer. That way I haven't accused him of doing anything, but I have said enough so the girls will keep an eye out for him.

I go to sleep thinking about Lizzie. I wonder if she will get into trouble for being pregnant and not being married. I'm never going to get pregnant without being married; that's how I ended up here in the first place.

55

I wake up early next morning. I seem to be waking up early a lot and failing to get back to sleep. My first thought is often, *Is Jonesy in her bed?* Then I remember she won't be, then I can't get back to sleep. Sometimes I'm awake for hours before the others get up. I just lie there staring at the ceiling, or I turn to stare out of the window. I'm staring but I'm not seeing, my eyes are looking but not focusing.

Mrs Paterson stops me as I'm leaving the cottage with Shona. 'Lesley, can you wait a minute?' she says. 'Shona, you go on without her; this is going to take a bit of time.'

When she says that, I feel sick. I immediately try to think of what I've done wrong. She and Mr Paterson have been so nice to me since Jonesy died that I've forgotten what it's like to be told off. Maybe now I'm going to find out.

'Can you go and wait for me in our living room?' she says.

I go into their living room, back with its smell and the phone I used before to call Detective Walker. I wait there for about ten minutes trying to work out what I'm in here for when the door opens. A woman comes in, followed by Mrs Paterson.

I stand up and try to work out who she is. She's thin – ill-thin – her eyes are sunken and her hair is thin, too, like an old person's. But she isn't old and her hair isn't grey; she's probably about thirty and her hair is a reddish brown. Her clothes are well worn, as if they were smart once, but over time have lost any hint of smartness.

'Lesley, this is someone who would like to meet you,' says Mrs Paterson, motioning to the lady. 'This is Margaret Jones. She's Morag Jones's mother, and she's asked if it would be all right to chat to you.'

I look at Jonesy's mum, and she looks at me.

Mrs Paterson says, 'I thought you would like to meet her; is that all right?'

I nod. I try to remember everything Jonesy ever told me about her mum, why Jonesy was put in here, why she hardly ever saw her. Her mother didn't even come to the funeral.

The woman comes over and holds my hands and looks deep into my eyes. 'I can see why Morag would have been good friends with you. You're a wee doll, aren't you?' she says, smiling and shaking a little.

'Take a seat on the sofa, you two, and I'll fetch you some tea.'

She lets go of my hands and we sit down at the same time. Mrs Paterson backs away out of the room.

Jonesy's mum picks up my hands again.

'You Lesley?' she says gently.

I nod.

'That's a bonnie name. My name is Margaret, everyone calls me Mags, expect Morag may have told you, aye?'

I nod. She hadn't. She had never mentioned her name.

The woman is speaking very softly and her hands start to feel shaky.

'D'you like it here?'

I nod.

'How old are you?'

'Twelve.'

'Aye,' she says, 'same age as Morag, heh?'

We both sit in silence after she says that. I don't know what to say to her. I don't know if it would be betraying Jonesy if I am nice to her. I don't think Jonesy liked her. I can't ever remember her visiting. Margaret Jones holds onto my hands and looks round the room.

Eventually the silence is ended when Mrs Paterson comes back in with a tray carrying a teapot and two cups.

When I see it is only two cups I realise Mrs Paterson isn't going to stay and I am going to have to talk some more to Jonesy's mum on my own.

'How are you two getting along?' says a smiling Mrs Paterson.

'Fine,' I say.

'I'll just pour you both a cup and leave you alone.' Mrs Paterson pours the tea into the pale blue cups and pushes the milk jug towards us. 'I'll be in the kitchen if you need me.'

When she leaves there is another silence, then Margaret speaks. 'Must have been hard for you?'

'It was. It still is.'

'How long were you two best pals?'

'For ever. We were always best friends.'

'And you shared a room?'

I nod. 'Same room,' I say, 'sometimes same bed.'

'Could you tell me about her?'

'Sure,' I say.

'The thing is, I didnae get to know her like you got to know her. They took her away from me. Said I was a bad mother, said I wasnae capable of looking after her. I *was* capable. I loved her. I'd have done anything for her, but they took her from me. Said I couldnae take care of myself. That's when I started with the drink.

'Always liked a drink, me, but see, when Morag came along I was good, I was real good. Me and her da didnae last too long. He wasnae a good man, so it was probably for the best, but see when they see a woman on her own with a baby, they're looking for a reason to take it aff you.

'Once they took her away I couldnae cope. Not with the one thing I loved gone. That's when I struggled. And when they see you struggling, well, they're never going to bring her back then.'

I can see the pain in her. Her hands are shaking even more as she speaks.

'When I heard what had happened to Morag, that was me gone. I couldnae continue. I heard the news and next thing I know it's days later. I couldnae tell you what happened in between. Woke up in the hospital. Said they'd found me in Dundee. I don't know anyone in Dundee. Never have.

'Och, listen to me going on, I shouldnae talk about me. I want to talk to you, you were gonnae tell me about Morag.'

She's wiping her tears away. I think of what she's said, of what she wants to hear. What would make her feel better?

'I don't know where to start.'

'Was she funny?'

'Oooh, was she? She was crazy. She was always doing daft stuff to make us all laugh. She was never happier than when she'd made us crease up with laughter.'

'That's nice. When I pictured her, I always pictured her with friends.'

'Aye, she would be with friends. She had friends at the school and at our cottage. She was a bit of a one. She wasn't like the others.'

'She was special?'

'Oh yes, she was special, all right. There wasnae another one like her. She was so full of energy.'

'I imagine you miss her very much.'

I start to cry too. I can't help it. I am just about to say that it feels like I am missing my arm, something that has always been there and now is suddenly not there, but I can't say it, I can't say anything.

'Och, I'm sorry, doll. That was a stupid thing for me to say, a stupid thing. Of course you miss her. I miss her and I never got to spend any time with her. I remember my best friend when I was your age. Bertha Campbell, thick as thieves we were. Went everywhere together. Such good friends. She moved away before we were teenagers. Never saw her again.'

I'm still crying, but a bit less. 'Sorry,' I say. 'When I

talk about Jonesy it just makes me so sad ... I always end up ... it's why I stopped talking about her ... but then when you stop it ... next time ... just comes out.'

'Oh I know, I know, I'm sorry, doll, I just wanted to get close to her in some way. Now she's gone you're the closest thing I've got to her.'

I nod.

'When Morag was born I'd never been happier. When I first held her I swore that day I would change. I knew I hadnae been the best behaved person before, but as soon as I looked into her eyes I knew I had to change, and I did. I got myself straight. She was a very wee baby, just over four pounds, but she was a fighter, and I was gonnae fight to give her the best life I could.

'And I tried, I tried so hard. I brought her home and Billy, her dad, he didnae know how to cope. When I'd got pregnant it hadn't been intentional, but he'd seemed happy, talked about mibbie one day marrying me. But he wasnae a nice man, Morag's dad, he didnae treat me well. And there's me looking after her while he was going out and cavorting. It was embarrassing. I was hearing what he had been getting up to, and then he was coming home after a drink and he was bad, real bad.

'I had to leave him, It wasnae safe for either me or Morag. We moved back to Hamilton, but I had no family I could stay with. It was no good. We were in this one-bedroom place, just me and her against the world. But Billy went spare. When he found out we'd gone he smashed the place to pieces.

'Anyways, one day the polis knock on the door, says we are in danger. Says they've heard he knows where I am, says he's coming for us both. I said, cannae they arrest him, and they said he's not done anything wrong. We moved to Aberdeen for six weeks. When we were up there the polis called and told me that Billy's dead. Got drunk, got angry, got in a fight, got killed. No witnesses but they think it was more than one person whit done it.

'I felt so relieved. You should never wish anyone dead, Lesley, but this is a man who won't be missed. Such a shame that he was the one who was Morag's dad.

'So I moved back to Hamilton and we're back in the one-bed flat. But Billy's mum starts putting round all these stories that I cannae look after the bairn on my own, and that it wisnae safe for Morag. I mean, that's her own granddaughter she's talking about. They took Morag away from me. Said she'd be better looked after if she was in care. I cannae tell you what that feels like, Lesley. There's no words for when somebody does that to you.'

She starts to cry.

'Oh, look at me. I'm sorry, doll.'

Mrs Paterson knocks, then comes in. 'You two all right in here?'

I nod.

Mags turns to me. 'Will you write to me?'

'Of course.'

She writes down her address, then stands up. I get up too and she gives me a hug; I can hear her sniffing as she does.

Mrs Paterson sees her to the front door. When she comes back she asks me how it was. I tell her it was nice to meet her but that she was a bit strange. She asks if I want to go to Jonesy's grave in Paisley later that day and I say yes.

*

After dinner Mrs Paterson drives me to the cemetery. I didn't know she could drive too, as it's always Mr Paterson who does the driving. We picked some flowers from the garden, so when we get to her grave we lay them down.

Mrs Paterson says she's off to find a shop to get some bread, so I sit down next to the grave so I can talk to Jonesy. There is no headstone yet. Apparently it's coming soon.

'Hiya, Jonesy,' I say, 'how you doing down there? Or is

it up there? I dinnae know if you are lying under all this or up in heaven.

'We've kept your bed in the room. I still havenae given up hope that you might come back to use it. The whole room misses you, it's just not the same any more. Shona talks even more now you've gone. I like her but I wish she'd shut it sometimes.

'Your mammy came to see me. She misses you even though she never came to see you. Sounds like your real dad was a bastard so you might have been lucky to not have been with them. She's awfy thin. Thinnest person I've ever seen. She looks like you could see right through her.

'School's been good, people were being nicer to me when we broke up. Remember when I said they didnae speak to me much and left me on my own? They talk to me now, and I've got friends there. No friends like you, though, no proper friends, just school friends.

'I'm gonnae get the bastard who did this to you, Jonesy, I'm going to get them so bad and when they go to hang them I'm going to pull that bloody lever and watch them choke.

'Dinnae tell anyone I said that.

'I think I know who might have done it; I think it might have been Mr Sharples, the caretaker. You cannae tell me, can you? Can you give me a sign? I told Detective

Walker. I like him. He's got a girlfriend and he's got her pregnant and now he's got to marry her. I said Sharples was a weirdy and, get this, he's a nutter too, saw a letter in his garage. And he's ugly, which is why he probably hates women.'

I hear Mrs Paterson walking up behind me. 'Got to go now, Jonesy. I'll come back to see you, don't worry, I won't leave you here alone. I hope you've made friends – knowing you, you will have. I hope you are stirring up the dead oldies down there. I'll be back, never fear, keep you in nice flowers. Bye, Jonesy. Bye, my pal.'

Mrs Paterson and I drive back to the Homes in silence.

It feels good to have had the chance to have a chat with Jonesy.

I hope she heard me.

56

Eadie comes to the cottage to get me the next afternoon. I'm wearing my best clothes. I haven't been able to concentrate all day for thinking about meeting the couple who might want to adopt me.

Eadie walks with me up to the tearoom. She tells me their names are Mr and Mrs Anderson. He is a doctor and she helps out at a school. Eadie says that because they are smart people, and I am bright, we will be a really good match. She says they will be able to help me with my schooling. Imagine being able to come home and speak to someone who could actually help me learn more.

I can feel my nerves as I walk. I think I am breathing too much. I tell Eadie I'm scared. She says they are good and kind people, and that I am a nice person, so I should just be myself – but what if they don't like the myself that I am? Plenty of people here don't like me.

When we get to the tearoom I can see a couple sat by a table at the far wall and I know it is them; they look so different to the type of people who are usually in the tearoom, they are neatly dressed, and I know this is a strange thing to think, but they look clever.

He has a long blue coat on, a black briefcase by his side, and brown hair which has faded back across most of his head. He has a moustache and glasses that make him look a little like a professor. What there is of his hair is curly and tight. She is wearing a patterned skirt with a cardigan on top. She has glasses, too, but hers are a fun shade of yellow.

As Eadie opens the door I suddenly pull back.

'What's the matter?' she asks.

'I cannae do it.'

'Sure you can, there's nothing to it.'

'What if they don't like me?' I say, shaking now.

'Lesley, there's nothing not to like.'

'There's lots of things not to like.'

'I'm sure they don't, and if they do, maybe they're just jealous.'

'They're no.'

'They are. But you're just looking at this from your

point of view, Lesley. The Andersons are going to be nervous too, they're going to hope that *you* like *them*. Unless you like them, they have no chance of you staying with them, so think of it like that. Nothing happens unless you decide it does.'

I look away for a moment, across to the main road that leads towards the entrance gate. Some boys are running around holding sticks, no doubt off to break something. I turn back to Eadie, breathe out slowly and say, 'All right, I'm ready.'

We walk across the room and I see some of the housefathers having a break from their cottages. One of them is Mr Roberts, the housefather of Cottage 14 who batters the boys, and I remember why I want to get out of here so much.

Mrs Anderson sees Eadie first and nudges her husband and they both get up and turn to face us.

'Eadie, so good to see you,' says Mrs Anderson. Her accent isn't Glaswegian, it's softer than from round here, a bit English, like they sound on the radio. I decide to make mine more proper.

'And you must be Lesley,' she says, smiling and offering her hand.

I lean forward to shake it and curtsey. I don't know why I curtsey, it's such a stupid thing to do. *You idiot, Lesley.* My face starts to heat up with embarrassment.

'We've heard so much about you, Lesley,' says Mrs Anderson, 'but Eadie didn't tell us how pretty you are.'

People never say I am pretty. I'm not ugly but people never talk about me as being one of the pretty ones. I think she is just saying it to be nice to me, but I don't mind, it's nice of her to say it.

'Hello there,' her husband says as he leans around Eadie and offers a hand too. He smiles at me and I can smell coffee on his breath.

'Hello, Mr Anderson,' I say.

'Actually, it's Dr Anderson – did Eadie mention I was a doctor?'

'Yes, sorry, Dr Anderson.'

'There's no need to be sorry, Lesley. Would you like to see my doctor kit?'

I nod and he gets out his listening device from his briefcase.

'This is a stethoscope,' he says. 'Would you like to try it?'

I nod again.

'You can use this to listen to everything that's going on in your body. Do you want to listen to your own heartbeat?'

I nod.

He attaches the listening bits to my ears and says, 'Right, put this bit where you think your heart is.'

I put it in the middle of my chest.

'Very good,' he says, 'but it's a little bit over to the left,' and points to the strap on my dress. 'Now try.'

I can hear it. My heart is going bi-dum … bi-dum … bi-dum.

'Can you hear two beats each time?' he asks. 'That's because there are two beats to every heartbeat. Did you know that?'

I shake my head.

'Because every time it beats there's a mini-beat first, so one half, the smaller half of the heart, beats first, then the bigger part beats, and that's the big beat.' He drums out the pattern on the table, with one hand doing a little tap, followed quickly by the other doing a big tap.

'Gerald,' says Mrs Anderson, 'she doesn't need a medical lecture.' She turns to me. 'Now, Lesley, can I get you and Eadie something to drink?'

'A cup of tea, please.'

'A cup of tea?' she says. 'How very grown-up.'

I smile.

We sit and chat for half an hour. They are definitely intelligent people, like Eadie.

*

Eventually I have to go back to the cottage for tea, but before I leave Mrs Anderson asks me if I would like to come to their house and spend the weekend with them. She says they have a dog and a cat they would like me to meet. They live in Airdrie on the other side of Glasgow. I tell them I would like to go very much.

As I leave Mrs Anderson waves me off and Dr Anderson smiles again. Eadie tells them she will take me back to Cottage 5, then come back for them. I say there's no need, I can make my own way back.

As I walk I am really smiling. I feel happy, I feel excited. I haven't felt happy or excited since before Jonesy died. I feel bad for feeling happy, but I can't help it. The Andersons seemed really nice and they seemed to like me. This could be my way out of this place; I could have a family and live in a proper home like a normal girl, in a normal house, with normal parents.

I could have my own bedroom to sleep in. That would be unbelievable. I wouldn't have Jonesy back, but I would have something for me, finally.

57

I'm on my way back from a walk around the fields when I see Shona sitting on the steps of Cottage 5. She spots me and comes racing over.

'You were right, you were right, you were right!' she says, almost out of breath.

'Right about what?'

'Two polis cars turned up; they went to see Sharples. They're with him now. Shall we go and looky?'

'Naw,' I say, then, 'Aye.'

I knew it, I think, *I knew he was odd and I knew I was right to say something.* I feel excited and relieved, but I don't tell Shona that it was me that told on him.

As we walk across the road to the farmhouse there's a big crowd of children standing about trying to get a look at what's going on. We try to get to the front but there's a policeman telling everyone, in very rude words, that we should go away now.

No one moves.

Then he says he will give us ten seconds, then he will call the Superintendent and if any of us are still here when Mr Gordon arrives, we will be punished.

That works and we all move away.

Shona and I walk back towards our cottage. We see Mary at the bridge over the stream so go and let her know what's happening. We sit on the bridge and wait. After about twenty minutes we see a police car leaving. As it goes past, we can see Mr Sharples sat in the back. His head is bowed down so we can't see his eyes but it is definitely him; he must be so ashamed of what he's done. There's a blue car behind the police car, which I recognise as Detective Walker's.

I get down off the wall and wave at him. He stops and winds down the window.

'I told you, I told you!' I say. 'Did you arrest him?'

'Lesley, I can't talk about this.'

'But I was right, wasn't I? It was him! I was right.'

'Lesley, what did I just say?'

'Sorry, sir.'

'Now please do not discuss this with anyone, understand?'

'Aye,' I say, but even as I say it, I know I am lying.

It is all we talk about that afternoon, it is all we talk about at tea, and all we talk about in our room. I finally tell the girls that I was the one who tipped the police off. They say they had thought it was him all along, too, but I know they didn't.

I go to bed feeling safe for the first time in a long time. I can't believe they let him live here all this time after he'd done it and he could have killed more girls. I think of the time I walked Petal with him; maybe he was thinking of killing me then, and when he said Petal could keep secrets maybe he told Petal what he had done to Jane and Sally. Then I think of what he did to Jonesy and I think how I hope they kill him now.

58

On Saturday morning I keep waking up to see if it is time to get up yet. I lie in my bed waiting for the sun to rise. Shona comes over to see how I am. With Morag gone, Shona is the girl in my room I talk to most, despite our disagreements before. She is excited for me.

I'm so nervous. I've borrowed one of Mrs Paterson's suitcases to pack my things for staying at the Andersons', and packed and unpacked it three times. I've never been out of the Homes for a weekend on my own. Some children get to spend the occasional weekend with relatives or parents, but my mum isn't one for that; she will only see me here. Gran talks about having me to stay but I think Mum is against it. I would like to have stayed with Gran.

Shona and I go down to breakfast, and after doing the tidying chores I run back upstairs to make sure I've packed everything again.

Eadie comes to the cottage to check on me. She doesn't live at the Homes and usually she doesn't work weekends in the summer holidays so it is kind of her to come to see me off. She says she was just passing so thought it would be nice to pop in, but I know she wouldn't have been passing.

Dr and Mrs Anderson arrive at Cottage 5 just after half past nine. They pull up in a dark blue car that looks new and spotlessly clean. They get out of the car and Eadie walks me over to them and starts chatting.

'Let me help you with that,' says Dr Anderson, as he takes the suitcase. When he feels its weight he says, 'You planning on staying a couple of months, then?'

I laugh nervously. I just wanted to make sure I had everything in case I needed to change clothes.

As we drive off, I wave goodbye to Mrs Paterson and Shona. The seats in the back of the car look like white leather. I sit in the middle and Mrs Anderson – she insists I call her Anne, but I'm always forgetting – keeps turning round to ask me questions. Dr Anderson – Gerald – watches the road while he drives, occasionally chipping in with a comment.

Mrs Anderson asks me a lot about school, what I like,

what I don't like. She asks how it was being the only person in my year at the Homes to go to the grammar school. I try to sound positive.

At some point I must have fallen asleep as next thing I see is their house. They have a bungalow, up a steep drive. Dr Anderson pulls the brake sharply to make sure the car won't roll back down, then we all get out.

I can hear their dog barking right away. Mrs Anderson sees that I look scared and tells me not to worry. 'He's very friendly,' she says.

'I'm not sure dogs like me.'

'Oh this one will, he's a big softy. You wait till you meet him. His name is Bertie.'

She opens the front door and Bertie comes rushing out. The cat flies out of the house at the same time, as if it is delighted to escape being locked inside with a crazy dog.

Bertie goes straight up to Mrs Anderson and rears on his back legs, pawing at her hips. He then rushes round the other side of the car to Dr Anderson, who tells him to get down.

Then he sees me, and comes up and starts sniffing me.

'He isn't angry, just interested,' says Dr Anderson.

Mrs Anderson says, 'Come away, Bertie!' and pulls at his collar. Bertie fights against her at first, but then does as he's told.

'This is our home, Lesley,' says Mrs Anderson. 'If at any time you want to go back, just let me know and we can drive you straight back to the cottage. We want you to enjoy your weekend with us, but we realise you don't know us that well and this could all seem a little strange. Right, let me show you to your room.'

The house seems odd. There's a smell as soon as you come in, like the forest smell out the back of the Homes. It hits me the minute I'm through the door. Also there are things on every flat surface in the hall. There are little model dogs on a shelf, a cartoon drawing of a golfer on the windowsill, and photographs lined up on a cabinet. Everything has something on it.

The room I am staying in is their 'guest room'; it has a double bed. I've never slept in one before and the first thing I think is, *They won't believe me when I get back.*

'Gerald will bring your suitcase in from the car. In the meantime, I'll just let you get used to your room. There's a bathroom across the hall, and the kitchen and living room are down there. But I'll give you the full tour later.'

Mrs Anderson leaves the room and I have a chance to look around. The window looks out to the neighbour's house. The wallpaper is a pale green, with thin light lines going down it. There are more things on the chest of drawers – little cat statuettes, this time.

After a while the door nudges open and in comes the

cat that escaped earlier. It walks straight into the room and jumps on the bed, then looks at me as if to tell me, *This is my bed, and don't you think of taking it.*

I hold out my hand and after a moment of thought it rubs its head and neck up against it.

'Hello yoooouuu,' I say. 'What's your name?' It's funny cos I am talking in my posh accent to the Andersons but I'm talking in my even posher voice to the cat in case it tells them that I'm no good.

It purrs and keeps rubbing up against my arm. I sit on the bed and it lets me stroke it. The cat and I have a good chat and it eventually walks onto my lap where it pads its feet. I think we have come to an understanding, and I will be allowed to stay in the room and sleep in the bed after all.

Mrs Anderson comes back, and says, 'So I see you've met Mog.'

'Yes, I think we've become friends.'

'That's strange. Mog doesn't take to people too easily; she must really like you.'

I smile at that.

'Now, what would you like to do this weekend? We could take a drive to the coast, we could go for a walk, or we could drive into Glasgow.'

'Ooh, Glasgow, Glasgow, please!' I say. I've never been there before and the chances to go to a city are so rare.

'Righty-o,' she says. 'If we're going to Glasgow we should head off now so we can get there for dinner.' She walks out to tell Dr Anderson that we're going to drive into town. I hear some discussion about whether he wants to go too, but when they come out of the kitchen they seem happy and so we set off.

There is a lot less talking on the way to Glasgow. I am so excited at the chance to go to shops and see the sights. When we arrive, Dr Anderson parks the car and Mrs Anderson finds a café she has eaten in before and they say they will just squeeze us in before the kitchen closes.

Mrs Anderson asks what I want from the menu and I don't know what to get so I say I'll eat whatever she's having, which is an omelette. Dr Anderson says he will have the same 'to keep it simple', then Mrs Anderson buys me a cola and we sit in a booth.

'Anything you want to see?' asks Mrs Anderson.

'Shops,' I say. 'Shops and maybe some more shops.'

Dr Anderson laughs and shakes his head.

'What sort of shops?' asks Mrs Anderson.

'Oh, clothes shops, please.'

'I'll see what I can do.'

The omelettes come and we scoff them down, Dr Anderson pays and we go walking down Sauchiehall Street. There are shops as far as you can see. Dr Anderson looks bored, but Mrs Anderson is as excited as me.

It's so busy. There's more people than I've ever seen in my life.

'All right, Lesley,' Mrs Anderson says, 'this is a one-off, but we are going to buy you something as this is a special treat.'

I want to hug her but I don't as I think she might find it strange. I think of how incredibly jealous the girls will be when I come back with something new.

We walk the entire length of Sauchiehall Street, going into the shops and inspecting all the different clothes. By the end I can see Dr Anderson wants to go home. He peers into a shop window with a big crowd of people in front of it, to see the football scores. Once he's seen them, he announces it is time to go. I haven't chosen anything yet, so we go back to the first shop and I choose a black skirt, and Mrs Anderson buys herself a scarf.

I want to write down everything that has happened so I don't forget it. I have to tell Shona and the girls everything.

59

The drive back goes quickly. I try to take in everything I see as I know I won't see it again for a long time. Who knows, though, if I come to live with the Andersons maybe I'll go to Glasgow all the time.

When we arrive at the house I can see Bertie the dog at the door already; he must be able to sense when the car is coming back. As soon as Mrs Anderson opens the door he rushes out down the drive, then to Mrs Anderson, then to Dr Anderson, then to sniff me. I am still not sure around him, he's just a bit over-excited.

Mrs Anderson says I should go to my room and try the skirt on while she starts tea, then if I want I can come and help her.

I try it on and look at myself in the mirror. I love it.

I am going to keep it hidden in my room for a week before I show the girls, then just wear it casually next weekend as if it were nothing. They won't know where I got it.

Mrs Anderson is making mince an' tatties in the kitchen. The mince is already on the hob and I help peel the potatoes. Dr Anderson sits in the garden reading his newspaper with a bottle of beer. When tea's ready we call him in and we all sit round the table.

They don't say grace. Every meal I have ever had at the Homes someone says grace. I almost ask them why, then I think maybe they don't believe in God either. I won't ask this time as it might be considered rude, but I am definitely going to ask them eventually.

The mince an' tatties are amazing. Cook makes it all the time but never like this, it just tastes so, so good. The Andersons ask me about the trouble at the Homes, but I just say I don't know much about it. Mrs Anderson says that after tea they like to have some quiet time listening to the radio, then maybe a quick game of cards, then I can go to bed.

We all sit in the living room and listen to the BBC on the wireless. Dr Anderson gets out his cigarettes and smokes two. Mrs Anderson explains how he likes to have a couple after his tea but rarely smokes at any other time.

After he's smoked the second cigarette, and the fog has disappeared, we get out the cards. The game is called Knock-out Whist. Mrs Anderson teaches me the rules and I love it. What a clever game. I lose the first one but win the next two. I think they may have let me win but it is great fun.

Eventually Dr Anderson declares I am too good and I will need to go to bed before his feelings are hurt. Mrs Anderson tucks me in and, after she's gone, I try so hard not to think it, I do everything I can to distract myself, but I can't help it, the thought just keeps coming back – one day, this could be my home.

Mog jumps up on the bed and curls up near my middle. This might have been my best day ever.

*

I wake up full of hope, which I haven't felt in so long.

After breakfast we don't have to go to church. No grace and no church is such a joy.

Dr Anderson gives me some of the newspaper to read, but after that it's time to pack and get back in the car. I say goodbye to Mog and make a mental promise that I will see her again.

We get back around noon, just before dinner. The Homes look somewhat greyer than before I left. It's a sunny day but the buildings don't reflect it. I don't mind, though, as this is not going to be my home for much longer.

I am excited about telling the girls everything that has happened. I find them round the back of the cottage. They stop what they're doing and rush over, asking loads of questions and I tell them what it was like and how nice the Andersons were. They seem excited for me; I am excited for me. I am trying not to be too excited, but I can't help myself.

60

The next day we are out of milk at the cottage. 'Go and get us some from the shop,' says Cook, giving me the money.

'Want to come with me, Eldrey?' I say. 'I'm off out to get some milk.'

'Nuh,' she says.

I think a month ago she would have come with me. A week ago I would have had three of them with me. They must think I'm back to normal now. I'm not, but there's only so long they can be that nice to me. And the adults seem to have stopped making us go everywhere in pairs. They used to shout at us if they saw us on our own, but now they seem to have given up.

I walk along Faith Avenue and I see a black car coming

towards me. It's flash, very shiny. I stop to look; so do other children. We don't get too many cars down these roads and we definitely don't get cars as nice as this.

I look to see who's driving, but they have a hat on and I can't quite see the face. I watch it go past then turn back and cross into Church Road.

As I do I suddenly spot Mr Sharples in front of me. He's carrying a large sack on his shoulder. He's seen me, and he's seen me watching the car.

I take a short breath.

'Hey, you,' he says.

I try to look away.

'No, you, I wanna word wi' you.'

I feel scared. He puts the sack down and walks towards me. 'You're the one that's been talking to the polis, right?'

I look at the ground.

'You think I had somethin' to do with those deid girls, right?'

I look up at him this time and nod, then back down again.

'You think I'm a weirdy, don't you? Think I'm a bit strange?'

I don't respond to this.

'Look at me.'

I look up again.

'Aye, so you do. I might be a bit different, and I'm no so good with people, but I didnae have nothing to do with them lassies, see?'

I nod vigorously.

'So dinnae go tellin' people that I did, cos I didnae.'

I nod again.

'On you go.'

A cold pulse goes down my back. I know I'm supposed to go get milk but instead I just turn round and run back to the cottage. I go straight to my bedroom and dive onto my bed.

Eldrey is in there with Shona.

'Whit is it?' she asks.

'Nuthin'.'

'You sure?'

'Aye.'

They leave the room.

Five minutes later, Cook comes in.

'Where's my milk?' she says.

'They ran out.'

'Ran out, eh? Could you no have told us, no?'

'Sorry.'

And I *am* sorry. I shouldn't have said anything to the police, I had no proof. I need proof.

61

I go to see Eadie. One other person is waiting to see her and it's Glenda McAdam.

When I see her and she looks at me I think I might be for it, but she says, 'Hullo,' so I say, 'Hullo,' back.

There is silence for a minute. I look at the wall. I can feel her staring at me but I am not going to stare back. Eventually she breaks the silence and says, 'Whit you here for?'

I don't know what to say. I try to think of a lie but it doesn't come quick enough, so I just tell the truth. 'There's a couple who want to adopt me, I think.'

'That's nice,' she says. 'D'you wanna go?'

'I dunno. Think so, think it would be nice.'

'You should definitely go; you'd suit a normal family.

Some of us are best aff here, but it would be good for you.'

I feel odd. She's being friendly. I've never seen her be nice, but then I have never seen her not surrounded by her scraggy friends.

'Whit are you here for?' I ask.

'Da's gone psycho again. He's attacked a policeman and gone missing. They're worried he's going to turn up here. Eadie asked to see me; she's worried about me.'

'Have you seen her before?'

'Oh, aye, come here all the time.'

'Really?'

For some reason her saying this makes me feel betrayed. I know Eadie sees lots of other kids, but I didn't know Glenda was one of them. She'd never said.

'Oh, aye, for the last couple of years. They worry about me cos of my family. Used to hate coming but now I kinda like it. It's a chance to get away from everyone.'

'She's good, isn't she?' I say.

'I dunno if she's good, I just know it's nice that someone listens to me.'

The door to the office opens. A scruffy boy of about eight or nine comes sprinting out. Glenda looks at me and says, 'Well, I'll see you later.'

'All right,' I reply and give a little wave.

Eadie puts her head round the door. 'Hi Lesley,' she says. 'You happy to wait?'

I nod.

'Good, get yourself a book. I'm sure I won't be too long,' and she shuts the door.

I don't get a book. I stare at the wall instead and try to work out if Glenda being there counts as a betrayal. It shouldn't, Eadie shouldn't have favourites, but still I thought she really liked me. She probably *does* like me; it doesn't mean she doesn't like other people. She could like Glenda, and Glenda is not very likeable, but then Glenda was nice earlier and maybe she's only horrible because she's from a bad family and maybe she's not bad herself, maybe that family just makes you bad, so it's not her fault.

I can't stop my thoughts going around.

After a long time the door opens again and Glenda leaves. She says goodbye to me as she goes.

It must be strange for Eadie; people go into her room feeling one way and come out feeling another. She's like a hairdresser for people's emotions.

I go into the room and sit in the chair. It still feels warm from Glenda's bottom. I've never said anything about Glenda or the fight to Eadie. Perhaps she already knows. Glenda might have said something, back when it happened.

'How are we, Lesley?'

'Good, I think.'

'And how were the Andersons?'

'Good, it was good, they were good. Yeah, really good.'

'So do you think you might want to live with them?'

'Yeah, I think, yeah, I think I would.'

'You need to really think about this, Lesley, because this is a big decision. You would be leaving here, and your cottage, and your friends, and although you won't never see them again, you certainly wouldn't see them very much. If you leave you would really leave.'

'I know,' I say. 'I have been thinking about it a lot. If Jonesy was still here it would be hard and I think I would say no, but she's not, and it's not the same any more. The cottage did feel like home, but now it feels like a place where I sleep and eat in between school.'

Eadie looks at me for a while. 'All right,' she says finally, 'here's what I want you to do: think about it for two more days, and if it's still a yes, either pop in to see me or write me a letter.'

I nod in agreement, but I know what my answer will be. I want to go live with the Andersons.

*

I am as good as my word. Two days later I go to see Eadie and tell her I have thought about it some more and that I definitely want to live with the Andersons.

She tells me that is great news and that she thinks I will be very happy.

The one thing that had been bothering me is that I won't get to see her any more, but she answers that question before I even ask, saying she will make sure she comes to see me once a fortnight either at the Andersons' house or at my school.

I feel relieved.

She says she will put the wheels in motion.

I feel happy but nervous and I decide to tell the other girls in my room. Shona asks if they want to take two girls instead of just one.

I think they are happy for me. Sometimes I think no one wants anyone else to do well or escape as it just makes those left behind feel bad. I can't think like that. I need to do this for me.

62

Shona and I are walking to the shop to get sweeties. Shona's mum gave her two shillings on her last visit. She didn't tell anyone but last night when everyone went to sleep she told me, and said that after breakfast we'd go and get a bag of sweets.

We're coming past the main road when I see Detective Walker getting out of his car. He sees me and looks down as if he hasn't. I tell Shona I'm sorry but I have to go.

'Mr Walker! Mr Walker!' I shout. He is still looking down, so I don't think he hears me. I run after him. When I catch up with him, he looks surprised.

'Mr Walker,' I say, 'is there any news? Do you have a new suspect?'

'It's *Detective* Walker, Lesley, and there's no more news at the moment. I was just going to see the Superintendent to give him an update.'

'So ... it wasnae Mr Sharples?'

'No, Lesley, it wasn't. He can account for his whereabouts for all the times of the attacks and there are people who can verify those claims, so we have ruled him out for the time being.'

'I'm sorry, I just thought—'

'Thank you for trying to help us, but you shouldn't judge people just because they are a bit different.'

'Sorry.'

'Like I said, thanks for your help, though.'

'Well, is there anyone else? Because they are still out there and people seem to have forgotten about that. People here are carrying on as if everything is normal and it's no. There's still a killer about.'

'Yes, Lesley, believe me, we haven't forgotten.'

'So you have other suspects? Who are they?'

'We have some people of interest, but I would be seriously undermining the investigation if I were to tell you who they were.'

'Oh ... all right.'

'Now, if you'll excuse me, I'd like to get in to see Mr Gordon. Thank you.' He smiles at me but he doesn't mean it.

I watch him go inside the executive building where the Super's office is, and think about waiting for him to come back out. I could help the police, I am the person who is here all the time, I am the one who sees what's going on. I was closest to Jonesy. I have to be of some use to them.

I stand in the same spot for the next five minutes, unsure of what I should do next, when I remember Shona and the sweet shop. When I get to the shop she's just leaving. I catch up with her but she says I can't have any sweets as I didn't come with her to buy them. I tell her I had to talk to the policeman, but it doesn't seem to matter to her.

She tries to walk a little faster and leave me behind, but I keep up with her, so she tries to walk faster still. In the end we are almost running back to the house.

I stop and let her get away. If she wants to be silly, she can; there are more important things than sweets.

'Suit yerself,' I say as she goes.

She doesn't speak to me for the next two days.

63

A week later I still haven't heard anything about the Andersons, so I go to see Eadie to find out what the news is.

As I arrive at the hospital building, I see a boy coming out with his face wrapped in bandages. You can see dried blood on his nose. It looks like he's had a 'doing'. If it isn't the houseparents it's the boys themselves 'doing' each other. For the boys there seems to be nothing more exciting than a fight. First the hope of the fight, then the actual fight, then the end of the fight, which is the point when someone usually gets badly hurt.

I still can't understand why they enjoy it so much; they are like animals. I look away from the boy, because he looks ashamed and I don't want to add to that by staring at him.

After he's gone, Eadie comes out of the building too.

'How are you, Lesley? How was your day?'

'Good. I went to the library at dinnertime and I'm trying to teach myself Latin.'

'What words did you learn?'

'*Valde bona*.'

'Oh excellent, *bene factum*.'

'Whit was that?'

'I said "well done".'

'Have you heard anything from the Andersons?'

'Sort of.'

'Whit do you mean, sort of? Have they changed their minds?'

'No, no, they haven't changed their minds.'

'Oh great, so it's still going to happen?'

'Shall we go to my office to talk about it?'

'Is something wrong?'

'It's best we talk in private.'

We walk to her office in silence. I already know it's bad news, just not what the bad news is. No one waits to give you good news.

I follow her along the corridor, she unlocks her office, and I walk straight to my chair. She takes her coat off, then sits in her chair and lets out a big sigh.

I want to just shout, 'WHAT IS IT? WHAT NOW?'
But I wait.

'All right,' she says, 'there's been a setback in the adoption. In fact, at the moment it looks like it is off.'

'But ... why?'

'It's complicated, I'm afraid.'

'Complicated how? Tell me. I can understand complicated things.'

'I'm afraid I can't right now.'

'Why can't you, if it's me it affects?'

'There are procedures in these situations, so that is all I can say.'

'Just tell me. Please.'

There's a pause. I can see her struggling. Then her face moves as if she's come to a decision. She takes a slow, deep breath, looks straight at me and says, 'Your adoption has been blocked.'

'Why?' I say. 'By who?'

'That is what I cannot tell you, Lesley. Please understand the situation I am in; if I could, I honestly would tell you, but I truly can't.'

She looks angry with me. I have never seen her look angry with me before and I can't understand why. First the adoption gets stopped and now Eadie doesn't even like me. It's the curse of adults again. Adults cause pain.

I get up and run back to the cottage, tears rolling down my face. All I can think is if there is no one I can rely on in this world, then I will have to rely on myself.

64

Life is continuing. I have to continue. I'm struggling to accept that I won't get out of here.

I would rather not have had the chance than have had the chance and have it taken away from me.

The days have turned into weeks and still I haven't gone back to see Eadie. Now it's the first week of a new school year – I was glad to see Clara again when we got back, but it feels like the summer holidays have taken their toll and while everyone else at the grammar school is fresh after the break, I feel exhausted. That's the kind of thing I would usually tell Eadie. I can't trust her now. The one person I thought I could trust and even she won't tell me the truth.

I don't know what happens to you when you become

a grown-up, what changes. There's not a single adult who won't let you down or lie or find some other way to make you suffer.

Ever since my mum gave me away at three weeks, I've been let down by grown-ups. Gran lied about my sisters and brother; the minister lies about God.

And if it's not them lying it's them either trying to do it to us like Mr Taylor, beat us for fun like Mr Paterson, or kill for some terrible reason like whoever the bastard is who killed Jonesy. We are just here so adults can cause us suffering.

Eadie was the one grown-up I thought would never let me down. How many times can people hurt your heart until it just dies?

Is that what makes you into an adult, having been so betrayed that you are dead and no one can hurt you any more and then you don't feel so bad about doing the same to others? Does getting older make you nastier, or do you have to be nasty to get old? Was Jonesy taken away because she was too nice? Does that mean when I'm older I will turn into a person who lies and lets people down and makes them hate me?

I hate grown-ups.

*

I still don't sleep well.

Ever since Jonesy went I either sleep, but have these really bad nightmares, or I can't sleep at all. Or both. I'll sleep, have a nightmare, then not get back to sleep.

I'll sometimes just lie in bed all night, staring at the ceiling, hoping my head will go quiet enough for me to drop off. Or I'll close my eyes and turn over, and keep them tight shut but sleep just won't come.

Mr and Mrs Paterson have always said that we're not allowed out of our rooms at night no matter what, but after Jonesy died Mrs Paterson said if I needed to come see her because I felt scared then I could. She said I should always know that she was just downstairs, so not to be frightened, and if it was getting too bad I could come down and sleep on their sofa.

I occasionally did. The girls in my room didn't know; I would sneak back up to bed before they were up. The first two times I did it I went into Mr and Mrs Paterson's room. Mr Paterson was a bit grumpy, but Mrs Paterson told him to shush.

After the second time Mrs Paterson said she would leave a blanket out for me each night so I needn't wake them; I could just come down and curl up on the settee.

I haven't done it for a few weeks as my sleeping had been getting back to normal but since the news about the Andersons, I have had some terrible nights. My brain won't switch off; it just keeps going over and over what happened. Was it something I did? Why won't anyone tell me the truth?

*

It feels like it's about two in the morning. I don't have a watch but I'm pretty good at guessing the time after waking up so much. I pull back my covers and creep out of the bedroom. The house is totally silent. I make my way down the stairs and into the Patersons' living room.

I walk quietly to the sofa, picking up the blanket from its place on the chair by the door. The blanket smells musty but I don't mind much and wrap it round me as tight as I can, then lay my head on the cushions.

The room is in half-light. The lamp outside our cottage is shining and the curtains aren't closed so the light comes into the room.

I can hear Mr Paterson snoring from the other room. I've heard it before and know it's him. Mrs Paterson actually snores a little too, but hers is pretty mild compared to him.

His is a weird one-in-every-three snore. He doesn't do it on every breath, or at least I think he doesn't do it on every breath, unless he's a whale. Whales can hold their breath for half an hour. If he is doing it on every breath it means he must breathe only once a minute.

I lie there listening to the sounds, hoping I can drift off. Last time I came down here I spent ages thinking, *How on earth can Mrs Paterson still be asleep lying next to that noise?* Has she got earplugs in? How could anyone put up with that? Anyway, next thing I knew it was morning.

So I listen to the sounds and wonder if Mr Paterson isn't next door but maybe a cow has come in from the field and is sleeping next to Mrs Paterson. It doesn't work this time, I'm not drifting off; my mind keeps going back to Eadie, to the Andersons.

I sit up, keeping the blanket wrapped round me, and shuffle to the chair so I can look out of the window. It's a very still night, no rustling in the trees, no rain. In six hours the village will be alive with the sound of children shrieking, running, fighting, kicking balls, calling names.

I watch as a fox crosses the path. It trots to the lamp-post, and stops as if to look around, then something scares it and it darts off. Then nothing again, stillness.

I try to get comfortable in my upright sitting position. A box near the sofa has some letters on it so I move them onto the floor so I can put my feet up but catch my leg on the edge of the lid. It makes my calf itch so I use the corner of the lid to scratch the itch. It goes, but a minute later it comes back, so I scratch so hard that it won't be able to come back.

It does, so I give up, put my feet down and look at the box. I open it to see inside, just to make sure I'm not putting my feet up on something fragile. It's filled with old newspapers, lots of them. The front page of the top one has the headline GUILTY! MONTROSE TO HANG. It's from the *Evening Times*.

I turn on the light next to me and examine the paper. It's from ten years ago. Beneath it are other newspapers or individual pages from newspapers. They are all about the Peter Montrose murders, the trial and then the hanging.

I read page after page, the details about what he did to those women. Much of it is the same information I read in the library weeks ago, but it's not just one newspaper, there are lots and lots of cuttings from different papers.

I hear a sound from the bedroom, so I quickly turn the light off, shut the box and put the letters back on top. I fold the blanket and put it back in its place on the chair before sneaking up the stairs and into bed.

Now I am never going to sleep; my head is racing with questions.

Why do the Patersons have all those newspaper

cuttings? What do the Montrose murders have to do with them?

I stay wide awake for the rest of the night waiting for the morning light to come. I don't go to breakfast and when it's time I leave the house without saying a word to anyone and get straight on the bus for school.

65

At school I can't concentrate. I don't hear what the teachers are saying. All I can think is, *Why would the Patersons have those newspapers?* Was Jonesy right? Did the police get the wrong man, and the real killer wasn't Peter Montrose, but Mr Paterson? Is that why he kept the clippings, so he could gloat that he'd gotten away with it? Maybe Mrs Paterson doesn't know about the clippings, doesn't know she's living with a killer? Or maybe she does know, and she's in on it, too?

Jonesy must have found the newspapers; she always was nosey. That terrible, terrible man; all that time being nicer to me and he knew what he'd done to her.

I borrow some money from Clara and at first break I go to the phone booth to call Detective Walker. He isn't there so I say I will call again at dinnertime, but I don't give my name.

He still isn't there when I call back. This time I say it's very important that I speak to him, but again I don't give my name.

All afternoon I carry on worrying. I have to go back to the cottage and face them.

During maths I say I'm feeling ill and ask to go see the nurse. I never miss maths, but I have to speak to the detective. I sneak to the phone booth and dial the number again. This time he picks up the phone on the second ring.

'Detective Walker, I need to speak to you.'

'Ahh ... Lesley, I imagine?'

'Yes, yes, I need to speak to you.'

'And what is it this time?'

'Mr Paterson, it's Mr Paterson, you know, our house-father at Cottage 5, I think he could be involved in it, perhaps Mrs Paterson too, but I think Mr Paterson might have done it.'

'All riiight ...' he says, stretching it out. 'So why do you say that?'

'Well, he had the opportunity to kill Jonesy, and he probably did Jonesy because she found out it was him, and she found out it was him because she thought that they got the wrong fella for the Montrose murders, and I was in their living room last night and I found lots and lots of newspaper clippings about the Montrose murders. I mean, why would they collect all that stuff? It's obvious, it wasn't Peter Montrose who did the murders, it was Mr Paterson. They hanged the wrong man. I cannae go back there, Detective, I cannae, he'll see in my eyes that I know and he'll do to me what he did to Jonesy.'

There's a long pause, then Detective Walker responds. 'Lesley, where are you?'

'I'm at school.'

'And what time do you finish?'

'Three-thirty.'

'And what time do you get back to the Homes?'

'Six o' clock.'

'Right, here's what is going to happen, Lesley. I am going to meet you back at the Homes, out the front of the executive building. When you get off the bus, do not go back to your cottage, and do not, I repeat, do not, speak to anyone else about this. Do you understand?'

'I understand.'

I knew it was the right thing to call him. He had said before to call if I knew anything and that is what I have done. I know I was wrong about Mr Sharples, but you have to keep asking questions and then you finally work it out.

I think about going to the nurse's office and following through with the lie. There's still twenty minutes of my lesson left, but I decide to go back to the classroom instead. When Mr Sanders asks why I'm back I say I don't feel so bad any more.

I go back to my desk, thinking about what the police will do when they arrest Mr Paterson. Will they arrest Mrs Paterson too? Will I have to move cottages? Will the others in Cottage 5 hate me for getting rid of them? They shouldn't, I might have saved their lives.

66

My heart is raging as I get off the bus. The journey was quicker than usual, so I'm ten minutes early and I stand round the back of the executive building. I watch the other children running around not knowing what I know, not knowing who is living amongst us.

At six exactly I go round to the front and see Detective Walker. He's wearing his suit even though it is a hot day and he walks up to me with a stern look on his face, a look that says I am in trouble.

'We should have a chat,' he says. 'You haven't been back to the cottage, have you?'

I shake my head.

'Good, because there is something important that I

need you to know; something you must *never* mention again. Do you understand?'

I nod.

'Shall we go and sit down there?' he says, pointing to the bench by the side of the road. I follow him and do as he says. The bench is slightly damp as it had rained a bit this afternoon, and the sun hasn't quite dried it out yet.

He seems calm, but I can sense that he's angry. I have seen this look in so many adults' eyes.

'Now, explain to me what it was that you found.'

I tell him about the newspaper clippings reporting the Montrose murders, and how Jonesy had wondered whether they had hanged the wrong man and the killer was free to commit more murders, and that is what they're doing now.

Then I say, 'When I saw those newspapers – I mean, why would you keep them if you weren't involved? Then I thought mibbie Jonesy had said something to Mr Paterson and he realised she knew and that's why he killed her.'

'That's what I thought you might have been getting at. Right.' He takes off his jacket. I can see the sweat patches underneath. He breathes twice, deeply; I don't know if he's doing it for show.

'When you work for the police, you learn that when you have a piece of evidence you look for all the different reasons it exists. You don't just pick the first one that comes into your head, or the one that fits your narrative.'

I put my hand up.

'Yes?'

'Whit's a narrative?'

'It's a story. So if you see something important, you don't automatically assume it fits your story in a certain way.'

'So, that's whit I've done?'

'Yes, yes, you have. There could be another reason for the Patersons having those clippings.'

'And there is?'

'Yes there is, Lesley. There is a reason, but I need you to swear, and I mean swear *on your life*, that you will not tell a soul what I am just about to tell you.' He looks me straight in the eye and I know it's serious. 'How much do you know about the Peter Montrose murders?'

'I know he killed eight women.'

Detective Walker nods. 'Yes. There's a bit more to it than that but, yes, he was convicted of killing eight women, although many of us think he killed nine. There were also two women whom he attacked but who managed to escape, and they gave evidence against him. One of those women was Mrs Paterson, or, as she was known back then, Miss McKinley. She was attacked by

Peter Montrose and she gave evidence that ultimately led to him being convicted. For that, the police force are very grateful to her.

'So, Lesley, I would assume that is why she has those newspaper cuttings. No doubt, it has been a traumatic time for her, with these recent deaths. It's hard when you've been through something like that.'

I feel awful, and though I try not to, I start to cry. He puts his arm round me and that makes me sob even more.

'I'm sorry, Mr Walker. I'm really sorry. I just thought it was Mr Paterson, and he can get angry sometimes and, whit with whit happened, and – he doesnae know, does he? *She* doesnae know whit I said to you?'

'Not yet. That's why I wanted to meet you here first, before you had a chance to go back to your cottage and tell anyone. Though I'm afraid I will have to let them know eventually.'

'I didn't mean anything, I just thought—'

'Lesley, it's natural ... You are a smart girl; you're always going to be looking for answers. It's just that this time you were wrong. It's what we would call an "avenue of investigation" – you follow up a theory to its end. That way you can rule them out and eventually you'll reach the avenue that leads you to the guilty person. We questioned all the housefathers and other men who work at the Homes after the murders to confirm their alibis, including Mr Paterson.'

'Whit's an alibi?'

'It's when someone can prove that they weren't in the place where the murder happened when it happened.'

'And Mr Paterson has alibis for Jane and Sally and Jonesy? That means he cannae have done it.'

Detective Walker smiles at me. 'That's correct, Lesley. You catch on quick. I think you could make a good detective one day.'

'You said that before. Do you really think so?'

'Sure, you've got brains, you're inquisitive. If one good thing came out of all this, it's that some day we could have you on the police force. Now, let me walk you back to the cottage to show there's no hard feelings.'

Walking back, I forget about feeling guilty and am full of the idea that I could become a police detective. None of them seem to be women but Detective Walker thinks I could be one. I could solve other murders. Science is over for me. This is what I am going to become.

At the steps to Cottage 5 he says, 'So, we are all right?'

'We are all right,' I say.

We shake hands like grown-ups.

As I watch him walk off, I decide two things: I'm going to be a detective when I'm older, and I am going to solve this case once and for all, and they will see that I will make a great detective.

I haven't made a mistake. I have eliminated a suspect. I am closer to finding out the truth.

67

I have forgiven Eadie. It's not her fault that the adoption was blocked. And she must have her reasons for not telling me who did it. I do believe she is a good person; she wouldn't have done that to me if she could have helped it. I shouldn't have been so hard on her.

It's Saturday so I decide to go to my morning meeting with her. My usual time is 10 a.m. but I head over now at quarter to as sometimes she finishes early with the kid before me, so I get to have more than half an hour.

The hospital smells different to all the other buildings in the Homes. The church smells of dust and damp, the big hall smells of sweaty boys, who often have games there, but the hospital smells like disinfectant.

I head up the first flight of stairs towards her office.

Her door is shut, so I sit outside. Sometimes if she is somewhere else in the building the room is locked and I just wait; she's never too late.

I sit and read the notices on the wall. At twenty past she still hasn't arrived and I start to get a little worried. She never doesn't show up. I wait another hour, and still nothing.

There's no note on the door. A couple of grown-ups walk past and I ask them if they've seen her and they say no.

At half-past eleven I decide to go looking for one of the nurses. When I find one, she says that Eadie won't be coming back. I ask her why and she says she couldn't say.

I am annoyed that she won't tell me why Eadie is away but also glad that there is a reason she isn't here; I was worried that something had happened to her. It seems to be how my mind works now.

Although I've skipped a few meetings because I was annoyed with Eadie, I never meant for it to be for so long. Now I know that I need my time with her each week – I rely on it. I sit back down and try to work out why she has gone, work through the avenues that might explain it. My immediate reaction was that she'd been killed, but I need to train myself like Detective Walker said; think through all the possibilities. If she had known she was going to leave she would have told me, she would have told all of us, so she must have left suddenly without knowing beforehand.

I remember that Glenda sees Eadie too, so I run over to her cottage. She's hanging around with her little crew. I nod at her and she nods back, then I flick my head to the side, to mean, *Come this way*. She starts walking with me and her friends come too. She stops and looks at them and shakes her head, and that's all it takes for them to stop where they are. She has such control over her friends it's amazing.

'Whit's goin' on?' she says.

'You seen Eadie?'

'Aye, Thursday. Why, whit's happened?'

'She's gone.'

'Gone? How so?'

'Gone. Nurse says she's no coming back.'

Her face looks how I feel. 'She cannae be gone.'

'She is so, no message for us, no nothing.'

'Tha's no fair,' she says. Glenda doesn't look angry, just hurt. 'Someone has to have got rid of her. She's too nice to run oot on us.'

'I know, but who?'

'Bastard Super, that's who.'

'No.'

'Aye, he never liked her, I can tell.'

'Aye, but not enough to get rid of her.'

We've reached the edge of the woods and stop.

'Whit we gonnae do?' she asks.

'We're gonnae find out who knows why Eadie's gone, then we're gonnae find out why she's gone, then we're gonnae get her back.'

'Aye right,' says Glenda, nodding.

'Right,' I say.

She walks back to her cottage and I walk back to mine.

That bastard Super, I think. *He must know, for sure.*

68

I'm in the kitchen on my own after school. I've just finished the crumble and custard that Cook left out for my tea.

The moment I finish the last spoonful Mrs Paterson taps me on the shoulder. I didn't hear her come in. 'Can I speak to you for a moment?' she says.

I sense trouble but I stand up and walk after her into her sitting room. 'Sit down,' she says, and I do.

I have the feeling I get when I know I'm going to get told off. I feel like I'm frozen and can't move, but I have to.

She sits down next to me and puts her knees together. 'Do you see my fringe?' she asks, pointing at her hair. 'Have you ever seen my forehead?'

I shake my head. I never have seen it as she always wears her hair the same way, ponytail at the back and fringe at the front. She lifts the fringe up, revealing her forehead and, up by the hairline, a four-inch jagged scar.

'Do you see this?' I nod. 'It was done by Peter Montrose. The other scars are behind my hairline so no one can see them, but I have to hide this one.

'It's not a nice story. He dragged me off the side of the road behind some bushes and hit me with the hammer. He hit me so hard my skull was fractured in three places. He didn't manage to knock me out, though he thought he had. As I was lying on the ground, he started to pull at my dress so I kicked him, as hard as I have ever kicked anyone in my life, then I staggered out into the road and was saved by the driver of a passing car. So that's what happened. And I keep those newspapers because I want to be sure they got him, and I want to be sure they hanged him. And when I get scared or have nightmares, I read them again. That is why I keep them. Do you understand?'

'Yes, miss,' I say.

'And I don't want you ever snooping through our belongings again. We let you sleep downstairs because you have had a hard time, but don't try it on, Lesley.'

'Yes, miss,' I say, drenched in shame.

'Also, Lesley ...'

'Yes, miss?'

'There's something else I want to talk to you about.'

The shame is now joined by fear as I wonder what else I could have done wrong.

'The Andersons, the adoption – I wanted to talk to you about that.'

I look at her eyes to try to guess what she is going to say. I feel relief as I know nothing can hurt me any more with regard to the adoption, I've already had the worst news I could get. This is something I've learnt this summer; sometimes things are so bad that it's simply impossible for them to get any worse.

'I gather no one has told you why it was stopped.'

I nod.

'I think that is unfair, Lesley. So I'm going to tell you, but you are not to tell anyone. Do you understand?'

I nod again.

'It was your mother. Your mother put a stop to the adoption; she says that she still wants the option to take you to live with her. If you go with the Andersons then you are unlikely ever to be reunited with your real family. So what she's done in cancelling it, she's done from a good place. She wants you back with her.'

'But I dinnae want to go with her,' I say. 'I want to be with the Andersons.' I try to breathe slowly. 'If she wanted me to live with her she's had years to do that, or is it only now someone else wants me? Why did she change her mind? What about what *I* want?'

'She's your mother, Lesley, and until you are sixteen, she gets a say.'

'Sixteen is ages away. Sixteen means I'm stuck here for ever.'

'It will go quickly, Lesley, I promise.'

'Well, the moment I'm sixteen I'm choosing never to see her again.'

'I understand.'

'What about the Andersons? Whit did they say?'

'They were obviously disappointed, they really liked you and were hoping it could be worked out, but ultimately they understood.'

I nod again. 'Can I go now?' I say.

'Yes, Lesley.'

I go upstairs to my room. The girls are all in there talking. I lie down on my bed and look at the wall. The others barely notice.

My head has too many thoughts in it again. To be wanted by someone you don't want to be wanted by. By someone who you did want to want you way back, but now you don't want them to want you and it's only now that they do want you. The people who do want you and you want back can't have you.

Is this going to be my life?

69

It's nearly time for tea when I hear the scream.

I'm sat on the front steps of Cottage 5 with Shona, Eldrey, Mary and Pam. Shona is saying that she has a boyfriend, but won't say who. Mary is begging to know who it is. Eldrey is staring off into space. Pam doesn't believe Shona and I don't know what to think.

The scream comes from Cottage 8, which is Glenda McAdam's house. It sounds like it's her doing the screaming. First I hear, 'Noooooo!' followed by, 'Daddy!'

I can see her out the front of her house. Her friends are standing in the doorway but she's on the grass. There's a man walking away, a big heavyset man, and it's more of a stagger than a walk. It's her dad. He's back again and he's drunk again.

I look at Glenda stood there. You can see she doesn't know whether to go after him or not. From what I've seen and heard, I would advise her to stay away. He is a bad, angry, dangerous man; Jonesy said so before.

I talk to Glenda more now that Eadie isn't about. She appreciated Eadie as much as I did. We both really miss her and are sad she has gone. Glenda doesn't know why she's gone either, but she's promised to tell me if she finds anything out. Sometimes when we talk, she mentions her dad and the drink, and how scared he can make her.

Pam runs over to Cottage 8 then runs back. She tells us that apparently he's come for the eldest McAdam lad. It seems there was an insult to the mother and now the dad is going to batter him.

Glenda is still stood there on her own, no one has gone to her, so eventually I walk over. I think the girls from Cottage 5 are a bit shocked as they still think she's my mortal enemy; they don't know that we've been talking and, although we're not friends, we do get on.

'Y'all right, Glen?' I say.

'Nuh.'

'Da gone crazy again?'

'Aye,' she says, kind of resigned. 'Been drinking again, said he's gonnae kill Tommy, says he's said something to Ma and he has to pay. I asked him what Tommy said.

He said it disnae matter. I think he can't remember, just wants to crack a heid.'

'How long's this gonnae go on?'

'Till one of the boys gets big enough to batter him back, I suppose. Or he drinks himself to death. No great options, eh?'

'Anyone called the polis?' I ask.

"Spect so, someone usually does. Just a case of whether they get to him afore he gets to Tommy.'

'Should we try to stop him?'

'No worth it, we'd only end up getting a battering too.'

We stand there looking in the direction Mr McAdam walked off in.

'Shall we go back inside?' I ask.

'Feels sorta wrong to, knowing my da is rampaging about.'

'Aye. Well, I'm off back to our cottage. Come over if you want to.'

'Thanks, I'll stay here for a bit,' she says.

'Right,' I say, and walk back to Pam and the girls. Soon we get called in for tea.

*

At the table, the girls ask me how come I'm friends with Glenda now. I explain that we aren't friends, but we have a sort of understanding and chat sometimes. They seem shocked. It makes me happy that I have surprised them. I haven't surprised anyone in a long time.

After tea Glenda does come over. The doorbell rings and Mrs Paterson answers it; she doesn't want to let her in, but I beg, so she says she can stay 'five minutes, but not a moment longer'.

Turns out the police did get Glenda's da, but only after he tried to batter Tommy; only he couldn't, he was too drunk, apparently. Tommy stayed out of striking distance and danced around him while he swung punches and shouted curses.

As someone who doesn't have a dad, I have been jealous in the past of people who have one, but as I've learnt, having one that's bad is worse than not having one at all. This is where not having one isn't so bad.

Poor Glenda. I think I'm starting to like her; she's not the person everyone thinks she is. When you get to know her she's actually good, I just don't think she's ever been able to show it.

That evening I can't stop thinking about Glenda's father. Imagine having someone that dangerous as your dad. Imagine not knowing if he was going to be nice or crazy when he visited; it sounds like he was never a nice man. It's no wonder they took the kids away. Glenda is probably safer here.

70

This is me, this is where my life is.

I am twelve years old. I have two sisters and a brother. I have never met them, I don't know if they know I exist. I have a mother who put me in an orphanage when I was three weeks old, who won't let me get adopted because she wants me to live with her family but hasn't done anything about it.

It looks like I have another three or four years in this place till I get to leave and I cannot wait. I did have Eadie, the one person I could rely on in here, but she is now gone.

I am basically alone. I have friends, but not great friends. I have Clara at school, and the girls in my room, but no one as close as Jonesy who was killed at the back of the house which I still have to live in. Two other girls were killed. Someone in the Homes probably did it but no one knows who and the police don't care about finding them.

People seem to have gone back to normal. I can't understand how. This isn't right, I am not the same person I was at the start of the summer.

If the police don't find the murderer, then are they just hoping it will all go away? Why aren't they doing more? Why aren't police about here all the time until the killer is caught?

My aim is just to get through each day, and if enough days go by, eventually I can leave. But only if the murderer doesn't come back and attack me. If no one seems capable of finding out who killed Jonesy, then I need to find who did it – the adults do not seem able. Finding out who killed her is the quickest way to me being safe. I can stop being scared and get revenge for Jonesy.

Mr Sharples is weird and creepy, but the police say he didn't do it. Mr Taylor can't have done it – even though he was going with Jane Denton, which was bad – as he was in custody when Sally Ward got killed, and he'd already been sent away when what happened to Jonesy happened. He can't have come back just to kill Jonesy, or someone would have noticed him sneaking about – someone sees most things around here. The

McAdams' da is too much of a drunk to be able to do it even though he is a terrible man. He'd be more likely to do that to one of his *own* kids, not one he didn't know.

I thought Mr Paterson could have done it as he can be nasty and Jonesy lived in his cottage and because of the newspapers. But Detective Walker said he couldn't have done it because he had alibis, and now I know why the Patersons have all those clippings about Peter Montrose, it was about Mrs Paterson, not Mr Paterson. Besides, Mr Paterson wouldn't have spoken to Jane Denton in years or known who Sally Ward was.

It must be someone around here, but who? Adults don't have the answers. When you ask them about God, they lie; when you ask them for the truth, they can't tell you. You have to find your own answers, not take their word for it.

I need to speak to Eadie about this. There is one person who will know why she has gone and when she is coming back. I don't want to speak to him as he scares me but he's the only one who will have real answers. He will know what's happened to Eadie, and he will know about the investigation.

I set off down Hope Avenue. I am walking quickly. Some girls say hello but I don't hear them until I have passed. I go into the executive building up the big stairs and I walk up to the secretary who is sat in front of a desk outside his office.

She looks tidy and proper, like she went to a school for manners.

'How can I help you, young lady?' she says, peering over her glasses.

'I need to see the Superintendent.'

'I'm sure you do but Mr Gordon is a busy man.'

'I know, miss, but it's very important.'

'Could you let me know what matter it relates to?'

'I cannae, miss, I cannae say anything, I have to tell him in person, please, miss, trust me.'

'Young lady, what is your name?'

'Lesley.'

'Right Lesley, my job here is to assist the Superintendent and one of the ways I do that is by not letting people bother him unless it's absolutely necessary.'

'But it is, miss, it is,' I say, louder.

The door to his office opens and Mr Gordon sticks his head out and gruffly asks, 'What's going on?'

'Ah Superintendent, I was just explaining to this young lady that it was not possible—'

My chance is slipping. She will talk me out of seeing him. I can see his granite face with the pockets under his eyes, his hard bald head and tight grey buttoned-up shirt.

'Sir, sir,' I cut in. 'I need to talk to you, sir, it's important.'

'Very well, come in,' he says, just like that.

I nod at the secretary to say, *See?* and she gives me a look back like she's chewing a nettle.

I follow the Superintendent into his office. The window looks out to the main gates and there is a map of the Homes on his wall. The large desk is stacked with papers. I can smell the authority in the room. He controls everything at the Homes from here, and if you are ever sent to see the Superintendent you know you are in for a world of sorrow.

His punishments are legendary. Rumour is, he's even given a couple of the housefathers a doing over their failure to control their houses. That's why the housefathers can be so strict, cos if they don't they are going to get it from him. It's a pyramid of beatings and we are at the bottom.

I feel terrified being in the room alone with him.

Mr Gordon points to the chair for me to sit down, and he takes his seat behind the desk, then leans forward.

'I know you,' he says, and my heart sinks. 'You're one of the girls in the Patersons' house, aren't you? Cottage 5? And you go to the grammar school?'

I nod.

'I believe you had a fight with Glenda McAdams last term, did you not?'

329

I nod again. 'How did you know?'

'It's my job to know everything that goes on in this place. I gather that you managed to emerge victorious, which is some feat. And it was your friend, young Morag Jones, who sadly died at the start of the summer holidays, correct?'

I nod again.

'What is your name?'

'Lesley, sir. Lesley Beaton.'

'Ah that's right, I knew it would come back to me. So, what is so urgent that you need to see me?'

'Sir, where's Eadie Schaffer gone? I'm worried about her.'

'She's fine. She's just had to leave, I'm afraid.'

'But why, sir?'

'The why is none of your business.'

'But she's just gone, without saying anything, she would have said something. Will she be back?'

'I don't think so, no.'

This hurts. It was bad to lose her, but to not have the hope that she will come back hurts more. I am tired of hurting.

'Was there anything else?'

I try to compose myself and say what I need to say.

'Well?'

'Why haven't the polis caught whoever it is killing

girls? I mean, how hard can it be? How hard are they trying? At first I thought it was Mr Sharples; he's strange, he has mental problems. But the polis say it isn't him.'

'I'm aware of your suspicions, but I can assure you that Mr Sharples was not responsible for any of the murders. He could account for his whereabouts for each time.'

'Then I thought it was Mr Paterson. There are all these newspaper clippings about the Montrose murders in the sitting room at the cottage and I thought he could have done it, being Morag's housefather. But then Detective Walker told me that he had alibis and about Mrs Paterson and I felt awful. At one point me and Morag even wondered if it was Glenda McAdam's dad. But I don't think it couldae been him. So who did it? They are still out there, why is no one doing anything?'

I sound angry. I don't mean to, but I can't help it.

'Lesley, the police have a huge team on it, we are doing all we can do.'

'But we're no safe. While the murderer is still out there we're no safe.'

'I assure you, you *are* all safe.'

And then I make my mistake.

'But we're not,' I say. 'You say we are, but girls are dying. My friend died, I could be next, and it must be someone at the Homes, someone who is here every day and they could murder another girl at any time. The polis can't seem to find them, so mibbie someone is telling them lies to send them in the wrong direction so the killer is free to do it again. And the person who speaks to the polis the most is you!'

There is silence in the room. The Superintendent stares straight at me.

'You're the one who can go anywhere in the grounds and not be suspicious. You can tell the polis the wrong thing. You can pretend to keep us safe and all the time have us where you can get us. It's you. It's you, you killed Jonesy!'

I find myself shouting, and I realise what I have just said, and I want to pull it back into my mouth, but it hangs between us and I know I am in more trouble than I have ever been in before.

His face goes red, steaming red. His nostrils flare.

'What did you just say?'

'Sir, I'm sorry, sir, I'm so, so sorry.'

'Sorry? I'm going to make you sorry. Miss McArdle, get this girl out of here.'

The door opens behind me and the secretary is stood there. I run out as fast as I can. I think he might try to grab me, and if gets me he will try to kill me, he has to, I know his secret.

I went in there thinking he was a bastard and came out knowing it. He doesn't care about the Homes children, he doesn't even like them, he thinks we are rats.

And we are. I scurry down the stairs, and race back to my cottage. We are little things he has to control to make sure we don't cause trouble.

As I run back it comes to me, like a vision, clarity. Like Detective Walker said, you look at all angles and from one angle you can see the answer – and I see it.

We have to get away.

71

I get back to Cottage 5. I need to speak to Mrs Paterson.
I need to tell her that we are in trouble.

She's talking to some of the bigger girls, telling them
off for something one of the girls has done in their
bedroom and how all of them will be held responsible.
The girls look like they just want the telling off to end,
but Mrs Paterson keeps going. I can't wait much longer.

Eventually she ends with: 'So if you do that again,
there is going to be serious trouble, do you understand?'
The older girls' shoulders relax as they realise it is finally
over and not that serious. At least Mr Paterson hasn't
been involved.

As soon as Mrs Paterson is finished, I run up to her.
'Miss, I need to talk to you. It's urgent.'

'Can it wait, Lesley? I need to get some things for the house right now.'

I can tell she is starting to tire of me, how much work I am since Jonesy died. I can see it in her expression; when she turned around and saw it was me her smile faded a little. But I need to really stress how much danger we are in, and for her to take me seriously. I am done with not having adults listen to me, or pretending they are listening to me then ignoring what I say.

'No, miss, this cannae wait, I need your help, I need it now.'

She looks at me and I can tell she's thinking, *Is this another one of her stupid wee ideas or is this something genuinely important I have to listen to?*

I stare at her. I try to put on my most serious face so she knows I'm not messing.

We are by the front door and suddenly I see through one of the glass panels that the Superintendent is walking towards the cottage. He looks really angry. I know he's coming for me, or to tell the Patersons what I just accused him of.

'Quick!' I say. 'He's coming!' and I grab Mrs Paterson's arm and drag her through the kitchen and out the back door just as I hear three loud bangs on the front door.

'Wait! Stop! Who's coming?' she asks.

'Mr Gordon, miss, he's coming for me.'

'What? Why is he coming for you? Why are we running?'

We go around the side of the house and I can hear the front door being opened and the Super shouting, 'WHERE ARE THE PATERSONS?'

'Quick, follow me,' I say, and I'm pleased that she comes with me without asking any more questions. We scuttle across the green, towards the church. Soon we are out of sight of the cottage. Mrs Paterson is breathing heavily, and we slow down to a walk when we get into the woods.

'What is going on, Lesley? What have you got me doing?'

I stop. We're near where Jane's body was found. I stand by a tree and put my arm against it to compose myself.

'Miss, I think it's him. I think Mr Gordon is the murderer. He can go everywhere, he can steer the polis in the wrong direction, he's got access to every cottage, he hates us kids, he could be seen with anyone and it no be suspicious, he's made Eadie disappear. Has he killed her? No one seems to be able to tell me where she is.

'I went to see him about Eadie but then I started to go on about how no one is doing anything and it clicked, and I told him I think it was him that killed the girls, and that's why he's come to the house because he knows

I'm right and he's gonnae try to do me in, miss! And you're no safe either as he might think that I've told you and then he'll have to get rid of you too. Miss, it was him all along! He was the bastard who killed Jonesy and I'm no safe in the house any more as he knows where I sleep and I can't tell Detective Walker as he doesnae trust me any more as I got those other people wrong and no one is gonnae stop him and I'm gonnae be the next one deid.'

My brain is working so fast I'm not sure I'm making sense, but I can't seem to stop.

'But why would the Super kill Eadie? Whit's she ever done to anyone but help them, and why would he kill Jonesy? Or Jane or Sally? I cannae tell the polis. Mibbie you should tell the polis, mibbie they will listen to you. Will you tell Mr Paterson? He could help us; he could drive us somewhere. Could you drive me to the Andersons? They could look after me ... Or my mum, you could tell her I'm sorry ... Or my gran, she's better – can we call my gran? She could come get me and look after me for a while, just a while, I promise I'll come back when it's safe. I won't run away, I promise, miss ... miss ... I just need help to get away.'

I can't seem to breathe properly. I am trying but I can't seem to get any air into my lungs and I'm dizzy and my face feels fuzzy like it's electric.

Mrs Paterson is looking at me. She is bent down and

she is looking directly into my eyes and she is saying something but it is slurred, her words are slow.

Why are her words so slow ... my lips are tingling ... and ... I can't ...

72

The first thing I notice is the smell of bleach. I was in the woods but now I am somewhere with bleach and strong soap.

I open my eyes and the room is very white. It hurts to look at it. Something has happened. I am in a bed in the hospital.

I'm not injured, nothing seems to hurt on my body, I haven't been beaten, I am lying in a bed with the sheets tucked tight, holding me in.

I look to my right and Mrs Paterson is sat on a chair and is holding my hand.

'Are you all right, dear? Are you back with us?'

I nod.

'You had a little episode, Lesley. You collapsed and we brought you to the hospital.'

I nod again.

I hear the squeaks of a trolley going past in the corridor outside.

We sit and don't talk for a while.

'Have you had anything to eat or drink today? The doctors think you may be dehydrated. There's a sandwich and a glass of milk here for you, and they have given you a sedative, too, to help you relax.'

I nod.

'Lesley, you have had an awful lot of terrible things happen to you this summer and I guess we didn't notice how much, what with your mum and the adoption, and Morag, and now Eadie going. It's a lot for anyone to take in.'

'But the Super? Does he know where I am?'

'He helped carry you here, Lesley. Mr Gordon is not a bad man. Believe me, he is the last person who would have done all the things you said. You thought it was Mr Taylor – I know it was you who told the police about him; I found the first version of your letter in the rubbish – then you thought it was Mr Sharples or Mr McAdam. You even thought it was Mr Paterson at one point? And now you think it's Mr Gordon. Lesley, you have to realise that this is something you can't work out.

340

It's not a maths puzzle to be solved. The world doesn't work like that.

'Sometimes you just need your brain to go quiet for a bit, not let it rule you. You are a special girl, Lesley, with a special mind that will help you do many things in life, but remember it works for you; you don't work for it.'

'Yes, miss.'

She squeezes my hand.

'They have said you can have this room on your own for the next couple of days, so you don't have to be on the ward with the other children. I need to go back to Cottage 5 now but you just take your time. Rest, sleep, let yourself slow down.'

I nod.

'And eat that sandwich, all right? I want you back to your old self in a few days' time. No rush, but we want the old Lesley back.'

I think I want that old Lesley back too. I was happy before this summer. Well, not always happy but I wasn't always scared, and I had Jonesy and I would give anything to feel like that again.

Mrs Paterson gets up and leaves and I take three bites of my sandwich, drink some milk and stare out of the window at the tops of the trees.

I feel myself getting drowsy again and close my eyes.

73

'Would you like something to eat, doll? Wee bit o' sausage and tatties?'

...

'Just checking your pulse, my love, nothing to worry about.'

...

'Freshening up your water, doll. You keep your eyes shut.'

...

'She's no awake at the moment.'
'Well, let me be the judge of that.'

...

'Lesley? Lesley?'
'Super, she's clearly asleep.'

*

I wake up.

Fear grips me as I open my eyes to see that Mr Gordon is stood at the end of my bed.

'See,' he says turning to the nurse, 'I told you she was awake.'

The nurse walks off. I don't want her to, I don't feel safe with just him and me in this room.

He stays at the end of the bed.

'Lesley, I wanted to check you are all right. Let's forget what was said in my office. I understand you are confused.'

I say nothing.

'I was one of the first people the police interviewed. As a man with access to all areas of the Homes, naturally the police needed to eliminate me from their enquiries, which they have done, for all three deaths. When Jane died, and then when her close friend Sally died, we were all wondering who was responsible. And then of course, your poor pal, Morag.

'No one has been more worried about you children. It is not just my job, but my duty to make sure you are all safe. Not being able to do that has been appalling. Anyway, I just wanted to come here to check on you, and explain the situation to you.'

I nod but say nothing. The nurse walks back in. 'Are you done with her, Super? She really needs her rest.'

'Yes, I am. Look after this lassie, she's a special one.'

He leaves the room and the nurse comes closer.

'OK, sit up, young lady, and take this medicine ... just pop it in your mouth ... sip of water ... another sip. There you go, all done ... back down for some rest.'

*

I stare at the ceiling, and I think about what the Super said, how bad it had all been for him.

He said they had been close friends.

I didn't know Jane and Sally had been *close* friends. Some of the kids had said they were pals, but there were so many different rumours and stories. How close were they?

I feel sleepy.

If they *were* good friends, then Sally probably knew what Jane knew. And Sally was probably killed for what she knew.

So it wasn't random. They were killed for a reason. The police must know this, but not what the reason is.

So Jonesy must have been killed for a reason, too. The same reason.

Not just some man wanting to kill girls. Jonesy must have known something they knew.

My eyes are heavy.

I try to keep them open. I must keep them open. I had it all wrong.

*

'Switching your lights out now. Nurse is on the ward if you need anything.'

*

Jonesy, what did you know?

*

'... there is such a thing as being too clever, Lesley. Ever heard the phrase "no one likes a smart-arse"? That's the one you need to understand.'

I feel my hand being held and stroked, and I know this voice and it belongs to Mrs Paterson, except it's not the posh voice she usually has. She sounds more like us kids, like this is the real her. My eyes are still heavy, and I keep them shut.

'You always were a special one, and it's no your fault, it's the way you were born. You're too clever and it's got you into trouble. You're like a wee dog with a bone, you. Dinnae know when to just leave it.

345

'It's none of our faults either. *We* weren't interfering with that girl Jane years back. He does it, and I'm left to pick up the pieces. He's sick. He knows it, too, it's why he drinks. But he doesnae stop it, it's inside him, and I'm the one whit's got to stop it getting found out or we're gone.

'And once Jane was gone, her pal Sally comes along. Stupid lassie asks me for help. Tells me she thinks Malcolm killed Jane to stop her talking, that she knows he'd messed with Jane and that we had to tell the polis. Well, no if I have anything to do with it, you willnae.

'It always comes down to the same thing, it always comes down to them or me, and it's no going to be me. I never wanted you to become one of them. I always liked you, but after what you've done I have no choice. You're trouble. Just like yer little pal. It wasnae her fault either. She overheard me shouting at Malcolm, telling him what I had done, telling him it was his fault I had to do it. She should never have come back at dinnertime, she should have stayed at school. But there she was, standing in the hallway. She heard the lot. She ran, but no quick enough.

'It wasnae her fault, it's no your fault, and it's no my fault. It's just the way it is. But I cannae have you taking this away from me. I got away from Montrose, I'm safe here, and I'm no having you destroy that.'

I open my right eye just the tiniest amount. I don't want her to know I am awake. I can feel her holding my hand and though what I see is blurry and the room is dark, she seems to be looking down at my hand, not at my face. It is very late, or it could even be so late it's early.

I know I am in danger. I know I have to get out of here, away from her, but I am stuck. The bedsheets are tightly tucked in around me. I won't be able to get out in one quick move. I need to loosen the sheets – but how, without her knowing I am awake?

She's still talking. She keeps saying she's sorry. Then she stands up.

I can feel her moving up against the side of my bed.

'I'm sorry, I'm sorry,' she keeps saying.

I open my eyes, pull my arm back, and jab at her face with outstretched fingers. I catch her right between the eye and the nose with everything I have.

She yelps and recoils back, and I am already pulling at the sheets to free my legs and then I am running to the door. I open it and run down the ward to the nurses' desk. It's dark as anything with just a small half-light showing me where to go.

There is no one at the nurses' desk. Behind me I can hear Mrs Paterson coming so I make a right and go down the flights of stairs until I am in the bottom corridor. Still there's no one about and no lights on.

I head for the main entrance. If they lock it at night I am done for, but it is the only exit I know from here.

I hit it at speed and it opens and I am out into the night. It's cold, my breath is steaming out and I need to work out where to go.

Think, Lesley, think.

But I can't. I can't work out who or where to run to; I just need to find someone who can help me, but the Homes are asleep and everything is still.

Mrs Paterson comes flying out the doors behind me. 'Get back here, you wee shite!' she shouts and I run, and all I can think of is Cottage 5, run back to Cottage 5, and I am running barefoot on the path then on the grass and my nightie is getting wet from the ground and I'm running as fast as I can and I am pulling away from her.

I cut across the grass, behind Cottage 32 and then back along the path but I'm slowing, and I can feel myself slowing and I have to keep going.

Eventually I get to Hope Avenue and I can see Cottage 5 and I run for it, and I know the front door will be locked as it always is at night but I head for it anyway and I'm going to make as much noise as I can.

I get to the front door and I bang on it with my fist – *bang, bang, bang, bang* – and shout, 'Hello! Wake up, anyone!'

I know Mrs Paterson will catch up with me soon. If

she gets to me before someone opens the door, I am finished.

No one comes, no lights go on, so I run round to the back door to the kitchen. Sometimes they forget to lock it. I step on something sharp and the pain shoots up my leg but I don't let out a noise in case Mrs Paterson is close by. I get to the back door and I can see Mr Paterson sat at the table by the wall, his head resting on his hand. He seems to be asleep again. I try the door gently and it's locked, but I know some of the older girls have hidden a spare key under a plant pot in case they come back really late.

I bend down to find the pot, lift it up and feel underneath for a key. There is nothing there. If I go to the front door again and bang on it, I will eventually wake Mr Paterson up; if I stay—

An arm grabs me around my neck from behind. 'You stupid girl. You stupid, stupid girl!' she spits.

And she's squeezing my neck, tighter, and she's growling, and I can't breathe.

I ... can't ... get ... any ... air.

Then she let's go, but it's only to spin me around and push me to the ground and kneel on me. And she starts choking me again, she's using her two thumbs on my neck this time, and I'm fighting to push her away and I'm trying to scratch her arms and pull them off but she's too strong and I'm going to die and I'm going to die where Jonesy died and I can't fight any more, oh Jesus this is it, this is where it ends, and it wasn't supposed to end so soon and I had things to do and I was going to make it out of here and her eyes are burning into me and pushing and pushing on my neck and I can't hold out any—

She stops, and the pressure stops and she releases my throat, lets out a grunt and then slumps on top of me.

There is a thud as her skull hits the path beside my head.

I am desperately trying to get air in, but the weight of her body is pinning me down. I can just see blood dribbling out of her mouth; warm liquid is splattered on the side of my face.

I look up and see Cook standing there, holding the biggest knife in the house.

She reaches down and rolls Mrs Paterson off me.

I am on my back with my breath steaming into the air. My neck aches like it's a rag that has been twisted dry.

Cook kneels down next to me.

'You all right, doll?' she says.

I cough, and wheeze and nod. I am not sure I can speak. I think she has broken my throat. A husky growl comes out.

I turn my head to the right, and I can see through the

open kitchen door that Mr Paterson is still asleep at the table, oblivious to what has happened yards away.

'I never liked her,' says Cook. 'There was something no right about them two. Always something strange about them, but nobody listens to me, nobody listens to Cook. I could see something wasnae right. I can tell. I can sense bad'uns.'

'What do we do now?' I manage to say.

'Get the Super,' she says. 'Explain what happened. Get the polis here. Get that bastard arrested.' She nods towards the kitchen.

She seems worryingly calm for a person who has just killed someone.

I look around to see if anyone is about, or if any lights have come on at the windows.

Nothing.

We are the only two people awake in the whole village. Mrs Paterson's body lies at our feet. Where there was rage there is now stillness, other than the pool of her blood getting larger and larger, soaking into her hair.

Cook walks quietly into the kitchen, turns the light off, then comes out and shuts the back door, leaving Mr Paterson asleep.

Then we walk together, my bare feet on the grass again and the cold breeze on my legs.

My heart is just slowing down.

'I dinnae trust him, and I didnae ever trust her,' she says. 'I seen his eyes when he looked at the young girls. He is a bad man, and she knew it too.'

'I think she killed Jane,' I croak.

Cook shrugs. 'Could be. The lassie used to live here, did you know that?'

I nod. 'When I was little.'

'She got her moved out when she was about nine. I knew something was up. It was Mrs Paterson whit decided she had to go. One day she just says she's no staying in this house no more, and she got moved.'

We continue walking. The lampposts are lighting the way towards the Super's house. His place is next door to the executive building. He will be angry at being woken up but he's the only one we can tell, and he'll have to call the police.

'Thank you,' I say, 'for saving me.'

'It's no bother,' she replies. 'Ah wisnae sleeping much, mibbie I knew something was up?'

'Well if you hadnae, I'd be deid by now.'

She puts her arm round me as we walk. 'Aye, and we cannae be having that for wee Brainbox. That's your name, y'know.'

'Is that what they call me?'

'Oh, aye.'

'We only call you Cook.'

'I know.'

'What's your real name?'

'It's Morag, like your pal.'

We carry on walking in silence, then we reach the Super's house and Morag bangs hard on the door six times.

74

A few days after everything, Mr Gordon comes to see me. We have a new housemother and housefather, Mr and Mrs McKelpie. They used to run another Homes cottage but retired a few years ago. They have been brought back temporarily until the Superintendent can find someone permanent to look after us. Another change is that Eldrey has been moved to another cottage. No one will tell us why, and she hasn't been to school since.

'Les!' shouts one of the older girls. 'It's the Super, for you.'

Two months ago if I had found out the Super was here to see me I would have turned cold inside, but now things have changed. I walk down the stairs and he says,

'Get your shoes on, I'm going to take you for a walk.' His voice is gentler than it usually is.

I can feel the eyes of the other children watching me. I put my shoes on and he closes the front door behind us. Normally if I was walking with the Super everyone would know I was in big-big trouble, but they all know what's happened; something like that doesn't stay a secret long.

'Where are we going?' I ask.

'Let's walk down the road, shall we?'

We walk out the Homes and over the bridge and past the bus stop that I get the bus from.

'It's been a rather eventful few months for you, hasn't it, Lesley?'

'Aye, sir.'

'I just wanted to check how you were doing.'

I think about how to answer this and in the end I settle on the truth.

'I don't know how I'm doing, sir. I just want things to go back to normal.'

'That's understandable.'

'I don't know if they will ever be normal, but I keep hoping if I can get to the end of another day then mibbie the next day will be normal. They have to be normal soon, don't they?'

'One day, but I can't tell you when that day will be.'

'I hope it is soon.'

We walk along in silence for a bit near the stream; the only sound is the water finding its way around the rocks.

'Lesley, I imagine you have some questions. I might not be able to answer them all, but I'll do my best.'

I have never seen this caring side of the Super, I couldn't have imagined there was one.

'Why would Mrs Paterson do that? Why would she kill Jane because *Mr Paterson* did things to Jane years ago? And if it hadn't been for that, Sally and Jonesy wouldn't have died, right?'

Mr Gordon looks off at one of the fields, as if he is trying to work out how to best put into words something that he thinks I might not understand. I understand things; he must know this by now.

'All I can tell you is what I think, what the police think now that they have arrested Mr Paterson – he has told them some, but not all, of the story. Mr and Mrs Paterson didn't have a ... normal relationship. Because of Mrs Paterson being attacked when she was younger, she wasn't able to do things a normal husband and wife do together.'

'Like make babies?'

'Sort of like that, yes. But Mr Paterson has a sickness – he likes young girls, which is very wrong. As far as I can tell, they had an arrangement where she didn't intervene.'

'I see ...' I say, then, 'No, wait, why did Mrs Paterson kill Jane, then? Had Mr Paterson been with Jane and Mrs Paterson was jealous of her?'

'It's a bit more complicated than that. Mr Paterson ... interfered with Jane when she lived at Cottage 5 several years ago, when she was much younger. You may be aware that a teacher was recently removed from the school—'

'Mr Taylor? They say he was going with Jane.' I don't tell the Super about the diary Jonesy found. That's our secret.

'Yes ... it may be that an inappropriate relationship with her teacher brought back memories of her time at Cottage 5. Jane realised what Mr Paterson had done to her was wrong, and she told him that she was going to tell Mr Taylor.'

I remembered Jane's last diary entry, written on the day of her death: 'Meeting T tomorrow, getting things sorted.' If she'd only told Mr Taylor sooner, they'd all still be alive.

'If that happened,' the Super went on, 'Mr Paterson thought it would be reported to the authorities. He would go to jail and Mrs Paterson would have to leave the Homes. He told his wife, and Mrs Paterson killed Jane to stop her speaking out. Perhaps she thought she would not be a suspect, being a woman. I understand that Jane's body was ... posed to make it look like a man had been involved.'

I nod. I remember when Jonesy said that Jane's knickers had been round her ankles. It seems so long ago.

'And Sally? Did Mr Paterson try the same thing with her as well?'

'No, Sally was Jane's friend. Jane had told her about what Mr Paterson had done to her when she was younger. After Jane was murdered, Sally made the mistake of telling Mrs Paterson that she believed her husband had killed Jane to stop her reporting his crime. It was a fatal error – Mrs Paterson killed Sally too.'

'Ah,' I say, as if I understand it all, but I don't. It's so hard to realise that someone you thought you knew so well could do that. The person who has turned out my bedroom light all these years, helped me when I was scared, but was capable of such cruelty. I could see why Sally had thought she was safe to approach, why she might need to be warned about her husband.

Now I understand how Mr Paterson had the alibis Detective Walker explained about. He really didn't kill Sally or Jane, and Mrs Paterson probably told lies about them both being somewhere else when Jonesy was murdered. The police thought the same person killed all three girls, so they wouldn't have looked too closely at Mr Paterson by the time Jonesy died.

I wonder if Detective Walker is in trouble now, him and the other policemen. He thought alibis were so important. Did they ask for Mrs Paterson's, or did they think only the housefathers could be killers?

I am silent for a bit. I suddenly think I understand why Eldrey is gone. Why she was always so quiet. Why Mr Paterson made her come to his study for a belting so often. But I don't say it out loud. If Mr Gordon says I'm right then that would make it real, and everything is already too real. I hope they find Eldrey her own Eadie to help her.

'Mr Paterson has confessed to Morag Jones's murder,' went on Mr Gordon. 'He and Mrs Paterson were having an argument about Jane and Sally, then Morag came home during the day. She overheard them shouting in their living room. He said he had no choice.'

I remember Mrs Paterson by my hospital bed, holding my hand. I hadn't quite understood what she was saying to me at the time. About my 'little pal'. About having no choice.

'But they did. They did have a choice.'

'I know that Lesley, that's how we think, but some people think differently from us. Some people are just evil.'

'Do you think Peter Montrose made Mrs Paterson evil?'

'I don't know, Lesley, some things you can't explain.'

That phrase sticks in my head like a flag. *Some things you can't explain.*

He's still talking but I'm not listening. I like things to be explained, I like to understand them. I *need* to understand them; things need to have a reason, otherwise we are lost.

Maybe that's why grown-ups lie, because they can't explain things. Maybe they don't know the answer and don't want to seem like they don't. Is that why they have religion and God and all that business? Because there are so many things that they can't explain that they have found a reason to scoop up all the unexplainable and difficult stuff?

I realise that no one has a clue what is going on and I am going to have to get used to that if I am ever to be happy again.

The world of adults is a mess. I think when I finally get out of this place it is only going to be more of the same. But at least I am prepared.

75

A few weeks after Mrs Paterson's death I received a letter:

Dear Lesley,

The Superintendent has kept me informed of what has been going on at the Homes. I have been unable to contact you as the rules of the Homes are such that I should not be in contact with the children, particularly once I explain the reason I have left.

The Superintendent has been extremely kind in making an exception in this case, given what has happened to you. I am sure you know now what a good man he can be, and the difficult job he has to do. He doesn't often let people see his good side, but it is there – I can vouch for that.

I want you to know you are so very brave and I am so very proud of you. What you have been through is awful, but I am glad you are concentrating on your studies.

I am so sorry I had to leave the Homes suddenly. It was never my intention to leave without saying goodbye; in fact, it was never my intention to leave, but circumstances meant that I was removed from my role.

I am six months pregnant. It is not something I intended, and I am not with the father any more. That I am unmarried and pregnant is something that the people who run the Homes consider a bad influence on you children, as so many, including yourself, were born to unmarried mothers.

I will be keeping the baby, but it means I will not be returning to work. The thing that disappoints me most about that is that I will not be able to see you again. You deserve the best, and any pain you are going through now will only go to making you into the exceptional woman I know you will become.

I want you to have the confidence to go out and make a difference in the world, because it's waiting for you.

Yours with love,
Eadie

P.S. If the baby is a girl, I am going to name her Lesley.

Postscript

The idea of this novel has been twenty-five years in the making. It started when my father suddenly died one Friday dinnertime in the gym at work. My mum was forty-seven at the time and the shock was shattering.

I was twenty-one and in the aftermath of it all I moved back home to be with her. We started to talk more than we ever had before, now that it was just me and her in the house together, and she would tell stories of her upbringing. She had grown up in the Quarriers orphan village near Bridge of Weir in Scotland. Until then I had known very little about her early life. I knew we didn't have grandparents on her side, but little else was explained.

The idea of the Quarriers homes fascinated me; that

you would have one thousand children in a purpose-built village seemed so strange. My mother did not realise that most children lived with their parents until she was about six.

There is a real Morag 'Jonesy' Jones, who inspired the character in this book. She is alive and well, and is still friends with my mum to this day. During the time when Mum was trying to put her life back together after my father's death, Morag came down to stay with us and help look after her. Seeing the two of them together was fascinating: Mum went from being my mother to a teenager, and helped me see what she was like as a young woman rather than just my parent.

Mum and Jonesy didn't actually know each other whilst in the Quarriers homes, but they moved in together shortly after Mum left at sixteen and became best friends straight away. They were so different from one another but both true survivors in what was a brutal place to grow up. I was inspired to write this by their courage, brains and bravery – they overcame the rough hand life had dealt them – and I wanted it published before the generation of people who had been in these types of places was gone.

Mum went on to have three children and seven grand-children, and became an actuary as, like Lesley, she loved maths as a girl. She is now retired and living in Surrey.

On the twentieth anniversary of Dad's death we went up to where we had scattered his ashes on Gleniffer Braes. Afterwards we drove to the Quarriers homes so Mum could show us where she had grown up and her 'cottage'.

After I had finished writing this book there was a development in my mother's story. She googled her own mother's name and found out that she had died a couple of months earlier. After waiting a period of time, and getting up the courage to do so, she wrote a letter to the eldest of her mother's other children, thinking that at seventy-two she didn't want to spend the rest of her life wondering *what if* she had tried to make contact with them.

They wrote back and after some confirmation of the facts my mother now has four sisters. They are in regular contact, she has met up with them, and she now has siblings for the first time in her life. They are the loveliest of people and I am so happy for my mum.

Lesley's mother in this book is completely fictional; that said, many unmarried women at the time were pressured into giving up their children by society; in fact, I have seen a handwritten letter from my grandmother to the Homes saying she only wanted her child in there for a couple of years as she wanted to be able to bring her back into the family. Although it took far longer, Mum is now back with her family.

This whole story is a tribute to my mum, who is an inspirational woman in the quietest, most dignified way. I wanted this book to show that courage comes in many forms.

This story is set in a fictional Scottish orphans' village in the 1960s. Truly awful things did happen in the real Quarriers homes. I haven't told that story here; that is for others to tell. Adults from Mum's cottage have been prosecuted and gone to prison for what they did. There were good people in the Homes trying to help the children there but there were also some very, very bad ones too.

If you were affected, there are support groups such as http://www.fbga.org.

Acknowledgements

The Montrose murders in the book are a reference to the Manuel murders, which occurred at a similar time, with a bit of artistic licence. I interviewed my mother extensively about her time at the homes. If I have got anything wrong, I apologise.

*

There are many people to thank for helping this book to publication. First is the High Priestess of Viper – Miranda Jewess, without whose help, insight, vision and this would not have got here. I would also like to thank Therese and the rest of the gang at Viper and Profile, who are utterly wonderful.

Huge thanks to Caroline Dawnay and Kat Aitken at United Agents for helping find a home for this story and for being so brilliant over the years: you are amazing.

Thank you Sheila McIlwraith, who helped hugely with an early iteration of this book, and Charlotte van Wijk, who was the first person to make me think maybe I had a story.

Thank you to the prereaders who saw an early version of this story: Simon Wort, Karen Yems, Vickie Ridley & Nik Upton – I really appreciate the help you gave.

Huge love to all the gang at Lucky's and the Saints for listening to me bore on about this book for too long.

Thank you to my mum, brother and sister, plus extended family and now new extended family. I hope to meet you all soon

Finally to Catherine, Felix, Alice and Mr B, thank you for your help, patience and for being the reason for everything. I am a lucky man to have you in my world and you make it all worthwhile.

About the Author

J.B. Mylet was inspired to write *The Homes* by the stories his mother told him about her childhood. She grew up in the infamous *Quarrier's Homes* in Scotland in the 1960s, along with a thousand other orphaned or unwanted children, and did not realise that children were supposed to live with their parents until she was seven. He felt this was a story that needed to be told. He lives in London.

If you loved *The Homes*, you might enjoy

'A mesmerising tale of secrets and lies'
VAL McDERMID

Not every child is a blessing...

The Rosary Garden

WINNER OF THE DUNDEE INTERNATIONAL BOOK PRIZE

NICOLA WHITE

Award-winning 1980s Dublin noir
Available in paperback and ebook

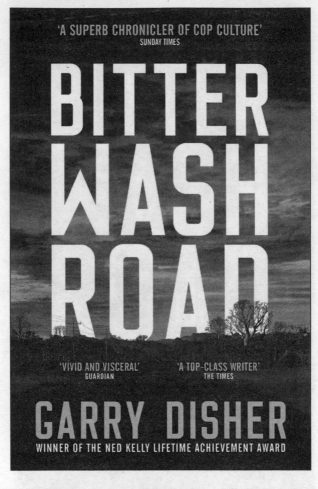

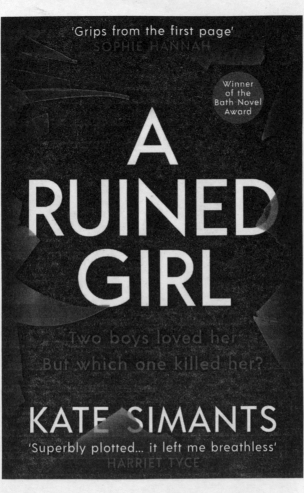

'Grips from the first page'
SOPHIE HANNAH

Winner
of the
Bath Novel
Award

A RUINED GIRL

Two boys loved her.
But which one killed her?

KATE SIMANTS

'Superbly plotted... it left me breathless'
HARRIET TYCE

A heart-wrenching and compelling
thriller set in the foster system
Available in paperback and ebook

MY DAD SAYS BAD THINGS
WILL HAPPEN IF I BREAK...

'Brilliant'
MARK EDWARDS

'Excellent'
WILL CARVER

THE RULE

DAVID JACKSON

'Horrific, hilarious and rather moving' *THE TIMES*

From the bestselling author of *Cry Baby*
Available in paperback and ebook